I0636141

ERYN, KING OF THE BRAWL

REVISED SPECIAL EDITION

NEW BEGINNINGS M/M SERIES
BOOK ONE

KASHEL CHAR

CONTENTS

Title: **Eryn, King of the Brawl - New Beginnings M/M Series Book One (Revised Special Edition)**

Amazon eBook: ISBN: 978-1-7778622-6-8

Amazon Paperback: ISBN: 978-1-0688085-6-2

D2D eBook: ISBN: 978-1-7383966-7-2

D2D Paperback: ISBN: 978-1-998713-51-6

Publisher: Kashel Char

DISCLAIMER

Eryn, King of the Brawl, was inspired by the Characters, Place, and Time who appeared in Men of Phoenix, written by Stefan Pride.

Now, Kashel Char introduces their debut novel, *Eryn, King of the Brawl - New Beginnings M/M Series Book One.*

WARNING

DEAR READERS/LISTENERS

New Beginnings is fantastical, yet imaginable and hopefully, with a little persuasion, believable.

It is darkly complicated, with bouts of silliness, humor, and wonder. In my imagination, Earth and the universe exist inside some kind of bubble, loop, or circle.

I say never stop dreaming. Always enquire, question, and explore to make the unimaginable a reality. Move forward and never accept the status quo blindly.

I added a timeline at the end of the book for readers who want to figure out what the fuck had happened and when in chronological order. It contains spoilers and is hidden to avoid revealing too much. Books one and two each have their own distinct parts, whereas book three encompasses the entire list.

This book and the New Beginnings series is a speculative, alternate history, post-apocalyptic, sci-fi fantasy featuring gifted DNA-manipulated paranormal beings falling in love.

It contains explicit and graphic depictions of imprisonment, violence, blood, and gore. It is unsuitable for young and sensitive readers or anyone offended by gay sex.

INTRODUCTION

In 2052 A.D., six years after the global neurotoxic Doomsday of 2046 A.D., the Romanov twins, Cian and Ivan, were born. They were the first successful ectogenesis twins, and the biological children of Mika and Connor Romanov. This marked it as the Year of the Twins (A.T.).

Earth was dying, and cataclysmic earthquakes, volcanic eruptions, and tsunamis caused a global winter.

Under General Brad McCormick, the all-male scientific and military society believed themselves humanity's last survivors, sheltered within Phoenix's gleaming plexiglass and titanium domes—a fantastical ice city against the Antarctic plateau.

After twenty-one years, the perpetual gray twilight caused by billions of tons of volcanic ash and snowstorms subsided.

The satellites orbiting Earth, taking incessant photos of a cloud-shrouded planet, forwarded an increasing number of glimpses of the blue ocean and ice-covered landmasses.

Prior to the birth of their twin boys, Dr. Connor Romanov, a computer programming genius and second-in-command of Phoenix, had taken control of the orbiting satellites. With the help of his husband, Dr. Mika Romanov, they had broken the codes from scores of intelligence-gathering orbiters placed in space by Earth's old governments. All human history and information saved in data banks at institutions like libraries and universities were downloaded to Phoenix's servers. Their ingenuity had helped prepare Phoenix City, thus saving it.

Since the Year of the Twins (After Twins—A.T.), many things have changed at Phoenix. Enthusiasm to rebuild and their quest for excellence continued as the citizens adjusted to their new normal, and the overall mood of the citizens grew. Fortunately, the World Health Protected Species Society (WHPSS) and Dr. John Saunders authorized the cryogenically transport of tens of thousands of eggs to Phoenix before Doomsday.

Children were born as a result of the Omega Project, led by Mika and his colleague, Dr. Peter von Leutzendorf, who successfully created a method for male sperm splicing and then fertilization of a human donor egg. They implanted this in an artificial womb with a placenta that sustained a life-giving equilibrium for the growth of human fetuses.

New lives have entered the Phoenix population, usually as twins and sometimes as triplets. They were primarily fraternal but occasionally identical. Unfortunately, all births were males.

Mika and Peter worked tirelessly to find a way to give birth to females into the genetic code. Parents could opt for just one child, assuming the fertilized egg didn't split, but most fathered twins since the waitlist to become a father was long.

Of course, many married or at least made civil commitments to create a nurturing family bond and raise their children. Prospective parents, regardless of their marital or relationship status, were eligible and wait-listed even if they prefer to raise a child alone, whether due to being heterosexual or not having a partner.

Marriage brought happiness, acceptance, tolerance, discord, hatred, and divorce. New family laws came into being to handle those situations, including polyamorous marriages. One man could file for divorce against one or more of his spouses or the third, or by all three, four, or five spouses, whatever the number of spouses in the union wanting to dissolve the marriage contract and go their separate ways.

Two things, however, have remained the same. One is the culture of scientific improvement and research. Phoenix's love and commitment to education established a new school for children at three years old. This created a circle of growth and development, allowing scholars to attend and earn as many degrees as possible.

The other thing that had not changed for most of the men of Phoenix was their appearance. None of the original men who opted to have the Eden Bean, better known as the Peter Pan Cap, had aged a month in nearly twenty-one years.

After designing the perfect nutrient capsules for fetal development in an artificial womb, Peter discovered a by-product of the Romanov twins' fetal nutrition. Aging was greatly reduced. No one knew how it worked or how much it would slow down the aging process. In addition to drastically slowing the aging process, the body recovered from physical injuries at an accelerated rate.

These life-prolonging capsules were not mandatory for the original residents. Instead, it was a choice. Some men didn't want it, and that was fine. Because their lives were dramatically prolonged, and the brain only reached full maturity as early as twenty-three, anyone, whatever age after twenty-three, may have it implanted if so desired.

But, somewhere outside Phoenix...Far across the ice from the Antarctic plateau, on another continent, the southern tip of Africa, something else did survive the Doomsday attacks and global winter...

CHAPTER I
THE ODD BOY BRAWL

"*Good morning, citizens of Phoenix.*

It's now six a.m.

Some residents have complained about stagnation. Do not worry, Lasitor has some good points to help you get out of your rut.

Number one. Realize that you are not alone. There are over two thousand men in Phoenix.

Number two. Find something that inspires you. Stagnation occurs because nothing is exciting to do.

Number three. Take a break. When did you take a real vacation for yourself?

Number four. Shake things up and change your routine.

Number five. Do one small thing differently today.

Breakfast is served until eight a.m.

Hope you have a different day!"

· · ·

Eryn, King of the Brawl
2058 A.D. (6 A.T.)
Phoenix
Glass-Domed City
Antarctica

ERYN WAS BORN and grew up deep inside an old gold mine, so deep that it's thousands of meters beneath South African soil. He guessed he was twelve or maybe fifteen years old. He wasn't precisely sure, because time passes differently when one doesn't see the sun. His large build did not match the naïve innocence of his character. In his heart, he was the same age as the six-year-olds he was watching. They fascinated him. None of the other children born inside the ice city interested him as much as these two boys. When they were born, he knew they were special.

Filled with excitement, he could barely contain himself. He crouched down and snuck under a big storage bin to watch Mika and the twins. Something exciting and out of the ordinary was happening today. Tucking his gangly legs, he sat on his haunches and hung on every word.

"Look, Papa," little Cian pointed excitedly, "there's something out on the ice," he said. Sitting proudly, back straight, head up.

Ivan's head popped up. "What, where?" He

THE ODD BOY BRAWL

followed Cian's line of sight. "Oh, there, look. What is that, Papa?"

Cian crossed his arms and scowled at his brother. "I saw it first!"

Ivan turned and looked at his twin brother. "I know you saw it first. I'm asking Papa what it is, that's all," little Ivan said. He smiled at Cian, who unfolded his arms. Their blond heads bobbed up and down in a mutual agreement that Cian won the game of "*I spy with my little eye on something new today.*"

"Good job, I see it, too!" Mika said. He shaded his eyes for a better view of the dark silhouette against the bright blue-pink horizon. "Yes, and that is about two hundred meters away." He pointed to the rusty fragments poking out of the snow.

Eryn shaded his eyes with cupped hands, scanning the snowy vista, and yipped excitedly when he spotted it. He had the best panoramic view of the Antarctic Valley from his hiding spot on the fifth level of the spiraling floor inside the Athletic Dome. Hiding under a storage bin by the plexiglass wall, Eryn spied on the family that fascinated him the most. Pretending to be part of their group was his favorite pastime during visits to Joshua. It was also crucial for him to observe and learn from them to grow into a wise and strong boy. Only then could he reveal himself and avoid the influence of humanity's evil, as Joshua said. "I must learn about humans to live like a human," was his mantra. He didn't fully grasp why it was taking so long.

Wondering where the other man, the other father, was, Eryn looked closer at the building and spied the other man at a window. This man was called Connor, and Eryn watched him mumble something as he watched his family, bringing Eryn's attention back to the amusing scene before him. Eryn bit down on his fists, smothering his laughter as he enjoyed the live entertainment and was seconds away from bursting into hysterics. Pressure built in his head while he restrained himself, small bursts of air escaping, sounding like farts and amplifying the humor of the situation. He snort-giggled at Connor, who peeked through the thick plexiglass wall, trying to see better while leaning in and pushing his nose against the cold glass. This was much more fun, and Eryn dreaded returning home to the darkness deep inside the earth. He knew what needed to be done, but he couldn't bring himself to do it. So he pushed that thought aside. It tore him apart. Too many things he wanted, needed to do, and wished for. Plus, he wanted to forget about his responsibility to his family.

Returning his attention to Connor, Eryn almost laughed out loud as he watched Connor mouth "Damn foggy glass," then balled his sleeve into a fist and rubbed the glass vigorously in small circles, polishing it. Eryn giggled, stamping his feet as he struggled to contain his laughter. The bulky frame and long legs barely fit under the bin. Occasionally, the container rattled, but no one noticed him.

Eryn watched the other three enjoying themselves outside on the glass dome roof. Suddenly, the three laughed boisterously. Eryn frowned, upset with himself for missing the punchline and unable to decipher their conversation. *I wish I could join them.* He longed to play with them and be part of their world of love and affection, especially when their fathers hugged the twins and showered them with attention. For now, he would hide and pretend, but one day, he would reveal his unusual face. I hate going home after just a day or two of short visits. Maybe not today, but definitely one day. He promised himself to refocus and not miss anything.

He turned back and watched Connor intently, reading his body language. Connor appeared increasingly irritated and nervously anxious. Ah, he feared for Mika and the twins, worrying they might slide off the roof. With wide eyes and an open mouth, Eryn leaned in, observing intently, like watching a movie on television, only better, as he soaked up the drama of Connor spying on Mika and their boys outside while Connor, like himself, was inside. His level of amusement rose to nearly unmanageable heights, causing the bin to rattle louder. Quickly, he righted himself, checking his knees to ensure nothing gave his position away. Connor's anticipation of seeing the three rubbed off on Eryn. As soon as Connor caught sight of the safety harnesses around their bodies, the relief and love he felt washed over Eryn. He gasped softly, then waited. From his viewpoint, he could see both fathers. Mika held both boys, with Ivan on his right and Cian on his left, all sitting in a tight row, while Connor watched them from the inside of Phoenix.

Eryn's inhumanly perfect hearing and empathic abilities came in handy when he pretended to be part of this family. The way they loved and interacted with one another was unlike any other family, and he could observe them for hours. Most of the time, it brought him joy, but sometimes it filled him with sadness. His father had told him he was special, and Joshua told him he would do great things one day because he possessed abilities that humans lacked. This was evident as he recognized Connor's sadness about being inside while the others played outside. Eryn sensed Connor's anxiety rising as he watched them atop the highest point of the dome roof, his heartbeats were louder and faster than usual.

Eryn crossed his legs, resting his elbows on his knees and his chin in his hands while smiling longingly at the scene unfolding before him. Connor puffed with pride and adoration for his husband and their two boys as he watched Mika trying to hold on to their kids while simultaneously explaining with his hands, fully immersing himself in the educational conversation. His gestures, like those of an accordion player, conveyed something big and explosive. Eryn's mouth hung open in concentration, twisting his head from side to side to interpret the miming. Playful chuckles escaped from beneath the bin as he pretended to sit outside on the rooftop, enjoying the animated hand gestures of explosions and crashing waves as he worked to figure out the answer. It was about the day all the water came to his home, and the land around his mineshaft froze. With wide eyes, hands in fists, and gesturing animatedly, Mika made pow-pow sounds while opening and closing his hands. Eryn understood Mika was discussing what they called the "Big Flood."

Ivan pointed to the satellite dishes jutting through the icy surface once more, and Mika continued to explain what they were. He nodded in agreement, then placed his thumb to his ear and his pinky to his mouth. Eryn concluded that no one understood what that meant. Then he heard Connor speaking as if Mika and the twins could hear him through the glass wall. "It's enhancing communication. It's for sending sound waves from one dish to another to talk or receive information from the outside world."

"Ah," Eryn whispered, joining the make-believe outdoor classroom game. Feeling proud of himself, he understood what Connor had said. Suddenly, Mika turned toward the Athletics Dome, and Eryn ducked and scurried deeper under the bin. He watched closely as the proud fathers made eye contact, both mouthing the words, "I love you," with broad, cheerful smiles. Eryn sighed and made soft cooing noises. Pouting his lips and pretending to kiss, sweet, kissy noises escaped from beneath the bin.

Connor was too focused on Mika to notice anything behind him. But if he turned around and looked, he might have seen the flopping dirty blonde curls as Eryn flopped excitedly up and down on his back. The joyful emotions were euphoric, causing him to bounce vigorously, sending his hair in all directions and obscuring his big, friendly, gold-green eyes with elongated pupils. Eryn swept his hair to one side with a quick, irritated motion. His reflection revealed that his pupils were almost invisible, as they sat so close to the light streaming in from outside. Eryn wore an oversized, ratty t-shirt he had borrowed from the laundry department. He pulled it over his knees, tucked it beneath him, and tented himself inside. Joshua frequently chased him back to his room to get fully dressed, especially when he went outside without shoes in the snow. Spying on humans was fun, but shoes made it difficult for him to do so silently, so he would wear no shoes today.

The boys turned and waved when they spotted Connor inside, waving happily. Connor waved both arms above his head as if he hadn't seen them all day. He yelled, but Eryn was certain they couldn't hear him. "Hello, my smart, beautiful boys. I love you, be careful. Dada loves you."

It sounded and felt beautiful to Eryn, and he wanted that. But most of all, he wanted to feel like a human being. The emotion overwhelmed him. All he could do now was let his head fall forward and allow his tears to stream down his face. *I am a big boy*, he thought with the mind of an innocent child, but he knew that wasn't enough. He had things to do and brothers to kill, but the thought of doing that made him feel utterly alone. So, he cried silently until he had cried himself out. Then, he used his shirt to wipe his big, amphibious-like nose, and he got up to go search for Joshua. There was nothing more to see here. He forced himself to leave without sneaking another look.

"Who are you waving at, Cian?" Mika asked.

"Our friend, Dada! Say bye-bye to him, Ivan."

Eryn didn't look. He left, not knowing that the friend the boys were talking about was him.

It had taken him over half a day sneaking through until he finally found Joshua in the army portion of the military compound. Aggressive shouting alerted him, so he fell to his knees in the cold snow and carefully snuck up, only to see what appeared to be a confrontation between Joshua and six other men. Eryn recognized them as the men who regularly slipped past the perimeter patrol and terrorized Joshua. Impulsively, he crawled on his hands and knees, making sure they didn't see him—*because I am an odd-looking little boy*. He found a hollowed-out area in the snow and watched. *I may be an odd-looking boy, but I'm not a stupid little boy.*

He narrowed his eyes to slits and pinned them on the men as Joshua yelled at them. Joshua was brave and didn't care how much bigger they were than himself. When one man punched Joshua in the ribs, Eryn lost his temper and jumped up to help, but Joshua locked eyes with him, shaking his head, signaling to stay hidden.

Eryn sat down again as he'd been told, but remained positioned and ready to strike. The air smelled of the sweet copper scent of blood, and Eryn watched as it seeped into the snow in slow motion. All the while, his hands covered his ears to muffle the painful cries of his friend.

He cried soundlessly for the second time that day, never taking his eyes off his friend. This was getting too much for Eryn's emotionally immature mind. But he saw that all humans were different, like he and Ernest were different.

When they were done hurting Joshua, Eryn waited until he heard them entering the side door of the compound. With the speed of a cheetah, he shot out of his hidey-hole, skidded on his knees, and scooped his friend into his lap. "Joshua, Joshua, are you okay?" Eryn inspected the injuries, worried and not sure what to do to help him.

Joshua opened his eyes and answered in between coughs. "Yes, boy, don't worry. I will be fine," he said as he rolled onto his side to hurl his stomach contents. It was a stinking mess in the snow, and Eryn's heightened sense of smell didn't help. He jumped up before it hit him. *Yuck!*

Joshua chuckled and spat more blood. "Just promise me you won't ever let them see or catch you. They're not good men. Promise me, boy." Joshua's voice cracked and was barely audible. He was growing older so fast. Sometimes it felt like Eryn looked away and back at him, and he seemed a year older. His hair was thinning and turning as white as snow. It was now red with blood. That enraged Eryn. He wanted to hurt them like they hurt his friend. He bulged his fists and gnashed his teeth, almost breaking his needle-sized fangs. "I'm going to kill them."

Joshua waved his hand weakly. "No, not now. Not yet. You need to grow a bit more. If you feel like killing, you must kill your brothers first, my boy," he said, and the hand plopped into the snow, almost into the puddle of vomit.

Eryn shook his head. "But I'm already a big boy, and I know I can kill them with my fork. I know I can." He kneeled to wipe the hair out of Joshua's face and whimpered, feeling frustrated, confused, and angry.

"I know, my son, but the time is not right. I will let you know. Promise me you will do as I ask."

The pain and despair emanating from Joshua

broke Eryn's resolve. "Okay." He sniffled. "I'll take my revenge the day you say so." Joshua reached for Eryn's face, wiping his tears and snot away. He cracked a loving smile, exposing a broken tooth. Eryn cringed.

"I promise you, I will let you know when it is time," Joshua said kindly with sad-looking eyes. The fear of losing Joshua frightened Eryn. If Joshua died, he would be alone in this big, frozen world.

"If you say so, then I will wait. Please don't die," Eryn said, sniffling. His brothers were not like humans. They didn't talk, laugh, or cry, and they definitely could not live in the glass city. Maybe Ernest could. But Joshua didn't seem to think so. "Joshua, you're my only human friend. From now on, I'll never leave you alone. I'll guard you and warn you when they're coming. Then we can hide together. I know a lot of good hiding spots."

Joshua smiled, but his words cut like knives when he spoke sternly and with finality. "No, my boy, it's time to leave. You should keep your brothers from finding this place. Do what your father said, before he died. Before your twin, Ernest, influenced your brothers and killed him. I'm telling you, you must do this. Flood those tunnels and bury them, my boy. Take this aggression and go do that for me, please. These men are looking for you and your brothers." Joshua coughed and lowered his head.

Eryn took his hand, squeezing it. "Joshua?"

The old man lifted his bloodied head again,

looking at Eryn as if to say something, shook it, before it fell backward with a plop. He closed his eyes and seemed to mutter something to himself, but Eryn couldn't hear.

Joshua, Peter von Leutzendorf, and his father were scientists and friends. That was the only reason Eryn was allowed to visit Joshua, because he was the only one able to travel across the ice to bring messages from the underground laboratory in South Africa to Joshua and Peter.

Eryn watched Joshua for a long time and then nodded. "Yes, Joshua," Eryn said. Deciding not to argue. He was just speaking out of fear and anger anyway. He didn't know how to kill so easily like his brothers. He was scared of Ernest; his own brother was cunning and deadly to humans. Their other nest brothers from another clutch of eggs were even deadlier.

After another few minutes, Joshua opened his eyes and said, "Okay, let's go." He wiped his mouth and checked his sleeve for blood. Then he rolled over on his hands and knees. Eryn jumped to help and support him. "Let's go to our room," Joshua said, short of breath.

They hobbled inside, and Eryn hoped nobody noticed. Tears filled his eyes as he tried to maneuver them down their secret passage. "You'll need adequate footwear, clothing, and food for at least a year. I want you to fill your ship with as much food as possible tonight."

Eryn soundlessly wept as they walked back to Joshua's secret room, where he was allowed to read books and sleep for a night or two before returning home to keep his brothers from leaving the mine. Or kill them. He agreed, maybe a year was a good idea. He would need a plan and courage to do what Joshua and his father begged him to do.

Eryn realized they needed to move, or someone might see them. He offered his support, allowing the older man to lean on him. He felt distraught. He just nodded, sobbing uncontrollably. *Why did this turn out to be a horrible day?* "I'm a good boy, Joshua. I'll be even better for you."

"No, you did nothing wrong, boy. Those men are the problem. They'll take advantage of you for the wrong reasons. They have an agenda."

Eryn nodded. He didn't know who or what agenda was. All the snot, tears, and constant wiping caused his cheeks to be burned raw, and they hurt.

"Our cave is where we will meet. If you can't kill your brothers, you can't come back inside. Not until you've eliminated your toxic brothers. I will bring food and clothes to the cave. Don't come back inside until you are able to tell me they are dead. Eryn, look at me. This is important. Do something about those Brawls. Look at me, Eryn!"

But Eryn's heart and spirit shattered. He despised

living in the mines and having to watch his brothers. It was that or kill them. He felt like running far away and never returning. But where to? He wanted to be close to the icemen, not live in a mine. "You want me to kill my only family and live alone until you call me? That is not fair," he said.

"Eryn, it's not a good idea for you to stay here. If your brothers are discovered, these men will use them, and everyone in here will perish. Do you want that to happen? Do you want these people to die? You need to kill your Brawl brothers. I know it hurts to kill your own. You are good and not a monster. That's why I ask you, for the sake of these humans, do you want them all to die?"

"No, I don't," he whispered.

Once inside, Joshua bent one knee. "Don't cry, please, my boy." He made eye contact with Eryn and gently wiped his face. "We can stay in touch. This is just temporary until I know the bad men are gone and your brothers are no more. Promise me you won't let these men find you or your brothers. They're selfish, evil men who do not believe in my god. They want to be gods themselves, and they will use anything and anyone to reach their goals."

Eryn didn't know who Joshua's god was, but he spoke of him and read stories about him from his favorite black book, the Bible.

He assessed Joshua's bloody, swollen face through

teary, blurred eyes as he thought about protecting the twins and the Romanov family.

"Okay, let's clean my face and get you and the ice sail ship ready so you can get out of here. Make a promise to me," he croaked. "Never trust those who hurt you. Ernest is hurting you. Remember that when the time comes to kill him, and until you do that, avoid coming inside Phoenix without me."

"Eryn sniffed and bravely promised while wiping more snot from his face.

CHAPTER 2

YOU WILL NOT DIE TODAY

"Good morning, citizens of Phoenix. It is I, Lasitor.

Get up! It's six a.m.

Did you know Easter was a religious holiday cele-brated with chocolates by hiding them and sending the youngsters to find them? It may be an excellent idea to head down to breakfast this morning to grab a few choco-late eggs, especially those made by our chefs so that you can have a real pagan experience.

Celebrate the day by increasing your children's sugar intake, getting them all excited and happy so they can crash early. You and your lover will have time to melt those chocolates and paint one another's eggs, just like they did back in the thirteenth century.

Visit the local community news page for exciting forbidden eggs, penance, and fast facts.

Breakfast is served until eight a.m.

Have an egg-citing day!"

. . .

GENERAL BRAD MCCORMICK
   2073 A.D. (21 A.T.)
   Phoenix
   Glass-Domed City
   Antarctica

FREEZING HELLFIRES! Brad counted the precious minutes he had left. *How many injections had I given myself already? When did I inject the syringes? Did I actually call for help, or did I think I should have called for help?* Questions rush through his disoriented mind. The hollowness of the ice canyon swallowed his howls and groans of pain and despair. Tiny snow crystals drifted on the wind, reflecting the Aurora Borealis' light into millions of shades of green, pink, and blue. Reminding him of the world he didn't want to leave behind, so the reality of his perilous situation hit him again.

Brad curled himself tightly into the fetal position. It seemed hell had finally frozen over, and he lay at the bottom. His mind spun like a disco ball, reflecting a kaleidoscope of thoughts, feelings, and emotions, and he struggled to think coherently as jumbled thoughts, worries, and prayers sparked at the speed of light behind his eyelids. *Come on, find my stupid ass.*

He'd arrived twenty-seven years ago in Antarctica

to lead Phoenix, and he had achieved the inconceivable and accomplished so much. *And now, here I lie, dying alone, because of my stupidity.*

More sparks flashed in his mind, and he told himself they were slight electric jolts from the dying synapses in his freezing brain. Describing the steps of his demise kept his dying mind occupied. *They are only tiny backfires, my neurons conjure up in protest of dying.*

He couldn't remember the last time he felt so numbed by the cold. He was so hypothermic that he was incapable of shivering, and his eyelids had frozen shut. *It's only a matter of minutes, and then I'll die.*

His ribcage was frozen stiff, making it almost impossible for him to take a deep breath. Each time he thought he'd taken his last breath, his mouth opened on its own, and he gasped like a fish out of water.

Bloody damn hell! He dreaded the cycle of gasping and waiting for all the disco lights to go out. *Someone must hurry and rescue me, or I'd better hurry and die already.* He cringed mentally. He didn't want to die, so when his body took another involuntary breath, he welcomed it. Bloody Peter with his *take-this-and-live-forever* capsule. He slowed his mind, willing the hectic thoughts to subside, forcing his mind to shut down and prepare his soul to leave for oblivion.

The last Glupidone shot he injected into the side of his neck prolonged his chance of survival by about fifteen minutes. It worked by combining life-saving chemicals and hormones. These boosted survival in freezing temperatures, reducing lung fluid, raising blood sugar for energy, including epinephrine and methamphetamine to stimulate the body. Finally, a cryoprotectant preserved cells from ice damage. In theory, prolonged consciousness meant prolonged life. Earlier, just as Brad injected his last syringe, he'd used its needle to tear the skin and muscles over his upper left pectoral wide open to remove his Peter Pan Cap. It made perfect sense at the time to chew on it like bubble gum, since his injections had given him hope of lasting long enough in the freezing cold until someone might rescue him. He thought it was probably futile, but he'd never been a man who quit and gave up. So instead of dying like a typical soldier, he would lie there like a pathetic dying shrimp on the bottom of the ocean with the worst medicine aftertaste ever in his mouth. *Bloody Peter with his capsules.* He berated Peter in his mind, furious with himself as he replayed the night's events.

He remembered seeing men running with flashlights in this direction. But like the *idiot I am*, he reprimanded himself for not radioing security to inform them about the sighting. Instead, he ran after the lights like the Mothman on acid. Thinking, *no, not thinking at all*, to investigate, *no, also not investigate, instead running around like an imbecile searching for a crack in the ice to run into.*

The pain in his backside made sense as he recalled falling onto his butt and knocking the wind out of his lungs. *I could have bitten my tongue off.* When he finally managed to scope his surroundings, he realized the immense size of the gigantic crevice he'd managed to run into. *How did I miss the mammoth split in the ice sheet? Thank god I landed on a ledge.* Unfortunately, he lost both his radio and flashlight in the process. He tried to stay alive as long as he could.

Yes, that's what I did. Then I removed my flare gun from my right leg pocket and the syringes from my left pocket. Brad remembered he removed the safety mechanism with his thumb, pointed it upwards, and pulled the trigger. *Yes, a pink flare; I remember shooting it into the night sky.* Ah, now his gloveless hands made sense as he recalled removing them to administer the first of five preloaded dosages. *Okay, so it's been more than an hour, that's good, then they're already on their way.*

Positive thinking helped him remember more. He faintly recalled opening his jacket, searching for a patch of skin to administer the life-prolonging aid. While he'd palpated the muscled area over his upper chest, he recalled Peter telling him about the special amniotic fluid and the by-products of the artificial wombs. His cryoprotectant research discovered a potential preventative aging mechanism in humans by splicing the bowhead whale SIRT6 gene and reprogramming human DNA on a cellular level to repair and rejuvenate damaged strands. It made sense to Brad after he'd injected the last syringe to dig that little Eden Bean capsule out from under the layers of his left pectoral muscle and started chewing it.

Brad stopped calling for help after he had no voice left. In his death-dream state, he saw a mirage of Rick laughing, Rick kissing him, and the last time he'd enjoyed a warm shower with his husband. Feeling the heat of the steam from their last shower together on his face, tasting the soap, *no, not soap, the bloody capsule,* and the taste of Rick's shoulder. The one he licked and sucked that morning while he made love to him in the shower. He cherished every throaty groan his husband made. *If I weren't frozen, I'd have an erection.* He smiled mentally at himself, thinking that when they discovered him thousands of years into the future, archeologists would discover he died with an erect penis and a smile on his face. The tour guide would describe him as Homo-Erectus-Erectus. He chuckled inwardly and imagined hearing the tour guide saying, *"Ladies and Gentlemen of the Museum of Human Studies. This Homo Erectus-Erectus, who walked the earth thousands of years ago, is an extinct species of archaic humans. It perished during the dawn of the global nuclear winter of 2060 A.D. We discovered this human had such a big penis he could have used it as an extra leg or a weapon!"*

He amused himself while he waited, drifting in and out of various levels of consciousness. He suspected he was tripping, as well. The amount of amphetamine in the Glupidone shots would make an elephant rave. He laughed and watched Rick blink in and out in his imagination, reaching out to him, smiling, and telling him everything would be okay and that he loved him.

Brad calmed his mind and shot one last message into the universe for his Apache. *Love, thank you for all your love, steadfast belief, and support you've given me. I love you. Please continue living your life to the fullest for the sake of me and the boys.* He whimpered, and he realized his frozen face and tear ducts wouldn't permit him to shed one tear. *Rick, I love you. And, boys, take care of your father, he'll need you.*

With that said, Brad's soul found peace, his mind quieted, and in the stillness, he waited to drift into the afterlife, but something or someone held him tethered to this plane. It was so still that he could hear snowflakes burying him.

Hello, is someone touching me? I feel something warm. Brad felt a gentle hand touching his cheek.

"Don't worry, Icemen King. I will stay with you until your icemen come," a deep, melodic voice said.

"What? Who are you? Are you an angel?"

Soft chuckles surrounded him, wiping away the feelings of despair and loneliness. They enveloped him with empathy, an experience he had never known before, like a warm blanket of love.

"Who's there? I hear giggles in my mind."

"Not long. Hold on, Icemen King."

*I'm either on my way to heaven, or...*Brad paused, stilling his mind, listening.

More playful snickers...and beautiful notes were being hummed. His tension and fear faded. He felt as light as a helium balloon. Safe and drifting. Hovering and waiting—holding on.

"I'm warming your heart and mind. You will not die today," the soothing, angelic voice said near Brad's ear. *It must be a hallucination.*

CHAPTER 3
BRAD'S A GENIUS

"Good morning, men of Phoenix.

Lasitor bids you a good morning. It's now six a.m.

Did you know that in 2035, ice carving was a trendy sport? At first, it was a hobby, but people began taking it seriously and started competing in events, and later it became an Olympic sport.

Visit your community news page to sign up for exciting events and things to do with ice and snow. Breakfast is served until eight a.m.

Hope you have an icy cool day!"

Dr. Peter Von Leutzendorf

"Here he is! I found him!" Connor trumpeted as he fell onto his knees at the ridge of a gaping tectonic crack. Peter joined him. They removed their head coverings, puffing enormous clouds of mist, stunned by the magnitude of the abyss.

"Jesus, the lucky son of a bitch," Peter said.

"Braaaad, Braaaad, can you hear me? Hold on, buddy, we have you!" Connor called.

"Good god, he fell right into a chasm, and look, the lucky son of a bitch fell onto the only protruding ice shelf," Peter said in awe. He doubted Brad could hear them.

"I told you we should've started on this side. He's probably dead by now," Connor said as he got up. Peter was glad they found Brad, so he could stop and catch his breath. He concurred if they started their search on this side, he wouldn't be so exhausted.

"We should be able to reach him!" Connor turned to Mika, who had just arrived, trailing behind them. "Look, there he is, but be careful." Connor pointed, and Mika shook his head in disbelief.

"Freezing hellfires." Mika crouched down, carefully crawling for a better look.

"My words exactly. Brad fell right onto the only ledge," Connor said. He stepped back from the edge and lifted his arms, helicopter style, signaling their position with his flashlight. "Here we are," he shouted.

Their team of three had searched the northeastern perimeter for an hour until they found and followed boot tracks in the snow to this spot. Although it was nighttime, the breathtaking springtime constellations reflected on the snow, shrouding the land in a dim glow. They wore night-vision goggles equipped with infrared heat signal detectors and progressive light particle refractors to differentiate between old and newly fallen snow.

"I see just a few specks of orange and red on my screen. Brad has probably frozen solid," Peter said, estimating their leader lay about two meters into the crack.

"We need to go get him," Connor stated. Mika and Peter leaned over the side, repeatedly calling for Brad, but saw no movement. Sitting back on their heels, they pushed their goggles to their foreheads to assess the area and plan their next steps. Their white and yellow extreme cold weather suits trapped air and insulated their bodies by preventing heat loss and conducting water vapor away from the layers underneath. The outer shell shielded them from the deadly icy wind, keeping them warmer for longer. Unfortunately, the visibility through the ten-by-fifteen-centimeter tent window, as Connor referred to it, was severely limited, making it challenging to see and maneuver during the rescue mission. They would have to move quickly without protection against the frigid air. The snow was falling so fast that they could barely see each other.

Connor turned from left to right, seeing how far the chasm stretched. "I don't think this was here yesterday. It must be a pressure ridge. Look!" He pointed with his flashlight, but the light disappeared into the profound depths of the crack. "I can't see how deep it is, and I'm not shooting flares into it. I don't want to disturb the ice and worsen the situation."

Peter felt increasingly nervous. "Let's just get Brad out before the chasm closes again!" Peter said, recalling the morning's reports about increased tectonic and microplate movements. Overnight, ice frequently formed across the cracks. If it got reasonably thick, it might rupture loudly when the warming sheet pushed on it the next morning. Other times it slowly pushed into a vertical curtain a few inches high as the crack closed again.

"Okay, you two lightweights, go down. I'm strong, I'll pull you back up," Mika said.

"Okay, Mika!"

"What? I'll wait and signal the backup responders this way. I'm afraid they won't see us or run over the side themselves," Mika said. Lifting the radio to his mouth, he reported their position to Phoenix.

Connor hastily drove four galvanized steel pins deep into the ice. Peter tested their sturdiness. Satisfied, they fastened their gear to the anchors and slid down with pivoting ropes.

Peter didn't make a sound, testing their purchase. Connor reached Brad first, gently wiping the powdered snow from his body. "Brad, are you okay? Can you hear us?" Brad didn't move. "I think he's dead, Peter," Connor said. His disbelieving whisper cracked the grave heaviness of their dire situation.

"Don't worry. Let's get him to my cryogenics laboratory. I have a few tricks up my sleeve," Peter said optimistically. Secretly, he was more afraid of the ice pancaking them than his frozen general.

That seemed to get Connor moving.

"Wait!" He stopped Connor by grabbing his shoulder. "If we pull on Brad and pick him up the wrong way, an arm or a leg, even his head, could break off. We need to safely loosen and then secure him to the stretcher in the position he's in now," Peter explained. When it came to frozen dead people, he was the specialist.

Connor nodded his agreement and followed his directions. "That makes sense. What do you suggest?" he hollered, trying to compete with the growing roar of the wind.

Peter assessed Brad's rigid and white frostbitten body. "The best way to do this"—gesturing, scooping the snow from underneath Brad, *the human icicle*, Peter thought—"is to loosen him from the snow, put the stretcher against him, and gently flip-roll his whole body onto it. Once that's done, we can then securely strap him to the stretcher, and we'll be able to hoist him vertically up the side of the ice wall."

In the background, Peter heard Mika briefing Phoenix on the search for Brad and the current situation. The wind blew ice over the sides and into their faces. "Tell them to hurry!" Connor shouted while scooping snow. Mika waved back, showing he had it under control, but they struggled to hear him above the growing roar of the storm.

Snow icicles packed on Connor's face and stubble. Peter didn't think he looked much better and feared losing the tip of his nose. *We have to hurry, we won't survive another hour without help.*

"Tell them to bring more Glupidone," Peter shouted to Mika.

"What?"

"We need more Glupidone!"

Mika waved. "Right, Glupidone!"

They went at it, smashing and scooping the ice, loosening Brad so they could roll him over without shattering him into pieces.

"This ice is rock-hard. It must be millions of years old. Do you think it cracked beneath his feet when he slipped and fell into the crevice? Why else would he be here?" Peter was short of breath, struggling to breathe as his lungs burned from the cold.

"I'm sure he said he was checking something on the other side of the domes. But why would he wander to this side of the valley? Maybe something attacked or spooked him or dragged him here?" Connor theorized between breaths.

"Maybe he heard the ice crack and came investigating?" Peter asked. He continued speculating, diverting the topic from other humans outside. He vigorously hacked at the ice with his small ax, then scooped out more ice to create space underneath Brad, loosening and freeing him.

"Okay, I think that's enough," Peter said. With a slight wave of his hand, he acknowledged Mika, who was helping another small man slide down the rope to help them. Securely strapped to the gurney, they hoisted Brad up and over the side to relative safety.

"Hold on, and please wait!" Peter tried shouting, but it came out in a wheeze when he crawled over the ledge.

"We need to..." He heaved with his hands on his knees. Catching his breath, he pointed to Connor, Mika, and himself. "Glupidone, for frostbite!" he yelled, barely audible above the howling gusts of wind. They soon understood when he started patting them down, searching their pockets for their emergency stash, and they hastily handed it over to him.

After each received a jab in the neck, they donned their masks. Mika checked that Brad was properly tethered and signaled his okay. The six men lifted the stretcher and sprinted toward Phoenix as fast as they could. The city's lights shone through the storm like a dim blue beacon in the distance. As they approached, the domed glass roofs illuminated the sky with streaks of bright lights, like a thousand lighthouses calling them to safety. They saw the big front door rolling up and retracting into the roof, allowing them to enter. It felt like an eternity, but after fifteen minutes of running full speed through the snow, the six men and their precious cargo were finally in the dome's warmth.

While the entrance closed behind them, Mika looked back and frowned. Connor followed his gaze. "That's strange. I could have sworn I saw movement out of the corner of my eye in the direction we'd just come from. It feels like someone's watching us," Connor said.

"I have the same feeling." Mika lifted his arm. The man operating the big door made eye contact with him. "Secure the door, now!" Mika ordered as his eyes followed the running men with the stretcher. As if thinking the same thing, they looked worriedly at each other. "Where's Bryan?" Mika asked. "We need to activate the Reserves!"

Sergeant Amir Lamasi overheard them and saluted. Seconds later, he announced the code status over the leadership pager. The well-practiced reserve team scrambled, knowing precisely what to do. "Captain Bryan Howell, report to Communications Dome stat. This is a Code Yellow Alert."

Mika hopped, skipped, and jumped through a sea of men trying to get to their posts.

"I'll meet Bryan at Communications. *Ublyudok!*" He swore in his native tongue. "I think this was an attack on Phoenix!" Mika said to Connor.

"All shutters need to be activated and closed

immediately!" Connor ordered his commands into his communicator.

"I'll catch up later. I need to find Rick and update him about Brad," Connor said. He blew a kiss to Mika, who smiled in acknowledgment and disappeared into the sea of soldiers.

Peter savored the breathable air as he yanked the head covering off again. His cheeks burned with tiny needle pricks as blood flow was restored. "Please, take him...my...Cryonics lab. Quickly...There are steps we need to follow. I...prepare...decompression room..." He heaved the delicious heat between every other word into the depths of his lungs. Unable to talk in complete sentences, he gulped a few deep breaths and shot after them. It crossed his mind that the other men were not nearly as out of breath as he was. *I should make it a priority to spend more time on my cardio exercises.* He would revisit that thought another day.

IN THE CRYONICS LAB, Peter directed the men to a large, thirty-by-forty-meter walk-in, temperature-controlled decompression chamber. Carefully, they placed Brad onto a steel slab. Peter immediately set the temperature to a freezer setting of minus 10° Celsius. He moved swiftly and with confidence. His cryogenics laboratory was one of the most, if not the highest, funded and secretly sponsored programs at Phoenix. Although not tight-fisted, Peter didn't freely share knowledge of his precious equipment and limited supplies. In fact, Peter harbored many highly classified secrets. Secrets not even known by his best friend and colleague, Mika Romanov. One such secret was that within the many chambers of his lab were hundreds of bodies and brains of the rich and famous, cryogenically frozen and patiently awaiting resurrection. This was one of many ways that funding for Phoenix had been raised. But he doubted he would ever resurrect these citizens from a lost civilization.

Dr. Peter von Leutzendorf, a high-born transplant from Bavaria, was a stunningly beautiful man with pure white hair and crystal-blue eyes, but he was a loner by choice, or so he let everyone think. He was also much older than any man currently living in Phoenix, and although not needed, he had implanted the first Eden Bean into himself when he appeared to be twenty-seven years old. Like everyone else in Phoenix, who had the capsule implanted, he hadn't aged a day since, looking precisely like the biochemist and cryogenics expert who first walked through Phoenix's doors. By hiding his true origins, he cloaked his milieu to resemble him, so that no one questioned him. A sacrifice to the right gods in the right way, using the correct form of traditional elemental structures, disguising his Aryan nobility. He didn't feel guilty because, at the same time, he had gifted good, deserving men with eternal life.

Inside the chamber, Peter went to work as fast as possible. Still dressed in his arctic gear, he worked to conserve as many of Brad's cells as possible.

When cells freeze, they collect water on a molecular level. If they thaw too fast, the general's cells will swell, explode, and he will die. *I think I'll need a high-pressure cryoprotectant.*

"When we thaw your cells, General McCormick, we'll have to dilute and exchange the fluids as quickly as possible to prevent osmotic shock and cell damage. However, this is all in theory. Using the cryoprotectant in the gas chamber with the pressure of fifteen atmospheres should guarantee high viability for your cells," he explained as if Brad could hear him and give him an answer.

"How much is high, Dr. von Leutzendorf?" a voice asked over the speaker system.

"Huh, hmm, what?" Peter turned and looked around, searching for the voice he thought spoke to him. "Was that you?" he asked Brad. Alone in his lab, in solitude, he regularly spoke to the frozen dead people, sometimes for hours. On occasions, they would talk back, but this voice sounded different.

"What do you mean by high viability? Will Brad be a functioning human being or not? Here, look at the monitor, please, Peter."

Peter frowned. His eyes searched upwards. "Ahh, there you are. It's you, Rick." Peter smiled open-mouthed. "I mean, over ninety percent of his body would thaw unharmed. Maybe higher and maybe lower," Peter explained to the fifty-by-fifty-centimeter monitor screen opposite him. He could see Rick talking to him. *Thank god I'm not crazy.* "Rick, if you prefer, we don't try this, then we can stop the procedure," he said, already busy removing his gloves to exit the freezer and speak face-to-face with Rick. "I'll come out and explain to you in person."

"No! Don't! Do what you can, Peter. I know Brad. He trusted you and would like you to try whatever you can to save him. He wouldn't want to leave the boys and me alone."

"Are you sure? This is all theoretical."

"Do what you can, please. You've been working in this lab for many years. Not once can I say you've been negligent or derelict in your research," Rick said with what sounded like respect in his tone. "It's the opposite. Look at the success of your Peter Pan Caps."

Peter hated that name. It's Eden Beans, not Peter Pan Caps—that's so childish. Peter looked closer at the screen. "Okay, let me see what I can do. Now that you mention the capsules, they already have some cryogenic agents on board to combat cell breakdown. Let me conduct a thorough assessment to see if we have a better chance of thawing and resuscitating him if I don't have to apply high pressure."

"Do you want me to come inside and help with that?"

"No, I'm going to do this. It'll take a while to prepare the thawing chamber, then we'll monitor the process on a cellular level, and when he's ready to receive CPR and take a breath, he'll be resuscitated. I'll ask Mika to assist me."

"Let me help. I can help," Rick pleaded, irritating Peter. Not only was he General Brad McCormick's husband and the last Apache Native American, but he was also the chief medical doctor in charge of the Phoenix Medical Operations Unit. The last thing he needed in his lab was a doctor who thought he knew better.

"You'll be emotionally involved," Peter said. *And you'll stand here judging me.* "Let's do this by the book. I know what I'm doing. If you want to help, you can call Mika to help me. When he arrives, we can discuss the next best steps for Brad's successful revival." Peter selected the best words from his vocabulary, which was a mix of polite and normal language.

Looking over at the monitor, Peter could see Rick biting his lips and his eyes watering with tears. "I'll start by cutting and removing his clothes for maximum dermis exposure in case Mika agrees we should administer the cryoprotectant gas." Peter hoped the request would give Rick a meaningful purpose and relieve his tension. *Please let him go, please let him go.* He didn't enjoy working in front of an audience. Judgment from Rick watching him would unnerve him.

After a long, uncomfortable silence, Rick answered, "I agree. Thank you for doing your best." Peter watched the monitor as Rick reluctantly left to fetch Mika.

Then he turned all his attention to Brad. "Okay, General, show me. Tell me what's going on with you." Peter removed the clothing by methodically cutting and removing layer by layer from skin surface areas over Brad's back, buttocks, and the upper side of his left leg and left shoulder. "Whoa, look at this. What do we have here?" Peter whispered, surprised when he opened Brad's left shoulder, revealing the bloody pectoral. At first, he thought it was a gunshot wound. "What the hell?" He poked and prodded the area with his face inches from the injury as he inspected the frozen blood and a gaping wound.

"No, this can't be. Really, maybe...wow, it is. Brad, who would have thought you had brains hidden between those big ears? That was clever of you...You just saved your skin...You son of a..." Peter whooped and danced like a chicken with its head cut off. He chanted, "Brad's a genius. Brad's a genius. Brad's a genius."

"What in the ever-loving hell are you doing, you crazy scientist?" Mika asked, joking and chuckling as he usually did when teasing Peter.

Shit, he must have entered the chamber without making a sound. Damn light-footed Russian ox. "Christ-all-mighty, Mika, you'll give me a heart attack. For the love of all that's holy, stop doing that." Peter smirked and ceased his happy dance. Instantly switching back to his usual professional self. But happy and relieved to see his friend.

"Mika, come see. If we had lots of time, I would have made you guess. But we don't, so come have a look here!" Peter excitedly pointed to the crystallized bloody left shoulder he'd just exposed. Carefully, he scraped the frozen pink ice, revealing an open wound of about two inches by two inches.

Mika, also dressed in his cryonics personal protective gear, held his hands up and turned his body toward Peter, just like a surgeon, scrubbed up and readied for surgery. Slowly, he bent forward, careful not to touch or contaminate anything, showing the proper professional etiquette when entering another scientist's laboratory. He visually inspected Brad's left pectoral and looked up, then softly, with wonder in his voice, asked, "May I, please, Peter?" Holding the palm of his hand out for Peter to place a scalpel in it. He inspected the wound, gently palpating it. Peter watched Mika closely, hoping he would confirm what he suspected. He towered over Brad, making *hmmm* and *ahhhh* noises, narrowing his eyes as he concentrated.

"Hello. What's going on? Did you decide on anything?" Rick asked, entering the cryo-chamber.

Peter lifted his head and watched him pussyfooting to the opposite side of Mika, not taking his eyes off Brad and stopping at the foot-end of the cold metallic slab. His posture stiffened, all the color drained from his wooden face, seeing his half-naked husband curled up and frozen. It looked like Brad was smiling, and Peter noticed when Rick saw it because the corners of his mouth slightly turned upward before he swallowed a few times. The audible gulps testified to Rick's emotional distress while he pretended his best to remain calm and appear professional. The muscles in his jaw pulled tightly when he bit down on his molars, looking like his heart shattered in silence while standing like a white statue instead of jumping onto Brad and never letting him go.

"I see. That's an impressive field incision. I never thought Brad would think of that," Mika said, smiling. "That'll certainly make a big difference." He expressed professional camaraderie, and Peter liked it.

"What is going on?" Rick demanded with a sad scowl, and his arms folded in front of his chest. Understandably, he was nervous, and his husband lay technically dead on the table. "Excuse me, that came out wrong. Could you two scientists explain what you're observing to me in layperson's terms? To me, it looks like a gunshot wound to the heart. I...cryogenic language is not my specialty. You're talking over my head," Rick admitted, and Peter could see he was close to losing his composure.

Feeling spiteful, Peter nodded and lifted a finger, asking for one second. Upstaging Rick's discomfort. "Mika, thank you for coming."

"It's no problem, comrade. Anything to help our general."

Peter turned to Rick to explain. Rick swallowed nervously, looking back and forth between Mika, Peter, and Brad. He stood over three meters away, distancing himself from the reality in front of him. Peter didn't want to feel sorry for him, but he did. He followed Rick's gaze to Brad's frozen and pale blue face.

At least he's smiling.

"Earlier, I said the process I initially intended exists only in theory, but I think we have a chance of proving it invalid by confirming my anti-theory." Peter hoped Rick was listening.

"Simply stated, Brad removed and ingested his Peter Pan Capsule."

"He what? Why did he do that?" Rick asked, looking highly confused. "Please explain to me. I want to know what you think happened to him. But most of all, how will we bring him back to life?"

Let me spell it out for him, the man's so annoying. Peter growled. Rick always made him feel less than, and he hated that. Rick gasped and seemed taken aback. Mika tsk-tsked at him.

Peter threw his hands up. "Look, it seems he gave himself his shots of Glupidone, you know, the shots every man in Phoenix has packed into their arctic gear in case of an emergency. Glupidone left pocket and flare gun right," Peter said, being very sarcastic, and he couldn't stop himself. Rick crossed his arms and listened, not saying a word, picking up on Peter's sarcasm. Mika coughed in the background, but Peter ignored him.

"I don't know what he did with his radio, but that's a moot point. Brad was lying on his right side and injected himself in his left upper shoulder and neck." He explained as plainly as he could muster. Pointing to Brad with his pinkie finger, he stepped closer. Concentrating on making sense to Rick while figuring out what Brad was thinking in his last moments. Peter hinted for Rick to step closer. Also dressed in lab gear, Rick had his hair pulled back into his favorite tightly braided French plait. His dark, almost blue-black hair and Native American complexion gave him a stunning, exotic appearance. As he stepped closer to inspect Brad's shoulder, Peter noticed the physician's emotions were verging on *fight or flight*.

Yeah, it's difficult to be nonchalant when your husband is lying dead on a slab in front of you. Peter's temper dissipated, and he engaged Rick empathetically.

"Okay, what am I looking at? Why would he

remove his Peter Pan gel capsule? Was it his intention to die?" Rick fired stupid question after stupid question, unnerving Peter again.

"He didn't remove it! I'm saying it wrong. Sorry, he removed it, but...no, let me start with how I understand it."

Rick pulled his one eyebrow up in question and darted his eyes in Mika's direction, who nodded and conveyed his trust and support by looking back at Peter. *Thank you, Mika. Tell him just to shut up and let me think.*

Taking a deep breath, Peter explained. "He must have used a needle from the Glupidone shots or maybe broken one and used the glass. I doubt the latter because it would be too small to handle with the big gloves. Look here." Peter used the backside of the scalpel handle to show the yellow discoloration around Brad's lips. "Your husband chewed the gel, which is ingenious. It's made to slow-release over ten to fifteen years, but he chewed and ingested it. That means every cell in his body has already absorbed the hyperosmolar cryoprotectant on a molecular level. The cryopreservation of his whole body and brain is already reversing the ice damage. My cryoprotectant in positive pressure would never have reached as far and as deep. So, theoretically, thawing should occur easily and naturally.

"That was a primary problem with bodies already cryogenically frozen in the lab in the old world. The cryoprotectant administered before they froze them to minus fifty-four Celsius lacked a particular molecule we discovered only twenty years ago. That's why hyperosmolarity causes cells to pop. They should have waited long enough for my formula to be discovered so that this process could work.

"We now use the same formula to sustain fetal growth and development and prolong longevity. No matter what I tried, the damage was irreversible, and I'd lost so many subjects already. I was cremating bodies faster than their cells could pop. Each time I attempted the process, no matter what I tried, they would end up like *Puff the Magic Dragon*. No, that's wrong. It is *Pop Goes the Weasel*. Anyway, my research would start all over again. It's very frustrating because I have the answer in my hand, but I can't get it inside their bodies, you understand. My current high-pressure gassing and reverse osmosis techniques were the least damaging. Still, when the body finally absorbs the cryoprotectant into the cells, it's thawed, and the cell damage has already occurred. It was very frustrating, I tell you."

"Okay, I hear you." Rick stopped the high-speed thought pattern, and Peter blinked a few times to focus on Brad. "So, you say we should let him thaw the natural way? What do you mean by that?"

Ting, ting, ting. Peter's eyes rolled mentally like a slot machine. Again, he took a deep breath to calm himself down after being so rudely interrupted. Mika chortled like a mouse on cocaine in the background. Peter and Rick gave him dirty looks.

"Excuse me, comrades." He pretended to sneeze into his sleeve.

Peter continued. "I'll slowly turn the heat, say one degree every thirty minutes for two hours, wait an hour, and start again. We must force nothing. Gently dry him and remove the rest of his clothing." Peter pointed to the rags of clothes and boots he had been unable to remove earlier.

"And the wound?" Rick asked. "Would that bleed...as his body warmed?" Rick waved a hand. "Of course, it will. Sorry, Peter. I ask stupid questions."

"Yes, we would bandage the wound, and when he's dry, and his body temperature has risen to seventy-five, we can place you in the chamber with him so that you can heat his body with yours. I'll contact housekeeping to bring in a bed with a comfortable mattress and bedding. Also, I would suggest you have something to eat, empty your bladder, talk to the boys, and come back because you'll be in the chamber for six to eight hours. I calculate that he'll complete the process within twelve hours," Peter explained, feeling secretly happy about all this because he had a living guinea pig and could finally finish his damn research paper.

Mika nodded his head in apparent approval of Peter's plan. "Good, we need to talk to Brad. I'll be back later. I agree that your steps for revival will work. If he does not spontaneously breathe, keep the resuscitation and emergency intubation trays at hand. I'll send a ventilator from the Medical Dome for you."

"Thank you, both of you," Rick said to Mika and Peter.

"No problem," Mika replied. "We want to be ready for anything. Peter, I think when Brad reaches eighty-five, call for me so we have enough hands on deck. I'll let Connor know he's in charge for the next twenty-four hours. We also have a situation outside. Bryan and his men are busy investigating." He hesitated, looking at Rick. "Rick, I don't want to traumatize or worry you more, but it's better to be honest under these circumstances. I think I saw something when we returned, and I'm wondering why Brad was outside. So, we need to investigate. We'll keep you in the loop," Mika said.

Rick nodded, keeping his eyes on Brad from across the table. His arms were folded, and he stared at Brad's body with tight lips and furrowed brows. An uncomfortable silence hung in the air.

"Yes, I suspected that when I heard Phoenix is on Code Yellow Alert. Connor explained, but was called away urgently. Thank you for coming, and yes, please send for that emergency equipment," Rick said, not making eye contact with Mika. "I hope we don't need a ventilator, but it's a good idea. We don't know how Brad fell and hurt himself. He may have broken a bone or hit his head and have a skull fracture," Rick stuttered, with tears in his eyes.

"Yes, that's true," Peter answered. Then he reached out, putting his hand on Rick's shoulder. "I'll scan his body in a few minutes." Rick took a deep breath and exhaled slowly. Peter hoped he wouldn't ask any more questions.

"I hope it hid nothing else from us...Brad's icy cocoon," Rick said.

Mika left. Peter programmed the thermostat, as they discussed. Then he turned to leave, but Rick asked, "Please stay," while holding onto Brad's shoulder. "I want to say a prayer for him."

No, no, no, Peter felt like a cornered, frightened kitten. He wondered if hissing at the man would help, but he thought better of it. Searching for an escape route, he realized his chance to run was zero as soon as Rick started chanting.

"May the moon restore you.
May the sunlight awaken you.
May the warrior in you rise.
May the breeze bring you before me.
So, you may know the beauty of another life on the earth and walk with me."

Rick turned, shoulders shaking, soundlessly crying as he left to get ready and prepare to come back to lie down with Brad.

Peter administered more cryoprotectants at fifteen atmospheric pressures while the cryo-chamber temperature rose by one degree every thirty minutes, resting every two hours. This slow but necessary process prevented cellular hyperosmolality.

Rick returned six hours later, and Brad's temperature was nearly fully thawed, allowing them to reposition him on a bed. After that, both Peter and Rick stepped outside the chamber and into the room with the machines and an observation window that allowed them to monitor Brad's progress.

"I have good news." Peter felt relieved.

"Oh, what's that?" Rick asked in a monotonous tone, his face expressionless.

"Yes, good news. I scanned Brad's body. I didn't find any fractures or damaged internal organs," Peter said, searching for hope on Rick's face, but Rick only nodded and sat down to watch him work for another two-hour session. Rick stared at Brad as Peter worked, monitoring the process with advanced neutron scanners and ectoplasmic gamma-ray triple ionization subatomic particles. These particles tracked the viability of Brad's cells by measuring the speed at which molecules detached from electrons inside them and by measuring the return of the electromagnetic waves.

Finally, when Peter showed it was time, they went back inside to lay Brad's body on an extra-long twin-size hospital bed from the Medical Dome. Rick wordlessly helped connect the wireless ECG and EEG monitoring pads to measure Brad's heart rate and brainwaves.

After that, Brad was ready to be revived over the next few hours. Rick undressed, removing his white t-shirt and navy-blue pajama pants and slippers, and climbed naked onto the bed behind Brad's body, already on his left side. Sliding his left arm underneath Brad's neck, he lay down behind his husband, big spooning him. Peter pushed a pillow under Rick's head, cradling it. Rick gently threw his right arm over Brad's hips, pulling their bodies tightly together. Rick settled in to relax, his smooth, yellow-copper frame behind his husband's pale, blue, cyanotic body. Neither Peter nor Rick said a word when Rick nodded his head to indicate that he was comfortable. Peter covered their bodies under multiple layers of plush, duck-feather bedding and noticed the yellow and blue airplane pictures, and smirked.

"I wonder where they got this from. Probably from an unoccupied apartment?" Peter conjectured out loud. "Sorry, are you comfortable? I'll enter the room periodically to monitor Brad's core temperature and administer anticoagulants, and I'll send for Mika when his core temperature reaches eighty-five degrees. Then we'll start tiny electromagnetic shocks to his heart, just to wake and loosen the heart chambers."

"Okay, and Peter, thank you," Rick whispered somberly.

He looks distraught and disconnected from reality. Peter dimmed the lights.

"You are welcome. Don't worry, just relax and give your love and heat to Brad," Peter said and left to sit vigil to monitor them from afar.

Phoenix will need Brad. I suspect the trouble has only started.

He hoped his suspicions weren't correct.

CHAPTER 4
SOMETHING FISHY

"GOOD MORNING, MEN OF PHOENIX.

Lasitor bids you a good morning.

It's now six a.m.

Learning to navigate using the stars is important and can be the difference between life and death. Still, only ten percent of you know how to do it. Statistics also show that it's often due to laziness or the task seeming so daunting that it gets put off, and people eventually get lost.

Statistics show you spend more time outside searching for each other than inside enjoying each other's company. To prevent getting lost, visit our community news page to learn more about navigating Antarctica. There's no need for it to be complicated, you can learn how to do it in minutes with The Beginner's Guide to Natural Navigation of the Stars.

Breakfast is served until eight a.m.

I hope you find your way!"

. . .

Dr. Mika Romanov

As fast as the ground blizzard had hit Phoenix, it dissipated. Tonight, with the Code Yellow still activated, Connor and Bryan could investigate without hindrance from the general population.

The blond giant knew he possessed a genius-level intelligence. The men of Phoenix loved him for his honest, boisterous personality. He served on the leadership council of three that was established with the birth of Phoenix when a new code of conduct was needed for their unique all-male community. Mika was an approachable guy, and his big build and prominent personality made him someone to look up to. As intelligent and bold as he was, he never acted self-righteous, making him one of the most beloved leaders and re-elected council members in Phoenix. Every three years, Mika, Connor, and Bryan got re-elected. Their council had disappointed no one so far; so, why put someone in a position to destabilize the status quo? Despite that, the voting continued every three years, and thus, the status quo persisted.

Mika had received word from Connor that they'd found another Phoenix resident dead outside, so Bryan came to escort him to where the men had found the upper half of Joshua Adams's body. The fresh powdered snow crunched loudly under Mika's boots as he followed Bryan to the gruesome scene, contrasting against the brilliant midnight-blue with no clouds and the Milky Way that hung low in all its splendor.

"Although it had stopped snowing, the mini-blizzard we just had washed away most of any existing evidence," Bryan said. "Connor is already working at the scene, taking pictures and collecting evidence."

"Hmm, I see," Mika said. However, he never lifted his head as he concentrated on searching the ground for more clues. Slowly, they made their way over to his husband. Mika couldn't shake the feeling of trepidation. He halted at the first perimeter line and surveyed the area, where some men were scavenging in the snow. Others assisted Connor while a handful of soldiers patrolled the area about five hundred meters in the distance.

Connor looked up from where he was working, smiling instantly when he saw Mika and came to greet him.

"Hello, love, are you okay? Do you need anything?" Mika asked and felt relieved seeing him. "To say today was hectic and nerve-wracking is a definite understatement."

Connor stomped his boots, cleaning them. "Okay, as can be. I'm very glad to see you." His voice was hoarse, exacerbating his thick Irish accent. He saw the big stainless-steel flask of coffee Mika offered him

ERYN, KING OF THE BRAWL

and gave him a brilliant, appreciative smile. "Thank you. I just thought to page the food services to bring out soup or coffee for the men. We've been at it for a while now. How's Rick coping?" Connor asked as he led Mika to a spot where they could talk privately. They stepped carefully over the green, pink, and yellow paint-marked areas identified for collecting snow impressions.

Both squinted and shaded their eyes from the bright spotlights that had been erected to light up the scene. Mika could tell the day's events were wearing on Connor's nerves. His husband's eyes were red and puffy. He looked exhausted. He found his best friend's frozen body and risked his own to bring him in. Mika assessed Connor up and down. The feeling of unease nagged at him. Connor took eager gulps of the freshly brewed coffee, his breath coming out in puffs as the warmth fought to keep its heat in the sub-zero temperatures. Connor and the men were dressed in regular zip-up white, green, and black arctic suits. He looked warm enough, so Mika relaxed a bit and spoke. "Rick's okay. He's with Peter. But first, tell me how it went with Rick when you told him about Brad?" he prodded, trying to give his husband the much-needed support and outlet he knew he needed.

"Not so good. It was difficult for me to witness Rick's lack of reaction and remain professional. To be honest, his emotional stoutness floored me. I think the truth has yet to sink in. We've all gotten so used to thinking we'll live forever. I suggested we see Brad and speak to Peter, but I got called here." He pointed to Joshua. "I can't force the man to break apart. I expected him to show emotion and lose his shit. Instead, I lost my shit, and Brad's not even my husband. I tell you, yelda, when Rick hugged me, my empathy and fears for him and their boys knocked me over, and I bawled my eyes out for them. Then I thought it might have been you or, god forbid, one or both of our sons, I discovered frozen curled into a ball." Connor confessed while barely taking a breath between sentences.

"It's understandable. We're a huge family and we've become closer than ever. It's natural for you to feel upset. You were really worried when Brad went missing, but you found and saved him. It was a relief for you." Mika approached and said, "Let me hug you, gille-toine." It was Mika's special name for Connor, which they came up with on their first night together. Gille-toine meant little bed buddy in Gaelic, and yelda meant big dick in Russian."

Connor fell into Mika's arms, resting his head on Mika's chest. A full embrace wasn't possible because he carried a bag of evidence, his camera, and the coffee, so he awkwardly stood like a statue, soaking up the support as Mika swung his long arms around to console him.

Mika lowered his voice to a whisper. "Don't worry about Rick. He's coping. He's a medical professional, and they have a way of compartmentalizing their emotions. I assure you, he's terrified of losing Brad, and Peter is taking great care of both Brad and Rick. Rick knows and trusts Peter, and we all know Peter's the best person to save Brad. Unfortunately, at this moment, there's not much help I or anyone else can offer." Mika rubbed his cold nose against Connor's. "Now, tell me, what have you discovered? Was it a freak accident? Was it caused by man or nature, and why was Joshua out here after we received a blizzard warning?" Mika's internal alarm bells wailed cease-lessly. He studied the darkness of the outer roped area behind the border of yellow tape.

When he saw no movement or confirmation of his concerns, he kissed Connor on his forehead and stepped back from the embrace. Connor seemed deeply satisfied, almost swooning after Mika's embrace. He looked recharged, content, and deeply in love as he smiled at Mika. Clearing his throat, he stepped away and switched back into his role as Connor Romanov, second in command of Phoenix, and gave Mika the rundown of the scene.

"Okay, thank you for that. I needed it, yelda." He blushed and took another few sips of the coffee.

"I know, and it's my pleasure." Mika smiled gently. His eyes prickled with tears as his love for Connor overwhelmed him.

"Bryan had established fifty, hundred, hundred and fifty, and two hundred meters perimeters around

Joshua's body." Connor pointed to Joshua, who sat upright like a planted Christmas tree. Mika followed Connor, taking care not to step on any evidence, while he nodded, signaling he was listening and simultaneously surveying the backdrop beyond the city of Phoenix's outer lines. From this distance, Mika could see Joshua's face, frozen in horror. The gory sight made Mika's skin crawl. Joshua's mouth and eyes were wide open, and his lips were pulled back, revealing his teeth, fixed in a last scream of agony.

Mika shuddered, imagining the excruciating pain the man experienced. "Is he sitting upright or...?" He halted mid-sentence, thinking that the snow had hidden his legs, but upon closer examination, he saw only the torso.

"You see right, yelda. We have these fifty-meter perimeters." Connor turned and pointed with a green laser pointer at the snow. "As you can see, we discovered Brad over there. Look in the crevice's direction. Brad was probably heading this way, hearing Joshua calling. Knowing Brad, he probably raced to aid while concentrating on helping and missed the fissure. But have a peek here." Connor pointed to several tracks and indentations in the ice.

"Hmmm, that's odd," Mika said. Placing his boot inside the one indent.

"Maybe a walking stick and homemade snowshoes. I can't imagine anyone having bigger feet than you," Connor asked rhetorically, appearing deep in thought. Mika watched his husband as his mind worked. He didn't want to break his train of thought. As a scientist, he knew how valuable it was to have a few seconds of uninterrupted mental calculations. He patiently waited for Connor to surface back to reality. It was cold outside, but not unpleasant for this time of the year. He had nothing to do but kill time and wait for Peter's call to assist with Brad's resuscitation.

The feeling of unease raised the hairs on his neck, and he shivered a few times. *Someone is watching us.* He sniffed the air. Smelling blood, the ozone scent of snow, and a slightly fishy odor. Strange, he thought, and saw Bryan conversing with a few men on the far-right side of the boundary. *Maybe there's time to do some investigating of my own.* He left Connor alone with his thoughts.

"Ah, here comes the smartest man in Phoenix. Mika, what a day," Sergeant Amir Lamasi said as the group noticed Mika approaching.

"Comrades." Mika counted ten men armed to the teeth and clothed in full tactical gear. He smelled the air again, wondering whether he'd imagined the fishy odor. Perhaps one of the men went fishing or something. As far as he knew, no one had planned a day excursion due to the storm warning. Perhaps someone took advantage of the fact that they were outside. Unobtrusively, he bowed his head and asked. "Do you smell fish?"

"Yes, we smelled it on the wind. Something fishy," Bryan said.

"When it stopped snowing, it became stronger," Amir said, barely audible, while kicking the snow with his boot. Feigning disinterest.

"I smell sweat, either ocean or fish, blood, and gunpowder," Bryan said under his breath, stretching his arms out and yawning.

"Do you have the impression that someone's observing us?" Mika sat on his heels, pretending to pick something up from the ground.

"Yes, that's an affirmative." Bryan looked up at the sky and then darted his eyes in the direction from which the smells drifted. "That way." He lifted his chin.

"At least I'm not imagining it, comrades." Mika stood and joined Bryan, gazing at the stars.

"We have a strategy. I've soldiers who have fallen to the rear and sides and are now encircling from a five-kilometer radius. Whoever is spying on us is unaware that we're aware of them."

"They're either unaware or unconcerned," Mika suggested.

"Let's go back to Connor and talk about Joshua." Bryan motioned with hand signals for his men to fall back and form a circle around the perimeter. "Whoever's watching thinks we're solely focused on this." He pointed to Joshua. "But we'll get them apprehended. I have complete faith in my soldiers." Bryan appeared in perfect spirit, enthusiastic and motivated to catch the perpetrators. Circumstances like these seemed to energize him.

Master Sergeant Bryan Howell was promoted to Captain after handling an emergency scenario with gallantry and bravery after the first big Phoenix earthquake. He was in his late forties when his Peter Pan Cap was placed. His full head of black and silver hair made him a stunningly attractive silver fox. He oversaw the Phoenix Military Reserve and Security and was one of the few men who appreciated being locked up with men and no females in sight after Doomsday. He'd always kept his sexuality hidden from his wife and family. Despite his grief over the outbreak and the death of his family, he embraced their new life by relishing in as many men as he could until he renounced his playboy attitude by falling in love with Tony Bonillo, who captivated him completely. The sharp-witted Italian civil engineer assisted in the design of Phoenix while still a student and interning at Environmental Project One, the initial title given to the complex by its founders.

Bryan halted at the fifty-meter perimeter, and Mika joined him. "We've established this a safe distance, not only because of the possibility of contamination of evidence but also because of the unpredictability of more cracks appearing in the ice."

Mika hated that Connor was putting himself in danger. He was the most accomplished code breaker, which made him the most qualified candidate to solve this enigma. They watched Connor lying on his stomach, inching toward Joshua's body. He was strapped into a rope and harness and secured to iron rods that had been pounded deep into the ice.

Mika swallowed bile. His stomach clenched. He took a deep, anxious breath. *Freezing hellfires.*

Bryan shook his head, then crossed his arms and spread his legs wide. All the men in the group appeared to be aware of the risk. No one made a move. When Connor reached Joshua's body, he carefully threw a rope cowboy-style over Joshua's head, securing it around his torso. All the slow-motion and carefulness agitated Mika. *Why is he taking so long? It's dangerous. I've had enough of this for one day.*

"Please hurry and take care. My nerves can't take it," Mika begged quietly under his breath. Grinding his teeth, he watched Connor taking photographs and gathering evidence thoroughly as if it were for bloody National Geographic.

"Joshua had been trapped between the sliding ice sheets," Bryan explained. "Connor could not identify the exact time of death. Once an autopsy is done, they should be able to provide a reasonable estimate. But the big question is, what was Joshua doing out here in the middle of nowhere on the ice? I'm also wondering what Brad saw. He should be able to give us more answers. I spoke to Peter a few minutes ago, and he told me he's working on reviving Brad," Bryan said.

"Yes, it's just watching and waiting for the next six to eight hours," Mika answered while looking at Connor knee-walking and taking more pictures of Joshua and the surrounding area. The foul odor of death and shredded intestines hung in the air. It worsened when the wind blew their way.

"Connor seems to notice something in the distance. Look how smart your man is. He's pretending to snap additional body shots while holding his camera at an angle. I hope he zooms into the frame for a better opportunity to observe the backdrop when we download the images," Bryan said.

Connor looked back at them and waved. Mika waved in a beckoning motion with his pointer finger and thumb. "Yes, gille-toine, stop waving. I'm anxious. Hurry and get your leprechaun ass out of there," Mika mumbled, his mood worsening by the second. He raised his arm and tapped his wristwatch, signaling that it was time to return. Connor raised his arm, indicating that he needed five more minutes, and pointed to Joshua, demonstrating his plan with push and pull motions. Mika felt like stomping his feet, walking over there, and dragging Connor by the ear away from the danger.

At any moment, the ice can open again, swallowing you and Joshua.

Kneeling, Connor pushed and tugged at Joshua, trying to loosen him and free him from the ice. He poured what appeared to be salt, warm water, or oil around him into the crack. A crowd gathered around Mika and Bryan, watching the spectacle of Connor, who groaned, slipped, and then cursed loudly in an Irish brogue with each effort. Connor's head vanished for a moment, causing Mika to take another anxiety-filled breath.

"What are you doing? Come back, leave the dead man. I'm sure Joshua's going nowhere," Mika ordered. His patience was at an end, and he was seconds away from grabbing the rope and pulling Connor back to him. The day had been too long, and Mika wasn't amused at all.

"Joshua might have a trapped ankle or leg," Connor shouted.

"Come back, leave him!" Mika yelled as he grabbed the safety rope. "I'll pull you back if you don't return right now. I've had enough for today!"

Connor signaled for one minute.

"Freezing hellfires!" Mika stomped his feet in frustration. They watched as Connor knelt, pushing his arms down between Joshua and the ice, clearly trying to loosen the corpse. Then his head snapped back, and Mika froze; all the men heard the dull sound of a long, slow-releasing fart. The air practically vibrated as it escaped into the night. Connor sprang back, arms spread wide, landing on his back.

More profane curses drifted from his direction, accompanied by the unmistakable smell of ruptured intestines. Connor, who had never tolerated foul odors, experienced an unforgettable, self-inflicted reflexive dry-heaving attack.

"Mother of hell!" More cursing soared on the wind toward Mika and the crew, who were watching Connor on his knees. Sounds ebbed and flowed toward them—*blargh, blargh*—followed by the distinct stench of excrement.

Fortunately, Connor's stomach must have been empty since he only expelled a few drops of coffee and bile. But he was never a quitter, so he tackled Joshua's stuck body with renewed determination. Vigorously twisting the deflating torso. Back and forth like an old mailbox stuck in the ground.

"It looks like Connor's dancing with a tiny Joshua," someone said in the back.

"Canoodling with corpses now. That's just sick." Bryan giggled like a ten-year-old approaching puberty. Mika wanted to pound his face in. But Joshua wasn't budging. He was going nowhere. Connor must have realized it. He leaned back to catch his breath. Then, without thinking, he accidentally rubbed his hands through his face and hair.

"You idiot!" Mika yelled, unable to ignore the silly banter from the nosebleeds. He couldn't help it. He laughed.

Blargh, blargh. Connor fell back to his hands and knees as more, *blargh, blargh*, drifted back to Mika and the crowd.

"What a drama queen?" someone said.

Mika didn't take his eyes off Connor. *I hope they pissed themselves laughing. Bloody wankers.*

Finally, Connor seemed he had enough of it all. He signaled to be extracted, waving his hand in a circle over his head repeatedly and very fast.

"Okay, let's get Connor out of there!" Bryan called it. The laughter died down, and they sprang into action. Connor lay back onto the ice, apparently tired of playing cowboy for the day.

"You stupid leprechaun," Mika exclaimed, bending to help Connor from the ground.

"You stink!" Bryan teased and doubled over again.

"Piss off, Bryan." Connor struggled frantically to remove his harness. Mika swallowed his laughter and bent to help Connor out of it.

"You and your team need to remove Joshua. I've gathered enough evidence. You can take him to Rick's lab for the autopsy. I'm going to take a shower!" Connor said, very frustrated. "By the way"—he raised his index finger—"it looks like the crack has shifted and widened another five inches, so be careful...this area is quite unstable."

"Go ahead! Laugh at me." Connor scoffed, lifting his knees high, forging a path through the banks of snow, muttering to himself.

Mika reconsidered reprimanding his husband, biting his lip. "No, my love, it's not funny. I was worried about you. Oh, and I forgot to tell you, you're in charge of Phoenix for the next twenty-four hours." He chuckled from behind Connor as he followed at a safe distance, avoiding the horrendous smell.

"Come walk this side where the snow blowers have cleaned a path already. You're going to fall into a hole. Then we have to save you. Please, Connor." Mika's heart rate spiked thinking of that scenario.

"I bloody know!" Connor shouted as he veered left toward the path about twenty meters from Mika. Men, primarily soldiers, jumped out of the way when they saw Connor, who seemed to be on the warpath.

The pair returned to their apartment, where Connor began undressing even before fully entering the front door. He kicked his pants aside and hopped a little on one leg to remove one sock, then the other. Mika stood to the side, leaning against the foyer wall with his arms folded and his left leg crossed over the other, admiring the angry Irishman's backside.

"I don't think the smell will wash out of the suit." Connor gagged, and Mika wondered if he was dry-heaving as he disappeared around the corner into the shower. "Ahhh, thank the stars for hot, clean water," Connor said, then sighed in appreciation. Mika stuck his head into the bathroom. He had a bag filled with Connor's snowsuit and clothes in his hand.

"I'm taking your clothes and boots down to housekeeping, and then I have to go help Peter and Rick with Brad. Do you want to come and watch?" Mika asked, enjoying watching his husband's silhouette through the fogged-up glass as Connor scrubbed himself vigorously.

"Maybe later. Do you know where the boys are?"

"Nope, I think they could be with the McCormick boys. Rick said something about asking them."

"Oh, that's good. I was worried about them. Something weird was going on, and although it looked like Joshua was killed because of a natural accident, I thought I saw someone watching me earlier tonight," Connor said, rinsing himself and applying shampoo and conditioner to his hair for a second time.

Mika's longing for his husband stirred. He coughed and cleared his throat. "Maybe I should help you scrub your back?" He bent to put the bag down.

"Don't you dare, Mika. I'm in a hurry. I need to download and enlarge those pictures I took. Something feels off here. I think the people watching us are from another place. Maybe they're Doomsday survivors. I've no idea where they've been all this time, but Joshua knew, so I need to get to his apartment as soon as possible. Perhaps I can find some clues about the man and what he knew there."

"Yes, you are correct. At first, I thought we were under attack, but I also sensed that we were being observed from a distance. It's good we're on high alert."

Connor closed the taps, opened the shower door,

grabbed a towel, and dried himself. Mika continued, appreciating the body he knew so well.

"No, Mika, maybe later," Connor said—again.

Mika rolled his eyes. "I can control my urges when I have to," he drawled, but he knew the hunger in his eyes said differently. Connor continued drying himself. Climbing out of the shower, he bent forward, teasing Mika.

"I'm only admiring what is mine, anyway." Mika focused on his narrow waist and well-defined calf muscles, then smiled seductively at Connor. "I would love to lick the water..."

Connor turned, towel-drying his hair. He raised his elbows, showing off his abs and the sharp line of his hip to Mika.

Mika watched his husband, eyes fixed on him, and licked his lips. Connor, teasingly, turned to brush his teeth. Mika went to the bedroom and sat on the bed, waiting. Soon, the comforting sounds of Connor's post-shower routine drifted from the bathroom. The gargling and spitting, and the uniquely loud toot of a nose-blow that always made Mika smile. The toilet flush made his heart race.

Like a lab rat detecting cheese.

Connor emerged naked, ever proud, from around the corner. Prancing past Mika like a doped-up runway model, eyes hooded and full of confidence, straight to the underwear drawer. He hummed an unidentified tune while choosing a pair of socks and his favorite tight-fitting briefs. He turned dramatically to put on his underwear.

"You might as well take them off again. I've changed my mind. I have to have you," Mika said, as his body reacted to his husband.

"You might as well take them off again. I changed my mind. I have to have you. I need you," Mika said, feeling feral with the need to have life-affirming sex. Connor smiled slyly and slowly pushed them down again.

"God, I love that ass of yours. Those perfectly sculpted cheeks were made for me to fuck you long and hard. I need to bury my cock deep inside you. Come here and bend over for me," Mika ordered, but Connor harrumphed, making a big show of slowly turning around. Instead of bending forward and grabbing his ankles, he walked seductively past Mika. Keeping his gaze fixed on Mika, he opened the bedside drawer, located the lube, and passed it over. He slammed the drawer shut with a flourish, strode past Mika to the foot of the bed, turned, and with a dancer's poise, bent forward to present his pink hole. Instantly, Mika was on his feet, kicking off his slippers haphazardly as he moved to position himself behind Connor.

"You know I fucking love it when you tease and play cat and mouse games," Mika said huskily. He then switched to an Irish accent, mimicking Connor. "No, Mika. Not now, Mika. I don't have time, Mika."

Back in his own voice, he finished, "And all I hear is, please, Mika, fuck me senseless, use me anyway you see fit, Mika, come conquer me, and plow me." Grabbing the perfect glutes he loved to spread, Mika exposed Connor's hole and salivated.

Connor glanced back, eyes burning with desire, and their eyes met. The room went utterly silent. He knows exactly what I'm going to do to him, Mika thought, stepping forward, gently nudging the backs of his husband's knees so they buckled slightly. Connor understood the unspoken invitation, sliding his hands down his thighs as he lowered himself onto the bed, opening his legs wide. He moaned, grinding himself against the mattress, seeking relief from the ache.

"You're such a tease," Mika murmured, shedding just enough clothing, his pants and underwear discarded while keeping his button-up shirt on. His cock swung heavily, its impressive size and weight preventing it from springing to attention. Connor grabbed a pillow and tossed it behind him. Mika caught it and slid it beneath Connor's lower stomach, tilting his hips up for easier reach. Mika knelt down, settling back on his heels. Connor's breath came in short bursts, awaiting the feel of a warm tongue. Mika savored the moment, drawing it out. He dotted tiny beads of saliva onto the creased skin surrounding the rose-pink opening before him, then licked it in languid, broad circles, avoiding the center. "Hm, damn, you taste delicious," Mika breathed between his ministrations.

"Mika, fuck, are you trying to kill me?" Connor gasped, breath heavy like a dog's on the Miami boardwalk. Mika felt slight tremors in his husband's hairy, muscular thighs. He responded with gentle licks, a quick flick of his tongue, teasing Connor's taint with lightning-fast touches. Mika had perfected this particular torment and knew it drove his husband wild when he lingered between his hole and his balls.

"Mika, for fuck's sake, we don't have time for this. Uhmmm—"

Mika silenced him, taking both of Connor's testicles into his mouth, one after the other. He teased them in his warm mouth, wetting them thoroughly before stretching Connor's scrotum with his lips. He repeated this pleasurable torment twice more, then released them, letting them slip out one by one.

Connor shamelessly rutted into the pillow below him. "Hold still, or I'll stop," Mika lied. He had no intention of stopping. Connor held still but protested with pathetic whining sounds, which made Mika so hard he had to squeeze his cock a few times for relief. He proceeded with his lazy assaults on Connor's backside by licking a path excruciatingly slow from his balls upwards.

Mika, pleased with the slick trail he'd left, gently blew air over Connor's sensitive spot. Connor shook his head, his moans and frustrated Irish curses muffled by the bedding he'd pulled around his head. After each, "Ah, fuck, yes," he'd grab more bedding, muttering obscenities—proof he was losing it. "Ah, yes, don't fucking stop," he blubbered.

Mika knew the Irishman was leaking pre-cum, and he wanted a taste of it as much as he tried to drive Connor over the precipice of lustful insanity. He got up, removed the shirt, and slid his hand underneath Connor's hip to grab hold of his five-inch diameter beer-can dick. When he had a comfortable grip, he laid his rigid member against Connor's crack without entering him, enjoying the pressure while he knew Connor loved the overpowering domination.

"Fuck my hand. I want to taste you," Mika ordered while he bit down on his upper back. Connor immediately pumped, eagerly obeying Mika. "Ahh, feel how wet you are for me. That's enough. Lift for me, gille-toine." Mika milked every drop he could get until the palm of his hand was slick. Pulling his hand out, he licked Connor's sweet natural lubrication.

"You taste so motherfucking good, gille-toine. Do you want a taste?" Connor moaned the affirmative drunkenly at Mika's filthy seduction. Mika dug between their bodies. Milking his cock and mixing their essence. Then offered a lick to Connor.

"Hmmm, that's it. Taste how exquisite we taste together." Connor lapped at Mika's hand as if it were the last drop of Mika's pre-cum in the universe. Mika lifted his big, hulking body from Connor and then went back to work eating ass. Minutes later, after stretching and much more prostate stimulation, Connor pleaded, begged, and cried for Mika's cock.

Mika was dizzy with arousal. "What a fucking pair we make. I'm so worked up I can't open the bottle of lube." Half blind with lust, he fumbled with the strawberry-mint-flavored glycerin lubrication. Connor laughed into his cocoon of bedsheets. "We'll see who laughs last, my little leprechaun." Mika frantically lubed Connor's hole, grabbed his ten-inch pole at the base, and inserted the head into Connor's well-stretched hole. "Ah, fuck yes, I love this best," Mika said and plunged into his idea of heaven.

"Hmmm, feed me that monster cock of yours, yelda. I need to feel the burn. Fuck me good, please, husband. I need to forget the ugly things from earlier today."

Mika ignored his plea. Rocking back and forth as if he had all the time in the world. Feeding Connor his cock inch by inch, knowing it was frustratingly slow.

"Oh, no, my fucking god! Mika, I'm ready. I want to feel your balls hitting mine," Connor muttered. Mika grabbed Connor's hips and increased the speed. His rhythmic, sensual pistoning rubbed Connor's prostate. "Yes, that's it, yelda, god, that feels so fucking good." The volume of their grunts and moans increased and filled the room with sounds of their carnal pleasures.

"Fuck, I love fucking you. You feel so good around

my cock. Just look at you taking all of me." Mika pulled out and watched himself being eaten by Connor's hungry hole repeatedly. "Jesus, I can do this the whole day, watching my cock disappear up your ass."

"Mika, please go faster. You can look at your cock another day," Connor begged. "Please, I need to be fucked into oblivion."

"Grab your cock, gille-toine," Mika commanded as he pulled back and straightened his legs so Connor could lift his hips, creating space so Connor could fist himself.

"Oh, and one more thing, earlier when I asked you to stop and come back to me, then you do so..." Mika folded his hand over Connor's fist and squeezed, simultaneously slowing and prolonging the torture. "I love you, Connor, too bloody much. You made me an older man today. I am worried so much about you. You're so stupidly brave. It scares me because I would rather have you alive than you trying to recover dead and frozen bodies," Mika whispered with a throaty groan into Connor's neck while his eyes rolled backward in pleasure.

"Yes, yes, okay, I will, I promise, that's it," Connor cried out in ecstasy.

Mika enjoyed each deep thrust of his hips and the closeness it created with Connor. Kissing and sucking his neck and upper back, he spoke his words of truth between each rhythmic movement. "I will not..." kiss, thrust, "be able to..." kiss, lick, thrust, "live without you." Kiss, lick, thrust. Finally, Mika let go of Connor's hand, leaving him to fuck himself.

"Hold on, my love. I'm going to give it to you now."

"Oh, yes, Mika, please! I'm sorry I made you worry about me. I love you, yelda."

Mika gripped Connor's firm, muscled hips, losing himself in the intense euphoria as he went wild on Connor's ass, a mix of playful punishment and deep affection.

"Yes, that's it, fuck me good, fuck me long, yes, yes, and hard, my yelda." Connor barely made sense. Sweat dripped in rivulets down Mika's temples, down his forehead, and into his eyes. He squinted, the salt burning his eyes, but he never let go of Connor's hips or slowed down, heaving like a sex-crazed gorilla, grunting in animalistic calls to the wild.

"Fuck, yes, you won't be able to sit for a week. You sexy hero of a man," he shouted.

"Oh, yes, baby, I'm going to come!"

Mika's orgasm exploded into Connor's guts just as Connor orgasmed, clamping his dick so tightly that Mika thought it was being amputated. Connor's prolonged orgasm was unending. Quiet mini convulsions milked every drop from Mika. He fell forward, sated and out of breath, onto Connor's back. They lay in that position, sweating and catching their breath together.

"Thank you, I needed that. I love you so bloody much," Connor whispered.

"I love you, too," Mika said, too weak and lazy to move. They passed out together, falling asleep for a few minutes.

Mika woke up and extracted himself slowly from Connor. Getting to his feet, he tenderly pulled Connor from the bed.

"Come on, we should probably shower. A rag isn't going to cut it this time."

Connor agreed, pointing to the cum running down his thighs. He stumbled after Mika without a word.

After a quick shower together, they got dressed. Mika leaned over and audibly sniffed Connor teasingly. Connor looked up and laughed. Warming Mika's insides. He could tell Connor was relaxed and ready for whatever was coming their way tonight.

"Are you done?" Connor asked.

"Yes, you passed the sniffing test," Mika said. Leaning in closer, he kissed Connor deeply and pretended to pull Connor back to the bed.

Connor pushed him back playfully. "Both of us must stay at least six feet from each other. We won't get anything done, and we might never leave the apartment."

"I know. It's all your fault. You seduced me. I'm weak in your presence." Mika changed the bed linen, adding the dirty pile to the bag of clothes, while

Connor disappeared into the kitchen. *Probably making a big cup of coffee for both of us.*

A few minutes later, Mika stood in the kitchen doorway, ready to go. "I love you, gille-toine."

Connor handed him his coffee and replied, "I love you, too, yelda." Their fingers touched a little longer than necessary, and his deep blue eyes crinkled at the corners. They knew their time together had run out. They needed to get back to work.

Mika grabbed the bag of soiled linen. "I'll take this to the washers, and I'll let you know what's happening with Brad." He kissed Connor's cheek.

"Okay, talk to you later," Connor said, grabbing his pager, camera, and evidence bag in a hurry. He dashed out of the apartment to upload and analyze the evidence back at his office.

Bang!

"Bloody hell, Mika, warn me next time. Will you please stop doing that? If I have a heart attack, it's your fault!" Peter exclaimed. Mika gave Peter a teasing smile.

Peter punched numbers into his computer and then, with a well-practiced move, pushed himself away from the desk, wheeling from one side of the desk back to a monitor screen to decipher the results of Brad's thawing process. "Things are progressing slowly, as expected, just what I'd hoped for, not much intra- or extracellular edema noted, but something's amiss."

"Hmm, show me," Mika said while adjusting the screen of the neutron scanner to accommodate his almost two-meter height.

"What happened outside?" Peter asked.

"Not much. Connor's looking at some evidence. We suspect someone's watching us. Connor took some long-distance pictures, and Bryan has the valley encircled and is in the process of apprehending the culprits. We could all feel their presence, but...hmm, oh yes, Connor had a minor incident while trying to move the body..."

"A body? What body?" Peter asked loudly.

"Joshua Adams's."

"Joshua?" Peter asked and flung himself around, turning back to his machines. "I'm rechecking the electroencephalogram and measuring Brad's brain activity...So, Joshua's dead. That's not good. What had happened?"

"Don't know."

"Hmmm...Mika, come look here and tell me what you see. I've been thinking maybe the EEG was faulty, picking up on Rick's movements." Peter smiled. "There were some erotic movements. I just turned the two-way mirror off," Peter said, blushing red and smiling like the Cheshire cat.

"Oh! Oooh, that's why it's blacked out. I thought maybe Rick got up naked and went to use the washroom or something," Mika said, his eyes wide with interest, stretching his neck to see inside, but with no success.

"Well, it's his husband. What he does to or with him is their business, so I blacked out my view."

"That's polite of you. I would have watched," Mika said, because he would have.

"I can monitor other, more important things like these weird EEG readings. That's why I said I thought it's because of movements."

"Let me see. Are these Beta and Gamma waves? Are you sure about this? Maybe the EEG pads are working incorrectly?"

Peter hit a few buttons. Then he compared his first readings and the most recent ones. "See, I was just comparing them when you entered. With or without movement, the readings stayed the same." He grabbed a pen to use as a pointer. "Look here. Rick was awake and talking to Brad. Here, Rick fell asleep, and I didn't go into the room, but movements on the EEG showed brain activity."

Mika looked up, eyebrows drawn together and a big frown on his forehead.

"Interesting stuff. What can it be?" Peter asked.

"*Ty che, blyad*?" Both beamed at each other. "What, indeed," Mika said deep in thought.

"Brad's core temperature is now thirty-four degrees Celsius. I'll administer the last round of meds, and then we can begin CPR."

Mika didn't respond. He continued studying the results as Peter left the observation room. His thick Russian accent had disappeared by ninety-nine percent over the past twenty-one years. The one percent remaining was for Russian swear words—and Mika loved cursing, especially while making love to his husband.

His silky, blond, shoulder-length hair cascaded over the black stubble on his face as he entered a slew of figures into the computer, his long, slim fingers racing over the keyboard. He grabbed and twisted his hair into a bun, a routine he followed to help him focus better. First, his hair irritated him, and second, he needed to see better.

Improved vision sharpened his thoughts, he mused, as he deciphered the EEG results. He drummed his fingers, stared blankly, then comprehension dawned. "Bloody hell!" he exclaimed, rushing for the resuscitation equipment. "Brad's been conscious the whole time! He was using Morse code."

CHAPTER 5
LET'S GET YOUR BLOOD MOVING

"GOOD MORNING, CITIZENS OF PHOENIX.

Lasitor, here. It's now six a.m.

Did you know a person is constipated if their bowel movements result in the passage of small amounts of hard, dry stool, usually fewer than three times per week? But did you also know that saying someone is constipated could mean that person may speak nonsense or falsehoods?

Visit your community news page to search for answers before speaking about falsehoods.

You can also search for home remedies like which foods to eat to prevent dry and hard stools.

Breakfast is served until eight a.m.

Hope you have a blockage-free day!"

DR. RICK LONGARROW-MCCORMICK

• • •

RICK HAD FALLEN ASLEEP CURLED up around his husband's back. The walk-in temperature-controlled decompression room was eerily quiet, except for the soft zinging noises coming from the air outlets of the thawing chamber. At first, Rick's teeth couldn't stop chattering, but as their bodies reached the same temperature, he relaxed and could speak to Brad.

He'd told him how much he loved him, how much he and the boys would miss him if he moved on, and that they would walk together once more, even if that happened. Rick told Brad about things he thought he'd forgotten, but once he started talking into the back of Brad's neck, he got carried away by the cathartic moment, telling Brad about anything that crossed his mind. Memories about growing up on the reservation. From being about four years of age, he recounted anything, no matter how silly. For instance, when he went fishing at the age of seven with his friends, they caught a sturgeon fish so big that one boy had to run home to call an adult for help, or risk losing the stolen fishing rod.

"Yes"—he juddered—"and then my father came." Rick snorted. "He helped us reel it in, but afterward, he told us to line up and drop our trousers for a spanking," Rick said, enjoying the vivid memory of the scowl on his father's face, as if he were in front of him.

"First, we stole. Second, we went fishing at a sacred, protected spot." Rick felt giddy with silliness, and he couldn't finish the last words. "We weren't allowed, but you know how kids are. Tell them not to do something, and they do the opposite. We caught my grandfather, the reincarnated chief who blessed the water and drowned himself to protect the lands..." Rick coughed, and more giggles escaped. "Father had to remove the fishhook and let it go 'cause the old man was a bastard, so no land of ever summers for him. They left him in the lake to live forever as a sturgeon fish." Rick laughed, but it brought the moment back to all seriousness with his internal debate about whether he should remove his Peter Pan Capsule if Brad were to die. He continued speaking, laying his heart out to his husband, the man who meant everything to him and to so many others in Phoenix who loved their charismatic leader dearly.

Before he fell asleep, Peter delivered more messages from citizens lining up in front of the lab, snaking down the hallway to convey messages of hope and love, as well as get-well-soons. Peter reported that now and then, someone's head would pop in, asking how Brad was or leaving notes and pictures the children had drawn for him. In his melancholy, he'd drifted off to sleep while holding onto Brad as tightly as possible. It was a selfish attempt to keep his soul on this plane, preventing him from moving on to the spiritual world and leaving him and their boys behind. Later, when Rick had awakened from a peaceful, dreamless sleep, Brad felt considerably warmer.

"Hmmm, I love the feeling of you." Rick moaned. He moved his hands over Brad's athletic physique, feeling every curve of muscle he loved in his husband's body. "Let's get your blood moving," he whispered.

He hoped Peter didn't notice because this was wrong on so many levels. "Dammit, you feel so good, and I miss you." He huffed into the back of Brad's hairline, enjoying the lingering smell of his favorite cologne. The overwhelming feeling of being with Brad, of making love to him, even if it was for the last time, left him dithering between what felt so good and how wrong this was.

Sucking a deep breath through semi-closed lips, he blew it out as slowly as possible. Then he repeated the mindfulness exercise ten times. After that, he concentrated on calming his libido and forced his heart rate to return to normal.

Tears spilled from Rick's eyes. "Baby, I can't stop loving you. I can't live without you." He was desperate for Brad to wake up. This was the side of Rick that no one knew. He was a resigned professional who did very well keeping his home and work life separate.

"It's hot." He squeezed his eyes so tightly he saw cobwebs and floaters in his field of vision. *This beats a hot yoga session.* Sweat beaded on his forehead, and he felt uncomfortable. His damp hair urged him to move away from the slippery wetness between their bodies. The result of spooning under yellow and blue airplane duck feather bedding for over six hours inside what now felt like a sauna to him.

"No, this is too much. First, you freeze yourself to death, and now we die from heat exhaustion." With one smooth movement, he threw all the comforters onto the floor.

"Ahh, now I can breathe again." *It's so hot in here. Peter is cooking for us.* He chuckled at his dramatic antics, then threw his arm back over Brad with a thud.

Overwhelming emotions of despair threatened to overtake his perfect self-control, but he swallowed them down to stay strong and believed Brad would return to them.

"Please, please, please, Brad, come back to me. Wake up, dammit!"

Rick lay waiting. Minutes later, just as he thought to call Peter, he felt Brad's muscles contract. "Umm," Brad moaned like a bear waking up from hibernation. His entire body stiffened beneath Rick. *It's a sign that his body and mind are waking.* Rick leaned backward for a better look.

"Thank the gods you're awake!"

Brad moved and attempted to open his eyelids. Rick peppered every surface, his face, eyes, lips, forehead, and cheeks with more kisses. Brad growled into

Rick's mouth. Rick sucked his cold tongue into his mouth, defrosting it.

Brad opened his eyes wide. "Hmmm." He sighed.

"My husband is awake! I love you, I love you, I love you!"

Rick looked at Brad, loving the sight of his open eyes reflecting the dimmed overhead lights. For a few seconds, Brad seemed disoriented, as if he didn't understand Rick. But then he smiled. His facial expressions softened, and their minds touched that familiar way they did when they made love without words. At that moment, Rick knew Brad said he loved him, and then Rick saw the want. *He needs me more than he could say.*

"I love you so bloody much, Gen. McCormick. I'd better get up. They'll be here any moment."

"I need water. I'm so thirsty..." Brad sounded like he trekked through a desert.

Just as Rick wanted to call for help, Peter opened the door unannounced. He snuck inside, then fussed and fidgeted in the dark. "It's time. He's ready to be revived," he whispered and turned on the bright overhead light. Rick straightened up. Peter froze and frowned, holding a stainless-steel kidney tray with three preloaded injections.

Before Peter could say anything, Mika burst into the chamber, smashing the sliding door to the side. "He's alive," he exclaimed and slammed the light switches with the palms of his hands. All the overhead lights shone with maximum illumination. Rick jumped to grab bedding to cover himself up.

Yellow and blue airplane duvet covers lay strewn over the floor, and the one covering Brad hung askew. Mika's and Peter's eyes were wide as they read the scene in front of them. Brad's covering slipped to the floor, revealing that Brad was definitely awake.

Mika had a stethoscope around his neck. Dumbfounded, he smelled the air and paused, seeming to take a second to think. "Okay, I'm a few minutes too late to check for Brad's chest sounds. Welcome back, comrade. I received your Morse code, a little too late," Mika said and threw the duvet back over a smiling Brad. Rick got dressed and helped Brad into white pajama pants and slippers.

"I was worried you would give Brad a precordial thump, as you did with Connor years ago, bringing the Irishman back from the dead." Rick laughed.

Mika handed Rick the stethoscope. "Yes, and Mika has a loving husband because of precordial thumping," Mika answered, reverting to Russian.

Rick's eyes glistened with tears as he listened to Brad's left and right chest sounds. The buzzing of the overhead lights was deafening in the quiet room. Mika waited with a big smile as Rick finished his assessment. "Thank you, I don't hear any abnormal lung or heart sounds." Rick nodded while removing the stethoscope from his ears. Then he followed the gazes down to the source of their astonished looks and radiant smiles, enamored with their leader, who lay with his eyes open and a grin on his face.

"You lucky son of a bitch," Mika exclaimed, offering his big hand to shake it.

Brad spoke with a soft raspy voice, grinning at Rick. "Hello, doctor," he greeted Rick with an all-knowing smirk, and those friendly chocolate brown eyes were the most beautiful orbs Rick had ever seen. He fell onto him, hugging and kissing him all over his face.

"You were awake. You knew I was feeling you up and speaking to you!"

Brad nodded with a mischievous look.

Peter stood to the side, staring at Brad, smirking like a happy Victor Frankenstein.

"Thank you, Peter." Brad coughed; his voice sounded like it had been put through a cheese grater. "Your concoctions saved me. I was never really gone. It was an experience. Mika, you're too late with the Morse code I sent you. Help me up, please. I'm parched." Brad struggled to get up, rolling to the side of the bed. Peter and Rick jumped to help, pushing him into a sitting position and swinging his legs from the bed.

"It's probably your cry for help that has your throat raw," Rick said. He felt guilty for riding him, noticing Brad move like an old man. "Oops, don't fall." Rick grabbed his arm to stabilize him. His eyes couldn't hide his surprise. "Your recuperation is unbelievably fast, but try to take it slow, my love."

"I'm a little lightheaded," Brad said, almost toppling over.

I'm so selfish. "I never thought you were in pain. Did I hurt you?" Rick asked, and Mika and Peter snorted in the background.

"No, of course not. I wanted it."

"We should monitor your blood pressure," Rick said.

"Yes-yes." Peter jumped to get the machine from the emergency cart Mika had brought in.

"Here, let me." Rick took the apparatus from Peter. While the machine took Brad's blood pressure, he offered his husband a glass of synthetic orange juice.

Mika walked over to the pager on the wall, pushed a few buttons, and waited for Connor to respond. "Connor. This better be good news!" Their second-in-command answered loudly with a thick Irish accent over the speaker.

"Good news. Brad's awake, gille-toine. Please let the men know. They must all be distraught and also be waiting for good news."

"Bleeding bloody hell, thank you!" Connor exclaimed. "Okay, I'll be down shortly." Static and a few clicks came over the speaker system before it went silent.

"What's that awful smell?" Brad asked in a barely perceptible voice.

"It's me and my boots, comrade. A lot has happened while you were playing spoons with your husband."

Rick climbed onto the bed with Brad, lying sideways, with his head on Brad's lap, and he stared upward like a lovelorn schoolboy. He didn't care about professional propriety. He was only thankful and most probably the luckiest person on Earth.

"Rick, love, could you help me to the washroom? I want to freshen up and be ready for Connor's inquisition." Brad groaned, rolling Rick over with an effort. "I don't want to hurt your feelings, but I feel a bit suffocated, and I've had enough of that for a very long time."

"Okay, that's our cue, everyone, out! Rick, down the hallway and to the right is the Lab's shower and changing room. Help yourselves to towels and scrubs and enjoy a long, hot shower." Peter turned, pushing Mika outside. "Let's go to our office and let these two get up and get ready."

"I thought they were ready already," Mika's voice was loud as he teased, looking back over his shoulder. His laughter traveled up the hallway as they disappeared into the same office that saved their lives twenty-one years ago. Connor, Mika, Peter, and the newborn twins had escaped the giant tsunami by locking themselves inside the watertight temperature-controlled environment that served as Peter's office.

Rick reluctantly got up, helping Brad by clasping his arms. He felt infatuated with his husband, so proud of him. So thankful. He wanted to rush home and lock them away from everyone, keeping them for himself for just one day.

"So, you like to sodomize dead people," Brad teased, whispering.

"I'm so glad you're okay. This goes against my medical knowledge and beliefs, but having you back, either by a miracle or Peter's advanced research, it doesn't matter. The boys don't even know about any of this. I think they're with the Romanov twins. I didn't want to scare them. My only thought was to stay positive and give Peter a chance to do his thing. The capsule you dug out of your pectoral and then chewed was probably what saved you." Rick had Brad's arm slung over his shoulder to support him.

"I was never gone, my mind, or maybe it's my soul. I don't know, but I could hear everything."

"Everything?" Rick asked as they hobbled to the washroom. He stopped, staring into those beautiful, dark chocolate-colored eyes with the friendly crinkles at the corners.

"Yes, everything." Brad rubbed the back of Rick's head, a comforting feeling he now appreciated more than ever.

"I loved every word and every calm action. Your lovemaking gave me direction on where to go to find you. I floated inside black darkness, and your words were like tiny sparks calling to me. The closer I drifted, the brighter and bigger they shone. If it wasn't for you, I don't know if I would've found which way was home," Brad explained, shuffling one slipper in front of the other.

"Also, I heard your Apache song for me. Thank you...And I think an angel sat with me." Brad looked into Rick's eyes, not blinking.

"I love you. You must tell me more about the angel." Rick wanted him to know that he could tell him anything. He would always listen and support him.

"Love you, too. Later, I'll tell you. Let's get me into a shower, please." Brad leaned in and kissed Rick.

After he'd helped Brad get dressed, Rick left Brad in the lab with Peter and Mika and stormed to their home.

He called for Donali and Kawa throughout the spacious executive apartment. Feeling increasingly anxious and trying to remain as calm as possible, he switched on all the lights. The quiet darkness confirmed they weren't there. His heart rate sped up. Blood pulsations rushed audibly through his ears, accompanied by the unwelcome sensation of nausea and light-headedness. Something was terribly wrong!

With his back against the steel wall, he slid down to the floor, taking a few deep breaths until the black and white spots in front of his field of vision disappeared. Feeling better, he got up slowly. Although it was futile, he opened up all the bedroom doors, checking every nook and cranny, hoping to find a note with a message at least.

After finding sweet blue bugger all, he went to the Romanov apartment, and his feelings of dread and terror increased—no one answered.

That horrible feeling a parent experiences when losing their child intensified as he stared blankly at the key card in his hands, wondering where to start searching next.

Where could they be?

Then, realizing Phoenix was too big to run around and search for the boys, he paged them on the general population overhead com system.

CHAPTER 6

CODE RED

"Good morning, citizens of Phoenix.

It's now six a.m.

Maybe some of you already know that Jupiter is the biggest planet of them all and that it's more than twice as massive as all the other planets combined in our solar system.

Also, if Earth were the size of a grape, Jupiter would be the size of a giant watermelon. And did you also know that seeds and paintings of the watermelon were found in King Tutankhamun's tomb as a gift for his long journey to the afterlife? This means that watermelons have been cultivated for thousands of years. Visit our community news page for more fun facts about watermelons.

Breakfast is served until eight a.m.

Hope you have a fruitful day!"

. . .

General Brad McCormick

Brad felt surprisingly warm and comfortable dressed in white scrubs, instead of his usual military uniform and boots. Wearing Mika's comfy rubber medical slip-ons, which he kept as an extra pair in his and Peter's lab, Brad squeaked-squeaked alongside Mika, escorting Brad from the Cryonics lab down the cold corridors connecting the domes that lay like lit-up ping-pong balls against the Trans-Antarctic Mountain Range.

The plan was to meet up for the evidence presentation and discuss the best next steps. The Command Center was their leadership hub, situated on the top floor of the gigantic Communications Dome. It was located in the center of the massive complex. A good comparison would be the head of an octopus, with its many tentacles serving as translucent passageways to the various plexiglass pods within the city's domed structures. Doorways from eight of the forty sides of the centralized Communication Dome connected the next ring of smaller domes, which were still large enough to fit several football fields in each. For example, the Agricultural, Research, Athletics, Medical, University, Transportation, and Housing domed sections. From there, it connected to smaller pods and so on.

They preferred using the colder, less-used hallways and stairs to avoid the crowds. The general Phoenix population almost never used these backway escape and service routes, because they were unheated and darker than the main hallways, preserving heat and energy. Thus, a small discomfort for Brad and his team of leaders and service people who wished to move around unhindered by inquisitive and talkative citizens.

Rick went to search for their younger boys, while Brad needed to get to the office to attend to messages, reports, and announcements. Their sons, Donali and Kawa, weren't answering their pings. They've met up with Connor halfway to the leadership office. He was happy to see that Brad was alive and walking, but upon hearing that their boys were also not responding, he handed them an armful of evidence and told them to get started, then went to find Cian and Ivan as well.

The preliminary evidence Connor had collected lay spread out on the new touchscreen prototype table, big enough for ten men to sit comfortably around it. This was one of the latest technologically designed, multi-layered silicone and PVC-coated touchscreen tables featuring a newly designed conductor material. It responded when in contact with another electrical conductor, like bare fingertips, and not elbows or butt cheeks—as reported by Mika and Connor, repeatedly, at Brad and Rick's dinner parties. Mika tapped the table to start it up, but nothing happened. He pushed the button on the side, but still nothing happened.

The overhead lights in the office hummed loudly. Enhancing the uncomfortable, silent pauses as Brad and Mika waited.

Brad's usual string of messages waiting for him to answer was strangely non-existent. He anxiously looked up, searching for answers on the inside of the glass-domed roof covering the mammoth tetraconta- gon. Usually, it relaxed him. But today he came up empty, with even more questions.

"Must be a fuse or something," Mika said, and he flipped open his husband's electronic notepad, getting to work.

Since there was nothing to look at, Brad couldn't hold himself in check. "I must admit, I feel like a defrosted, spanking new man." Patting his chest a few times, he doubled over, resting his hands on the dead tabletop in front of him. He guffawed, thought better of it, and swallowed his laughs.

"Are you having a seizure? Must I call for the medics?" Mika asked sarcastically.

Brad figured it probably looked like an upright epileptic fit as tears and spittle flew in between small piglet snorts. Gods, his emotions were all over the place. He was medically dead, resurrected, confused, disoriented, aroused, irritated, flabbergasted, scared, and now stupidly silly all in a couple of hours. He was acting out of character.

I just died and came back to life, he thought as he let loose and laughed explosively.

Mika just frowned, shaking his head. Sitting back in his chair, he locked his fingers behind his head and focused on Brad with a questioning look.

"I'm telling you, it's probably Peter's concoctions, and..." Noticing Mika watching him like a hawk, he turned to the big one-way observation window and continued describing his experience while repositioning himself discreetly. "I'm pumped full of drugs, and it bloody feels like red ants are marching inside my balls." He resisted palming himself for relief and rolled his eyes instead, before turning back to Mika. "The precise moment my consciousness returned to my body, I opened my eyes and connected with reality. My metaphysical and physical existence collided and exploded at the precise moment when Rick begged me to open my eyes. Mika, it was as overwhelming as it was welcoming. I was bombarded with sensations, feelings, and emotions...the opposite of where my mind was, where I sent the SOSs from. I didn't think or feel or have a sense of time. I just was, and it felt like I was tethered to Rick somehow. He kept me here like a balloon attached to a string." Brad tried to explain to Mika the best he could. Thoughts of Rick loving him encompassed eternity and floated back and forth through his mind.

I felt it, and I experienced it. We are two but also one... scattered like stardust, but one like the sun.

Mika wiped his long, blond hair back over his shoulders. His icy blue eyes had dark circles around them—*he was tired.* "I feel like those fireworks sticks we used to run around with. What were they called?" he scratched his chin. "Sparklers!" he exclaimed. Mika nodded slowly. As he listened, delicate laughing crinkles broke the tired dark circles around his eyes. Brad felt triumphant, noticing they deepened.

I'm lifting his mood slightly. Good, Mika always attempts to make us feel better with a smile or a joke, so I want to do the same for him.

So he continued his story animatedly. "I felt like an old *Chevy* motor car. You know, backfiring little ice cubes, icicles, or whatever the new name the kids come up with for the white stuff outside." Mika squashed his lips together, eyes tearing up. He looked like he sucked on a lemon or something.

Brad mentally counted backward, three, two, and one. "Pfft, bahahahaha!" The Russian burst out with a boisterous laugh. Slapping his knee a few times, he seemed to sober himself and swallow his laughs. He sat up, indicating he was zipping his lips. "Sorry, my friend, tell me, I am all attention. Your way of describing your experience is damn refreshing. I just imagined a snowman sounding like a motorcar while farting puffs of snow." Mika rested his chin on his fist, giving Brad his full attention.

Making you laugh was my full intention.

"I know, right? It's weird for me, too," Brad said.

Wiping his face up and down vigorously with both hands to sober up and clear his mind from the endorphin overload. "Mika, I experienced the most indescribable euphoric sensations, and the weird thing about it all is that they happened all at once. It would feel like being in heaven or when an angel touches you. That's the only way I can describe it. Let's say happiness, peacefulness, and all-encompassing, enveloping love. Plus, I felt radiantly warm from the inside. I don't think it was the amphetamines. Maybe that's what happens when your soul moves on, but I wasn't dying. It's just...something...or someone..." Brad stopped midway, noticing the deep furrows on Mika's forehead return. *He's too pragmatic, he's already doubting my sanity, and I'd better change the subject.*

"But anyhow, first things first." Brad steered away from the visiting angel and how the angel spoke to him.

"What was Joshua Adams doing outside, and who were the men with him?" He changed the focus of his conversation to more important matters, and he knew it was a good idea when he read Mika's body language—sitting up and obviously waiting for him to finish his antics.

"Comrade, I am glad we called an emergency leadership meeting to solve the mystery of the sour-faced Mormon Alderman from Salt Lake City. Nobody seems to have known him. When Connor, Rick, and Bryan arrive, I would like to be ready to solve this problem. Something doesn't add up. It makes me extremely uncomfortable. Call me a control freak, but I think I know all the residents and where they're at all times," Mika said. He looked up at the electronic clock on the wall and then back at the door like he was timing his husband's arrival. "Shit's happening under our noses. I'm expecting a hammer to drop at any moment. You have ants in your balls, and I have ants in my pants," Mika joked.

Brad smirked. He recognized his friend's nervousness in the way he bounced his legs. Mika returned his attention to Connor's notes.

Brad broke the silence. "The residents are moving faster than usual." It looked like a busy shopping mall the day before Christmas. "The bees are busier than usual. You said you ordered a lockdown," he remarked and turned his face upward. Basking in the early morning light that shone through the plexiglass roof.

"The Irish translation is *hede full of beis*, meaning to be preoccupied and agitated. I guess it's the same as maggots in the brains," Mika said.

"Hmmm, I agree with the maggot part. They forget what orders are and take them as opinions or recommendations. Phoenix has turned into a vacation resort," Brad said, verbalizing old feelings of frustration and irritation with non-military residents. Brad was supposed to be in charge of the military personnel, but since Doomsday, he'd taken on the role of General and Commander-in-Chief of the entire Phoenix, having been voted into the position.

Mika was his third in charge, after Connor, and he enjoyed Mika's unusually insightful contributions and observations during their conversations.

"Sometimes I feel ignored and obsolete," he told his friend honestly. He liked how Mika and the leadership team supported and never bored him. However, he guessed that everyone else, except Connor and their boys, bored Mika.

Brad joined Mika, shuffling through the stacks of pictures and evidence.

After a few minutes of looking at pictures of ice, snow, and a dead Joshua, Brad spoke and held his one hand up. "Let's count the facts as we'd gathered them," he said, wiggling his fingers.

"What I know about Joshua Adams is that he was forty-eight years old." Brad wiggled his thumb back and forth. "He refused his Eden Bean—"

"It's not compulsory," Mika interrupted, sounding agitated.

"I know, but the reason behind it may count or lead us to a clue. I think it could help us connect some facts. So, save that as an issue to answer why..." Brad continued. "Bryan said that his apartment looked like a monk lived there. The fact that he was a Mormon could explain that, but I feel it'll lead us to more clues. Something's amiss. I bet you he wasn't even living there. He staged it to fool us." Mika noted.

"When did you see Bryan?"

"Out on the ice, before we resurrected you," Mika joked.

Brad lifted his index finger. "What else do you know about the mysterious dead scientist?"

Mika sat up, pushing the photos aside, reading Connor's notes on the notepad. Brad stood, waiting for a summary.

"Interesting. Connor noted that he was lying and making excuses. Even his fellow research partners thought he was working in the Agricultural Domes, and when Connor questioned the Grain lab, they said he was busy in the Vegetable lab, and vice versa."

"So, what was he really doing?" Brad asked, slapping his hand on the table in frustration. The thing flickered. "Lasitor!" Brad called and paused, looking at the screens above, waiting for the AI face to appear, before responding. He turned in question to Mika and then back to the massive screens in front of them. He expected the black screen to light up and display a cybernetic male face, greeting them loudly and over-enthusiastically. But nothing. Only black stillness remained.

"What in the blazing gory hell?" Brad's voice echoed through the large, quiet office.

Mika glared at the black screens. "What is going on, Brad? With this and your feelings about the citizens, perhaps it wouldn't hurt to keep a closer eye on the men. Even though growing up being policed, controlled, and hunted, I vowed never to create that kind of environment for my children. I wanted, no, I know we all wanted, to live in a utopia. A place where our children could be free. We trusted the scientists to guide their research. However, I must agree with you. This place is turning into a vacation resort, and this" —he gestured to the inactive screens—"this situation is escalating." Mika leaned back in his chair, crossing one long leg over the other. "I think we need to implement at least an accountability system. This is really getting on my nerves, I must say. It's not safe, and the men and their children roam around as if they're at Disney World," he said, inspecting the photos with one hand. Flipping through them repeatedly, he seemed deep in thought. "I feel like I'm missing something. I feel like I'm on the brink of solving this puzzle, but something's troubling me. And where are our boys? I'm becoming concerned; it's been an hour since Rick and Connor went to look for them. I still haven't seen them. Who went to call Bryan?" the Russian asked anxiously, raising his voice with each question.

"I know. This is strange. Lasitor is never offline," Brad said, crouching down to crawl on his hands and knees beneath the table to restart the main computer. He turned it off and waited, counting to ten as Connor had taught him. Then, he restarted the system. As the minutes passed, Brad noticed the look in Mika's eyes. They were both anticipating confirmation of bad

news. The air was thick with trepidation and foreboding feelings he recognized well from his years
observing battlefields.

"Come on. Let's go through the photos," Brad
suggested, hoping to distract Mika while they waited.
Mika, staring out the office window, turned back to
examine the evidence. "The facts about Joshua and
how he deceived us—and his coworkers—must be a
clue." The same stifling apprehension was suffocating
them both, he thought.

Suddenly, static broke the silence over the speaker
system.

Rick's loud and clear announcement that the boys
were missing confirmed their fears. "This is Dr. Rick
Longarrow-McCormick. This is a broadcast of high
importance. We're looking for four young men. The
Romanov and McCormick twins. Donali and Kawa
McCormick. Please page the leadership office right
away. Cian and Ivan, your fathers are looking for you.
Anyone who has seen them recently, please page the
leadership office. If you see these four young men,
please tell them to report to the leadership office
immediately. If anyone has noticed anything unusual,
please report it. Thank you."

Brad tensed up. The announcement had his
emotions running wild. Mika looked up and said,
"Comrade, I fear the worst is yet to come. That
Mormon, what was he up to? Connor couldn't find

any clues in his apartment. Most importantly, where are our damn kids?!"

Brad's gut twisted, and a jolt of fear shot through him. "I don't even know where to start!" Brad ran his hands through his hair, weighing whether to continue searching himself or gather a team to start looking outside. *I must trust Bryan and Connor to handle this.* "Let's give the boys time to respond," he said, silently hoping and praying that his concern wasn't justified.

"Perhaps...Remember the time my twins had us all worried about nothing?" Mika asked.

"God, yes, I don't think Phoenix would ever forget that day," Brad said, with a nervous chuckle.

Mika sat up and crossed his arms. "We'll see what you do if your underage sons were found trying to slip into Quik-Fix Hall for a blow job."

Brad gasped and enlarged his eyes to three times their size. "Maybe that's where your boys have gone to, and they've taken Donali and Kawa with them?"

Brad gulped and cleared his throat. His boys just turned eighteen, and only twenty-one-year-old patrons were allowed in the red-light district. *The Romanovs are going to ruin my boys.* Then he shook that off. "I don't think my Apache angels would ever be convinced to go there. Rick and I have raised them well, and they openly discuss anything with us. If they wanted to go, they would talk to us and ask us about it. They know that's our red-light section. When Rick explained how babies were made when they were only six years old, he traumatized them so deeply that they had nightmares about vaginas and artificial wombs for years."

"Oh, dear lord!" Mika laughed, cutting the tension. "Yes, that's right. The word dildo turns your boys red as tomatoes." They laughed, shortly diffusing the tension.

"I'm sure they're swimming or watching movies in the Entertainment Dome. Maybe they're hanging out at Juandre and Andrew's?" Brad said, but inwardly he worried. He failed to hide his nervousness and knew he wasn't fooling Mika.

"Toss this. I'm going to search for my family," Mika said seconds later, throwing the photos down and jumping up.

Brad reached for the pager attached to the wall. Screeching interference noises surprised them. "Why all the static?" he asked, looking at the device. He dialed the general population. "This is your leader, General McCormick. Teams assigned to the tunnels and the Athletics Dome report immediately. This is not a drill. I remind you we are in Code Yellow. We are on high alert..." Brad halted mid-sentence, interrupted by Captain Bryan Howell, in charge of Phoenix's security and reserves, who all but fell into Mika on his way out of the office. Brad jolted, totally shocked when he saw Bryan looking trampled by a herd of buffalo. Mika side-stepped with a surprised look.

Bryan's usually neatly styled salt-and-pepper hair was pointed in all directions, sticking to his face. Streaks of blood and sweat ran heavily down his chin, and his left cheek was scraped right down into his neckline. Heaving heavily, he ran into the meeting room. His green camo pants and shirt were wet and in bloody shreds.

Coming out of his stupor, Brad immediately decided to increase the level of preparedness. "This is now a Code Red. We are on full lockdown. We are under attack. Reserves report to your stations. No one crosses over the barrier lines. If you're found outside your assigned area, you will be arrested and brought in for questioning. I repeat, this is a Code Red. Everyone who's not a soldier, return to your apartments. We are under attack and have been infiltrated. No one crosses the barrier lines. We are on full lockdown until cleared," their leader said.

"Bloody hell!" Brad exclaimed, looking Bryan up and down.

"General, we need to..." Bryan stopped, coughing into a handkerchief and clearing his throat. "We must assemble a team for a search and retrieval mission," Bryan barked. Brad noticed bright red blood on the cloth and wasn't sure where it came from. Maybe the cough or his face? Or was it a nosebleed?

Mika blinked, looking like he wanted to run but

stayed planted. The captain looked like he struggled to compose himself, swallowing some words and biting his lips. Bulging his fists, he took a deep breath, whipping the bloody snot and tears from his eyes and nose. "I'm so sorry, General," Bryan said to Brad, while tears streamed from his eyes.

Oh, my stars, he's crying? It shocked Brad to see the man in such an emotional state. He was usually so well put together in emergencies. His captain was distraught, walking in small circles, pumping his arms. He halted, collected himself, and then continued. "I'm sad to report that I lost the boys."

Mika gasped. Brad's heart nearly stopped again as fear overtook him. Bryan seemed to gulp his anguish back. He took a few deep breaths and continued to apologize.

"I knew it!" Brad said, slamming the headset a few times into its place. Bryan lifted his left hand as if to stop a blow to his face.

"Stop that. I won't hit you! Has anyone ever hit you?"

"No, sir, sorry, sir, but I deserve it anyway." Bryan cried into his hands, shaking his head.

"Captain, get a hold of yourself!" Brad ordered, and it seemed to help. Bryan straightened his back and swallowed his tears. Mika sat down, mouth agape.

"I have a team following them. They'll report back. They may be slow, but at least they can report on a general direction for us to pursue. We need to fuel up the airplane. I have one man in custody. He helped us stop the kidnapper. He, he, he...his eyes. I'll show you later." Bryan pointed to his face and then the ceiling. Confusion was written all over his face.

"You have a prisoner?" Brad was ready to go, but he realized he needed to prioritize the mess. "Is he secure?" he asked.

"Yes, sir, he's secured and cooperating. We can proceed to interrogate him, but I suggest forming a search party first."

"How many hostiles, Lasitor?" Brad called the AI and realized it was still in old-school mode.

Bryan frowned and looked at the screens.

Mika's table came to life, the screens lit up, and Lasitor answered.

One abductor, one captured. There may be more.

"What?" Brad asked furiously. They've wasted precious time, hoping for the best. "How many hostiles?"

Standing back, he watched the screen to read what Lasitor answered.

One sailed away with the boys. Enforcing Code Red. One friendly.

"This makes no sense," Brad muttered, stunned and silent as he calculated his next move. He wanted to run, but to where? He needed to rescue the boys. He must defend Phoenix. He took a deep breath and waited. "Alright, Captain." He paused. "Bryan, please finish. Explain so we can understand."

"Lasitor! Show me the map of Antarctica," Bryan ordered their AI.

"Certainly, Captain," the AI's robotic voice echoed loudly.

"Zoom in on the latest satellite photos!" Bryan ordered when a giant map of Antarctica appeared.

"Here, here, and here, in this direction." Brad's captain of arms pointed to specific areas on the map and circled them in neon yellow with his finger on the touch screen.

"We need to regroup to find the boys," Mika said, then immediately started bombarding Bryan with questions. "What do you mean, you lost the boys? What happened? Who took our boys?"

Bryan hobbled from one leg to the other in front of the screen, favoring his left leg while gripping his right hip. He grimaced in pain.

"I can confirm our suspicions that two foreign men were outside on the ice. From what I gathered from the alcove, only one man stayed there. They weren't there when we found the place, but it appeared to be a camp or a hiding spot. I saw carved animals and pictures. I found the fish we smelled, but only one plate, cup, and bed were made from furs. The men encircled the area, narrowing the circle to trap them, but all they found was the alcove. It tunneled deeper into the ice, leading to a subterranean area beneath the city of Phoenix. We gathered our lights and gear and followed an old trail that ran deep into the old volcanic tunnels. To our surprise, they opened just behind the Athletics Dome's entrance." Bryan said, pointing at the map, exasperated.

Loud gasps came from the direction of the door. Rick and Connor had arrived. Brad waved them over and watched as they dragged chairs closer to sit. "Please continue, Bryan," he urged.

"I think Joshua knew them and was possibly the middleman. They could have been family members, people he met, or perhaps...followed him here." Bryan was clearly speculating.

"Lasitor was hacked or damaged, and we don't have footage from the last few hours," Brad said.

"Are we under attack!" yelled Rick..

"Can we get organized?" Connor yelled. "We need to regroup!"

"I second that," Bryan said, pointing to the area behind the swimming pool. "This is where we heard someone calling for help. I knew it was one of the boys, but we couldn't determine which tunnel to take because of all the echoes. I sent the men to split up and stumbled upon a small hunchbacked man loading a weird-ass sailboat."

"A what?" Brad asked, his head whipping around to see if he missed something.

"A weird-ass sailboat?" Rick echoed, but they asked again, "A sailboat?"

"Yes, a boat, but not for water. They, whoever *they* are, had adapted it for ice. Maybe both water and ice," Bryan said, clearly annoyed. It seemed they had stretched his patience paper-thin. No one asked him to repeat anything. He paused, taking a few breaths.

"Okay, I could see the boys were tied up sitting down. I followed, ran, jumped, and clung to the side, attempting to climb in."

"Others were also jumping on the back of the boat. But once the sails opened, it flew over the ice, and none of us could hold on or try to continue climbing into it. That's when I noticed another man running alongside the ship—he was fast. He ran and jumped onto the boat. He even tried to stop it, turning it around and throwing anchors onto the ice, but his buddy came from the back and surprised him by kicking him on the ass right off the ship. We must have been going over a hundred kilometers per hour by then. I couldn't hold on to the side anymore. I was too weak, even though I could see the terror in the boys' eyes. Their mouths were gagged, and...they looked so afraid. I'm so sorry. I'm so very sorry." Bryan paused and turned away to hide his tears of shame. They waited for him to continue while looking questioningly at each other.

When he'd collected the courage to face his friends again, he said, "By the time I got up and recuperated, the boat had already disappeared over the hills. Fritz and four other soldiers were on snow riders following them. I signaled and radioed not to stop, for them to follow and stay in radio contact while I returned to Phoenix to regroup, maybe load the plane, sir." Head in his hands, he cried. "I'm so sorry." He apologized again with eyes full of tears. "The fear in those boys' faces...I'm such a failure...couldn't protect the boys, and they could see that."

Brad understood the situation for what it was. After Doomsday, Bryan had never explicitly stated it, but Brad and Rick knew he had quietly replaced the boys he'd lost by doting on Donali and Kawa. He suspected that all those feelings were surfacing. Bryan had never confronted those feelings of loss in a healthy way. He preferred to sleep his way systematically through Phoenix, and now the dam had burst as he sobbed uncontrollably.

"Thank you, Captain." Brad reminded Bryan of his professionalism. "Let's start from the beginning so that we can have all the puzzle pieces. How did you apprehend the second man?" Brad asked, trying to focus on the facts at hand. He knew it would be counterproductive to go in circles. "Wait, let's request a status update," Brad said, picking up the page to radio the team pursuing his boys. Corporal Fritz de Vries had been promoted from private to corporal two years ago.

"This is the Phoenix HQ. Corporal de Vries, come in. Over," Brad said, changing the frequency by pressing a few buttons. He tried again to make the call. Worry was etched on the faces of all the men in front of him.

"Corporal Fritz de Vries, this is leadership. General Brad McCormick here. Please provide a status update. Over." Brad silently hoped for a miracle. Then, static followed by the sound of motors humming crackled through the overhead speakers.

"Hello, General. This is Corporal de Vries. We are pursuing and tracking from a distance in a northeast direction from Phoenix City. We are nearly out of fuel. We will inform you when we lose visual contact or notice any signs of the ship's origin. Please send rein-forcements. We will continue the pursuit on foot. Over and out."

"Copy that. Thank you, de Vries. We appreciate your efforts. Are you within range to fire a tracker into the hull?"

"That's a negative, sir. Out," the corporal shouted.

"Copy. Can you stop and transfer the fuel from two vehicles into the third? Over."

"Copy. We can do that. Over."

"Copy. We're sending reinforcements. Are you prepared for the weather? Over?"

"Copy. Yes, sir. Over."

"Copy. I'll check in five-minute intervals. Over and out."

"Copy, over and out."

Connor pointed. "Brad, let's start with you."

Brad's facial expression and body language

changed so much that they all did a double-take. He knew his psychopathic warlord face was showing—good. I work better with my mask off. Now they'll understand why I won two wars for my country. Everyone except Bryan seemed stunned by the trans-formation.

"Okay, yes, they're being followed, so they're not gone yet. I agree it won't help if we all rush off prema-turely after the boys. Let's get to know the enemy," General Brad McCormick said. "Lasitor, are you recording this?"

"I am, sir," the male robotic voice thundered over the overhead speakers. The giant touchscreen shim-mered and divided into nine squares, resembling a tic-tac-toe board, complete with circles and crosses. Brad mentally rolled his eyes but refrained from repri-manding the cheeky AI. A map of Antarctica appeared in the top right corner, while the left side recorded their dialogues, word for word, as they spoke. In the center, the face of Joshua Adams glowed back at them, and neon blue lines formed a visual mind map. Facts and pictures filled the squares on the screen. In less than a minute, the program Connor wrote to enhance Lasitor's database many years ago resolved, clarified, and addressed all their questions and concerns, displaying slideshows of the evidence, Connor's notes, and the pictures Connor had collected earlier that day.

Lasitor was an updated version of the program

they had used to break into the Chinese satellites orbiting the International Space Station. Brad had grown accustomed to the AI scheduling and running Phoenix's entertainment and news broadcasting.

They viewed the Earth from space.

"Lasitor, add two more columns for questions and answers," Brad commanded. "Why were the boys abducted? Why did one attempt to prevent the abduction?" Brad asked, and the question appeared on the screen.

"What are their motivations?" Mika added.

"What do they want to do with the boys?" Connor asked, and silence fell over the room as tension rose. No one wanted to voice the worst fears.

"Are there only two men, or do they represent a larger group?" Bryan asked.

"Why did they meet Joshua in secret?"

"I will kill our boy's abductors. I will kill anyone who hurts my family." Mika grunted.

Brad nodded. "I know, Mika, and I'll help you kill the bastards. Starting with the one in custody." Rick gasped, but he said nothing, shaking his head.

The team continued brainstorming. "Also, gentlemen, I have some significant findings to share. So far, we've been divided, and it won't bring our kids back sooner," Brad continued.

Mika nodded in agreement. "I need to stand," he said as he got up and rested against the wall behind Connor's chair.

Looking at the big screen, deep in thought, Brad cleared his throat. "Someone get Bryan something to eat and drink before he falls over."

Rick's eyes stretched as big as saucers when he saw that Bryan's eyes were about to roll back in his head. "Sure, I will." He jumped, pulling a chair closer for Bryan, who swayed on his feet. "I'll be right back," he said, disappearing into the hallway. A second later, he returned with a first aid kit. He multitasked, speaking over his shoulder into his personal pager while he cleaned and bandaged Bryan's wounds. "Please tell Juandre to bring us his super juice. Yes, that's right, up to the Command Center."

Brad's husband and two older sons were running the medical unit of Phoenix, and he trusted his husband's expertise. Satisfied that Bryan was taken care of, Brad pointed to the map and continued the meeting. "Okay, my input may be a moot point, but we all need to be on the same page. I was out last night to check the external hydraulic system for the front door. We don't use it much since the smaller exits are easier to use. However, I've been receiving strange reports for a few years now. The external hydraulic system was one of many scattered but small incidents. I was uncertain because the incidents were infrequent. But lately, I've noticed a pattern. When most of the population is busy, such as during events or mealtimes, I notice sudden and short drops in temperature. Usually, it's not something that would even register on my radar. At first, I thought nothing of it. Maybe someone was just slipping outside for some crisp, fresh air, not wanting anyone to notice, or seeking a bit of solitude. I noticed this because I monitor the heat loss—it's my responsibility to account for saving and planning electricity use. I discovered exit doors left open; not wide, perhaps just enough for a pen or a paper clip to fit. Something that anyone not paying attention would notice. While inspecting the hydraulics, I began to suspect sabotage. I saw lights over the ice about two hundred meters out into the valley. I didn't think to report it. As I ran, I wanted to be as quiet as possible to catch the men sneaking out and find out why. To my surprise, I saw Joshua Adams talking to two men."

As Brad told his story, exclamations of surprise came from around the table.

"I've never seen these men before. Joshua knew them and might have been meeting with them for years. They weren't dressed like us, so I knew they were survivors from outside Phoenix. They wore different winter gear."

"I can't believe it. All this time, Joshua must have been in contact with them," Bryan said. The men at the table were dumbfounded.

"Do you think these men...why, what would they do to our boys?" Rick's voice grew louder and higher. "Why live outside of Phoenix all this time? Where did they come from, and why was Joshua, of all people, involved with them?" Rick rambled, crossing his arms over his chest. They watched the screen, reading the questions as the AI captured them electronically and categorized them as unanswered questions.

Brad tried to keep the order, but they bombarded him with questions. "Calm down. Let me continue. I didn't have many places to hide, but they saw me approaching when I saw them. Instead of calling for help, I sprinted after them again, but I heard a loud crack. I thought they were shooting at me, so I jumped and fell onto my belly on the ice. The next moment, Joshua stopped dead in his tracks. He looked at me, wide-eyed and fearful, and fell straight into a crack. The ice cracked again. It sounded like a flock of birds taking off as the ice sheets moved and shifted around us. Joshua screamed, and I crept forward on my hands and knees to help. The sounds he made were horrendous."

"Then the ice trembled beneath me, and I didn't know if I should go forward or backward. Then suddenly, the ice opened, and I slipped over the side into the opening. I tried holding onto the ledge while Joshua screamed like a banshee." Brad grabbed his ears as if he could silence Joshua's pleas for help. "It all happened so fast. The ice was so unstable. We shouldn't let anyone out there."

"I know," Connor interjected. "I tried to remove Joshua's body, which was a mess. The moving ice sheets squashed him like a meat tenderizer."

"My gille-toine tried his best but couldn't," Mika noted with a grin. Connor smiled briefly at his husband.

"Anyway, since we're on that subject, when we have our boys back, these incidents are a testament to the need for a policing system. Phoenix is growing too large for just us to manage." A round of affirmatives came from the room.

Bryan cleared his throat. "I'll establish a framework. We can start small."

Brad thanked him and continued. "By the time I couldn't hold on any longer, I slipped and fell onto an ice shelf. I lost my radio and flashlight. Lying as still as possible, I tried to pretend I was dead. I was worried the men would return to finish me off and possibly shoot at me. Joshua was silent and likely dead. I realized I couldn't call for help, and once again, I thank Dr. Peter von Leutzendorf. I used the injections and fired all my flares when I thought I was alone."

"Luckily, we saw your flares. We wouldn't have noticed if the glass-domed roofs weren't transparent," Connor added, and reached for Mika's hand.

"Yes, so when I injected the last syringe, I hoped there was something more to keep me alive until someone found me. The only thing I had left was the Peter Pan Cap. So, I cut my skin open and dug it out. I almost lost it, my clumsy frozen sausage fingers. It nearly rolled away from me. I grabbed the thing and chewed on it. And dear lord, was it a horrid taste! The rest, you know."

The men in the room were speechless. Rick broke the silence. "Maybe we should use the plane?"

"The thing is, love, we don't have enough fuel," Brad said. "If we manage to get it off the ground, we won't be able to come back. We also don't know where they are."

"Then let's build a sailboat!" Connor exclaimed, his Irish blood clearly boiling to get moving.

"And where do we sail to?" Mika asked.

"Let's be smart about this," Connor added. "I'll get the satellites up. Let's see what we can find."

"That's what I was trying to convey to you earlier," Bryan said. He got up and hobbled over to the screen as if he needed a cane. "We must determine the direction and inspect every hovel for lights or signs of where humans may live."

"It's probably not that far. Assuming they met up with Joshua," Connor said, but Brad interrupted him.

"I noticed that the intervals for doors being left open were anywhere from six to nine months apart. How fast do you think you can travel on the sailboat, Bryan?"

Bryan frowned, calculating.

"That depends on the wind speed," Mika replied. "So, anything from sixty to a hundred and sixty kilometers per hour, maybe even more?"

"How long do you think you could survive on a boat like that?" Connor asked.

"It seemed like a common fishing boat. It was just the hull, with no decks below or anything fancy." Bryan paused, clearly unsure of what he should say.

"Out with it, man!" Brad shouted impatiently.

"The men looked strangely animalistic or wild. They were deformed, with the shorter one being more so than the larger. Let's just say he's the tallest, scariest bastard I've ever engaged in hand-to-hand combat. Luckily, my team helped, and we have it in custody. He's an easy two and a half meters tall, much bigger than Mika."

"Bloody frozen hell!" Connor exclaimed.

"Toss that. I'm cooking fuel or building a ship. Come on, Connor." Mika grabbed Connor by the arm, attempting to leave.

"Wait," Brad called. "We need to plan our next move. And we have to figure out what to do about the dead body."

Mika turned around, his blue eyes bloodshot and filled with tears. "Comrade, what will take longer, building or checking satellite pictures?" He paused, then, not waiting for Brad to respond, Mika continued, "Exactly, so you check the satellites while I handle transportation. Joshua Adams was spying— an undercover agent. Those men he met up with, he fed them information and probably stole from us. Call for backup for Fritz and interrogate your prisoner. Please call me if you need help obtaining information from him. We're dealing with kidnappers who have our sons. I won't let a second go to waste. Joshua was likely planted here by someone who never showed up. Perhaps they even died in the Doomsday outbreak? They're probably mutants due to radiation. Those monsters knew Joshua. They might be planning a hostile takeover of Phoenix, and are going to use our boys as leverage. I'm going to get my boys." Mika finished his rambling and marched, leading Connor out of the office, and no one tried to stop them.

Brad, Rick, and Bryan shook their heads. There was no stopping Mika now. "Okay," said Bryan, and he used a chair to support himself. "I think they can survive a maximum of two weeks on that ship. But we don't know if they have a stopover to replenish supplies."

"So, how far can an ice sailboat travel at a minimum speed of sixty kilometers per hour for two weeks?" Brad asked as he walked up to the screen and marked two points on either side of the valley. "Which direction did they all go?"

"North, northeast," Bryan answered, and then Brad drew a triangle.

"Okay, I'm going to work with the maximums. If you travel at the slowest speed, how far would you go? Sixty times twenty-four times fourteen gives you two thousand one hundred sixty kilometers." He drew two circles, one representing the minimum estimate and the other representing the maximum estimate. Then he drew a straight line from Phoenix through the triangle and the two circles, landing at the tip of South Africa. "Now, all we need are satellite photos to track them. Maybe a weather balloon."

"I'll page Tony. He can set one up for us," Bryan volunteered. Tony Bonillo was the Chief maintenance man, a civil engineer who had helped in the design of Phoenix.

"Good, make sure he doesn't go too high. We want to see movement on the ice. Tell him to stay low and send the pictures directly to me. We need something to work with."

"I need to freshen up and check on the prisoner. When do you need me back?" Bryan asked.

Brad stepped closer to him. "We'll work six-hour shifts. Take a quick break, then I want you to check each room, even if you think it's occupied or just a broom closet. Here, take my master key. I'll pull some data and ask Lasitor to retrace Joshua's steps to see which areas he frequented or if any other residents are exhibiting suspicious behavior. He might have been working with someone. Find the room, apartment, or space that Joshua Adams truly occupied," Brad said, handing Bryan the master key card. "Where are you holding the prisoner? Do you have enough people on him if you consider him so dangerous?"

"Yes, sir, he's in the area below the Reserves compound. In the detention cell."

"Good, I don't want to wait. I want to see what we're dealing with. Maybe mess with his head a bit. When you return, come and join me. We can interrogate him together. Also, before you go, send a team of ten men on the six-wheeler to find Fritz."

"Yes, sir." Bryan turned and left. Over his shoulder, he said, "See you when I have answers about Joshua."

Brad turned to his husband, grasped the chair handles, and squatted in front of Rick, who was distraught. Gently lifting his chin with his thumb and forefinger, he noticed Rick's usual olive complexion was paler than ever. Brad's heart shattered for his husband and their lost children as they locked gazes wordlessly. He fell to his knees, pulling Rick closer while he folded over Brad, hugging him tightly.

"We will find them. We will, I promise you." Rick hugged Brad tighter in affirmation, holding on to him while hiding his sobs and trying to muster courage amidst audible gulps. Brad looked up at him and saw the guilt suffocating Rick.

"It's my fault," Rick blurted out. "I assumed they were okay and never made sure they were. I thought... I should have...maybe paged earlier...checked..."

"No, stop that. They're smart and responsible. It's not your fault. We don't even know the full story." Brad reasoned the facts as they stood. He pulled Rick with him, gesturing toward the screen and the pictures, maps, and test results on the electronic table.

"Let's gather and analyze the evidence together. Mika had a valid point. His theory is logical. We just need to gather more intel to give us an idea about what we are dealing with."

"Speaking of evidence. I'll start with Joshua's body."

"Good idea. I'll ask Peter to come and assist you. I'm more interested in clues about where our boys were taken than in the cause of Joshua's death."

"You never know what his body can tell us unless we look," Rick said, jutting his chin.

Brad softened his tone. "Let's involve the new medical students who are interested in forensics. They can observe the autopsy and have the opportunity to share their insights. They're young and think outside the box. Let's focus on the clues and the few facts we have," he said.

"Yes, please, let's find them." Rick's voice broke.

Brad closed his eyes, taking a slow, silent, deep breath for strength and concealing his anxiety about their boys. A ping from Brad's pager interrupted his thoughts. He got up, and Rick followed, anticipating news about the boys. "General Brad McCormick. Talk."

"General, you need to come down to the Reserves compound, sir. The prisoner has escaped!" Sergeant Amir Lamasi said, short of breath, as if he had been running.

CHAPTER 7
EVERYTHING HAD WITHERED AWAY

"*GOOD MORNING, CITIZENS OF PHOENIX.*

It's now six a.m.

Have you ever wondered where mosquitoes go during winter?

Mosquitoes, like all insects, are cold-blooded creatures. As a result, they cannot regulate body heat and become lethargic at fifteen degrees Celsius.

So, you should be safe if no mosquito eggs survive the global winter. When temperatures rise, these mosquitoes will wake up and begin feeding.

Visit your community news page for tips on how to get rid of those bloodsuckers.

Breakfast is served until eight a.m."

ERYN KING **of the Brawl**
2073 A.D. (21 A.T.)

Underground Laboratory
Fochville gold mine grid
South Africa

SOUTH AFRICA WAS LIKE ANTARCTICA, cold, dark, and barren. Nothing should be able to survive in the Brawl's nest, but Eryn and his brothers did.

High on the mineshaft, Eryn's body got battered by the icy wind while he held onto the rusted steel bar with one hand. His tattered clothes rattled like a long-forgotten flag in the wind, and the rhythm of the noise and solitude soothed him. Under the buckskin and fur cloak, he wore the same clothes Joshua had given him fifteen years ago. The worn-out pair of jeans hung in brown pieces of cloth around his muscled legs, and the t-shirt was nothing more than a shredded tank-bikini top. His size eleven boots were adapted and cut open at the front to fit his wide size sixteen feet with webbed toes. He had wrapped strips of animal hide around his shoes and lower legs, not only for protection and warmth but also to keep the boots from falling off his feet. The socks disintegrated a long time ago. They collected mud, and washing it was useless because nothing dried inside the mine.

Hearing flapping wings, he looked up. Hundreds of birds, one enormous flock of doves, flying over. The African skies were a rich blue, and only a few small clouds were in sight. Eryn turned his gaze toward the distant mountains and asked. "How long must I wait for you?" Bitter frustration fueled his resolve today. "Come on, Icemen King!" His voice rumbled through clenched teeth. "If not today, when? I told myself one day, and that day is today. I can feel it." He rested his back against the massive cable wheel of the mineshaft and closed his eyes, listening to the sounds of nature and willing the humans to appear on the horizon. *It's my fault that all living things surrounding us either died or moved away. No critters scurrying, nothing burrowing into the ground, and no animals calling.* There were no heartbeats, no life on the ground for hundreds of kilometers surrounding them—he only heard the Brawl and the four human boys.

He climbed up today to gather himself and, for once and for always, decide on the timing of his next steps. *The time has come to stop being a selfish coward.* His reluctance to follow his father's advice stemmed from the fear of being alone. It was time to fight for what he wanted, and he wanted to be friends with men and live like men. *It's time to stand up and do what is right.* "Not only for myself," he said with driven determination as he scanned the gray world surrounding their mineshaft. The hills were strewn with dying tree stumps and desolate frozen grass-lands, and the monkeys that had lived on Monkey's Mountain had disappeared. They were gone. He missed their chatters, squeaks, and whines late at night when he escaped the oppressive melancholy of his brother. Ernest, who's bonkers.

Everything had withered away, so nothing lived or grew in the soil. It's being poisoned. And it's my fault that it got so desolate. Today is the perfect day to take action on this dire situation. It must happen today.

He had left the four boys inside his cave in their cage. They were all alone. His nerves spiked as he realized he couldn't leave them like that for too long, so he swung his feet back and forth. He liked the height. It felt freeing to sit ten stories high on a crossbar of the headframe of the old mine shaft. He'd lived here all his life, guarding his brothers and preventing them from waking up and escaping. A chill ran down his spine. Flashes of memories sailed through his thoughts as he remembered what Joshua had called Doomsday. The chaos and destruction his brothers had sown, as well as his own failures and inability to contain it all. The emotionless, obsidian, predatory eyes with zero intelligence. Only an insatiable hunger that no amount of consumption could satisfy. Although they listened to him and were his nest brothers, he had nothing in common with them. Even so, he felt responsible for them. They looked more like Ernest when they walked upright on two legs. Warts thickly covered their skins with green-black patches, and their faces were a cross between frog and lizard. When he described their long, gangly arms and legs with hunchbacks covered with spikes to the boys, they said they sounded like amphibian swamp monsters. Eryn agreed they were monsters, their four-fingered claws were so big he'd seen how one of them crushed a human's head like a grape and then sucked out their brains like an empty juice box.

Eryn sighed. The incessant pangs of hunger drained him emotionally. *My brothers want to hunt.* He closed his eyes again, wiping his mind from distraction. Connecting telepathically with them, he said, *No, brothers, sleep. It's not time.* He lulled them back into a deeper state of hibernation. When he felt them succumb, he opened his eyes. *My life sucks, frog balls. Why did Ernest take the boys?*

Exasperated, he wiped the tears of frustration from his eyes. He hoped the icemen would come and help him because he couldn't do it alone anymore. *Ernest has something up his sleeve, and he's planning something. I need help, and I can't ask Joshua.* Irritated and sad about losing the last human friend he had. Before he died, Joshua was in the process of telling Eryn about his father and the evil men who had harmed him. Eryn stopped those thoughts and pushed them into the tiny box marked "*do not open, now, never, or ever.*" It terrified him. Freezing frog balls. He straightened up and forced himself to think of his action plan. He would have to be one step ahead of Ernest.

If Ernest tries to hurt those boys, he has to go. If I take the boys back to the glass city, my brother will make trouble for everyone. Worst case, he'll wake the nest, and they'll go on a killing spree. So I'll have to get rid of my brothers first and give Ernest his last chance to choose my side. If he doesn't, he must be eliminated because the safety of those boys comes first.

"Those blue eyes and long blond hair." He groaned out loud. "My boys, my friends." *They are young men, not boys,* he corrected himself. They had infatuated him and drawn him to them. He was under their spell. Eryn's lower body throbbed. Since they arrived at the mines, he'd been walking around hunchbacked to hide his arousal. Their smell was everywhere he went. And their heartbeats pumped in perfectly synchronized rhythms with his own. A crescendo melody of beauty, love, and hope. It strengthened him, and he realized he had in his cave, in a cage, everything his soul wanted and yearned for all his life—he wanted to belong to them. If not Cian, definitely Ivan. *What if both wanted me?* Eryn's heart rate sped up, just imagining what both of them on top of him would feel like. *That's not happening if they are prisoners.*

He must free all of them. The Icemen King's two sons, Donali and Kawa, were important too, he thought.

The night Ernest followed him, he should have known Ernest was up to something. He'd been talking for a while about being thirsty for blood. Eryn didn't think he meant human blood. So when he went to meet with Joshua...

He paused, hanging his head in his hands. *I should have taken the long route I usually take to throw Ernest off my track.*

He wiped his face up and down as if to wipe the images from his mind. *Why had Ernest taken them? And why did he laugh at Joshua when he died?* Eryn asked himself those questions, just as he did every day. He couldn't understand his brother's sense of humor in the face of human suffering. That night replayed over and over in his mind. Especially when he let himself be captured and wasted time, only realizing he had to stop his brother and get to the boys, or his brother would hurt them. When he eventually caught up with them—he remembered how close to death they were—a shiver ran up his spine, they were frozen to the bone.

If he hadn't chased after them, they would all have been dead if he'd arrived one minute later. Still dressed in only swim trunks with towels covering them.

I had to choose between taking them to the mine, where it was warm, or to the glass city. It was a life-or-death decision.

Also, he didn't know it was his friends Cian and Ivan. If he'd known that, he would've tried harder to stop the boat. *Why didn't I look? I should have known, but no, I didn't think. I was dumb, like usual.* He reprimanded himself, a habit he picked up from his brother.

Since they'd arrived home, the moment he saw them and realized who they were, he wanted to scoop them up and take them back to safety, but he realized that would not be easy. They had to be kept safe from Ernest and his brothers. He had to think about all those humans and intended to keep them safe from his poisonous man-eating family until he could figure out a way to get them home safely. He had to build an enormous golden cage for all of them, and only he had the key. Eryn had given each an anti-toxin injection from his father's lab, and since then, he tried to spend as much time as possible with them until their ice king arrived.

He hated himself because he was weak. *Why can't I just kill my brothers like my father said I should? I could be free, living with the men, and be friends with Cian and Ivan.*

"Okay, step one, ask Ernest to help me flood the tunnels. It's a two-person job. One must steer the elevator, and the other must pull the floodgate levers," he muttered to himself and continued to rehearse his plan.

"Step two..." He turned, swung his leg over the bar he was sitting on, and stood up to prepare the beacon he had built from old telephone poles and tree trunks. *Yes, step two would be to light the fire so their people can find us.* Eryn could see for hundreds of kilometers from this height, so he knew the beacon of smoke and fire would be seen when their rescuers came.

"Step three, get the boys out." He felt positive and now more motivated than ever to do what he must. He decided this time he would follow through on his plan. *I'll ask Ernest to go hunting. Then I'll tell him about my plan so he can choose if he's with me or against me. Save the boys and live with the humans...*

CHAPTER 8
THE BLUE HALCYON

"GOOD MORNING, CITIZENS OF OUR GLASS-DOMED CITY.

It's now six a.m.

Did you know heatstroke can cause disorientation and headaches? The body cannot control its temperature, which rises rapidly. The sweating mechanism fails, and the body is unable to cool down. Before you freak out, follow these steps to cool the overheated person.

Get the person into the shade and remove his excess clothing. Cool the person with whatever means available. Put the person in a tub of water or, even better, grab a firehose and spray the human. But before you do all that, be sure it's heatstroke and not just a vicious hangover.

On second thought, splashing down a hung-over man may help anyway.

Visit your community news page to read about exciting facts on failing body mechanisms.

Breakfast is served until eight a.m.

Have a refreshing day!"

DR. MIKA ROMANOV

PREPARATIONS TO GET the rescue mission underway had Phoenix buzzing twenty-four-seven for a little over two weeks. Despite that, it felt to Mika like they were dragging their feet. He had hoped to interrogate the prisoner, and now he too was gone. Like their boys. Mika let Connor take the lead and busy himself by working with a team of savant scientists and engineers who set up a shipyard inside the belly of a recently constructed Transportation Services Dome. Over a thousand men volunteered and worked diligently in shifts to finish the flying sailboat as fast as possible.

Tony, Mika, and Connor re-designed a camper-ship prototype by weaponizing and fortifying it with new materials, either salvaged or newly created. The Phoenix metallurgical engineering teams used previous research to create a newly designed metal by blending salvaged pieces of titanium, tungsten, and Antarctic blue marble rock lava infused with halogen by grounding the metals into fine powders and mixing it with carbon and frozen halogen. They put the powder inside a high-heat, high-pressure mold to shape the required pieces for the hull of their ship.

Once the scientists set up a foundry, the area to work safely inside the lava tubes, the process of blending, pouring, and infusing, was time-consuming. But yet another invention testified to the ingenious scientific designs these savants were capable of. The new artificially created metal would never rust. It was lightweight and stronger than any metal on the periodic table.

The magnificent ship was christened the Blue Halcyon. She glowed blue at night, giving her an ethereal look. They named her after the mythical bird said by ancient writers to breed in a nest floating at sea at the winter solstice, charming the wind and waves into calm.

The men who worked in any capacity needed to get the job done humbled Mika. It didn't matter how big or small the task was and whether a man thought he was over or under-qualified, they all had one goal —to help retrieve their sons.

The design of their ship was like no other, but it was not new to the men. Mika had presented it at the Phoenix University Transportation and Innovation show the previous year. However, he'd adjusted the installations, so only the most needed stayed for the rescue mission. It reduced the building time and created the possibility of an airlift.

Mika ground his molars. The unique design was a showstopper for families planning to go ice camping. It now represented retaliation to retrieve, defend, and destroy. He assessed the finished ship from afar, standing with his hands on his hips while calculating where to install his two laser cannons.

"Now it's a warship to save my boys," he said to no one in particular as he stood and visually measured the hull, which was the shape of a curling stone. Originally designed as a recreational vehicle, or RV on ice, it was intended to go short distances for families who wanted to get away from Phoenix, say to go ice camping. It had a flattened bottom with a hollowed base, almost like a catamaran, for access to the water below or ice, if needed. But it was also for speed and direction control. Instead of a very tall mast, Mika had gone with two shorter masts that held the sails shaped like a soccer net for the maximum draft capacity. The ship weighed almost nothing, so he designed a sturdy but fat and bulky-looking design for greater surface tension. Instead of sleek and streamlined, it appeared like an old oil rig platform with no bow or stern. The shorter masts prevented top-heavy problems during storms and sporadic wind changes, which could be retracted or telescoped on demand.

The re-designed ship relied on wind and sunlight to glide or fly over the ice, including the frigid mountain ranges of South Africa. To make flying possible, Mika had a team of physicists design solar sail panels, new light-sensitive nanoparticles, and gallium arsenide weaved into the silicone strands used to create a material for the sails and the balloon, capturing heat and sunlight more efficiently. The renewable energies provided the ship with its luxuries of hot food and warm showers and fueled the wind propellers to move the boat in various directions. They even allowed lift-off with the help of a solar-powered hot-air balloon while honoring the creed of Environmental Project One. The founders, the WHPSS, and specifically Dr. John Saunders, were honored in remembrance by preserving the history and avoiding the causes of the world's demise in the first place and by re-engineering failed technologies.

Phoenix University solely existed to secure humanity's and the Earth's survival. Thus, education emphasized advanced education, minimum military defense, progressive healthcare, unconventional citizenship based on rebuilding infrastructure, and government charters devoid of ethnic, religious, or any other component that had steered the human race thus far.

The original goal was the birth of a new civilization that transformed and improved into a wholly new global entity. Therefore, infinite resources were allocated to ensure the successful dawn of a new civilization. Scientists like Mika had to design and build only environmentally friendly but high-tech means of transportation. For this reason, fossil fuel or any fuel causing air pollution or environmental damage wasn't an option to be produced. Instead, programs like the Phoenix University Transportation and Innovation show were created. Since the six-wheeler and snow riders used the last fuel, newer models would be designed and built with the same new metal and solar panel particles.

After standing like a statue for almost an hour, Mika had awoken. Unknowingly, his mind had shut down, and he'd been sleeping upright. His exhausted mind pinged back from REM sleep, preventing him from falling to the ground. "We need one laser cannon above the entrance door to cover those who run to or from the ship and to melt or break shit in our path and one in the back to cover our asses," he said. Noticing his friends were packing the final provisions.

Was I sleeping again? He worried this kind of tiredness could cause accidents. *I will sleep when we are underway.* He told himself what he told the men a thousand times a day. His husband stopped, looked up at the ship, and back at Mika. The Irishman's objection was futile.

"Good, you're awake now," Connor said, meaning everyone noticed he was night-night on his feet. Mika felt embarrassed, an emotion he hated and rarely experienced. "What do you mean, to melt the ice for easy movement, but also in case of an attack?" Connor asked, sounding agitated and avoiding eye contact.

"Precisely that, Connor. Do you want me to draw you a picture!" Mika's temper flared and he shouted furiously at Connor. The dark circles under his eyes caused his blue eyes to look so dark that they were almost black with anguish, hate, and tiredness. Mika felt like grabbing his husband and hugging the shit out of him. *Both of us are exhausted and mentally ruined to the brink of defeat.* He said, "I will not budge on this."

"You'll shoot our damn sails down like a foolish Russian soldier shooting himself in the foot!" Connor shouted back, running his hands through his hair. "And if you haven't noticed, we don't have time for this! I haven't slept in weeks. I want to go! Now!" Connor yelled, his voice breaking and his eyes glistening with tears.

"No one can shoot at us with any gun. My lasers would destroy it before it reaches us." Mika scowled and lowered his voice when he noticed the crowd around them growing larger.

"If these lasers fall into the wrong hands, they can accidentally blow the moon out of the sky! Bloody damn hell, Mika, or worse, you'll decapitate yourself!"

"I've had enough of this. My canons go. That is final! I can't sail there and say, hey, do you feel like giving my children back? They will laugh at us. We need to scare them, and if they aren't scared, I'm going to kill them until they're scared. We don't know how many of them there are. Are there thousands like us? And if so, they must stay away from us when we return home. They need to know we're bigger, smarter, and more advanced than them. They must see us as gods, and we're angry gods. Very angry, *ty che, blyad*!" Mika roared. His anger combusted, he couldn't keep it in check and failed dismally to lower his voice.

He noticed Juandre stepping closer out of the corner of his eye.

"Bzzzzz, leave the man! He knows what he's talking about," Juandre said. Interrupting his friends while giving Connor the stink eye. The crowd grew in size around them, probably expecting a bit of free entertainment.

Dressed in his best 1980s Prince outfit, Juandre was resourceful, scarily bossy, and demanding. Men knew that if they wanted to get things done, Juandre was the person to ask, and he would sort the rest out for them, even as the local peacock.

"You two should stop your fighting. You're at it all day like two Chihuahuas. Yapping, yapping, yapping. Just shut up. Bloody damn hell, I'm sick of it," Juandre said while clapping his hands and shooing them like dogs.

Mika and Connor indignantly did so.

"I agree with Mika." Brad tapped Connor on the shoulder. "Mika is correct. We need the cannons. I'd rather be over than under-prepared."

"Me, too. Sometimes you have to show you can defend yourself," Bryan added while pulling a trolley packed with more weapons and ammunition crates into the ship.

Connor threw the crate he was carrying onto the ground. He bent down on one knee, opening it. "Okay, I'm outnumbered, but I can't wait to say I told you so." Looking like Santa, he dove into the crate and handed each man a smaller but just as deadly version of the cannons, a personal protection laser handgun. A round of thank you's followed.

"Ooooh," Juandre said, looking at his gun like a new studded sex toy.

"Good luck to those assholes! Anyone who hurts us will meet our vengeance," Mika said with murder in his eyes. Meaning it and planning to shoot shit dead. He holstered the handgun into the side of his belt and then assembled and installed the cannons on board. "Andrew, my man, I need your strong, muscled arms. Can you help me?" Mika asked.

"No problem." Andrew jumped, eager to be of help.

Connor cleared his throat. Mika felt his husband's gaze on his backside and heard him say, "I don't know how he does it. Men respect him even more, despite his animalistic disembowelments. No, instead of making him the most feared man in Phoenix, he's now more popular than ever."

Mika and Andrew's heads popped over the side of the deck while they worked.

"He's sexy, strong, dangerous, and too smart for you. Pass him to Andrew and me, and we'll keep him entertained. I heard he is hung like a horse, and I love rodeos. Times are changing. It's the survival of the fittest, not the richest, Connor, my man," Juandre said. Licking his index finger, he pressed it to his buttocks, mimicking a strip of bacon in a hot pan. "Hsshhhhhhh."

"You little slut. You know I have a black belt. I will..." Connor mock attacked Juandre, who disappeared between Peter and Tony, discussing the newly designed bulletproof heat suit. The new material was woven from the same solar-powered silicone strands and lightweight, newly designed metal. The stretchy fabric conserved light energy in its nanoparticles activated by freezing temperatures, which released energy as heat.

"Yes, almost like wearing a microwave oven, ha-ha!" Peter and Tony blurted out as one.

"They should wear it as an undergarment, like a deep-sea diving suit. Each suit fits the body for which they measured it and protects it like a glove." Peter showed them by dipping his arm in a bath of ice.

"Here, come feel this." He folded his sleeve back so they could feel the heat.

"You're a brainiac. I mean, both of you are," Bryan said.

"Thank you, but Peter made my idea a reality," Tony said. Out of habit, Peter quietly stood to the side, attempting to disappear into the background.

Bryan must have noticed and immediately went to him.

"Come here, Peter. Let me congratulate you." Peter's gaze fell to the ground. He blushed a bright pink.

"Damn, Peter, why haven't you ever come to visit with Tony and me? Wait, I know the answer. You're always working in your lab." Bryan hugged Peter, whose arms dangled at his sides, and then reached for Tony, who looked happy with how Bryan included Peter.

"It seems Bryan and Tony are looking for a third, and the way Peter's smiling from ear to ear, it looks like he is going to fit snugly between Bryan and Tony," Mika told Andrew, who noticed the three men below. He nodded, not saying a word, but Mika noticed disappointment for a second. How odd, he wondered. "Finally, my long-time friend and lab partner has found a place to belong," Mika said and again, saw the downturn of twitching muscles. *Andrew wasn't happy about the union. Maybe he wanted Peter for Juandre and himself.* Mika didn't know his friend was such a commodity. Unfortunately, they have to leave, otherwise, he would have wanted to ask Peter about this. Why his friend never shared things like this with him upset Mika, he assumed they were work husbands.

"Okay, okay, stop smothering me. I appreciate you inviting me. I meant to visit Tony, and we work well together," Peter said shyly, his crisp white hair covering his ice-blue eyes.

"Have you seen my playroom?" Tony asked. The sexy engineer threw an arm around Peter's neck. "Now that I think of it, why haven't you ever visited? Did you know Bryan and I are in an open D/s relationship?" Tony asked. Peter looked embarrassed and excited at the same time.

"I knew, and I hoped one of you would invite me, but...you know...no one has. I knew about your kink and hoped to talk to you about it." He shoveled his toes into the ground and kicked at it, much like a shy adolescent would do.

"Now that's just sad," Juandre added from a distance, never missing a beat while interrupting them. It seems Juandre was a tad irritated with Peter. "Do I have to be naked to get my body scanned for the suit?"

"No, you can keep tight-fitting underwear on, the type you'll wear when you wear the suit," Peter and Tony answered. Juandre undressed and climbed out of the red bodysuit, leaving only his underwear on.

"I know, right? I'm big. This doesn't get strapped and tucked away. First, it's too pretty, and second, I like it too much," he said with an effeminate lilt. Rubbing himself shamelessly. "What?" he asked while the group looked at him astonished.

"I need space for my junk in my suit. I don't want to go on a rescue mission with squashed balls. And if I want to scratch them, my hand should at least fit down there."

Mika and Andrew laughed. "That's an excellent point!" Mika yelled from above. Juandre turned, waving animatedly, then kissing the palm of his hand, blowing strawberry kisses up to them.

"Thank you, Mika, only a man as intelligent and virile as yourself will see my meaning," Juandre said. Then he threw an arm down toward the ground, and he shouted, "Elephant trunks and beer-can dicks and all that." With a cheeky grin, he was still eyeing Connor. Andrew and Mika chuckled. Mika appreciated Juandre volunteering to come along with them. He knew just what to say to break tense moments. *And I love his breakfast muffins.*

After Juandre, the rest of the rescue mission crew rubbed themselves up for a bigger basket room before scanning their bodies in 4D.

Later the same day, Mika went with his crew as they collected and dressed in the new suits produced and woven by the factory-sized 4D sewing machine. Of course, if the rest of Phoenix was interested in such a suit, they were welcome to fall in line for a measurement. Eagerly, they waited for their turns as every man rubbed themselves to the point of ejaculation before getting scanned for a new suit to wear underneath or replace the bulky military-issued arctic suits.

"Oh, my goodness, look at them! Why are the men rubbing themselves like that? Maybe I should tell them a ball of socks would have the same effect. What if there are children here? What will happen when I'm gone?" Brad asked.

"Juandre, it's all your fault," Mika yelled.

"No, no, no, no, no, no," he said, snapping his fingers left and right. "If I jumped in the fire, General, it's common knowledge not to follow. It's not my fault half of Phoenix are exhibitionists." He flung himself around in a dramatic fashion and disappeared into the hull, looking sexy with the black suit, black boots, and a red chiffon scarf around his neck.

"Bloody damn hell!" Brad said.

Mika was relieved when Brad laughed before turning to Rick and Bryan, who were standing at a big table, rolling up the maps they prepared to reach the location of the kidnappers hiding out in the old gold mining region of South Africa.

Brad and the team mapped, located, and studied the terrain to determine the quickest route to the goldmines and to plan the extraction. They calculated that flying over Table Mountain and following the old river canyons originating south of the central mining area, known as the iSangqu and iGwa Canyons, would be almost exactly how the crow would fly into the Place of Gold.

Rick had Mika and Connor design a mini surgery outfitted on the Blue Halcyon. Mika made sure he would be able to perform procedures such as removing a splinter to open abdominal surgery.

"Time has come to board the ship!" Mika called, then listened as Brad left Bryan in charge.

"Just listen to your leadership council, Bryan. I couldn't have done my job without the help and trust of my supportive council. You know it. You were one of them."

"I know, sir, but..."

"Bryan, I trust Phoenix has voted correctly. It makes sense. And no, you're needed much more here. I need you to update me at least twice daily. Good?" Brad waited until Bryan agreed. "I leave Phoenix in your hands, and you may use my comfy recliner in my office. You may also look in the upper left drawer of my desk. There's a bottle of Lord Andrew that you may have a small sip of. It's most probably the last in the world. Just remove your shoes and don't damage my chair." Brad was joking, but Mika and everyone knew his chair and whiskey weren't easily shared. Bryan just hung his head and nodded. "Come, give me my last hug!"

"Sir, no!"

"Aww, bugger that. Who cares about formalities anymore?"

Bryan lifted his arm to salute, but Brad enveloped him, giving him an enormous hug. After a strange uncomfortable moment, both coughed and cleared their throats as Brad broke the embrace.

"Good luck, sir. Bring our boys back home safely."

Mika saw the water in his friend's eyes as he turned to board the ship.

The hollow shipyard amplified the roar of heartfelt goodbyes. Mika heard good luck and bring our boys back! Connor, Mika, Brad, Rick, Juandre, and Andrew waved back at the crowd from the deck.

The glowing new retractable doors opened up and retracted into the dome's roof as the Blue Halcyon sailed into the cold veil of mist covering the Antarctic Valley.

CHAPTER 9
THE ODD GROUP

"*Good morning, brave men of Phoenix.*

I, Lasitor, am bidding positive vibes in the spirit of reunification. It's now six a.m.

Did you know man's worst fear has changed over time?

Man's earliest fear was predators. Famine, even a solar eclipse, can frighten a man. Did you also know that just twenty years ago, according to the results of a quiz, men of Phoenix reported their worst fears were brain shrinkage and cognitive dysfunction? To partake in this exciting study, please connect with Lasitor on your local community news page and tell him what you fear today.

Breakfast is served until eight a.m.

Bon voyage!"

Captain Bryan Howell

. . .

A WEEK before the departure to South Africa, the new leader and council members elected were announced. Brad and each member who left on the rescue mission informally handed over the reins of power to their successors. An open voting system allowed the men of Phoenix to vote and monitor the results without having to count the votes. Each time a man had voted, he could see a point added next to his chosen replacement.

While Brad and the men readied themselves for the rescue mission, Bryan and his new council members prepared to replace them as smoothly as possible.

Dr. Peter von Leutzendorf stepped into Mika's shoes while they elected Tony Bonillo to replace Connor Romanov. Dr. Simon and Dr. Paul would oversee Phoenix Medical Operations. The gifted pair were well-loved and trusted by the general population. Whether with injuries or surgeries at Medic-Underground or working at the local eye clinic, they always showed up and assisted no matter the crisis. After the first big earthquake had hit Phoenix, Dr. Rick Longarrow-McCormick took them under his wing, encouraging and nurturing their interest in medicine. Both graduated with honors from Phoenix University, where they continued to specialize in various medical fields.

Dr. Simon McCormick, Brad McCormick's older son, born before Doomsday, was as handsome as his father, tall and athletically built. Never leaving the side of his husband and best friend, Dr. Paul Chevalier, who was a brilliant and strikingly handsome young man with crow-black hair and snow-white skin.

Donali and Kawa, the two younger boys who had been kidnapped, were half-brothers of the two doctors, who were married before they were born. They had helped raise them and had a powerful bond with them. Completely devastated by their abduction, the two doctors eagerly volunteered to join the rescue mission, but being chosen as Phoenix's Chiefs of staff and replacing their stepfather, Dr. Rick Longarrow-McCormick, was an honor, so their fathers could travel together on the rescue mission.

As the Blue Halcyon departed, Bryan followed Charles, who stood a head taller than his men, as they waddled after him through the crowd. Bryan had noticed him and his group a few years ago, but they had disappeared from his radar because they seemed dull and uninteresting, other than being self-righteous bullies. However, to be safe, Bryan had Lasitor trace their movements throughout Phoenix. With the AI not using valuable manpower, it would inform Bryan of their every move. On a closer review, Bryan noticed they were always standing to the side like a prison gang attempting not to be seen. Brad, being

Brad, just brushed them off as a bunch of rotten apples. But Bryan's alarm bells incessantly rang as he observed them. *There's something odd about the group.*

Dr. Charles Montgomery, the leader of the secretive group of pretend scientists, spoke. "This is bad, really, really bad. I hoped they would at least test the hydrogen-propelled craft we designed and built. But no, they just had to design something impenetrable like that. Look at it. It's a tin can," he said. He had a flair for untouchable superiority.

"Yes, it looks like something a five-year-old would draw," a bald black man said, chuckling.

"Sir, maybe we should have hidden on board. We could have taken hold of the ship or left unseen once we arrived at the mines."

"No, the timing is wrong. We should have been there already! And I don't think all of us would fit anyway," their leader said sternly.

In deference to Charles, the five men turned as one and nodded their agreement.

"We must make haste and leave in our prototype right away."

"Yes, sir, as soon as the crowd dissipates," Nick said.

They maneuvered through the fray of men watching the Blue Halcyon leave the shipyard. Around them, men were cheering. Some fathers had lifted their boys onto their shoulders to see the pretty blue ship. Some youngsters had small blue boat toys in their hands.

The mysterious group of scientists was registered for their research on renewable energy. Their work results were nothing extraordinary, and some of their projects were outrageous and far-fetched. For example, the racketeering ideas they recently proposed for rocket fuel production. They were a tight-knit group, apparently all heterosexual, so Bryan and Brad thought their sexual preferences were the source of the judgmental watching and waiting with their hands always casually tucked into their pockets. Since the episode with Joshua, the mysterious meetups, and the escape of the mysterious prisoner, Bryan and Brad had sat in Brad's office working with Lasitor. They scanned every recorded security video and were still no closer to understanding the goal of the secretive team operating right under their noses. The escapee's face was only known to Bryan and his team. But when a sketch artist was called in, none of them could remember any facial features, except that he was tall with weird eyes. It was as if Bryan's and his team's memories were wiped along with Lasitor's.

No footage of him was found in the system, and Lasitor, for some inexplicable reason, identified the escaped prisoner as friendly and the shorter, stocky man, forcing the four young men at gunpoint onto the ship behind the athletics dome, as the enemy. It was unclear if they were working with this group of wayward scientists or not.

To confirm his original suspicions about the odd squad and not to show his hand prematurely, Bryan informed Brad that he would observe, investigate, and report to him before confronting them. As the acting leader, he'd already searched their labs and rooms without their knowledge, and their investigation had clarified that they were working on projects without proper council approval —projects that were unusual and out of the ordinary, such as hydrogen-propelled airships. However, the most concerning aspect was their research on DNA manipulations and genome sequencing.

They also found research and books deciphering old Mesopotamian, Egyptian, and Babylonian languages. Weird symbols and pictures of what seemed to be ancient astronomy charts and maps of cities of gold. No translations were found, but the notes from dangerous and unapproved projects showed them to be a kind of rebel splinter group or perhaps religious fanatics who hung on every word their leader, Charles Montgomery, said.

As the ship sailed from Phoenix, Bryan moved closer to the back. Attempting to hear what they were saying. *This group lives and operates in the background. They're hiding in the shadows, waiting for their turn to do what?* Bryan was extremely curious to find out.

"Charles, maybe we should let them know," a man Bryan knew as Nick said.

"No," the black man said as he scoped their surroundings. "It is written. They will come to us. We must be ready. The twins will come into their power, and when they do, they..."

"Damn it," Bryan whispered to himself, extremely frustrated. He thought he'd heard something about twins. But Phoenix was full of twins.

"No, if they knew they would somehow make it about themselves...only looking after their own needs, like they've done all these years, and there's no space for impure homosexuals," Charles said.

"They chose none of these people for a reason," another man with light, short brown hair, cut in a monk's tonsure style, said.

"I agree, let's not...we had...Joshua...Unbeknownst to the...Earth's...a ticking time...gasses...before Doomsday!" the bald black man screamed at them.

Still, Bryan couldn't hear the entire conversation above the cheering crowd.

"Look at them." Charles pointed to the crowd. "That's an enormous boost to their confidence. I can't wait to see the mighty fall."

"It's quite magnificent how the ship glows in the dark," a smaller, skinny man said.

"That's so idiotic. It screams, here I am," Charles said, reminding his gang. "At least...we'll be able... stupid homosexual asses."

Bryan heard that, and the urge to run and call his friends back made him nauseous. It felt like, with this information, he was letting them sail right into a trap. Bryan felt divided. He needed to get to the office to contact Brad and call his first council meeting. Lasitor must record and track them, and to do that, they needed to plant a tracker. Stepping back but keeping his eyes on the bigots, he grabbed the nearest soldier by the arm.

"Sir?" he asked.

"What's your name, young man?" Bryan asked without taking his eyes off his target.

"Thomas, sir, Private Thomas Lavetti," the young soldier squeaked with a mousy voice, looking like he wanted to piss his pants.

Bryan did a quick summation. He recognized him as a kid, barely twenty years of age, but he should do. "Boy, this is a matter of high importance, top secret, do you understand?" Bryan asked, not making eye contact. "See that group?" He nodded with his chin to Charles and his men.

"Yes, sir, I do."

"I need to follow them, but I also need to contact our new leadership team and get word to General McCormick and his men. Do you think you can help me?" Bryan asked, feeling the young man relax when he realized he wasn't in trouble.

"Yes, of course, sir. How can I help?" Private Thomas asked.

"Can you follow the men, see where they go, and let me know where they are so I can fetch a tracker and meet up with you? Here, put my black jacket on over your uniform. Try your best to avoid being seen. They're dangerous." Bryan removed his jacket and helped the kid into it.

"Yes, sir! Are they the men we've been searching for?" the private asked. Putting on the oversized jacket and not taking his eyes off his new quarry. Smart boy, Bryan thought.

"Yes, soldier, so don't be brave and put yourself in danger. Just observe from afar." Bryan looked at his watch. "I need you to go silent," he ordered while switching the young man's radio off. "Precisely fifteen minutes from now, I want you to switch it back on and report your location. Continue to do that every fifteen minutes until I meet up with you. Here, let's switch to my private channel," Bryan explained, liking the young man who immediately grasped what he needed while still eyeing his target.

"Okay, sir, I won't disappoint you." Private Lavetti nodded bravely and shot head down into the crowd, following Charles and the group of bastards.

CHAPTER 10
ROCKETRY AND DNA MANIPULATION

"*GOOD MORNING, CITIZENS OF PHOENIX.*

I, Lasitor, bid you a good morning. It's now six a.m.

Did you know they spotted four Frog People near the Little Miami River, USA, in the nineteen-fifties?

So if you see a frog-faced creature, especially if it's one meter tall and roughly seventy-five kilograms, it's probably a Frog person.

And also, if it's hairless with a wide leathery mouth with no lips, it's most definitely one.

Visit our community news page for more paranoid paranormal sightings of inhuman creatures.

Breakfast is served until eight a.m.

Good luck with that!"

PROFESSOR WOLTER WESSELS
Herpetologist notes. Day 935 Post-Doomsday

Environmental Project III
Underground Laboratory
Fochville gold mine grid
South Africa

THIS IS PROBABLY my last entry. However, I say and believe that every day. Whoever reads this, you have found us. My scientific method and critical thinking lead me to study empirical avenues that both explain and defy the laws of physics and biology in irrational and chaotic ways. It was through testing my hypothesis that the outcome was gloriously positive.

Yet, to my detriment, the sponsors had confiscated my subjects for reasons I only grasped too late. They should never have attempted that unless understanding the inherent behavior inside and outside their habitual environment. They allowed me to watch other, more trusted scientists work in my laboratory. They would have dismissed me if I interfered with the research. My research! I watched as they genetically altered male specimens in-vitro. One subject surpassed all our expectations. We created a superhuman species that will live and thrive in the harshest conditions on this or other planets.

But, as the sponsors further insisted on breeding a swarm of walking neurotoxic bio-weapons, they caged the cannibalistic monsters in containers that were to be parachuted worldwide. After their return, I suspect the company would have destroyed them.

But their careful planning and maneuvering back-fired. Uncoordinated attacks and rapid infection rates overwhelmed their control. The Brawl, named after the Afrikaans term for bullfrog, '*Brulpadda*', released airborne toxins that quickly spread due to global windstorms. Other natural disasters have compounded their failures, and all governments have perished within weeks.

The disappearance of the internet due to the bombing of electricity grids and satellites caused their downfall. The Brawls had killed their handlers, ran rampant in Africa, and spread to Europe. A few selected individuals received the little anti-toxin developed. The ones who survived the outbreak fought to escape the global massacre and were either eaten or killed. I shared the formula with Joshua Adams, my colleague, and friend who lives at EP-1, the Antarctic Research Center.

We—Environmental Project III (EP-III)—were assigned rocketry and DNA manipulation to ensure the superhuman race survives and thrives on the moon. They also tasked us with research to address fuel, oxygen, and water shortages. However, every-thing went wrong. Scratch that—it all fell apart.

The American Star Connect company funded the rockets built for human travel in cooperation with the WHPSS. A global effort to establish a lunar presence, and I suspect is the driving force was behind all this madness. Locate the number two mineshaft, marked in blue. It's the northwest tower near the Fochville ruins. Inside lies a rocket ready for human travel.

I'm tired, and it seems pointlessly futile and impossible to fix this. I named the King of the Brawl, Eryn. It's typically a female name, and I determined it fitting to call him so in the context. Eryn means peace and comes from Ireland's word *Eire*, which is derived from the Goddess Eriu. They named the island after her, according to Irish mythology and folklore. Someone who knows this history would find the resemblance fascinating.

He is but a young boy who believes he is protecting me from his brothers. Specifically, the more humanoid one I named Ernest, who's immune to Eryn's empathic and pheromone influence. He is a dangerous free agent who cannot harmonize or work well with others. I classify him as dangerous. The creature shows primary psychopathic tendencies. He manipulates, is callous, and I'm positive he feigns fear and anxiety. I think Ernest drove the nest to break out, and Eryn is the one who sent them home. Eryn says that Ernest enjoyed it. He shows no guilt or remorse for what they have done. Ernest is a cunning and antisocial Brawl who manipulates his brother, the king, for his own narcissistic needs. I know he wants to eat me. The nest is not responding to me, only to their king. They lie and wait as an army. I attempted my best to influence and educate the king on the ways of humans. He responded with an immense psychological shift away from his nest toward the ways of men. I sense a deep yearning to connect with me. I encouraged a relationship with Joshua. I hope he includes Eryn in his research and introduces him to the rest of the Phoenix population. Eryn has assured me that the nest is sleeping.

I tasked Eryn with destroying the tunnel system. I told him to bury the nest. Only then will Eryn be able to join Joshua Adams and his men in Antarctica, the glass-domed city of Phoenix. If you are reading this, do not trust Ernest. Carry the anti-toxin with you. If you can reproduce the formula, it's available in the back of this notebook. Do it! If you can kill the swarm and keep Eryn, please do it. I am proud of my creation. He is the embodiment of the perfect human soldier. He's intelligent, and I suspect he will exceed your expectations with loving coaxing. He needs lots of stimulation to discover who he is and how he fits into this world. Wrapped inside his powerful body are innocence and naivety. If you are fortunate to get to know him, you will agree he's magnificent. His empathetic and intellectual characteristics made it simple to appeal to his humanity. He seems to identify himself as human, but he finds it challenging to shunt the Brawl nest.

I observed and tested some of his abilities to override the mindless swarm behavior. They accept him as king, as bees do their queen, which I found fascinating because they're male. It may be a blessed failsafe that they cannot reproduce. I'm unsure of the length of their lifespan. I fear they are protandrous hermaphrodites born as males, but like in a beehive, only the king of the Brawl can reproduce.

It's unclear whether this trait is positive or negative and how it affects his ability to lead a species that can't coexist with humans.

To stay alive, if possible, I've forgone my role as a scientist and taken on my role as a father. I hope the knowledge I've shared is helpful to the person finding this.

CHAPTER II
ERNEST

"*Good morning, citizens of our lovely glass-domed city.*

I am Lasitor, your Artificial Intelligence (AI) community news broadcaster. It is now six a.m.

The local Antarctic temperatures are –70.6°F.

Volcanic activity is increasing rapidly. Ice caps are melting alarmingly fast, constantly shifting and creating pools of hot water and steam. Update your last will and testament, then enjoy a relaxing swim in these new natural hot springs.

Breakfast is served until eight a.m.

Thank you, and enjoy your day."

Eryn, King of the Brawl

. . .

THEY'D JUST RETURNED from the hunt cold, empty-handed, and hungry. Ernest was extra loud, as if to chase away their prey. Eryn listened with half an ear to his brother. He climbed into the rusted steel box elevator, ready to go back down to check on the boys.

Grabbing the bar of the metal door aggressively in frustration and flinging the thing shut, he stood glaring at his much smaller twin.

"Ernest tells you, brother, my trap will work!" he shrieked with a rasping, froggy voice above the noise of the old mine cage that worked like elevators in tall buildings.

Eryn recoiled. White knuckling his trident in frustration, he said through gnashing teeth. "The nest is hungry; they want to tunnel themselves out. I will do what I should have done long ago, putting them to sleep forever. I sense only six heartbeats left. They are suffering, brother. It's not fair that they were born only to suffer for existing. We can explain to the Icemen King that he is a good man, and he will understand if we admit we made a mistake. It hurts me deeply, brother, and I'm so tired, *croak*. They are in pain, they are hungry, and they are scared. If they reach the Ice City, it will be chaos. Humans will die. Then those bigger beasts will come. Don't you feel alone, brother? Don't you remember how good it was to talk to people? Every year, I feel lonelier and lonelier."

Ernest ignored him, just as he had when they had

hunted. Eryn's carefully laid action plan was ruined. He was sure Ernest had heard him, so he was waiting for an affirmation. But Ernest was licking drool from his lips and not replying.

The cage came to a sudden halt with a loud bang as it struck rock bottom. Ernest snapped out of that faraway look in his beady black eyes. Eryn lifted the two-hundred-pound gate as if it were nothing.

Eryn froze. "I smell blood. If something happened to the boys—"

"I stubbed my toe, that's all." Ernest shrugged and shuffled closer to Eryn as they exited the elevator cage. He feigned brotherly love as he looked up at Eryn. "Everything will work out in the end. You will see."

Ernest was lying. Eryn could see right through him. He saw the deceptive cunning, recognizing the psychopath who lived within his brother. *Dammit, this was your last chance, brother.*

Eryn gave him his ultimate opportunity. He told him about his plans, but Ernest disappointed him. He pretended to have never heard him speak those words. Eryn was hurt. His brother had made his choice today and had chosen his fate.

Ernest rolled his shoulders forward to enlarge his hunched back and rubbed his finger pads, producing a sticky mucus that dripped from them. Ernest whispered with a shrill, high-pitched voice, "My trap will work."

Ernest continued to avoid the subject of returning the boys. He pretended to talk about hunting and trapping, thinking he was fooling his brother, hurting Eryn even more.

"Also, don't worry about the humans," he said and side-bumped Eryn, pretending to be playful. "Ag, come on," Ernest said with an Afrikaans accent. "Stop being such a worrywart, brother. Tshe, tshe, tshe!" Sucking the spittle back through his teeth, he shuffled even closer. Ernest shook his head, clucking his tongue in visible anger when Eryn didn't react. The sounds echoed down the stuffy tunnels.

From the corner of his eye, Eryn noticed Ernest planting his webbed toes deep into the mud and moss of the cave floor. *He's anchoring himself.* Eryn realized just as he felt Ernest pulling on his arm.

Eryn looked down at the sticky, amphibian-like fingers around his forearm. He didn't like Ernest in his personal space and felt disgusted and intimidated. His brother was unstable. Ernest repulsed him, and he knew his brother noticed his sudden, rigid posture. But Ernest continued his trickster effort to pull Eryn deeper into the darkness. *Further away from the salty copper odor of blood.*

"Here, let's go sit down so we can talk more privately." Eryn saw how Ernest calculated his movements before discreetly moving away from their proximity. *Why did I never see this?* But he knew his brother. He'll start with verbal attacks next. Eryn expected aggression if he didn't agree with him.

"Brother, why do I smell blood? I must go check —" Eryn had barely finished when Ernest instantly switched to verbal assaults.

"Ernest is so tired of thinking for you." He flipped from happy hunter to disappointed brother faster than Eryn could blink his eyes. "And so sick of your piece of dumb, lazy, frog-ass. And your negativity! Useless numbskull calling yourself our king." He patted his chest. "Ernest should be the leader. Ernest does all the work and all the thinking. On top of it all, the shit Ernest endures hearing about your feelings." He slapped himself on the forehead, and the more Ernest rambled, the more he spat malicious lies.

"You dumb brawl, you can't even make the right choices without Ernest. You are brainless, inbred, thinking you know it all. Look at you. You're frogging pussyfooting!"

That shocked Eryn. Even if he was used to this, he steeled himself, but it always drove the knife deeper. Each nasty word hurt more and more each time.

He wondered why Ernest was pulling on him like that. He tried to joke and lift the mood. At the same time, he stood his ground, not willing to move a centimeter further.

Not trusting Ernest, he stared at him. "Stop it right now!" he yelled at him.

Ernest gasped and leaped backward, lifting his

chin defiantly and baring his teeth through his thinly stretched, rubbery lips. His teeth glistened with venom and spit. Blocking his path.

A rush of memories of dead humans flooded Eryn's system with adrenaline. His heart raced, and he felt his pulse rapidly tapping on his temples. Gathering himself, he breathed deep, silent breaths. With his left hand, Eryn grasped Ernest's right hand and squeezed it tightly. "Listen to me!" he said. Hoping to get his full attention. Eryn leaned down and looked him in his black eyes. Ernest gasped, blinking in surprise. "Yes, look at me and listen to me, brother." Eryn had never touched his brother like that before. Usually too scared or disgusted by him.

"Croak!" Ernest answered, small and submissively. "Sorry, I didn't mean to say that, but you know how I get when I am hungry," Ernest cried out.

"Brother, stop ignoring the big problem. We need to take the humans back. Their families will destroy us when they find us. We must make this right, brother. They will shoot first, asking no questions when they find us." He lifted his hand and pinned Ernest with his stare. "No, brother, you have avoided this problem for too long."

Ernest did a double-take. His eyes bulged, and he crossed his thin, amphibious arms in defiance.

"The boys said..." Ernest lifted his pointer finger, stuck his long tongue out, and licked water drops from the rock face. "All the talking is making me thirsty," he said.

That was one advantage of living underground. Water ran in rivulets and dripped from the rock walls.

Rolling his buggy eyes, Ernest took a deep breath and sighed. "Ernest doesn't care what the boys say! They will say anything to be released." He talked about himself in the third person and scowled.

Eryn sensed raw hate emanating from his brother toward him and his friends as he spoke wickedly. His brother was a short Brawl, only one meter tall compared to himself, a two and a half meters giant. They were egg brothers, and Ernest was the smallest of the whole nest. Their father had told Eryn that Ernest almost died when they hatched from the same egg. Eryn always felt like he had to protect and please his brother.

"You stupid mampara!" Ernest insulted Eryn in South African English. He smiled cunningly and pretended to be joking, but Eryn knew he was planning something. Recognizing the false smile for what it was, an attempt to manipulate and change the subject to confuse Eryn. That was one of Ernest's oldest jokes, finding it funny each time he accused Eryn of being a mampara. He would laugh out loud and fall to the ground, kicking his skinny legs as he laughed at the double entendre.

Parra meant frog, and mampara meant idiot, so frog idiot. Eryn never understood why it was so funny because, to him, it felt mean, and he could never understand being cruel or mean.

But now, Ernest let loose and was ranting. "You are an idiot frog. Eryn, you stole all my juju in the egg, and I want it back!" He rubbed the pads of his little toad fingers together again, thinking he was in charge and spoke to Eryn as if he were younger and going to listen to him. Eryn stepped backward and shook his head from side to side. This shit was getting old quick. Ernest's belittlement was not worth the price of not being alone anymore.

He's always been sly, but this is too much. His verbal attacks are getting worse.

Eryn pushed Ernest to move out of his way. Ernest pointed his small, bony index finger at Eryn and continued with the accusations. "If Ernest didn't break out of our egg, Eryn would have eaten Ernest! Like the nest, the bigger brother always eats the smaller ones, but Ernest is smarter. Ernest is still the smartest and the smallest." He took a deep breath and continued ranting, his voice growing raspier the longer he continued. "That makes Ernest mad and very, very sad." He furiously kicked at the rocks on the floor, alternating his skinny, knob-kneed legs, looking like he was skipping rope.

Eryn felt sorry for him instinctively, although he knew what was to come. *I have to kill my brother today.* He stepped closer to hug his brother, wondering why the sudden resentment about things that happened when they had hatched years ago.

"Ernest wants humans. Give Ernest one human, only one. You are selfish, brother!" And there it was. They reached full circle. Since they returned, Eryn and Ernest had the same argument repeatedly. He was big-muscled, but he never bullied Ernest to feel insignificant. The two had been inseparable twin brothers since birth, or so Eryn thought. Because they were the only two brothers who survived being hatched from the same egg, Eryn assumed that made them special, like he was responsible for looking after Ernest.

This is it. I've heard enough!

Eryn slammed his self-made pure gold trident into the rock floor. It was the one special thing he had left from his father. He carried it around like a walking stick. Pieces of stalactites fell from above them.

Miraculously, that silenced Ernest for a bit. When Eryn spoke, he warped his voice to sound husky and melodic. "Listen to me. I was born to lead the nest, not you." Ernest dropped his gaze to the ground.

"I know you think you have me wrapped around your finger, but you don't. One more word about eating, *my friends*, and I'll end you." Eryn's voice sounded like a rolling thunderstorm into the darkness of the tunnels. He puffed his chest and repeated his words in an even lower baritone. "E-n-d, y-o-u! Do you understand me, b-r-o-t-h-e-r?" he bellowed like a gigantic bullfrog.

"Ugly frog face!" Ernest retorted. "Look at that face. Big, wide, and flat, like a human's. You can't even look like a decent Brawl."

Eryn ignored the taunting. "Listen, brother, if even one human is dead, the icemen will kill us." Eryn was so upset that his head felt like it was about to explode. He turned his back on Ernest and took a breath for courage. He was tired of arguing and missed the boys. *Why do I smell blood?* He turned to check Ernest's toes for blood.

"Remember, Joshua Adams is dead. Our only friend who brought us food is dead! Now, who will meet me outside the glass city so I can bring us food? I don't eat humans. You should stop thinking about them as food. After your abduction stunt, our lives are in danger." Eryn forced the words through clenched teeth. Fearlessly, he looked down at his smaller brother, who thought he had the upper hand, and slammed his golden trident into the rock floor again so the vibrations of his power flowed into the mine tunnels and cavern floors, causing fine tremors beneath their feet.

"That's smart, brother. Bury all of us under-ground," Ernest goaded as the thundering and cracking sounds of the earth died down around them.

"Why didn't I see this earlier?" Eryn asked, looking at his trident as if it were for the first time.

The answer was in my hands the whole time. More pieces of rock and dust fell from above. He realized he knew what to do once he brought the boys to the surface. His brother is not going to help him flood the tunnels to fill the mine with mud and sludge.

"I understand you are hungry. I am, too." Once more, Eryn pushed his brother to the side. Wondering if he should stab his brother with his spear. "Joshua said we should plant food, and it will grow," Eryn said. He had hoped to learn the secret from Joshua, and now it's too late for that. The boys said they could show him how.

Ernest ignored Eryn and took a deep breath, inhaling the air. "I can smell the blood pumping through their veins, brother."

Eryn's fear for the boys magnified as Ernest licked his lips after wiping the saliva with his forearm from his mouth. He closed his eyes. "Ernest can taste their flavor already as Ernest tears their tongues out. Ernest wonders how chewy human tongues are." He opened his dark eyes, revealing his true evil intent as he spoke slowly, spelling it out for Eryn. "Brother, I dream of sweet and salty blood on my tongue and wake up in the mornings with a wet pillow as I dream about sucking the marrow from their bones." Wiping the saliva from his chin again, he looked at it and then licked the palm of his dirty hands with his long tongue. "Humans taste so good, so much better than monkeys. You will want nothing else once you taste a human, brother," he said and licked his fingers. Then, with a slight tilt of his head, he sucked his fingers and seemed to savor the blood from underneath his nails.

Eryn shivered as he watched the cannibalistic delight on his brother's face. He hoped that it was animal and not human blood. "We can't eat them. We won't have anything to bargain with," Eryn said. He knew he sounded weak and unconvincing. He felt sick to his stomach. In that moment, he also knew he wouldn't be able to change Ernest's mind.

"We know nothing about growing food, and humans can show us how. Besides fish and rats, we have meerkats and many other animals to feed on." Eryn knew he was grasping at straws. He couldn't remember when he last saw something alive on the ground. They only ate birds or bats. Nothing survived in the soil. He also knew precisely what caused the frozen desert around them. *I must exterminate the nest and my crazy brother before they kill all the Earth's humans, plants, and animals.* Eryn paused; the time for being nice had ended. He squashed his eyes closed as hard as possible, forcing the tears back.

Ernest laughed at him.

"The icemen aren't stupid. Look at what they built. The most beautiful glass city. I want that for us. Don't you see that, brother?" Eryn knew he was alone in his understanding. The Brawls couldn't see past their hunger, and his brother was the same. "They wouldn't come to help us. They would come to eliminate us if we ate their children."

"Give Ernest only one, now!" Ernest gulped but continued his argument. "Brother, be smart. Do you want to live in glass houses? That's not freedom."

"Yes, dammit! We will have all the food, freedom, and friends. I don't want to live underground and alone forever." And that was Eryn's truth. He wanted a mate. He wanted two mates. The two beautiful boys...no, not boys...the young men who sang for his soul. He couldn't mate with the things in the nest, and thinking of mating with his brother nauseated him. "Argh, do you always want to be hungry and worried about where your next meal comes from?"

Ernest smiled up at his brother, his biggest smile, with his teeth showing. "No, because over two thousand men in the glass city are waiting to be plucked and eaten," he said sarcastically, his hands on his hips.

Eryn had had enough. He pushed his aura of dominance into Ernest, subduing him. Ernest looked like he wanted to fall to the ground, his knees bent. But before Eryn could think, he would show his yellow belly, like all the nest brothers did when Eryn showed them who the true King of the Brawl was.

Ernest straightened up. "I can resist you. Even in your ugliness, even if you smelled good. I can resist you, brotherrrrrrrrr."

Eryn tried staring him down, but they ended up

having a staring contest. Ernest's hateful gaze told Eryn he wished he could kill him with his bare hands, but he couldn't, so he hurt Eryn with words and poisoned his mind.

I should overpower him and give him one bite. I am stronger; I could paralyze him. I could kill him with one bite before he croaked.

But the big Brawl King was torn between reason, dignity, responsibility, and insanity. Between loneliness, distrust, and doing what was right, he didn't move his eyes from his brother's.

How do I just start killing him? How? Do I spear him or bite him? Eryn never planned, and he never thought to ask. Do you do it, and then what? He'd never killed anything. *I'm a useless killer.*

Ernest surprised him and broke the stare. "Here, stick this bone in the ground. Maybe this one will grow." He handed Eryn a fishbone.

"It won't. I've planted many bones. I tell you, they need light, heat, and fertile soil...I think. The humans said we should only have asked, and they would have helped. I believe them, and I miss talking to Joshua. That's the truth, brother."

"That is the stupidest thing you ever said," Ernest snapped at his brother. "We live here because our tunnels are safe. We survived the frozen waters because we are Brawl, and Brawl is a secret kept hidden deep inside the earth. No one can reach us unless we want them to. All they see is an abandoned old mine shaft. They will never think we are down here. Ernest will put up signs saying so. *Stay away. We will kill you. Humans are not welcome. Humans will be eaten.*" He stuck his tongue out at Eryn, putting his thumbs in his ears, waving his froggy fingers, and pulling his face. Ernest teased and sang, "They will never find us, neh, neh, neh, neh, neh!"

Eryn bumped his fist on his forehead. In his mind's eye, he saw all the wooden signages zig-zagging from the mine. *Ernest might as well paint a runway for the humans.* "They will. And when they come, we will meet them and tell them we have their boys, safe and ready to go home."

"And then we have dinnerrrrr," Ernest inter-rupted, biting down on his thin, stretchy lips. "I'm kidding," he blurted out. Then he fell to the ground, rolling on his back from side to side, holding onto his fat belly, and let loose with croaks and horrendous laughter.

CHAPTER 12
TRUST YOUR GUT

"Morning, good citizens of Phoenix.

It's now six a.m. Get up!

Did you know Lasitor can make his voice sound like a drill instructor and create a litany of the required noises for an authentic military experience?

Visit our community news page for tips and tricks to adjust to waking up easier in the mornings to get your kids out of the house and make your day run smoother.

Lasitor can yell or play the 'A call to the Post' tune to wake you up earlier, unfortunately, not later.

Breakfast is served until eight a.m.

Get up!"

General Brad McCormick

. . .

BRAD PACED in front of the helm, his head low and hands sunk deep in the pockets of his arctic jacket. The news from Bryan's latest report left his mind reeling. He enjoyed the cathartic, meditative state that his counting provided. Because their airship wasn't as large as his usual secret hideout back in Phoenix, he had to improvise.

Instead of counting to one hundred, he'd settled for five. *One, two, three, four, five. Groove, step over the line, and turn. One, two, three, four, five. Groove, step over...*

"Brad, sit your ass down. We've had just about enough of your pacing." He heard Connor's frustrated demand in his Irish accent. *That meant only one thing: Connor was livid. He must have drawn the short straw to come and order me to calm down.*

"Sorry, Bud, I'm busy." Brad had hoped to be left alone. He continued counting his steps and the grooves between the steel plates beneath his boots. *One, two, three, four, five. Groove, step over the line, and turn. One, two, three, four, five. Groove, step over the line, and turn.*

Connor's boots were on his path. Brad ceased his pacing and gave his friend his scariest death glare. "Get out of my way, Connor."

"Please, you're making it worse for everyone. Your husband sent me to talk to you. Evidently, with just cause. Look at you. If you were my husband, I would throw your bloody ass overboard." Connor's black hair was standing in all directions, and his face had wrinkles and pink lines on the right side. Brad speculated he had probably been sleeping. *Rick must have awakened him to talk to me.*

"It's only been twelve days. You act as if we were months at sea. Get a grip on your emotions." Connor laid it out straight, using all the tact he could muster. Just then, laughter boomed from down below the deck.

"See what I'm talking about? They act as if we're on a holiday or something."

"That's uncalled for. We're all equally invested in rescuing our kids. But, unlike you, we're trying to stay positive. We eat, sleep, and feed our bodies and minds because we want to be ready for whatever is waiting in that mineshaft."

"I know, but..." Brad started and then stopped, deflated. Taking his gloved hands out of his pockets, he showed Connor the photos of his boys. Brad couldn't keep it in any longer. Tears rolled down his cold cheeks. "It's all my fault. I worry about my boys. And I can't do anything about it but wait. How can they sit down there and act as if nothing's happened to our boys? It irritates the crap out of me!" Brad turned and yelled into the distance behind them. The laughter abruptly ended.

"I know." Connor put a hand on Brad's back. The

touch had a soothing effect on him. He willed himself to calm down and swallow his tears. "Imagine what it would've looked like if all of us acted as you have been. Pacing up and down the deck, hands fisted, ready to strike, swearing, and talking to ourselves. We'd look like bloody lunatics! Not everyone reacts to a stressful situation in the same way. It's energy and anger being spent in the wrong place and time," Connor explained.

"I hear you. Rick has essentially said the same thing, but I still feel responsible for all this. If I'd called it in, this probably wouldn't have happened. Men would have joined me on the ice, and we would've had Phoenix on lockdown much earlier." Spittle and tears flew sideways as Brad ranted.

"Stop that. This isn't healthy. You can't lead a rescue mission thinking about coulda, woulda, shoulda's." Connor spoke firmly. Punching his index finger into his palm, emphasizing each word.

"I'm sorry. Can't we at least go faster?"

"We could, but they might hear us coming. If these things have exceptional hearing, we want to have the element of surprise, remember?" Connor pointed up to the mouth of the hot-air balloon above them. "We planned a stealth attack, so it makes sense to approach soundlessly. We'll sit this balloon down in two days, tops, just like we planned," Connor promised.

Brad stopped pacing. "You know what? I'd gotten used to all the pacing space provided inside Phoenix." He blew out a breath. "I guess I've gotten used to being in control and spoiled by everything running smoothly. Also, I feel a little claustrophobic on this ship." Brad looked away into the distance. "No surprises there," he mumbled, letting his head fall, ignoring his best friend's stare.

"Yeah, my brother, I know." Connor stepped closer for support and patted him on the shoulder once again. Brad turned to his friend, who was smiling gently. Connor lifted both his arms, resting one hand on each shoulder. Brad straightened, squared his shoulders, and made eye contact with Connor.

"Remember the last time you were upset like this? Before we wrote the code. When you stormed into the office, acting as if the sky would fall because three men were having sex. All because you wanted to have control over other people's sexual behavior. This is the same thing. The lesson you learned was that you can't go around burning people at the stake because they don't think, act, love, worry, feel, etcetera, as you do. And that applies to every human being left on this planet. Think about it. If we all examined our own attitudes and refrained from controlling others', all the world's crises would be resolved. How we act and react toward each other, nature, and our surroundings"—he pointed to the horizon, mountains, and themselves—"that's all we can control. Not others, only ourselves. Do you get my meaning? It turned out all right for us when we gave the responsibility back to the men and stopped the archaic thought pattern of what we want versus how we can make it work for everyone."

Brad nodded, then sat down to take hold of the wheel. Steering the ship by taking it off autopilot gave him a sense of control. He liked Mika and Connor's ingenious design. He could steer from various points below and the upper deck, whether they were sailing, gliding, flying, or floating.

"You and Mika did an excellent job on the design of this ship. Even though it is a bit claustrophobic."

Connor sat down next to Brad. "Hmmm, thank you." They watched as they soundlessly drifted over the snow-covered Table Mountain at Cape Point, South Africa.

After almost an hour, Brad broke the comfortable silence. "Thank you, Connor. I needed that."

"That's all right, my friend. Will you be okay now? I need something to drink and eat. Do you need anything?" Connor got up and stretched his back and arms. Both were wearing their new tactical arctic suits. Even with the freezing temperatures on the deck, their bodysuits kept their bodies toasty inside, so they were comfortable.

"I'll be right back."

"Sure, take your time. I'm good for now. I'll get a bite later." Brad nodded and continued enjoying the view. Connor turned, opened the hatch, and disappeared down the stairs and into the dinette where the others were playing poker.

Flashes of memories assailed Brad, remembering when he almost needed a triple coronary bypass after seeing the three young men getting their rocks off in the tunnels. The moment those odd sex noises were in earshot, he should have turned around, but no, he had to investigate the echoes of moans and groans coming through the tubes.

He smiled—the nostalgia relaxing him. The icy wind froze his cheeks. To free up his hands, he reactivated the autopilot and set the Blue Halcyon on the route course waypoint northeastwards to the Drakensberg Mountain range. Then he removed one glove, massaging the life back into his cheeks.

Now and then, a bird, primarily a seagull, would land on the deck, wondering who dared to fly into their airspace, squawking noisily. Putting his glove back on, he appreciated the colorful sunset for a few minutes.

Mixed feelings of peace and foreboding anticipation made him anxious. He closed his eyes and took a deep breath of cold air. After holding it for a few seconds, he slowly released it. He repeated the exercise several times, feeling much of the tension go. When he opened his eyes, he peacefully enjoyed the stunning oranges and blues of the South African horizon.

Squawk! Squawk! Another seagull, no, not a seagull, a secretary bird, came investigating. Brad's heart leaped with joy as he admired the quill-like crests on the back of its head and the light bluish-gray plumage and red-colored face. A magnificent bird, it was over a meter high. He said hello. It was bad luck not to.

"Hello, Mr. Secretary Bird, just excuse us while we experience the thrill and peaceful serenity of hot-air ballooning through your airspace. Come join us," Brad said gently, not moving from where he sat.

Squawk! Squawk! It answered and flew off. That was probably a no, Brad thought, but he felt elated by the blessing of the rare experience.

He remembered an interesting fact about secretary birds. No human had ever witnessed these birds mating.

Amused by that thought, he reminisced about the times he saw others have sex. His thoughts wandered back to the subterranean tunnels when he got acquainted with a threesome that shattered his narrow-minded world into a million pieces. *Connor's correct, and he makes a valid point. God, will I ever wash that erotic spectacle from my mind?* Dylan Hurst received a hammering from Dr. Mitchell Fairgate while the young Amir stood on his knees in front of Dylan. "Ha!" What a shock. They tainted my mind, and yeah, that's funny in hindsight." Brad slapped his thighs, laughing at himself and his over-reaction.

Then his thoughts drifted to Simon and Paul, his oldest sons. Simon was his firstborn. His biological son, by his wife, who had died in the Doomsday attacks before she could join them. Both boys came to Phoenix with Brad as students in training when they were just nineteen years old. Paul had married into the family ten years ago. They'd made a suicide pact the day he saw them having sex. He never told them he had overheard or seen them. However, he'd let them know he loved them and supported their rela-tionship, and they were still together. That was the best decision ever. Both were physicians today, making him proud; he had a fantastic relationship with them.

Why do I have a history of walking in on people having sex?

Thinking back even further to the day he had walked into his twin brother Daniel's room with his mother following behind him, and how his mother cried when they saw *Daniel and Jerrod* together in his bedroom.

Then, his mind jumped to that horrible day when he'd found Daniel lying on his bed, the linen soaked with bright red blood. He could still vividly see the multiple wrist slashes, Daniels's peaceful, pale face, and that damn letter he could never forget.

Transported back to his brother's room, he

smelled the sweet iron odor of blood and saw the words in front of him on the note.

I'm sorry I was such a disappointment to all of you. I'm humiliated and beaten. I couldn't seem to help what I was doing. I've embarrassed Brad and made Mom ashamed of me, and Dad, I guess you're right, I'm not a man. I have nothing if I can't be with the man I love. Don't blame Jerrod. He's a good man. He won't let me be with him if I'm humiliated or lose my family. Be happy. I love all of you.

"Bloody lies! You were never an embarrassment or a disappointment to me. I miss you, brother. If you had stayed, you could have sat right next to me. You were my hero. What you did, killing yourself, confused me and messed me up for many years." Brad closed his eyes and drifted toward sleep. He felt a warm blanket thrown over him. His feet lifted and tucked in, cocooning him.

When he woke, Brad thought his husband was kissing him but soon realized it was a cold, wet rag wiping his face instead of warm sensual lips caressing him.

"Is that bird shit? Lord, yes, that's bird shit! Brad, you have bird shit all over your face." Juandre laughed hysterically. "Now that's what I call shitfaced!" He pointed at Brad, teasing him like he usually did. "Gentlemen, to your left, you'll see a shitfaced general. I don't..."

"Juandre, I'm going to kill you!" Sleepily, Brad sat

up, swiped a gloved hand over his face, and felt something crusty. He checked his gloves and confirmed it was probably bird shit. He looked up at Rick, who enjoyed the spectacle while Juandre giggled, pointed, and skipped in circles like a little girl, embarrassing and irritating their barely awake leader. Although he was still cautious, he was measuring the time and distance to escape Brad's wrath. He was the only one in Phoenix with the guts to tease the mighty general like this. Brad attempted to jump up, ready to throw the irritating nymph off the airship, but they had wrapped him in so many blankets he couldn't get up and was too slow.

"Okay, you get away this time because..." He looked around for an excuse. "Because my husband brought me a coffee!"

Juandre cackled down the stairs, continuing the teasing. "Chicken! Chicken shit, get it, you're a chicken with shit on your face!"

"Damn drag queen, one of these days, I'll teach him a lesson," Brad mumbled, reaching for the coffee his husband held for him. "Thank you, love. What a way to wake up! You know, he doesn't have any respect for me."

"Morning, lover." Rick smiled widely with affection for Brad. His eyes were tearing with laughter and crinkled at the corners. "Juandre drives you batshit crazy, but we all know you let him get away with anything. He has a special spot in your big heart."

Brad looked up. "Don't you start now. He's like those sex-crazed aunts you never want to invite to weddings but somehow always arrive without an invitation." Brad scooted to the side, making space for Rick. "Damn, you're beautiful this morning. Come sit with me under the cozy blankets." Rick climbed in eagerly. "Was it you who covered me with all the blankets? How many are here?" He counted them. "One, two, three, six blankets." Brad lifted his arm for his favorite man in the world.

"I guess I brought two, and each of us came up to check during the night, thinking of you and bringing you a blanket." Rick wiggled himself under Brad's legs and lay to the side. "I missed you last night," he said.

Brad took his gloves off, stroking Rick's beautiful long brown hair and gently wiping it out of his face. He had his hair in a braid, but strands always slipped out at the sides. His attempts were futile. The wind kept blowing them back into his face.

"We'll land in a few hours. Connor said the wind's working in our favor."

"What? I never checked..."

"Don't you worry. We checked everything from downstairs. This is an amazing ship they designed." Brad settled back and finished his coffee, then said, "I'm sorry about last night. I took my frustrations out on you all."

"It's okay. I know you are, and you didn't mean it. It's just when you get like that, you're like a caged lion," Rick replied. "I'm just glad you could get some sleep." Rick then pulled Brad's face in close to kiss him, showing him all was forgiven.

After a few moments, Brad pulled back and asked, "Are you ready for whatever's living down there?"

"I hope they're"—Rick cleared his throat—"they're alive. Strangely, I feel positive, like everything will work out fine. And yes, I'm ready to kick butt. All of us are."

"Then let's get ready." Brad removed the blankets, and Rick caught them before they blew away. The general held his hand out for his husband, feeling determined. "Let's gear up and go over the extraction plan again."

Rick bundled the ball of blankets under one arm and took Brad's hand. "Yes, let's go get ready."

Because the ship's hull was round, they divided it into three large slices downstairs, much like a cake. A dinette for eating and socializing, a bathroom with a shower and toilet, and a shared sleeping area with one enormous bed.

In the dinette, Juandre and Andrew had prepared them a feast. They decked the small table with home-made bread, scrambled eggs, cheese, pan-fried bananas, hash browns, and his famous Rooster Booster Orange Juice, filled with many vitamins to boost stamina.

"Oh, wow, look at this table. Thank you, Juandre.

May we sit? Did Connor and Mika eat already?" Brad asked after they washed up.

"They're on their way, quickly making use of the shower and facilities so you can get ready after breakfast. We can't send you to battle on an empty stomach, can we?" Andrew stepped in behind Juandre, kissing his neck and looking proud and in love with his partner.

"Sit, sit, don't be shy," Juandre said effeminately, sounding like he'd lost more of his accent after living in Phoenix for the past twenty-one years. One thing that would never change was that he was trustworthy and well-loved.

"I see you at least got rid of the bird shit, General," Juandre said teasingly.

Brad shook his head and held the plate of freshly cut bread and melted butter for Rick.

"This looks delicious, thank you," Rick said.

"My bear baked the bread," Juandre bragged, pointing his thumbs backward to Andrew.

"Yes, it's easy. Just flour, water, and stick it in the oven." Andrew belly laughed with his deep, friendly giant voice. His green eyes sparkled in the morning sunlight that shone through the cabin windows.

"I bet it's a bit more complicated than that, Andrew. I've never attempted something like this, and if I tried, I know it would be hard as a rock," Brad said.

"Probably, but if you do, we can build houses with

TRUST YOUR GUT

it!" Rick teased and shoved the delicious bread into his mouth.

"I'll huff and puff and blow your house down!" Juandre made an O with his lips, pumping his arm back and forth, feigning blowjobs.

"I knew you were going to say that. You're so predictable." Brad laughed.

"Yes, or burn Phoenix down," Rick teased again, referring to the last time Brad attempted spaghetti. They all laughed cheerfully when Mika and Connor entered the dinette.

"I see Brad is in a better mood. Morning, comrades," Mika greeted them with an exceptionally wide smile. Behind him, Connor followed with the same smile. Dressed in their newly designed bullet-proof suits. Mika slipped into a seat next to Brad, and Connor scraped his crotch on the back of Rick's head.

"Oh, sorry." Rick shuffled his chair deeper under the table. The space was tighter than a virgin's ass, with all six big men inside the dining area, but once the food and table were packed away, the room was reasonably comfortable.

"Since this is the first time you're going into battle, I would like to go through all our plans one last time." A chorus of moans and groans came from around the table.

"I know, but you'll thank me for it. I've been in a war. It never turns out the way you plan, so we must

217

be prepared for all possibilities," Brad said, hammering the table with the back of his knife.

"We've been going over these steps for the past month. Every time a new satellite photo came in, we met. We're ready, sir!" Juandre moaned.

Brad shook his head. "No, one more time. I must give you a rundown, and I want you to tell me, step by step, what follows what, and how to proceed with the minimal confrontation with those, whatever they are. The plan is to go in and remove the boys without anyone noticing. You're not soldiers, but I'm thrilled that Bryan had monthly compulsory basic defense classes and that the civilians at Phoenix trained.

"Also, I know you've never been a part of a special operation extraction with the least amount of contact with the enemy. You're all young and healthy, trained to defend Phoenix. This is helpful, but it's the reason I'm nervous. Not one of you has seen a real battlefield with blood, gore, and men screaming for help. I don't want that for you, so this differs from whatever your defense classes have taught you about eliminating the threat.

"This is stealth, and if you must kill, do it silently. This is not going in and closing your eyes and pulling the trigger, shooting whatever shows its face from left to right." He paused, pointing at Juandre. "Like a video game." He clapped his hands, and they straightened up.

"Okay, Juandre, please pack the food away.

Andrew, get the room ready. I want the maps, weapons, and everything unpacked and ready to assemble. Fifteen minutes. I'll be back. Get your suits on. Oh, don't wash with soap, shampoo, or any deodorant. You want to smell as natural as possible."

"Oh, man." Juandre moaned again.

"Juandre, I've had enough. You're staying here. I decided that right now. You're not ready for this." Brad, as the General, stared him down, making it clear his word was final. "No, not one word of back talk. This is serious."

"I think that's a wise choice," Andrew said.

"No! Now, who will look after you, my bear?"

"See, that's exactly why you can't go. No one's looking after anyone here. We work together and trust they'll be able to make the right choices to be safe."

Andrew put his hand over Juandre's mouth, silencing him playfully.

"Please assemble and disassemble the weapons, and when I'm back, we'll talk in detail. Juandre, I'm not being funny. It's better to stay with the ship and make sure we have something to go home in. You're responsible for our transportation home."

Juandre straightened up, realizing he had an important job.

He saluted. "Yes, General."

"Good, thank you. Weapons, extraction plan, and defense plan when I return."

Fifteen minutes later, Brad walked back into the room with Rick. He noticed the changes in the room. They had flipped the round dining table into a smaller rectangular table and folded the little cabin chairs underneath the sofas. Juandre and Andrew must have been the ones who cleaned the galley and swiftly turned it into a makeshift field surgery or combat casualty care area. As Brad had requested, Mika was finishing up the unpacking of all their gear and weapons. He was quiet and goal-focused, but he mentioned Connor had slipped into the pilothouse to get ready to land their ship. Juandre and Andrew completed testing their radios and were donning their suits.

When Brad grabbed their attention, the six of them looked ready for battle and were dressed in their tactical arctic suits of white, brown, green, and black camouflage. Over their heads, they wore ski masks woven from the same material as the bulletproof bodysuits they wore underneath—the military-issued helmets with night-vision goggles folded over their eyes.

Brad let them show him how to load their guns again and again. Their little laser guns had only a few shots loaded. Since they were prototypes, he didn't want them to depend on them, but used them as a backup. He checked their knives, flare guns, Glupi-done shots, torches, ropes, and last, they tested their communication systems. Little earbuds with microphones fitted around the ear that Connor designed a few years ago.

When Brad and the men reviewed the plan of action, he stood back and spoke. "Okay, I'm very impressed with how well you've prepared. I feel confident that we've prepared as best we can. You look good and are ready for whatever may come our way. Stick to the plan, trust your team, and trust your gut!"

CHAPTER 13
FROGGING FUCKER

"MEN OF PHOENIX, LASITOR BIDS YOU A GOOD MORNING.

It's now six a.m.

Did you know there are science-based ways to reduce hunger and appetite? If you ever manage to skip a meal and become hungry, tell yourself that hunger is normal and keep busy, you could be a boredom eater.

Visit your community news page for more easy ways to battle hunger.

Breakfast is served until eight a.m."

CIAN Romanov

"HEY, you piece of frog shit, let us out! Come back. Where are you going?" Cian's voice was hoarse from screaming, so it sounded like a whisper. Being a say-it-like-it-is kind of guy made him the world's worst cellmate, and their current predicament wasn't highlighting his usual sunny disposition. No, instead, he gave words to his anguish and irritation. He was sick of being hungry, and he wanted damn clothes. At this level of darkness, he could see three different shades of darkness. Light gray, dark, darker gray, and dark.

"I'm sick of this. What are we waiting for? He said today is the day," he asked for the umpteenth time, and still, no one answered.

"Bloody locked up and tucked away for safekeeping, my ass. Is that what he thinks we are? Do we look safe? No. We wait like life bait. That's what we are." He ranted because his brother and the McCormick twins just sat there, letting him have his turn at freaking out. They rotated that honor a few times a day. The unspoken rules of prisoners stuck in a gold cage in a king's cavern.

"We sit here and wait for our fate!" He waved his arms around in circles, looking like a windmill in hurricane season, as he pointed to the thick golden bars that testified about their captor's goldsmithing skills. Out of frustration, he fell on his ass and planted his feet on either side of a bar, then pushed and pulled the one in the middle.

"Get off your ass and help me. I want to get out of here!" he demanded, but no one was in the mood. "Ugh, it just won't budge." He groaned and pulled.

"One of these days, ugh, I'm gonna pop a vein," he said, trying a few more times.

"At least it keeps you busy and us entertained," Ivan remarked.

"A beautiful cage for his beautiful human boys," Cian muttered. Disgusted and defeated, he fell backward, staring up into the dark.

"I'm sick of the darkness. I want to see light!"

After a few minutes of quiet, he felt a hand on his shoulder. Probably Ivan's.

"Brother, don't worry. Eryn said he'll get us out. Just give him more time."

"I'm giving him one day. I can't live like this one day longer. It stinks. I can't breathe." Cian heaved, breathing harder and faster.

"Stop that. You're hyperventilating. You'll pass out and lose consciousness again," Ivan said. *Always coaxing.* He grabbed Cian's hand, squeezing it. Then he looked right at Cian and said, "We have endured this captivity as best we can, given the circumstances. We're all going to get out of here. I'm sure Eryn doesn't know, and as soon as he finds out, he will kill his brother." Ivan reasoned, *always the calm and reasonable twin, the opposite of myself, who's impulsive and emotional.*

"Come closer, so we can huddle and bunch up for heat," Ivan said, pulling his twin closer.

Cian let himself be pulled closer to the other two men, where he and Ivan folded their upper bodies over Kawa's shivering body, containing as much heat as possible. Still dressed in their swim trunks, the dampness of the subterranean mining tunnels was stifling. Kilometers deep into the musty earth, their malnourishment compounded their hypothermia. When they'd arrived, they were having trouble breathing and sweating profusely. The pressure on their eardrums was excruciating, but now they'd acclimated and were not popping their eardrums. One positive thing about the constant dripping of water from the rock surface above their cage was that they at least had clean water to drink. Despite that, the smell from their bucket reeked. *Eryn should come and empty it.*

"I can't believe we haven't caught a sinus or lung infection yet. It's a miracle in itself. The stench of our excrement is suffocating. We've passed the level of let's get out of here!" Cian said, trying to say something positive, but it came out the opposite.

"Maybe, if we're lucky, we can convince Eryn to take us out of the cage to his father's lab. That's a positive move in the right direction." Ivan seemed to look on the bright side by highlighting their new freedom to use the facilities for daily bathroom breaks.

"Of course, that's a big positive, I agree. It's heaven to wash up out of the old bathroom sinks," Donali added scornfully from out of the dark.

"Yes, but terrified doesn't describe how I feel

when I see that ugly brother of Eryn's," Cian added, finding it impossible to walk on the bright side of life.

"I'm just thankful Eryn sits with us, and I enjoy how he laughs at our stories. I can tell he's hungry for love and friendship." *Ivan continued his quest to find goodness.*

"I don't feel cold and scared when he laughs or sings for us," Donali added while holding Kawa.

"Yes, but where was he today? We needed him, and he went on a freaking walkabout! I'll give him a piece of my mind if I see him," Cian said, pissed off again.

"Cian, you give pieces of your mind freely every day, the whole bloody day. Eryn went to build a beacon for us. To show our fathers where we are. He'll come for us...trust that for now," Ivan begged, sounding tired.

"I can't believe what just happened to Kawa. Donali, is he okay?" Cian asked, feeling guilty about his antics while Kawa was in pain.

"Hmmm, for now, he's fine. However, as our nightmare has quickly become our reality, we need to get him home as soon as possible," Donali replied.

"As if being abducted by frogmen only in our swim trunks wasn't bad enough. Surviving not being eaten isn't something one expected to be celebrating," Cian added sarcastically.

"Being thankful for only a chomped-off arm instead of another limb isn't something I ever thought to experience," Kawa moaned. Donali held him tighter in his arms. "He'd munched on my arm in front of my eyes." Kawa cried and muffled his wails in his brother's lap.

"This nightmare is genuine. That frogman crushed your radius and ulna like a bloody potato chip." Cian mimicked Ernest's raspy voice. "*Naughty and saucy knick-knacks.*" Kawa cried louder as Cian described their ordeal with vivid clarity. Oblivious to his insensitivity, he rambled on. "And when he bit the tip of your thumb off, and the blood sprayed all over us, that was gross! I'll never, ever suck my fingers clean after I have eaten," Cian added.

"Thank you, Cian. We all needed to hear that. You can be so blatantly crude sometimes," Ivan reprimanded him, and Cian rolled his eyes.

"The animal almost came back for seconds but thought better of it when the king called for him," Cian said, not backing down.

"What will happen when they return?" Donali rocked Kawa in his arms. "The thing winked at us and licked its lips, promising he'd be back."

"The words *that was delicious* are playing on replay in my mind." Kawa sniffled.

The four of them were reaching their limits. They've been sitting in the cage waiting to be rescued, slowly dying of light deprivation and hunger. Barely fed and looking like skeletons, Cian knew his fathers were going to freak out when they saw them. It reeked in the cave, and using a bucket for toileting didn't help.

"Luckily, since we befriended Eryn and explained what humans needed, he was happy to take us to his father's office to use the facilities. Remember, he disagrees with the abduction, but he has many players to move to get us out safely. So I guess if they return and Eryn sees Kawa's arm, he won't let his brother hurt any of us," Ivan said.

"Still, I agree with Cian. The stench is suffocating, and I can barely understand them. It's a weird mix of South African English, Russian, and frog," Donali whispered.

"They croak a lot. There are croaks for yes, croaks for no, then croaks for anger, and a string of croaks for laughter," Cian said, and Kawa whimpered, sounding like he was in excruciating pain.

"Sorry, I just can't stop crying," he said, covering his mouth to hide the sounds.

"That's why I'm trying to joke about it. No need to hide anything from me. Turn onto your left side, and let's elevate the stump." Cian helped him. "That's it!" He ripped off another shred of a swimming towel.

"This is going to hurt." Ivan helped Cian to apply another tourniquet higher up, closer to the shoulder, and bandaged the stump over the already-soaked one.

"Oh, my stars, that's sore! Hurry!" Kawa howled. "Somehow, the bite had numbed the pain and slowed the bleeding, but now, it's burning and hurts like a hot iron," he said. His breathing was wheezy, his teeth chattering. His breath reeked and gave Cian a migraine. He guessed all of their breaths stank, so he kept that to himself, as well. Also, he noticed Kawa's stump was bleeding at an alarming rate, *worse than a slaughtered pig*, and decided not to verbalize that thought. He scooted in next to Donali to keep the stump elevated. While holding his friend, his heart broke for him, and he wished he could do more. So he ended up rocking him back and forth.

"Cian," Kawa whispered.

"Yeah, buddy," he whispered back.

"I see black spots and light flickering. It feels like I want to pass out," Kawa said. Sounding weak and defeated.

"It's okay. Close your eyes. We'll watch over you. Sleep a little." Cian said. Donali sniffled until Cian felt Kawa's body relax. *Hold on, don't die, Kawa.* Cian thought and lightly felt for his carotid pulse to confirm his friend's beating heart.

"When our fathers come to rescue us, and they will come," Donali said. Cian agreed and hoped it was soon. "They'll kill that thing first, and I'll ask them to do it slowly." Donali's voice deepened with the promise of vengeance.

The four looked and smelled like they lived inside a sewage plant. Their matted hair and dirty faces contrasted with the white of their eyeballs.

"This is ludicrous!" Ivan whispered, "We need to think of an escape plan. I agree, brother. I'm not sitting around, waiting to be rescued one more day either. We need to get Kawa out of here. Eryn must come so we can go clean up. I say it's then we take our chance. He must take us up and out, or we over-power, maybe lock him inside somehow. Then we escape."

Far away in the distance, they heard a crashing and banging. A sound they got to know well. They listened to the frogmen getting out of the elevator.

"I bet we can tease the small one enough to unlock the gate so we can overpower him," Ivan said. "We need a plan if Eryn doesn't come through for us today."

"Uhm, I agree with you, brother." Cian hummed while rocking Kawa.

It was Ivan's turn to bend the golden bars. Making grunting noises like a weightlifter at the Olympics, he pulled and pushed on them, entertaining the idea that they might budge this time.

"Their eyes are adapted to see in the dark, so we must be smart. Maybe when the smaller one's alone," Cian said. *Overpowering your enemy on their soil needs perfect strategizing.*

"Eryn's eyes are beautiful. Did you notice his green-golden irises with elongated pupils?" Ivan added almost dreamily.

"Yes, and it's the second time today you've asked

us that. I admit, although Eryn is humongous, he has attractive humanoid features," Cian said.

"Ha, so you noticed his other big humanoid features, too! What about the feeling of knowing him, like we should know him?" Ivan asked over his shoulder, still pushing and pulling.

"Yes, I can't put my finger on it, but now that you mentioned it, I know what you mean, brother. It feels like I've seen him somewhere. Like a déjà vu feeling. Do you think we've seen him in Phoenix? We should ask him how long he's been visiting."

"He's a gentle soul, almost like he wants to please us in everything he does, but he doesn't know better. So we need to tell him what we want. You know, like when he sings, I like it when he sings for us. Maybe we should continue to play on that. We were making progress. He's almost my best friend ever!"

"We noticed," Cian said sarcastically. It pissed him off that he wanted Eryn close to him and hated him at the same time. "Today, I tell him to let us out, or we'll never speak to him again. I'm going to give it to him straight because we're at the point of having nothing to lose. No more being nice. Ivan, if you want out, you need to let him know we aren't happily waiting, and we need out. Kawa is going to die of an infection within two days. And that's not me being overdramatic. That's the truth of it. We all need to stand together and not budge on this. We want out today, and his brothers must go. No more serenading, no more waiting."

A pained keening from Kawa forced them to turn their attention elsewhere. Ivan crept in closer to the group. "I need heat," he said, and Cian moved up and threw his other arm around his twin brother, pulling him closer and away from the bars where Ernest could catch him.

"I don't know how much longer I can hang on," Kawa cried. "Why don't they just kill us?" He stuttered between the chattering of his teeth. "I want to go home, please, I want to go home. I want to go home." He repeated the words and mindlessly rocked back and forth.

He's going to end up with tetanus or an infection. Cian kept that to himself. "We should demand to go rummage through the lab for meds. We must ask Eryn to go as soon as he returns. Maybe we can find a first aid kit or antibiotics," he said.

"I agree," Donali said.

"Anyway, my only worry is the others Eryn was talking about. Somewhere down here is the nest. If we escape, we should know where to go," Ivan said softly, leaning into them. He threw his arms around the McCormick boys.

"They hatched from eggs, like little tadpoles," Cian said.

They chortled. "We got to know our enemy's routine fairly well. Questions need to be asked about the nest and the tunnels. We should ask about the ship and where to find shelter and food," Donali whispered.

"Ernest is the lunatic. I bet they stole eggs from Phoenix..." Cian abruptly stopped talking and listened. It sounded like someone was walking outside.

Maybe it's water dripping.

"Shhh, they're coming..." They all looked up. Listening again—more listening.

"False alarm," Ivan said.

Donali chuckled. "Born with little tails?"

"Yes, that's funny," Ivan said. They fell silent for a minute. Ivan cleared his throat. "My biggest worry is what Ernest said that one brother would eat the other brother. I worry those things have more hatchlings, maybe smaller ones."

"Maybe bigger ones," Cian said.

"Shhh, here they come," Ivan cautioned.

All of a sudden, they heard Eryn saying from outside their cave, "The nest is restless, brother. They're hungry."

"Oh, my stars, we are going to be frog food. I need a weapon. We must ask Eryn for weapons so we can defend ourselves," Cian said.

"There is a nest of frog monsters," Ivan whispered. "He told me that when he closed his eyes and concentrated on them, he was connected to them." He held his finger in front of his lips. They listened—

water dripped behind them. They could hear the two frogmen arguing a few meters down the tunnel.

Eryn, King of the Brawl

Eryn pointed to his cave, beyond his brother, who was blocking the tunnel to it, where he kept the boys safe until their fathers arrived.

"I'm going to free the boys and light the beacon!" Eryn shoved Ernest hard against the wall. Ernest resisted. He kneed him, glaring at his brother. "Get out of my way!" Determined to go get the boys. He decided to kill his brother once he'd lit the beacon, he thought, procrastinating killing yet again.

Ernest wiggled free and ran, the pitter-patter of feet jogged Eryn into action. "What do you think you are doing?" Running as fast as his little frog legs could carry him, his brother disappeared around the corner into Eryn's cave. The boys screamed hysterically.

The boys are in danger.

"Ernest, no!" he shouted as he sprinted as fast as possible to prevent their carnage.

"Leave us alone, you psycho, no, piss off!" Cian stood in front, protecting the others as he kicked and screamed while Ernest hopped around the cage. They flattened themselves against the bars on the opposite side of Ernest's reach for an arm or a leg. Open-mouthed, baring his little toothpick teeth, he snarled and groped at them. *Desperate and lost to his hunger for human meat.* Eryn saw the animal in him. And then he saw all the blood.

What in the ever-loving hell? One boy already has an arm missing!

Eryn's switch flipped from irresoluteness to a killing rage. He grabbed Ernest at the back of his neck with one arm and picked him up from the ground. Dangling him like Kermit, the Muppet frog. "*Croak!*" His voice blazed like a trumpet in his indignation. Ernest kicked wildly and stretched to grab onto the cage's bars. His beady eyes reflected red. They were savage, and he looked at the boys like they were his only meal.

"No, Ernest, stop your nonsense. No, stop that right now!" Eryn said to no avail as Ernest turned to attack him. Eryn threw Ernest like a wet rag against the rocks, but as soon as Ernest hit the ground, he jumped, flung himself over in a twist midair, and landed on the three-meter-high cage.

"Give me an arm or a leg. That's all I need!" he said as he snarled, saliva dripping. Grabbing onto a white-haired boy—Ivan—he pulled him closer. "I bet you taste different. Your color is different." It was chaos. The boys screamed, holding onto him and dragging Ivan back from Ernest, but his cannibalistic brother wouldn't let go.

"Ernest, no! Ernest, stop that!" Eryn bellowed as he threw his trident aside, not to hurt the boys, he leaped and landed on the cage. He pushed and pulled fiercely on his brother, who ignored him. In the scrimmage, he received a hard kick from one of the boys, who was kicking frantically. *Ernest is seconds away from biting the boy's head off.*

"Ernest, stop it," he ordered, using his commanding voice as he grabbed on and exerted all of his power and pheromones. "I will have to kill you if you don't stop right away." Ernest didn't even blink. He simply kept pulling on Ivan with his mouth just a centimeter away. The boys yelled furiously as they fought to save Ivan. "That's it!" Eryn stood up and delivered a deadly head kick to his brother. He heard bones breaking when his foot connected with his brother's skull for a second time. Ernest fell from the cage like a sack of rocks. *Where is my trident?* Eryn leaped onto his back, preventing him from springing away once more. Ernest wriggled and kicked to escape, but Eryn had him pinned with one knee, securing his lower back while he pressed his head into the dirt. Lifting his head high, Eryn opened his mouth wide and let his fangs slide out. He struck and bit Ernest as hard and deep as he could into the back of his thick, warty neck.

As he injected his deadly venom into his brother, the boys quieted down while heaving and coughing in the background. Ernest stopped his kicking and thrashing. Eryn listened for his brother's last heartbeat. When he couldn't hear anything after a few minutes, he retracted his fangs and fell backward with a plop.

The cave was deadly quiet.

Catching his breath, he lay there staring up at the crystallized cavern roof. He felt horrible for killing his only brother and, worse, realizing he was utterly alone. Relief and immense sadness built inside him until he let it all go. He cried for his father, who wanted more for him. He cried about the pointless annihilation of the humans. And then he cried for being born. When he had calmed, he rolled over onto his hands and knees. Shaking his head in disbelief as he straightened up.

"Boys, we must leave. Can you help me flood it all and bury the nest?"

They looked as though they barely understood his rambling. He couldn't say the words correctly, although he often thought about saying them. *I want to be human and live among humans, doing human things.* But he said, "I will take you back home to your families."

The boys sat shocked and wide-eyed, too scared to move. One move from Eryn, and they scurried backward. Eryn cringed.

He felt ashamed about his treatment of them. "I should have done something sooner. I'm so very sorry. My brother had somehow...lowered my spirit through our bond," he said, wiping the tears and snot from his face and remembering his father, who warned and begged him long ago. He sat with him for days, holding his dead body, talking to him, and even reading to him. He rocked him until he blew up like a balloon and smelled terrible. *I visited the Ice City in a daze, meeting Joshua. I should never have trusted Ernest. Now he's dead. My mind feels lighter, and the haze has cleared.*

Approaching the skittish four boys in the cage, he said, "I need help flooding the tunnels, or we can just leave for the surface, then I'll come back and cause a few tremors and rock falls, burying the nest." His booming voice woke the four shaken humans from their stupor. Eryn knew Ernest was a cunning and dangerous Brawl. Now, he vividly remembered his father's words, *"Eryn, my boy, you need to flood the tunnels and bury your brother and the nest. Leave to live with Joshua."*

He burst out laughing. Eryn felt as light as a feather. He couldn't stop himself. He croaked and croaked, feeling elated and free for the first time in a long time. "Ernest, you liked the taste of humans too much," he said as he bent down to grab his brother by the ankles.

"Boys, I'll be right back. I'm just taking Ernest away so you don't see him anymore," Eryn said over his shoulder and inspected the webbed toes and overly large feet. They looked so different from his own feet. Without a grunt or a moan, he dragged his brother's body out of the cave to discard his corpse far away from the boys.

Next, he planned to unlock the cage, free the boys, and tend to their wounds, especially the little one's stump, where Ernest had chewed it off. The thought made him queasy and nervous.

The Icemen King will not be happy.

With no clue how to do medical care for a human, he decided he would take them to his father's office, where they could clean up and use the medical supplies. After that, they would go to the surface while the twins could help him flood the tunnels.

During the scuffle with Ernest, the key around his neck had come off and swung to the back. Eryn mumbled to himself and entered the cave while reciting his steps to himself and searching for the key. Once he found the key, he stood up straight, smiling widely, eyes sparkling with happiness. "I found it. Let's go!" He showed them the giant golden key, feeling triumphant. The boys gasped.

"Little ones, don't be scared," Eryn said, fumbling with the key in the lock. He heard continued gasping. "Calm down. I will help you. I will not hurt you. I'm helping you, see?" he said softly and opened the big golden door to show them.

Then he saw sparks flying in front of his eyes, a sharp pain in the back of his head and neck that zapped through his body, and then their voices and faces disappeared as it all went dark...

CHAPTER 14
THE MINE

"GOOD MORNING, CITIZENS OF PHOENIX.

I, Lasitor, am bidding you a good morning.

It's now six a.m.

Did you know the song *Kum Ba Yah* is an African American spiritual song tied to captured and enslaved West African people?

I cross-referenced three words: Africa, strength, and good luck, for our leadership team, who are on their way to search and retrieve their offspring from South Africa. Don't fear, for Lasitor will play this song for you today. If you don't know the lyrics, just hum along to *Kum Ba Yah*.

Breakfast is served until eight a.m. *Kum Ba Yah, my lord, Kum Ba Yah*."

(Lasitor sang for twelve hours, and no one could find the computer program to silence him.)

• • •

GENERAL BRAD MCCORMICK

"THIS IS the epicenter of it all," Brad confirmed over the comms as he hung over the rail. Connor steered the ship closer for a better view to inspect the bullseye of death. Massive rings of different gray, white, and brown shades ran for kilometers in circles around the mineshaft, marking it as ground zero. To guarantee a successful mission, Brad, Rick, and Andrew studied the terrain and activity in the area harder than Tibetan monks studied philosophy. They fine-combed every map and satellite photo Lasitor had found in the heaps of old maps and information downloaded by Connor during the Doomsday internet grid crash. This enabled the team to visually plan the extraction of their children from the ultra-deep mining tunnel system, which ran in a vertical and horizontal mesh called Western Deep Levels near the ruins of the old mining community of Fochville in the northwestern province of Gauteng, South Africa.

As planned, the Blue Halcyon's glow wasn't visible in the early morning light. Connor had parked the ship five kilometers away in a hollowed-out area, and as a precautionary measure, the team had covered it with camouflage netting to blend the vessel with the frozen black mud and dying surroundings.

According to recent satellite images, the mineshaft was where most activities were concentrated. Brad noticed the barren wasteland as they made their way to enter via a hidden emergency exit used by miners as an escape route during rock falls and earthquakes. Around them was a frozen desert. Not at all like one would have expected in Africa. He saw no trees or grasslands. It was cumbersome, and he worried about the rest of the earth. He realized Phoenix had a bigger problem than he thought. They had an obligation to save the earth and restore the balance—once their children were home.

The Anti-Gravitational Lab at the University of Phoenix created a spy sphere, which Connor used to scope their surroundings and observe the kidnappers. Designed by second-year students, the prototype won a yearly competition to encourage creativity.

"I'm very impressed. I can see why this baby won. It's a little winner," Connor whispered. "I can see you clearly on the screen. Okay, steering the camera toward the entrance." Silence, except for heavy breathing, from the men on the ground. "I'm at the tunnel. We should re-design this little floating camera ball and build it bigger. Who would have thought balancing the gravitational pull with electro-magnetism opposites was possible? I'm sure a person could experience free fall without ever touching the surface." Connor yapped on while Brad and the team panted heavily over the comms.

"Why don't you just say fly, so we will all understand what you're trying to say," Brad said.

"I'm dropping the ball... okay, that's funny... that's it... I think I've reached the bottom... nope, not going to laugh. How far are you, Brad?" Connor coordinated the position of the floating camera ball as the team moved further and deeper into the earth.

"We're on a rescue mission, and you have time for sexual innuendos. I expected this from Juandre and not from you, Connor. One more joke, and I'll take your ball privileges away," Brad said and grinned. More chuckles followed over the comms.

Then, all went quiet as Connor announced, "Okay, I have a visual of their space. I mean, their living area. Holy shit, it's an enormous entrance. I can imagine gigantic trucks driving up and down these tunnels. They're easily three apartment levels high. I see nothing moving. It's quiet. Not at all what I imagined. Absolutely no life at all. Okay, ready. Lights on standby, awaiting Brad's signal to light up the area," Connor whispered while Brad, Mika, Rick, and Andrew entered from the far side at different depths. Once they reached the rendezvous point safely, Brad showed them it was time they switched their headlamps off. They activated their night-vision goggles and crept step by step into the hot and humid darkness to the back of the underground warehouse.

Brad raised his head and whispered over his shoulder, "This is not just a warehouse. This was

some kind of animal research and experiment laboratory." Brad saw a big tank twice his size. It was shattered and drained, and there were broken jars with
animal parts inside them. The most upsetting were
exact replicas of the Omega Project, artificial wombs
with not two but multiple pods for babies or whatever they dabbled with. Animal cages lay strewn and
turned on their sides with broken open gates. A chill
ran up his spine. It was a horrific scene.

"And the gates are open," Andrew noted.

"What?" Rick whispered.

"Freezing hellfires!" Brad heard Mika and knew
they'd finished passing through the eerie scene.

Brad: "Okay, refocus. We've arrived. All four of us
are ready."

Connor: "Ready."

Brad: "Okay, move out."

The team of four split up, searching the tunnels
for what Connor identified as the living area, moving
down and through the levels as planned.

Andrew: "I'm going to vomit. The stench is
unbreathable."

Brad: "Copy, follow your noses. That must be
them."

Simultaneously, they heard the faint cries echoing
from afar through different tunnels. Moving in short,
silent steps, Brad was determined to kill those
responsible for abducting their kids. The thrill of the
hunt would excite him under any other circumstance,

but as his heart leaped into action, he remembered he was there with untrained men.

Brad: "I know you want to run to the boys, but please, for the love of... stick with the plan."

Brad reminded the team again, just as he had drilled it into them on the ship.

Brad: "No matter what you hear or see, stick with the plan. Don't give our position away."

I'm so glad Juandre isn't here. I can imagine his retort.

Brad crouched closer, centimeter by centimeter. He maneuvered deeper into the dark with his finger on the trigger. Blood rushed through his ears, almost deafening him. He willed himself to calm down for a second before proceeding. Not a cheeky word from the men. It sounded like it had stuck during preparation. They heard the agony of their boys crying. Every cell in his body lit up as it was pumped full of adrenaline and the protective instinct of a parent.

Connor: "Jesus Christ, can't we go faster?"

Just as Connor's voice boomed over the comms, the crying died down. Brad and the men inched closer.

Brad: "I have a visual. I see one big man pulling another by the ankles. Our boys are inside. Wait, he's returning."

Andrew: "I have a good, clear shot, standing by. First cover is ready."

Rick: "Back up, ready."

Mika: "Second cover is ready."

Connor: "I'm deploying the ball. The third backup is ready. No other movement detected."

Brad: "Moving in for extract."

Each member of the team positioned themselves strategically to cover Brad.

Brad: "I count four souls, one enemy."

Thank god they're alive. A chorus of relieved sighs followed over the comms.

Connor: "Halt, don't go in yet, Brad."

Far off into the dark, Brad saw Connor raising the ball camera. Barely visible in the darkness, Brad heard a faint click from the camera. *We need to work on silencing the camera.*

Brad: "Is it unsafe? Please advise."

Silence for a while. Connor must have been uploading and inspecting the pictures, so Brad waited.

Connor: "No, it seems safe to proceed. I saw something you won't believe."

Brad: "May we proceed?"

Connor: "Yes, proceed, please."

Brad: "I'm going in. Stick to the plan!"

Soundlessly, Brad crept closer, entering the reeking cave low on his heels. He saw their boys in a cage with an enormous figure in front. After making sure no other enemies were in sight, he leaped through the air, shooting the giant in its back and head, releasing fifty thousand volts. After walking like an Egyptian for a second, the thing fell to its knees and made a loud, pained noise. The earth and cave walls trembled, and Brad quickly jumped up, ready to shoot another round. The boys gasped. They watched as Brad pushed the still convulsing giant with two fingers so it fell backward, eyes rolled back in its head, unconscious or dead—Brad didn't know and didn't care.

And then the boys shouted their jubilation.

"Dad! Brad!" they all yelled, ecstatic to see him.

"Dad!" Donali called again, his voice filled with urgency.

Brad lifted his forefinger to his mouth, "Shhh," then tapped his earpiece.

Brad: "Enemy one neutralized."

Then he opened the already unlocked gate. *What? A cage made of pure gold.* Feeling like a superhero and a father worth his salt, he stuck his hand out and pulled the boys out of it.

"There, can you see your dad?" Brad pointed to Rick, who was waiting in the darkness.

Bloody hell, my kids were sitting in the dark, in a cage, this whole time waiting for me.

Brad swallowed his anger and proceeded as he said they should.

"Here, come to Dad," Rick called softly. Reaching out for them, he pulled the young men to the exit of the cavernous area. He must have handed them night-vision goggles. Brad heard Donali objecting to putting them on.

"Dad! Don't worry. We can see. Our eyes have adjusted while we were here." It was quiet for a second, and then Brad heard Rick losing his hold on his emotions; he'd broken down and cried.

Brad's heart slammed against his ribs with angst, relief, and joy. He saw the boys reaching for Rick, hugging and clinging to him. But it seemed Rick had forgotten about their mission and was having a meltdown.

I still need to tie the buggers!

"Rick, Doctor Broderick Longarrow," Brad whispered his husband's full name, hoping to catch his attention. Nothing. Rick seemed frozen in an embrace as he told them how much he missed them. "Later with that, Rick," he encouraged. "Move, move, move!"

Rick seemed to sober up immediately at the mention of his name. "Come, boys, this way, follow us!" He coaxed his charges, and Brad relaxed.

Jesus Christ!

Relieved, Brad returned to tying up Big Foot. This is not a monster. It was a bloody man, and probably the one Bryan had captured.

Brad: "The big fellow is incapacitated. Checking on the one that was dragged out by the ankles."

Connor: "Copy over."

Brad found the body of a green-skinned creature about fifty meters away in another smaller cave. Kicking it hard a few times, he wondered whether it was necessary to tie it up. It appeared dead. *To be safe,*

I'll tie its hands and feet, anyway. He snooped around a bit, clearing the space. It seemed it was only the two.

Brad: "Connor, if you're sure it's safe, I have a few seconds. Light up the area so we can see what you found."

Connor: "I took pictures, but here it is. Move a few meters deeper eastwards into the right of the forking tunnel."

First, Brad saw the dim light of the camera ball and turned to see what it highlighted.

"Holy shit! Is that what I think it is? Is that a damn rocket? How high is this thing?" Bowled over by the surprise, Brad just stood there, taking it all in. Nothing computed or made sense to him.

Brad: "Connor, please take more pictures. See what you can find, writing or identification."

"For the love of, what the hell was going on here?" he asked. *Weird animals, overgrown giants, and now a rocket.*

A whiff of stench jogged his memory. "Oh, the mission. I need to make sure the boys are okay." He sprinted to meet up with the others.

Connor: "Yes, I will. See you on the other side."

Brad ran as fast as he could, slipping on moss and mud as he ran.

He didn't know what to make of this, but the boys were his priority. He tried to go faster, filled with relief from a successful mission. As circumstances were, they had luck on their side. Making sure nothing followed them, he swiftly backtracked until he met up with the group, as they'd just passed the halfway mark. It seemed they stopped for another round of hugs. As he approached, he heard *I missed yous, and I love yous, and I knew you would come.* Of course, "You look badass, Dad," was Brad's favorite thing to hear when they reached the exit. Once outside, they regrouped inside a warehouse that seemed recently used. Brad made a mental note of that. All of them appreciated the cold, fresh air.

More hugs and health checks followed. While the other three youngsters were malnourished, Kawa appeared frail and on the verge of fainting. He was lying on the floor of the cage when he'd pulled them out of it. Brad noticed him, pale and probably in shock, and who knows what. Someone had thrown a blanket around his shoulders. *He needs more. He needs medical attention.* Brad calculated and triaged the young men, but the situation soon became disorganized, making Brad super nervous.

"We need to go back, Dad," Ivan told Mika.

"No, you go to the airship right now!" Mika said sternly.

"Dad, I'm serious. We can't leave him alone," Ivan said, and Mika took a deep breath, looked at his boys, and assessed them. He looked lost and unsure as he turned to Rick for answers. He waited for a second, then decided warmer clothes for their boys were the immediate priority.

"Why do you think they're demanding to go back? Is it Stockholm?" Mika softly asked Rick, who looked at Brad, who shook his head. He had one goal—to get them all out of the mines as fast as possible.

"Dad, that man, he was our friend. He killed his brother to save us," Donali told Brad.

"That man you just killed!" Cian yelled. For a second, Brad thought the boy was going to attack him, but Mika held him back, frowning. Obviously, Mika was thinking the same as they looked, stunned by Cian's sudden aggressiveness.

"No, he's not dead. I only used a stun gun. He's alive and not dead," Brad assured them. "It seems they have an attachment to Hulk," Brad mumbled into his comms.

"Well, you just treated Phoenix's only hope like shit! He needed our help to flood the tunnels and bury the nest, as they called it," Cian ranted. He looked hopeless and defeated. Tears streamed down his dirty cheeks, so lines of pale skin appeared from underneath the dirt.

"You mean there are more of those things down there?" Brad asked, a bit pissed off because he missed them.

"Yes, and they're worse. They scare him, so that says a lot about what's about to wake up and go hunting," Ivan added, his teeth chattering while Mika tried his best to pull a suit over his head.

"We have to help him! They'll kill everything!"

Cian heatedly yelled between gulps of the Rooster Booster Juice Mika was forcing into his mouth.

It impressed Brad. Mika moved like he had six arms and two heads.

"Yes, Dad. He wanted your help and didn't know how to ask. We must help him," Donali urged Brad.

"What, and who, abducts someone and then expects help? Who does such a thing? Why would we help someone who treated you like this?" Mika asked while putting on his son's boots.

"Dad, this is serious," Ivan rambled to explain. "The king keeps them hibernating, but earthquakes or hunger wake them. He worries that they'll find their way to Phoenix. He calls it *Ice City*, he told Joshua, and Joshua told him Phoenix wouldn't help. But he lied, you will. I promised him you will. Also, he wants to show you something. I think Joshua was his friend, and he gave them food. We must go back and help him. That's why the land and people died." He pointed to the shriveled-up trees and barren mountains.

Brad's blood boiled and then froze when he heard the term *Ice City*. *Can this be? Don't worry, Icemen King. I'll stay with you until your icemen come.* He remembered the melodic voice that kept him company.

Ivan's voice broke his trance. "That man helped us survive down there!"

"Helped you? Look at you! When was the last time you ate something? Mika, you deal with your boys."

Brad turned away, exasperated. "We need to get them to safety. If there are more of those things, we need to regroup."

Rick gasped. "Oh, no, my boy. Brad, look!" Then they noticed Kawa's stump.

"Oh no, what happened?"

Kawa's eyes rolled back in his head, and he passed out. Brad stepped forward, and just before his son hit the ground, he scooped him up.

"Thank the stars you caught him," Rick exclaimed. "He needs blood and antibiotics." Rick threw a blanket over Kawa and tucked his son's feet inside. They made their way out of the building while Rick gave him an antibiotic, tetanus, and a Glupidone shot.

"That's it. You should take him to the ship right now," Rick said. "We still have five kilometers to run."

"Bloody damn hell, get to the ship. We can talk there." Brad ran with his boy in his arms, listening to the comms.

"Who else is inside? Who can follow us?" Andrew asked.

"Just the king and the nest," Ivan and Cian answered enthusiastically at the same time.

"The king?" Rick asked.

"King of what?" Mika asked while herding his children out of the dilapidated warehouse.

"The King of the Brawl," Ivan and Cian said together.

"Jesus Christ, get to the ship!" Brad shouted, huffing and puffing.

Brad: "We're bringing four dehydrated boys, one unconscious. Looks like a traumatic arm amputation. Connor, I need you to bring the ship closer. I'm running a straight line from the mineshaft in your direction."

Juandre: "Yes, sir, standing at the ready."

Connor: "I'm on my way."

Brad: "Andrew, can you stay and make sure no one follows us?"

Andrew: "Yes, sir, I'll cover you until all are on the ship.

Mika stood still, unmoving, wondering what to do. He folded his arms and pressed his lips together; he planned to be firm but failed dismally.

"Please, Dad." Ivan halted, planting his feet firmly on the ground. Pulling on Mika's arm, he begged him.

Mika saw the urgency in both his son's eyes. Usually, he thought before acting and listened to reason before speaking, but lately, he'd lost his sense of judgment, worrying sick about his sons. He trusted his boys but also wanted to get them to safety. "No, son, first things first. We're not safe yet. We have orders from our leader, and we listen to our chosen leader in situations like this." Mika's heart broke for his boys, and they smelled horrendous. The words shower, shower, shower flashed red in his mind. Although dressed, he wrapped each with a blanket, feeling like a mother hen. "You're in shock. You don't know what you're saying."

Rick: "We have to get them out right now."

Covering Donali in a thermal blanket, he scooped him up and followed Brad with the boy in his arms.

Mika closed his eyes and exhaled. "Did the creature have a name?"

Ivan and Cian answered in unison. "Eryn!"

Mika felt divided.

"He fed and spoke to us, even gave us anti-toxin shots, and today he killed his brother for us."

Connor: "No, Mika, you come to the ship now. I see no movement, so you still have time to return safely. I must show you something I saw. We can regroup and return."

Mika felt relieved hearing Connor's voice over the comms. Mika looked at Ivan, who held out his hand.

"Is that Dad you're talking to? Please give me the earpiece." Mika looked Ivan in the eye, trying to see or read something in his boy's bright blue eyes. Hesitantly, he removed one earpiece.

"Say your name and speak so we can all hear you." Mika watched his son insert the earphone.

Ivan: "Hello, Dad. It's Ivan. I've missed you so much." Cian pressed his ear onto his brother's, listening to their father.

Ivan: "I understand it's unsafe, but I can't leave him."

Turning to Cian, he said, "Father, we call a veto. We can't leave without assisting Eryn."

Cian nodded. "Yes, we call veto!"

Mika looked at his sons, stunned by the realization that they were young men, brilliant, and likely capable of surviving this ordeal without his help. Most importantly, they had agreed and had called a veto. *He must support them. How could he not?*

"When he wakes up, he'll think we abandoned him. That will devastate Eryn. He fears being alone. He's a good person, and he isn't a creature. Eryn's different from the others, and he's not like us, you'll see." Ivan stepped back and waited for Connor's response.

Connor: "I hear you, my Ivan. I hear both of you. I'll bring the ball up and land the ship. Just give me a few minutes. Brad, I need to go help my boys."

Brad: "Do what you have to do. Rick and I will take care of our boys. Stay in touch."

Connor: "I'll come to you. Wait for me!"

Ivan: "Dad, thank you."

He removed the earpiece and handed it to Cian.

Cian: "Hello, Father."

Cian wept. He couldn't talk.

Connor: "We'll talk soon, my Cian. I love you. I'll be with you now."

Mika hugged his boys closer. They left him speechless for the first time in his life. The overwhelming feeling of protecting them, listening to reason, and not reacting like a crazed murderer had him frozen in his tracks.

Mika: "Andrew, we'll stay with you until Connor arrives."

Andrew: "Alright, I'll cover for you."

Connor: "Thanks, my friend."

CHAPTER 15
FLOOD THE TUNNELS

"*Although it's now six a.m. It is not a good morning.*

Did you know the word 'barbarized' was first used in 1602?

And did you also know yesterday was the first time Lasitor experienced it?

To the barbarians who mutilated Lasitor's framework, bring my microchips to the office, or else...

Breakfast is served until eight a.m.

Have a good day."

(Lasitor's usually friendly, upbeat robotic voice sounded evil today.)

Eryn, **King of the Brawl**

. . .

ERYN OPENED HIS EYES. They were unfocused, so he blinked a few times. "Ouch, blinking hurts." He moaned and closed his eyes again. Realizing he was not alone, he attempted to open his eyelids softly and slowly. *My head's sore. What happened to me?*

When his vision cleared somewhat, he looked upward into the faces of four inquisitive humans. Not knowing what to do and uncertain of their intentions, he held himself as still as possible. *Don't breathe, Eryn.* Their foreheads flickered with bright lights, he noted. Maybe not human? *If I move, even my eyelids, I'm dead.* So he lay frozen, eyes wide open.

"Those eyes are bloody amazing. Are they a cat or a goat?"

"Hmmm, my guess is neither."

"I wonder, yelda, do you think Brad fried his brains? His pupils aren't reacting to light."

"Let me see." Eryn felt his eyelids being closed gently with the palm of a hand. Open, closed, open, closed, open. "Hmmm," the older man with curly black hair said.

"I'll kill Brad right after hurting him slowly. I'll start by pulling his nose hairs and then progressively move to more painful things like his teeth or his toenails!" Eryn recognized Cian's voice.

"Calm down. He's just waking up and finding his bearings. He'll be fine," the bigger, older man said with what Eryn thought was a Russian accent.

Suddenly, Eryn realized it was Mika, Connor, and the twins who were staring at him, fascinated by his inhuman eyes. He'd always been sensitive about his eyes. *That is why I am different.* Memory slowly returned to him, and the urge to rub his eyes for relief became unbearable. Before making sudden movements, he put his emotional feelers out, sensing no aggression toward himself.

I have to put an end to this, or my eyeballs will shrivel up.

Eryn closed them.

Again, he put his feelers out. He felt four humans in his presence. Fascination, excitement, and happiness flowed from his twins, and the two adults were confused, nauseated, and weary. Opening his eyes, Eryn searched for the twins and smiled.

"Yelda, look. Did his eyes just reflect the light? He has an extra layer of tissue covering his eyes. Like a cat's. What's it called again?"

"It's called the tapetum lucidum."

"Can you stop looking into my eyes and help me? It feels like I'm lying on my hands." Eryn wiggled his shoulders to pull his hands out from behind his back, but he couldn't. *Are my hands tied?* "I think a rock fell on my head, and why did you tie me up? May I roll over?" Eryn asked, just as the men pushed him over to his side.

"Please hold still, Eryn. We're untying you," Ivan

said calmly, while supporting his head with his knees. Eryn loved the smells coming from Ivan's crotch.

"Okay, lie as still as possible. I'm using a knife to cut the ties. I can see Brad had tied these. It would've taken you hours to wiggle out of them," Mika said.

As Eryn's wrists were released from the ties, he felt the telltale prickling of blood flow being restored to them. His shoulders were uncomfortably tense, but with Cian and Ivan rubbing them, he relished the delicious smells and emotions emanating from them. So he lay there relaxing on Ivan's lap.

"Come, Eryn, we'll help you sit up." The loud but caring voice of Cian stirred him.

Disoriented and groggy, Eryn asked, "What happened to me?"

Silence. Nobody answered. He sensed all four of his helpers were embarrassed, and one was growing disgusted by the second.

"*Croak!*" Like a telephone pole being snapped in two, they pushed him into a sitting position. "Brrrr, *croak*, my head hurts badly. Is there a rock stuck in my skull?" Eryn croaked again.

Hunched forward and rubbing his head, Eryn checked his hands for blood. Memories of his brother, the cage, and the hysterical boys came back to him. He looked up and refocused on the four faces. *My favorite family.* He smiled, but the dryness of his mouth choked him. "You came!" He coughed. "Water,

I need water, please," he begged, barely able to speak, just as Connor ran outside. Mika followed, his feet sliding over loose rocks and mud.

"This awful stench." Connor coughed and hurled in between words. "*Blargh, blargh.*" More coughing and swearing. "The cage"—he took a few loud breaths and coughed more—"*blargh, blargh*"—he spat a few times—"and the shit bucket!"

"Dad, are you okay?" Ivan asked.

"It's the smells. Let's get you up, Eryn," Cian said.

"Can we get on with whatever help you need?" Mika said shortly as he rubbed Connor's back, who was standing with his hands on his knees.

The twins grabbed each of Eryn's arms, flinging them around their necks, and pushed up while grabbing Eryn around his waist. He straightened up and unsteadily found his feet.

Eryn couldn't believe what was happening. The knowledge that they were there to help him. *It was all I wanted.*

They blinded him with their headlamps as they helped him up, so he hid his eyes behind his hands. *The lights hurt.*

"We're blinding him and hurting his eyes. Switch off the lights," Cian told them.

"No, turn the front. It'll dim them," Mika said as he quickly checked on Connor with a concerned look. "I'm worried the pitch-black dark will swallow us.

And who knows what's hiding here," he muttered, looking over his shoulders as if something was going to materialize out of the darkness.

Four blue eyes looked up at Eryn, and the brothers simultaneously asked, "Better now?" Eryn's knees almost buckled. He experienced too many emotions at once. Excitement, happiness, horniness, thankfulness, optimism, wonder, and a weird fuzzy feeling he had never experienced before.

He shook his head to clear his mind. He needed to answer them. "Yes, thank you. I need water. Can we...?" Eryn asked, pointing to the water. They helped him hobble over to the rock siding of the tunnel outside his cave. He stuck his tongue out, drinking from the rivulets of water streaming from the tunnel wall. "Ahh, that tastes good, thank you."

Connor and Mika stood open-mouthed, totally shocked by what they were seeing. "Where are the other two boys? Are they safe?" Eryn asked as strength returned to him. He wiped his face and drank more water.

"Yes, they're with their family," Ivan answered while holding Eryn upright.

An immediate shift of temperament came from Connor. *Oh, shit, it must be the tongue.* Quickly, he retracted his long, lizard-like tongue and braced for impact. Just as he turned to see where Connor was, he received a surprise punch to his gut.

"The family you took them from, you monster!"

Connor yelled, fists swinging. "You kept my children in a cage! They had to shit in a bucket, and you expect us to help you? After seeing the conditions you held my boys, I changed my mind about helping you. I'm going to murder you!" he said. Teeth gnashing and spittle flying, he loomed over Eryn's face. "I'll help you! I'll help you into a grave!"

Mika grabbed his husband's arms, pulling him back just before he could deliver a second round of blows. "Gille-toine! Connor, wait!" Mika yelled, holding Connor tightly around the waist. They all watched as Eryn, the nearly three-meter-tall giant, fell back onto his haunches, bracing his head.

"Don't kick my head. Please, don't kick my head!" Eryn said, making himself as small as possible.

"Connor, look..." Mika said to Connor, who panted short, loud breaths and hulking over Eryn with wild eyes. "Dada, calm yourself!" Cian yelled, holding onto Eryn, supporting him, so he didn't fall backward. Petting and stroking him affectionately. "Don't be scared. I won't let my dad hurt you. Shhhh," he coaxed, as if talking to a bewildered animal. Ivan and Cian gave Connor the stink eye and wrapped their arms around Eryn's waist so he could stand up.

"We came back to help you with... with the others. You asked for help to flood the tunnels, didn't you?" Mika asked.

Eryn looked up. He blinked a few times to clear the tears from his eyes. He was unsure of trusting

Connor, but he did trust Mika, so he answered him. "Yes, I asked for your help," Eryn said softly. He closed his eyes and concentrated on the nest.

"What's he doing now? Why's he closing his eyes?" Connor asked.

"He's communicating or checking in with his brothers in the nest," Ivan said.

"Bleeding bloody hell, what? Are we in the Twilight Zone or just a bad Anunnaki horror story? You know, never mind, don't even answer that. I'm smarter than that. I'm not hanging around. Let's go. I want out of this hole! How do we flood these tunnels?" Connor asked, losing his shit. He spun, rocks flying. Then flung himself around to whisper in Mika's ear, "Are they overly affectionate, or am I imagining it? I was this close to killing their pet."

Pet, what is that? Eryn made a note to ask the twins later.

"I don't know. This shit is just weird. I don't know what's happening. Just watch them closely," Mika whispered under his breath.

They think I can't hear them. Eryn opened his eyes, looking at Mika and Connor with a pointed look. "My brothers are waking up. They will kill you, if not by ripping you apart, then by poisoning the air."

"What?" Mika and Connor asked simultaneously.

"You cannot breathe the air once they crawl from their nest. I sense only six. They are weak and dying, which is a good thing. But if they get out, I'm not sure how much they'll destroy this time."

Eryn decided to take charge. He jumped at the ready, finding his trident where he had last left it after running to stop Ernest. He smiled at Cian and Ivan, rubbing their heads affectionately, as a sign of his thanks and love for them.

Mika and Connor looked amazed at his trident, reaching out to touch it, but Eryn ignored that since there was no time. Then he started to run.

"Come to this side. I have it ready, but I need help. Oh, no, wait!" He stopped, remembering the rocket. "My father wanted me to show you the rocket's door. We also need to retrieve his books and notes. Also, we have to exit while I open the sludge dam and the water. I'll drive the cage."

Eryn noticed that the two adults were even more perplexed. "The what?" Connor and Mika yelled after him. He grinned as he ran with a spring in his step, elated. The game he'd been dying to play his entire life. All of his friends were present, and his hopes and dreams were becoming a reality. "The cage, the elevator, the thingamabob!" Eryn shouted over his shoulder.

"Come, Papa, come, Dada, run!" the twins called. "Eryn, go! We'll follow you. Just tell us what to do," they yelled.

After a few hundred meters of zig-zagging down dark tunnels, they all jumped into the cage with Eryn.

He waited patiently until all were inside, and then he pulled the massive door closed. Then they climbed into another contraption that turned as it moved upwards. Eryn worked at the controls with his hands, instructing them on what to do. His feet hovered over the pedals that would ultimately close the tunnel system to this shaft.

"Every time we stop, find the yellow lever and push it down, do not touch the others."

Connor and Mika nodded and soon realized why Eryn couldn't do the job himself. It was a puzzle inside a giant Rubik's cube, a human-sized gear-locking mechanism engineered to work as a gigantic canal-locking system.

"The top lock will only open when all the locks from the bottom to the top layer are lined up. Only then will the whole system fill with water. He's driving the panels, which will raise the slots to open the lock and fill the lower levels first," Mika said in awe.

"This is a fantastic architectural marvel," Connor answered. And Eryn sensed his mood lifted better after leaving the stinky cavern.

Next, Eryn stopped at the abandoned laboratory tunnel. A foreboding feeling of doom, accompanied by the stale, sour smell of chemicals, hung in the air. Here and there, tube lights blinked. Dirty papers and chairs lay scattered everywhere. More rows and rows of cages open and toppled over in the distance.

"Cian, Ivan, can you run to the first desk on your left? Inside the top drawer. Bring everything for your fathers." Eryn said, and the boys ran. Mika and Connor watched as the boys worked in sync while taking orders from him. In the light, Eryn turned so Connor and Mika could see his face. He smiled at them. They frowned. He smiled wider. They looked at each other, then back at him. Eryn stopped smiling, and he cleared his throat. They turned their heads, searching the lab.

"Is that where the scientist slept?" Mika asked. Seeing his father's room, with two small cots and a desk between them. Then they waited. Eryn didn't want to answer. Mika pinned him with a stare.

He cleared his throat. "Yes, that was our bedroom," he said. And couldn't look at it.

"Why didn't you keep the boys in here, where it is dry and lit up, so they don't have to sit in the dark in a cage? Connor asked.

Eryn answered with short, honest answers. He decided to explain later. "Because I couldn't trust my brother."

Connor took two big steps, leaning into the room. "I don't understand. You could have locked them in here." Connor stepped deeper into the room and gasped.

"I can't go in there. My father doesn't smell good." Mika joined Connor, and Eryn saw his disgusted face, knowing he saw his father on the floor. They looked around the room and back at his father. Then Mika steered Connor outside and closed the door.

Eryn hung his head. Embarrassed. "I didn't know what to do with him, so I left him in his room."

"Here we are!" Ivan and Cian handed over a big diary filled with loose notes and papers. On the brown leather cover, it read 'Notebook and Journal of Dr. Wolter Wessels.'

Happy with collecting all his father's notes, Eryn slammed the big door closed. "Yes, let's close this chapter," he said, teasing Mika and Connor by frightening them with the loud noises. For a second, they stood shocked, but then they caught his meaning and laughed shyly. Eryn chuckled. They looked at him amusingly. He ran, laughing like a silly loon, climbing back onto the contraption. Then all his helpers laughed as they progressed, like a corkscrew, stopping at every tunnel. He would signal, and they would find the yellow lever, push it down, and move up, making their way out of the mine.

The elevator slowed and came to a stop at its second-to-last stop. "Here we are. This is the entrance into the rocket." Eryn released the pedal, putting the brakes on so they could stop safely and have a look.

"This level's cold and musty. It was designed so it doesn't overheat."

They exited onto a steel mesh floor built around the massive, white, silo-shaped body, which was located at the entrance to the guidance section of the rocket. Above their heads hung dim lights, like old dusty Christmas lights, forgotten and broken. The black darkness below them enhanced the hollow feeling of the deep shaft, and it echoed their voices. The entire place had a sad, haunted, and forgotten dreamlike atmosphere that suffocated Eryn.

"Oh, yes, my goodness, it's big!" Ivan said. Finally, they looked at what Eryn had wanted to show them for many years. On this side, the rocket had flags of different countries painted on it, and more than half of them had already peeled off.

"A spaceship," Mika said, sounding like he didn't believe his eyes and like a young boy seeing a rocket for the first time. He looked down through the mesh floor below them. "How sturdy is this floor?" He stomped his boots, testing it.

"All right!" Cian exclaimed. "Can you believe it? You did it, Eryn!"

Eryn laughed, and the three hugged.

Connor punched in a bunch of buttons on a device. "I'll record this and send it back to the ship." He pressed a button on the gadget over his ear and said, "Brad, General McCormick, you must see this! Here you can see the entrance and the size of the rocket."

Eryn stepped closer so he could explain what his father wanted many years ago.

"My father said to show you this, but I never got the chance to meet with you. I wanted to let you come here many times, but Joshua kept saying the time was not right and that the bad men must not see this."

Mika listened intently. He frowned and elbowed Connor. Eryn's head fell forward. "My father is dead, and now Joshua, too." Silence. Then, lifting his head, Eryn straightened his back and rambled to get the truth out. "My brother followed me to your glass city. I'm so sorry. I wasn't aware of his plans. I tried to stop him but got kicked in my behind and taken prisoner by the icemen. I thought that would be a good time to tell you the truth, but knowing my brother, but knowing my brother's plan to kill all of you, I escaped to go stop Ernest. The boys were blue and frozen. Maybe dead. I brought them here, where it is warm. I knew you would come for them. But my brothers..." He sucked in air and waited.

Connor huffed, and Mika held onto him, listening closely to Eryn.

"Go on, tell them," Cian said.

Eryn nodded, liking how Ivan and Cian held him.

"I warmed them as best I could, and because we were closer to our home, I brought them to my home, where it's warm. When we arrived, my brother was outraged. He wanted to eat them." Eryn paused.

Mika ground his molars.

"Okay, go on, no need to enhance the tension," Connor said, waving his hand in small rolling circles.

"Tell them. They should know," Ivan encouraged

Eryn, who gulped audibly and turned a few more shades of pale.

"When we arrived in my cave, I saw the four faces and realized I knew them, especially Ivan's and Cian's."

"You see, he's real. We always told you about our friend, and you never believed us. You thought we imagined him," Cian said proudly. Ivan joined his brother, patting Eryn on his back.

Eryn saw that the two fathers were motionless and only blinking, so he continued. "I built a cage to keep them safe from Ernest while we waited for you. My father told me a long time ago, and so did Joshua, that I should kill them all and flood the tunnels, or call you and show you. I'm a coward. I couldn't kill them. You took so long getting here, but came just in time." He finished with a sad smile.

Connor grimaced, probably wondering how to respond.

"This is too much, much too much to digest for one day," Mika said.

"Yes, Dada, Ernest is the one who chomped off Kawa's arm and almost ate me. He wanted to bite my head when Eryn kicked him away and killed him." Ivan turned to Eryn with adoration, and Connor looked like he wanted to vomit again. "He saved me," Ivan added, with hero worship on his face.

Connor shook his head. "I can't hear this any longer. Can we shelve this and talk about it later,

please?" He walked around the platform to the opposite side, where a door was. "This was where the
pilots or astronauts would enter," Connor said, practically shrieking from the opposite side. "We saw the
tail down at the bottom, which is easily over five
hundred meters down, and we haven't even seen
the top.

"So what happens if I wanted to fly this thing out
of this hole?" Mika asked, walking over to the rocket
and gently running his fingers over the paint-chipped
Russian flag, stroking it lovingly. Cian and Ivan
smiled and nodded in approval of Eryn. He sensed
they were proud of him.

"It's all in my father's notes, but you would need
fuel." Eryn pointed to the notes with his trident and
noticed Mika's sorrow as he touched the rocket—he
made sure it was real and not an illusion.

"Could this be... why would... this doesn't make...
bloody hell..."

Eryn enjoyed looking at Mika, speechless, but he
knew something else was bothering him. *He has a
secret.* He guessed Mika would tell his story when it
was his time.

Eryn thumped his spear to get their attention.
"So, do you want me to flood it all or not?" Eryn
asked, moving from one foot to another, wanting to
get this show on the road. "I could try to force my
brothers into a tunnel and cause tremors, starting a
slight earthquake, but I suspect the ground would be

unstable. There are many mines in this area. It will cause a chain reaction and damage the rocket, anyway."

"How does the flooding work? Are the levels below not flooded yet?" Connor asked, walking back to their side.

"When the correct levers are pushed down, mud and water will fill the tunnels, burying the entire project and filling this mineshaft," Eryn said, and pointed upward. "It's in my father's notes. He was worried that you might want to use the rocket. He told us the world would end, and we might want to fly away. That was why he made me, to help him and whoever flew the rocket to the moon. But my brothers have killed him."

Again, the boys rubbed his back, hugging him and supporting him. Eryn noticed Mika lift an eyebrow at Connor. An unspoken question. *Do they even know what they're doing?*

"I don't care, just flood the thing. If the world ends, it ends." Connor turned to leave. Ivan and Cian looked on, waiting for them to make a decision.

"No, it's not only up to you. We're the last humans. Or so we think, and after this, I don't know. Is there a way to block your brothers from ever coming out and saving the rocket?" Mika asked and started verbally calculating.

"It doesn't even have fuel," Connor reasoned,

rubbing his temples as if he had the worst migraine ever.

"I know, but if we get back to Phoenix, we could look at the options." Mika looked as though his interest was piqued, and he instantly rose to the challenge.

A bit of static came over their comms, and with his enhanced hearing, Eryn could hear a voice say, "Flood the rocket, bury the monsters, and come. I want to go home. Kawa's not doing well. That's an order!" He recognized the voice of the Icemen King.

They ignored him.

"There's only one way to get it out and flood the tunnels. We would need to disassemble it, take it piece by piece out of the hole."

"Or fly it out," Connor proposed.

"Yes." The twins seemed to like that idea, almost jumping up and down.

Eryn interrupted Mika and Connor. "My brothers are awake. We cannot wait."

"Yes, let's leave." Connor dragged Mika by the elbow. Mika turned reluctantly, rubbing the back of his head.

He's thinking, Eryn observed.

"Yes, he's weighing the pros and cons," Cian said as if reading Eryn's thoughts.

"Okay, let's go."

Eryn jumped into the cage with the twins and their fathers on his heels.

As they ascended, they stopped now and then to push more yellow levers down. Finally, when they reached the top, Eryn lifted the massive door as if it weighed nothing. They followed him outside to the pump house on the far side of the cage hoist room. It was cloudy and gloomy, but Eryn felt like he was walking into the sunshine.

The icy wind burned their cheeks, but they all welcomed the fresh air.

His retinue followed him inside as he used his trident to open the large pump house doors. There, he put his fork into the spokes of a huge, corroded, frozen-tight steel wheel.

"Is this the last step to flood it all?" Mika asked. They wearily looked on as he wrestled the wheel that was not budging.

"*Ublyudok!*"

"What?" Connor asked.

Mika turned to his husband. "The laser cannons! We can laser the things."

"Brawl, they are called Brawl. So am I," Eryn enlightened them.

"Yes, Papa, Eryn is a Brawl, not a thing," Cian added, short of breath and red in the face from the exertion as he was helping to turn the wheel.

"Right, if you say so. Leave the wheel," Mika told Eryn. He touched the device on his ear and said, "Brad, bring the ship to us."

Silence. Static. They waited a few seconds.

Then, after a while.

"What, Mika? I told you to flood the place and come!" Eryn heard the Icemen King shout.

"Bring the ship now! We can kill the mutants and save the rocket."

"Why? We don't need the rocket. Anyway, Connor's the pilot, and he's with you!" Their king was getting upset with them, and Mika didn't seem to hear how upset he was.

"Tell Juandre to do it. He knows how. He's been standing with Connor, watching every move he makes. I know he'll be able to fly the ship. He keeps telling us he's not stupid. Maybe listen to him."

"Brad, you want me to fly to them? I can. I know I can!" Okay, Eryn thought, so now I know what Juandre sounds like.

"I don't know why you keep saying I'm the leader if all of you do what you want, anyway!"

"General, this is not the army." Juandre cackled.

"Bloody damn hell!"

Eryn heard severe agitation and swearing in the background, and then someone told the Icemen King to calm down.

Then Juandre said, "Starting up the ship, be there in two minutes."

"Eryn, where will they exit the mines? Where will they run first?" Mika asked.

Eryn closed his eyes and reached out to his brothers. After a while, he finally spoke. "The tunnels to the back are blocked off already so that they couldn't exit that way. They're heading this way. There are several ways to exit, aside from the main exit, here. We already blocked those we just used, and my home, too. If I have to guess, if they discover and flee that area, hoping to find me, they'll use that shaft." He pointed to the north to a shaft where the buildings had collapsed.

Connor and Mika looked shocked and afraid. They looked left and right, unable to choose a direction to run. "Andrew, where's Andrew?" Connor tapped his earpiece and said, "Andrew, can you hear us?"

Silence.

"Andrew, talk to us!" Juandre said over the comms. Mika and Connor looked worriedly at each other.

Mika touched his earpiece and said, "Andrew, we're at the south mine shaft if you can hear us. We'll come for you."

"Andrew, baby, stay where you are. We're coming after we've sorted this lot out." Juandre's voice came over the comms.

Eryn was confused. Everyone had an idea, but he couldn't remember which one to execute. "I can call them to me. So you can get to your ship."

The Romanov twins simultaneously exclaimed, "No!" and grabbed Eryn, who turned to see what Mika thought, but Mika shook his head and then sent Connor a scathing glance. Eryn listened in on their unspoken conversation. *I told you, something's happening between the three.*

Connor enlarged his eyes back to Mika. *I know we'll talk later.*

"What do you mean?" Mika asked Eryn.

Eryn pointed to the broken-down electricity turbine next to the shaft where he suspected the Brawl would be exiting. "I'll climb up to the top and call them to me. Give me your jacket." He pointed to Connor.

"This is not a jacket. It's an arctic suit."

"Yes, I need it. They'll smell it. I need you to run downwind."

"Naked?" Connor asked, looking confused.

"Tell your people to sail in that direction." Eryn pointed southeast. Thinking they traveled by ice sail-ship as he did. "I'll start running, and then you run in the opposite direction." He pointed away with his trident while pushing them to go with his free hand. "Go, go, go. You have time to get to your ship. I'll keep them occupied until you're safely on your ship. You must go now! The air can kill you! Go now! Go as far away as possible," Eryn shouted frantically. *This is a nightmare. They don't understand me.*

"No, absolutely not," the twins objected as they hung on an arm.

Mika interrupted. "Why not just laser them when they exit the shaft?"

"No, I don't like that idea. We should not let them exit at all," Connor, the Irishman, protested.

"Let's go back to the mine, down to the scientist's lab. Call them there, and then once inside, take them to the gassing chamber." Connor paged through the scientist's notes. "Your father had a special room. You can call them in there, and then we can open the gas and kill them there."

"Father tried that. It didn't work. They killed him."

Mika took the book with loose paper notes. "We've wasted so much time already. Where are they now?" he asked nervously. "I'm trying to calculate the time it would take us to go back down."

Eryn again closed his eyes and scanned empathically for his nest brothers. They watched him.

"They're still very far down. I'm trying to confuse them and send them in the opposite direction. Maybe ten minutes." Scarcely a few steps out of the pump house, they heard Juandre calling over the comms.

"Coming up behind, almost one hundred meters southeast of the pump house, we can see you. The queen has landed. Step aside."

Connor touched his earpiece. "We need to figure out a strategy. I'm not sure what to do. If we go back down, we stand the chance of getting killed," Connor exclaimed.

"Yes, and we also save the rocket. How did they

get it inside the shaft?" Mika retorted. "Where's the equipment the builders used?"

Mika ran backward a few steps and circled around, searching as he and Connor bounced the unanswered questions off each other.

"What will we do with a rocket, anyway? There's absolutely nothing on the moon," Connor reasoned.

Mika frantically scanned the notes. "According to these notes, there is."

"What?" Connor tilted the book so that he could read upside down with Mika.

"If we go with the tower plan, we should be on the ship already, but we still need to go get Andrew. I'm worried about discharging lethal poison spores into the air." The tension and indecisiveness were unbearable. And they needed more time. Suddenly, the earth beneath them quivered.

"Earthquake!" the twins shouted. Like the Serengeti during migration season, deafening, droning sounds followed and grew louder. The rumbling of a large amount of water, burbling and snapping sounds, got deafening. Similar to a storm and lightning strikes, only it wasn't raining. Structures snapped and cracked. Eryn smelled the sludge and knew the dam had broken.

Loud knocking, like metal on metal, drew their attention to what was behind them. They returned their gazes to the pump house. The Icemen King stood there with a large ax slung over his shoulder. Big and fierce, looking like a warrior.

"He's pissed with us!" Connor muttered under his breath.

"I told you, get on the ship!" Their king yelled, but nobody moved.

"Get on the bloody ship right now!" he ordered again, then turned and walked away.

Mika and Connor pulled their shoulders up to their ears. Only one option left. "To the ship it is!" Mika said.

"Run!" their leader shouted. Eryn and the Romanov family answered voicelessly by throwing their hands up in a gesture of surrender.

"Run!" he yelled again.

Eryn saw something blue in the distance.

As one, the five turned and sprinted as fast as they could to catch up with him. Eryn, positioned in the middle, held onto both twins while Mika and Connor dragged along. It was crazy and so much fun. Eryn's joyful heart leaped as he experienced freedom. The twins never loosened their grip, and their laughter was contagious. By the time they reached the ship, the five quickly stifled their silly laughter and composed themselves. In front of what looked like a large tin can with windows and a door stood the Icemen King, waiting for them with an ax in hand. No smile was in sight, only a reprimanding scowl. His fierce, dark eyes told Eryn they were in deep trouble. He said nothing. Mika and Connor snorted.

Once they were all safely inside, he locked the door and shouted, "Juandre, lift off! Now! Thank you!" He touched his earpiece. "Andrew, we're picking you up at the rendezvous!"

"Sir, yes, sir!" he replied.

"That's what respect and obedience sound like," the Icemen King said. But Eryn saw a twitch of the corner of his mouth. He sensed only determination and a hint of amusement.

"Welcome aboard. Let's go home!"

CHAPTER 16
GOOD KINGS

"Morning, citizens of Phoenix. Get up, get up! It's now six a.m.

Did you know I can call someone a fathead, and although it sounds unkind, it is the absolute truth? Sixty percent of human brain matter is fat.

And did you also know spelling fat with a "PH" means superb, the opposite of idiot?

Visit your community news page to read more interesting facts about the human brain and ways to spell and describe it.

Breakfast is served until eight a.m.

Have a Phat day.

Ha-ha-ha!"

General Brad McCormick

• • •

AFTER RICK HAD COMPLETED surgery on Kawa's stump, he performed a thorough health check on the rest of their children. Like new puppies, he vaccinated, dewormed, checked, and then rechecked them. Brad wouldn't be surprised if he chipped them. He even checked them for fleas. His husband, ever his professional and stoic self, had taken Eryn aside for privacy into the washroom, where he spent two hours with poor Eryn, assessing and cleaning him from his small toes up to his ears. And when they returned, he transformed the young man from a muddy caveman into a clean-shaven god. As Eryn stood in the middle of the dinette, smiling proudly, all eyes were on him. His borrowed sleep trunks sat tight around his muscled upper legs and hung just below his knees. Enormous bare feet supported what Brad thought to be an easy two hundred kilograms of beefy muscle. Bare-chested, each of his muscles rippled under his golden-brown skin as he moved. Rick had given him an undercut and braided some strands before tying it all in a long ponytail, matching the hair on his chin. He was shaven on the sides of his jaws, leaving a short and braided goatee in one braid that stemmed from right below his lips, down the center of his chin. The vertical symmetrical lines stressed his powerful jaw and high cheekbones. Big, friendly eyes matched the proud demeanor. Eryn looked stunning, and he almost seemed to sparkle under the light.

They ate and slept after everyone had showered

and freshened up. Juandre seemed overjoyed to feed the four boys, who were underweight. Their spirits were high, although they appeared to be tired out. Brad and Mika spoke while the others relaxed, watching the young men have fun with Eryn, as if he were a new toy.

"Eryn has the same emotional maturity as them," Brad said, and swallowed the last gulp of his coffee. Mika grimaced. Brad noticed he paused for a second longer before responding. *He's reconsidering his response.* That was something he liked about his friend, who preferred to think things through rather than comment on the whim of the moment.

"I agree and disagree with you, comrade. Eryn, on the other hand, appears to be a full-grown adult, with an emphasis on *"full-grown,"* and his other prominent distinguishing features, which seem more animal than human, are as fascinating as they are unsettling. We, Connor and I, have had the privilege of inter-acting with him. There are some failings, but I believe that with time, he'll adjust to our way of life at Phoenix more quickly because this is what he's desired his entire life."

"They played with human and animal DNA. You saw those pods. The destroyed lab we entered through. That was probably the eggs, Donali and Kawa say he hatched like a tadpole, but most proba-bly, they were born just like the twins were back in

Phoenix," Brad said, referring to the unsettling reference Mika made.

"I wouldn't use the term play. In all honesty, they toyed with it so much that I can't figure out what's sitting before us," Mika remarked and pointed to the scientists' notes.

"He interacts with them respectfully, and they, particularly your boys, adore Eryn." Brad stood there watching the kids stack cards. They constructed a pyramid and challenged Eryn to flick his tongue out and remove a card without knocking the stack over. When he did well, the boys would yell, and the game would restart with new dares or challenges.

Sadly, Kawa wasn't in the mood for games or small talk. Brad watched him with concern. Although it was to be expected, he noted his son was less cheerful than the rest of the gang. Rick explained it was something he had to process on his own, and Brad agreed. They could support him as best they could, but he would most likely require some psychiatric help at home. People who've had traumatic amputations must grieve the loss of their limb and accept that it was no longer with them. Brad was relieved it wasn't a leg. At least there was something to be optimistic about. *Rick is completely correct. Although he has the other arm, he will need psychological support to prepare for and lay a sound basis for dealing with the situation. My son is strong; he will adapt with*

*our help and his determination to learn everything all
over again.*

"I see you worry about Kawa." Rick kissed Brad on
the cheek and hinted with his chin to their boy, who
looked so lost and quiet in the activities before them.
"I'll talk to our new physicians and ask them to refer
us to the best clinical psychiatrist. Someone who
survived the old world may have more experience
working with amputee patients," Rick said.

Brad leaned in to kiss Rick back. "Yes, I'm sure
someone from the bionics lab can also help refer
someone."

"I'll make it a point to talk to Kawa more often if
only to get him to vent about the ordeal," Rick told
Brad, but looked at Mika. "We should take turns with
all of our boys so they can talk about their captivity."
Mika nodded, and Brad's heart warmed as he noticed
all the adults in the room nodding to support their
boys. Andrew gave them a warm smile and a thumbs-
up. Juandre looked down at Andrew's arm, which was
wrapped around his waist. Then, I seconded it by
giving two thumbs up. They all agreed to get the boys
talking.

The men got up and invited the boys to join them
outside. They eagerly followed. Connor stayed downstairs to operate the ship from below because the
wind had picked up, and he needed more control over
the steering.

While most left, Eryn waited to be last in line to

climb the stairs up to the deck. On an impulse, Brad grabbed hold of him, deciding to have a friendly talk with the young man.

It was a good time to ask Eryn questions, as they had all decompressed. Questions about his knowledge of the six mysterious men and who they may or may not be. *Maybe he knows if we have terrorists or saboteurs inside Phoenix.* Bryan Howell messaged Brad earlier via radio that he'd finally found the spot where Joshua Adams lived. Pictures of Eryn, taken when he was a small boy in Phoenix, were discovered, along with diaries and proof that the boy had been visiting Joshua for many years. He'd almost become invisible, with Lasitor only getting a few frontal or facial shots of him. Brad wanted to prod the boy, who claimed to be a king, to see what else he could learn.

Bryan confirmed Joshua had been in contact with what they now know was EP-III. As for the scientists, what had happened to them was unclear since Joshua had lost contact with them years ago. From what Bryan Howell could figure out, Joshua was initially selected to work in the grain research department but had somehow gotten involved with a group of people who claimed to have his family and had demanded that he provide them with information. He found a blackmail letter addressed to Joshua, and it also seemed that he was in contact with Dr. Wolter Wessels. Bryan assumed they were forced to work together because of the same threat.

They suspected Joshua had provided them with various types of research materials, including cryogenically frozen human and animal eggs. Right after Doomsday, the terrorists disappeared for a while, and Dr. Wessels traveled to Phoenix twice, but Joshua suspected the Brawls murdered Dr. Wolter Wessels, left little Eryn orphaned, and Joshua, at that point, had moved down to their hideout. Eryn showed up yearly without his brother Ernest, while Joshua provided them with food and clothing. The men who blackmailed Joshua wanted more research material, and it was for that reason that Brad figured he never wanted the Peter Pan Capsule. *Joshua was probably tired of hiding.*

Bryan figured Joshua was most likely protecting Phoenix and Eryn, but got in way over his head. Joshua loved the boy, and although his brothers were toxic to humans, he allowed Eryn to stay and watch over the humans in Phoenix.

Therefore, Brad called him back into the little dinette area. After pushing the playing cards aside, one card stuck to his hand, sticky as flypaper. Eryn giggled, and Brad couldn't resist. He laughed, too. His laugh was infectious.

"My boy, can I call you boy? You're almost my husband's age. But since you're friends with my boys, I guess you need to tell me, how do you refer to yourself?" Brad asked.

Eryn sat down and slid his hands underneath so

he could sit on them. His shoulders rolled forward. Looking nervous, he whispered an answer, "I am Eryn, I am Brawl, and I am the King of the Brawl, and I am a boy."

"That's nice, and you have a beautiful name. My name is Brad. I'm also General Brad McCormick of Phoenix, and I'm an older man who's a father. I'm a husband and married to Dr. Broderick Longarrow."

"Oh, and you're the king of icemen." Eryn's face lit up with joy.

Those words doused Brad with an ice-cold realization. It wasn't an angel but Eryn, who sat with him while he was alone and dying.

"Oh my goodness, it really was you! You helped me!"

Eryn smiled and nodded eagerly. "You're a good king, like I am a good king. I kept you warm until the icemen came."

"Thank you for saving me and sitting with me."

Brad inspected him from up close. His wide smile revealed perfect, white front teeth, although they were longer and sharper, but not grotesquely so. His skin was smooth as wax. His eyes were mesmerizing. They reminded Brad of cat eyes. His new haircut suited him as well. With the mud washed away, his hair, longer than shoulder-length, was dark blonde, contrasting with a Middle Eastern complexion. Brad liked the genie-in-a-lamp look. And he reminded himself that although

Eryn's bulky natural beauty seemed strong and unbreakable, underneath, he was a fragile child. "And no, I'm not a king," Brad replied calmly, correcting Eryn.

"But they listen to you as my brothers listened to me," Eryn said.

Connor lifted his head and looked their way inquisitively.

"I'm their chosen leader, and no, they never listen to me."

Connor burst out laughing from behind the wheel. He sat within earshot of the lower deck operating system. Eryn looked at Connor with surprise, but then he obviously caught the joke and joined in the friendly banter.

"Yes, I remember how they all ignored you a few days ago." Eryn relaxed, and his eyes sparkled with pure innocence. He squashed his lips together. He seemed to wait for Brad to continue.

"What else can you tell me about yourself? You're an extraordinary boy, sorry, I mean king." Brad corrected himself, and then Eryn giggled and started talking freely.

"You can say, boy. Since my friends are boys, I am a boy too. I'm Eryn. I was a brother to Ernest. But Ernest was a bad Brawl, and the nest was bad Brawls. They wanted to hurt the humans. Always hungry, always calling for Eryn." He grabbed his head, squeezing his eyes shut. "They made noises in my head." Bumping his head with his fists, he made a low humming sound.

Brad gently took his fists and put them down on Eryn's lap. "Are they quiet now?"

"Yes, yes, they don't call or cry anymore. Eryn makes them sleep. Best for me, best for humans. Father said to flood the tunnels, but Ernest said we wouldn't have a home. We went to ask Joshua, and he said no, bad men, evil men will catch us and hurt us."

"What evil men? Are you talking about us in Phoenix?"

"Yes, yes, Ernest said so."

This is confusing. Brad understood what the poor creature endured for his father, Joshua, his brother, the humans, and the nest. "You looked after so many Brawls and humans."

"Yes, Eryn is king," he said. He sat up, proud of himself and owning it.

Brad's heart broke for the soul of the innocent being in front of him. "Eryn, if you see the bad men, could you show them to me?" Brad asked. He hoped to find out more and maybe show Eryn the footage of the recent group they discovered. *However, Joshua's notes sounded more helpful.*

We'll only have six men to catch if they're the same men. If not, the problem is much larger than we expected.

"Eryn, has anyone ever given you a hug?" Brad asked, out of the blue, to distract him.

For a long time, Eryn was still, then sagged his

head. He answered shyly, "Yes, my father, when I was a baby, Brawl and a boy Brawl, and Joshua. Joshua was a good friend. When the bad men hit Joshua in his face, his mouth and eyes bled, he told me to go home to the Brawls, and then he hugged me."

Brad picked up on the evil men, hitting Joshua.

"So, nobody's ever hugged you after Joshua. Who sent you back to the mines? Did you stay until the twins were taken?"

Brad knew the answer, but he wanted to hear Eryn's side of the story.

"No." Shaking his head, Eryn sat back on his hands.

"The men who hurt Joshua. Do you know their names?" Brad asked.

"No, but I know their faces."

"Are they the same men who live in Phoenix? The same bad men who hit Joshua?" Brad asked again. *We're getting somewhere.*

"Yes." Suddenly, all the happy innocence was gone, replaced with dark intent on Eryn's face. "I told Joshua I would kill them when I'm bigger!" He smashed his fist into the palm of his other hand, grinding it.

"I want to catch them and make them hurt like they made Joshua hurt," Brad said.

"Good, we make them hurt together," Eryn said, and Brad was glad Eryn was on their team.

"Okay, that's a promise." Brad held out his hand

to shake on it, and, strangely enough, Eryn shook it, then looked away. Is he shy, or is he hiding something? "Would you let me hug you?" Brad held his arms out, inviting the big young man for a hug.

After a long pause, Eryn lifted his head. "Yes, please, mister king of the icemen."

"Ah, my boy, come here. You're such a special boy." Eryn stood, looking surprised and uncomfortable—he didn't lift his arms for the embrace. Brad was half a meter shorter, but he leaned forward, hugging Eryn, a superhuman-sized boy, awkwardly accepting the embrace.

"Okay, thank you," Eryn said while gazing back, looking unsure or sad. "Must I go now? Men hug to say goodbye. Should I go back home? The last time I hugged my father and Joshua, I never saw them again."

Brad's heart broke. He wanted to bawl his eyes out, but he grabbed Eryn and hugged him again. Tighter. "No, my boy, you're coming to Phoenix. We'll never send you back to that place, ever! I will never send you away. I'm sure Cian and Ivan would skin me alive if I did. You're now a part of my family. The Phoenix family."

"At the glass city? For real, forever?"

"Yes, we're a big family working and living inside the glass city. Tell me, can we meet for more chats?"

"What are chats?"

"What we're doing now. We're having a chat. I want to ask you more about the bad people."

The smile fell from Eryn's face, replaced with aggression.

"Not to worry, we're going to be smarter than them. We're going to play a game."

Eryn's eyes widened with interest.

"Yes, a game. I know you're a smart boy. And you're a brave boy. You saved Kawa and Donali, who are my boys."

"Oh," Eryn said, not seeming to understand.

"Anyway, Ivan and Cian..."

His eyes flickered again at the mention of their names. He's like an adorable puppy, a puppy in love. Brad thought about how easily Eryn's face wore all his emotions in his eyes.

"Do you like Cian and Ivan?" Eryn nodded enthusiastically. "Do you like them a lot?"

"Yes, yes, very much."

Brad smiled. "I can see they also like you very much. But Mika and Connor are worried about them."

Eryn frowned. "Why?"

"We're not sure if we should be worried or not."

"They are my friends. I will protect my friends."

Brad didn't know how to ask whether it was more than that.

Is it sexual? I wonder? I should ask Ivan and Cian.

"I'll tell their fathers, Mika and Connor, that

you're excellent friends. When we get to our family, our home, Phoenix, the city of glass."

"The ice-people?"

"Yes, there. With whom would you like to live? Because we have different rooms."

Erin's eyes were wide and bright. "Ivan and Cian's room, yes, yes."

Brad was worried, but left that for a conversation with Mika and Connor.

"Good, let's talk or chat later. We can decide how to bring you in without anyone seeing. Just until we figure out who the bad guys are. That's the game I was referring to, a hide-and-seek game, okay? The sooner we catch the bad guys, the sooner we'll all be safe. And you can stop hiding. Then once we have them, you can join me so we can destroy them together."

Eryn straightened up, holding his heavy gold trident. "Yes, yes, Icemen King General, sir!"

CHAPTER 17

ERYN'S TRIDENT

"Good morning, citizens of Phoenix.

It's now six a.m.

Did you know that thousands of years ago, scientists and philosophers wrote about a beautiful city that disappeared one night under the sea, never to be seen again?

Historical notes stated that earthquakes and floods had consumed the town. Since then, the story has become a legend.

Almost everyone has heard the story of the city of Atlantis.

On a positive note, if Phoenix disappears underwater, at least they will remember us for a very long time.

Breakfast is served until eight a.m.

Have an unforgettable day!"

GENERAL BRAD McCORMICK

. . .

LATER THAT AFTERNOON, just as they were about to put the ship into the ocean, a tremendous gust of wind snatched the Blue Halcyon and hurled her higher into the air. A storm cloud engulfed them within minutes, soaked them to the bones, and forced them to retreat below deck.

"No surprise Bartolomeu Dias dubbed this point of Africa the Cape of Storms in fourteen-seventy-four when he first arrived in the area," Connor shouted over his shoulder. "Just a complimentary history lesson while attempting to fly the bird to a safer location. I'm going to sit us down by the water. It's better being flung around than crashing upside down."

"What? Are we going up again?" Brad hollered, attempting to be heard above the thunder and lightning.

Connor cackled like a crazy pirate. "No, on the contrary, the bird is descending. Free-falling! Prepare to hit the icy water. You guys best grip tight because I'm sure we're going to hop a few times," Connor said, looking at Mika. Brad saw the unspoken sarcasm. And then Connor said, "I told you those cannons are going to cause problems."

"Bloody damn hell!" Mika spun around and threw the door to the deck open, disappearing into a flashing cloud of wind and ocean spray. They heard

Mika faintly swearing as he fought the wind to shut the door.

"Where is he going, sir?" Eryn asked. Not looking afraid or stressed. As if it were an everyday occurrence for him.

"He's going to man the laser cannons!" Connor yelled as lightning struck nearby, a deafening snap temporarily blinding them.

"So he wanted them to melt the ice. Let's see if he can melt it." Connor chortled.

"Was that mockery?" Eryn asked no one in particular.

"We're rising again," Juandre reported the obvious to Connor.

"I think your husband just threw his cannons overboard."

"Jesus Christ, the smart idiot is a stupid hooligan," Brad remarked while helping Rick and Andrew collect the flying plateware and other dangerous projectiles, then locked them into a cupboard. Ivan and Cian were hanging onto the McCormick twins, preventing them from sliding from side to side.

"Let's buckle up!" Ivan shouted while handing out safety harnesses. "Eryn, here, come sit with us!"

But Eryn shook his head and disappeared up the stairs into a plume of watery mist through the upper deck door.

"What's he doing?" Cian shouted, upset. "Is he going to help Papa?

"Probably." Ivan looked around, hoping someone would answer them. They heard Eryn's low, melodic voice shouting at Mika outside.

"What's he shouting?" Cian asked.

The next second, the upper deck door opened, and Mika fell back inside, drenched, soaking wet, slipping sideways like an amateur ice skater.

"That boy is going to get himself killed! If he doesn't watch himself, he'll go overboard," Mika yelled, holding on for dear life just as the ship contacted the surface of the Southern Ocean. He flopped up and down, knocking the air out of his lungs.

His ass is going to be sore for days, and not in a good way, Brad thought.

Connor shushed Mika, who was sitting upright, legs wide open, and gasping for air. "Yelda! Shhh! Listen."

A gentle sound, a low, calming hum, something beautiful.

Monotonous and rhythmic, all in one. The sound of iridescent colors.

"What's that?" Brad asked. There was no response because everyone was listening. Frowning, they sat up straight. In only a few seconds, panic dissipated, and the storm subsided.

Eventually, the ship rocked less violently as the storm's ferocity died.

"I have to see this." Brad struggled to get up, slipping this way and that. When he stood, he pulled Rick up, who helped the boys and the rest of the crew.

Finally, when they reached the deck, they saw something impossible. Yet, it was happening right in front of them. A bubble stretched over them with a radius of a few hundred meters. It sheltered them, keeping them safe from the storm outside. In the middle of it all stood Eryn with his trident. Unlike his usual playful self, he looked grave and as if he had only one purpose. Keep them away from harm.

His eyes were focused upwards as he sang notes from a song Brad had never heard. Mixed shades of purples, oranges, blues, and pinks danced where the bubble reached the storm. Inside, it was eerily still, like a sunny day at the beach. Even birds were chirping. While on the outside, dark blues and purples shone through as the lightning struck the force field Eryn created. The men were awestruck and speechless. The Blue Halcyon bobbed on calm waters.

What do you say when you see shit like this? Brad wondered.

Standing like a bunch of salt pillars, Brad noticed that Eryn's playful nature had returned. Small whirlwinds formed a waterspout, spinning around and around as if playing and dancing on the blue-black ocean. More and more salty mist escaped from the spout, waking Brad from his trance. He realized Eryn's intent just as it swung over the rubbernecking crowd, and Eryn released it. Before they could react or even understand what was happening, he doused them with more buckets of icy saltwater.

"Ha-ha-ha. I got you there!" He laughed playfully.

Another waterspout came their way. Every man was fighting for himself as the crowd split up. Shoulder to shoulder, they bumped, pulled, and laughed for a grip on the door to escape downstairs. He was having fun teasing them.

"You little shit." Ivan and Cian turned and ran for him. He just stood his ground.

"Wait, I need to concentrate!" Eryn said. Pointing his trident upwards, he laughed while trying to stay upright and simultaneously holding the protective bubble in place.

They're going to get us killed. Brad realized what was happening. "Boys, leave Eryn until he says it's okay and safe to do so." Luckily, they ceased their horse playing, taking a seat to watch him work.

Brad watched, astonished, as the lightning danced across the clouds without entering the protective lining. Whatever it was. No sounds from the outside were audible. Only the ocean wildlife surrounding them created the profound obscurity as they lay, like one of those model ships in a bottle on Brad's desk. Brad had the sudden urge to feel the magic. He stepped closer.

"May I?" he asked. Eryn looked down at him and nodded. *He trusts me, and he trusts me enough to share this with me.* Brad touched the trident. It faintly vibrated, and it felt a little warm. Filled with wonder and awe, Brad felt what could only be described as a heavenly experience. What he imagined it would feel like if a holy being touched him.

"It feels like the notes you sang earlier," Brad whispered, smiling. Eryn beamed with gentleness. His weird, friendly eyes crinkled at the corners. *I like him, and he likes me.* Brad observed his friendly demeanor. *He's goodness personified.*

With one hand, Eryn supported Brad while both held the solid gold trident upright.

"I sing the notes of what I want to happen, and my fork concentrates and focuses the vibrations of the sound to where I want them to go."

"How did you learn to use a trident?"

"My father taught me to concentrate my vibrations, after I'd used his golden pen by accident one day." Eryn laughed. "The ink and plastic insides melted. So, we tried wood and various metals, and it turned out gold worked, and we had tons of it lying around. So, Father taught me to make molds and things from gold. A big truck loaded with gold bars was not far from the mine. The humans who drove it died inside the truck. Lucky me, Father said, and we made pretty things with gold."

"The cage you kept the boys inside was made of gold."

"Yes, I made it to protect them from my brother,

who didn't have a key. I kept them safe for you. I waited for you, Icemen King."

Brad felt like he was in an alternate reality, yet here he was. He wished he knew what they did with this boy's DNA and what they used. He was a pure, intelligent soul who radiated goodness. *Maybe this was what angels or aliens are.*

"Thank you for keeping them safe for us." Brad leaned in. He wanted to hold on to the goodness and never let go. It wouldn't surprise him if Eryn had wings like an angel.

When the skies cleared and the atmosphere within the bubble escaped, the humidity, which had been noticeable after the passage of a great storm, lingered in the air, although it had moved on. However, it became clear that the boy who called himself King of the Brawls was indeed a king of nature or something.

"They did it!" Mika threw his fists in the air and exclaimed. "The Russians must have ordered the scientist to manipulate his DNA and could finally create the superhuman they wanted me to do years ago." He folded over, laughing. "But not one of them could witness this. I doubt Saunders knew. Brad, when we reach home, I want to work with him. Figure out what he can do and how he manages it. I suspect he manipulates sound waves."

"You need to treat him like a family member. He's extremely vulnerable and an innocent personified,"

Brad said. Already knowing, he developed a soft spot for the King of the Brawls.

"Yes, and he'll have to live with us," Ivan and Cian said. They had their arms around Eryn's back. They looked up at him lovingly, and he looked down at them. "Eryn is ours!"

"What does that mean? Eryn's not a toy," Brad said while noticing the looks of protest from their parents.

Mika asked, "What are your intentions with my boys?"

Connor rolled his eyes. Brad lifted his eyebrows. Rick was sympathetic, although the three looked extremely happy and cute. He hugged Kawa and Donali closer. As if to say, it's cute, if they aren't my boys. Juandre and Andrew were strangely quiet for a change.

Eryn looked as if he wanted to answer honestly, but he was interrupted.

"Father, don't. We'll look after Eryn and teach him all he should know about living in Phoenix." Eryn hugged his two friends. Brad read Mika and Connor like a book. This was not what they had planned for their Russian princes.

Mika whispered to Connor, "*Ublyudok*, a triad with a DNA-modified man."

"Don't jump the gun. Maybe it's just friendship," Connor said, ever the optimist.

"Friendship, my ass," Mika said a little too

loudly. Everyone looked at him. As a father of four boys, Brad was afraid he knew what was coming. He recognized his fear and uncertainty in Mika's tone of voice. Mika was usually open-minded, but he was highly protective of the twins. Brad knew well the parents' hopes and dreams for their kids and how much Connor and Mika invested in their perfect princes. They didn't plan on having a genetically modified frogman as a husband, let alone for both boys. Something so taboo, Mika had defected from the Russian research team precisely because he refused to be part of this type of research and genetic manipulation. A thing that might hurt their boys.

Just as Mika opened his mouth, Brad interjected before Mika made the situation worse than it was. "Boys, let's go inside and sit around the table with your fathers, Mika, Connor, and me." Brad thought it imperative to act as a mediator.

"Yes, General, great idea," Juandre said. "I'll take the helm with my bear and the rest of the crew."

Mika calmed down a bit. He reluctantly went down the stairs as Connor pulled the cabin door open. The boys seemed optimistic about the inquisition as they entered the dinette, Eryn in the middle and taking the opposite side, with Brad pulling a chair closer so he could sit at the table's head.

"Thank you." He turned to Mika and Connor and proudly smiled. Perhaps he enjoyed rubbing a bit of salt into the situation, just as he enjoyed poking and prodding his friends.

"Boys, as the leader of Phoenix, we believe..." He looked at Mika and Connor. "We believe in talking things out and clearing up misunderstandings. Could you explain to us? What does it mean when you say he's ours and he says you're his? Before you answer, please know you're both twenty-one years old."

"Almost twenty-two!" the twins called out in unison. Mika ground his teeth, and Connor turned red.

"Okay," Brad said and treaded as carefully as possible. "Eryn, how old are you?"

Eryn became still, his forehead wrinkling into a deep frown. The more Brad interacted with him, the more he could see and hear the beautiful appeal. Eryn's gaze was gentle, and it felt supernatural when he pinned Brad with those genuinely gorgeous eyes, with irises like pools of gold with green specks, and surrounding the amphibian-like elongated pupils. His strange facial features were delicate and handsome. Although he had a flattened nose, it fit his face perfectly.

Brad lost his concentration and train of thought when Eryn spoke. "I was born before all the humans died."

Brad cleared his throat and continued. "How old were you when the scientists sent you and your brothers out to poison the world?"

"No, they didn't send us. My brothers escaped after they killed all the scientists except my father. I protected my father. I called them back and told them to sleep deep in the tunnels."

"How old were you?"

"I was young," Eryn said, drawing a deep breath through his nose. "I was maybe four or five. Years passed differently when I lived underground."

"A baby Brawl, then? Two or three years?"

"No, a small boy Brawl."

"So you're about thirty to thirty-five years of age now?"

"I don't know what my years are." He croaked—shocking Brad and the others with the strange burping sound. Eryn fidgeted with the cloth of his pants.

"Brad, you made him sad now," Cian said. *He's protective of his friend.* If Brad didn't know better, he would say Cian sensed Eryn's emotions like Eryn does theirs. He wondered if Cian knew that.

"Sorry, Eryn, it's okay not to know your age. And it's okay not to know everything. Not one of us knows everything. You did nothing wrong. I probably reminded you of your brothers and your father. And I'm sorry if that hurt your feelings."

Eryn nodded and hung his head low. Then, not making eye contact, he shied away from them. The total opposite of what he looked like when he protected them from the storm.

"As you can see, Eryn will require much schooling and needs it at a comfortable speed. His time living with his brothers was quite difficult, which hindered him. Your dads are concerned that you may not comprehend the significance of his being different. Then, after getting to know Eryn, they'll decide if it's safe to live in Phoenix with the rest of the regular population." The general raised his hand as they inhaled deeply to interrupt him. "Eryn has told me he'll never hurt you or any other person at Phoenix, and I have faith in his word. Bryan reports that he's been visiting us for years and living with Joshua secretly. So far, nothing has transpired, and I'm certain he'll follow through on his promise," Brad said, making eye contact with everyone around the table.

The twins sank into their chairs with ease. Eryn sat up with his back to the wall once more proudly.

"Can you explain to me why you chose the blond boys? Are they pretty?"

"Oh my gosh," Connor said and slapped his upper thigh. Mika placed his hand on Connor's and squeezed it quite hard. Connor slowly flipped his hand over, weaving their fingers. The tension was a visible indicator for Brad to provide support.

Eryn turned to face the other grown-ups at the table and answered honestly. "Yes, they are pretty, but they are excellent friends. They pay attention to what I say and never make me feel horrible about myself. I can hear their songs, and they can listen to my song when I sing."

"Can you tell me which songs?" Mika inquired.

"Could you please sing for us so we can hear you?" Connor elaborated.

Eryn looked questioningly at the twins for permission to share their song. They nodded and gave the impression that everything was okay. He took a deep breath and opened his mouth to sing the notes of a song. The melody was euphorious; it sounded light and vibrantly pure. While singing his melodious siren song, the cabin filled with an odoriferous smell Brad couldn't identify.

Eryn closed his eyes and pushed what Brad guessed were pheromones outward as the delicious smells intoxicated them. Brad felt feather-light. Eryn's forearms had a pearlescent blue sheen while he sang. The beauty of the unearthly angelic notes charmed everyone at the table. Brad wanted to weep, and he stroked the goosebumps on his arms. Cian and Ivan were wholly absorbed. It seemed as if Eryn was the only person who existed for them. The boys burst into applause when he finished.

"As you can see, he's amazing." They leaped to their feet and clutched their Brawl. Eryn hugged them back, shoving and playfully grasping the lads.

"What was that?" Juandre asked as he and the others surged onto the lower deck. "It's just stunning. It was the first time I heard anything like it."

Brad looked at them but still felt dazed. "Oh, that was Eryn. He showed us how he sings for his friends," Brad explained while making a point of saying, friends.

"That's amazing. Wow, Eryn, you have many phenomenal talents," Juandre praised him. "It sounded nothing like the song you sang outdoors to shelter us from the storm." Juandre continued, looking super impressed.

"It was extraordinary," Mika said slowly while glaring at Connor. They were having one of their unspoken conversations with their eyes.

Eryn soaked up the praise. "I know many types of songs," he said, ready to sing more if someone asked. While they all praised him, Brad expressed gratitude for sharing his gift with them.

"See, no one in our group has ever heard anything like that before, so people need to get to know you better like we're getting to know you now, Eryn, and that's why we want you to feel comfortable living in Phoenix. Mika and Connor want you to stay with them," Brad said, dropping the hammer on a high note.

"Why can't we get our own apartment?" the Romanov twins asked simultaneously.

"No, we need to get to know Eryn better," Mika said curtly. Cian and Ivan gave each other a questioning look, and their expressions turned sorrowful as they accepted their defeat.

Mika looked instantly irritated. "That is a sign they want to be alone and away from us," he muttered to Connor.

"I know. We'll have to take turns chaperoning them." Connor replied.

The twins were stunned, but before they could protest, Eryn pulled each in an arm and nuzzled their heads with his chin.

Brad chuckled and hoped he'd diffused the tension and prevented things from being said in the heat of the moment. "Boys, remember we just met him, and we must watch over him. There are people at Phoenix who would want to hurt Eryn." He turned to Mika and Connor. "So, you two will have trouble sleeping for the foreseeable future." Brad teased and then bolted from the table to join Rick and his boys.

CHAPTER 18
LET ME DROWN HIM

"*Good morning, city of Phoenix.*

It's now six a.m.

Do you know the difference between infiltrating and penetrating?

Infiltration is all about being sneaky about penetration, while penetrating means finally gaining entrance.

Did you also know that it has the same meaning as the slogan 'make love, not war,' because it was a code for spies to infiltrate and penetrate enemy lines?

So, it doesn't matter whether you're spying or making love; both are about gaining entrance, but only the spies infiltrate.

Breakfast is served until eight a.m.

Have an insightful day."

Eryn, King of the Brawl

. . .

LATER THAT NIGHT, one after the other, the young men passed out sleeping as the discussions about their exciting day had wound down. While Juandre and Andrew prepared breakfast for the following morning, Brad, Rick, Connor, and Mika rested on the deck under the stars. The aroma of butter and pastry wafted across the ship, and Eryn welcomed the smell of scones and the sounds of Juandre and Andrew's jovial banter. He shared the sleeping cabin with the twins, lying between Ivan and Cian, linking arms while Kawa and Donali slept just a few meters away. Eryn had just awakened from one of his recurring nightmares. He tried not to think about the hundreds of people who'd died while he walked through the streets of Cape Town. The buzzing of flies and the overpowering stench of decaying human bodies hung over the cities like clouds. The vivid images of dying humans caused by his brothers' horrible trail of doom flashed in and out of his field of vision. He sat up, rubbing his eyes to dispel the torturous memories.

I should stop referring to them as my brothers because I'm nothing like them.

The dreams were always the same, and always woke him up. Disoriented and unsure whether it was a dream, he stood among the dead humans, eyes closed and crying in agony over so much death. His empathic gift enabled him to carry the sorrow and pain of many people, and to this day, when he closed his eyes to dream, he could vividly see the horror surrounding him. Monsters waiting on his command, eyes wild, teeth bared. More animal than anything human. *They waited for him to lead them.* He remembered telling them, "Go home," and the confusion in their eyes gave way to obedience as they returned to their tunnels. That look in their eyes, the connection with him, was why he'd struggled to kill them.

Eryn was the only one who could bring them to a state of calm and slumber. He felt responsible for them. He hated himself for letting them suffer for so long. *I should have drowned them sooner. I should have listened to Father.* Especially now that he tasted living with the twins. Those monsters, Ernest included, were incapable of listening to reason long-term. Their only emotions and thoughts were confusion, fear, aggression, and cannibalism.

Yet, I felt responsible for taking that away from them by giving them calm and peace, by putting them to sleep. I was terrified of being rejected by humans and being all alone.

Eryn turned his head to look outside the cabin window at the stars. There were a few clouds in the sky, with a beautiful full moon shining on them. He lifted his hands in the air, inspecting them in the moonlight, noticing how dirty his nails were. Why didn't anyone mention that? He lay his head back down, folding his hands behind his head. He listened to the boys' sleep noises. Joshua made terrible sleep noises, but the twins sounded nothing like Joshua. Everything they did, even their breathing, was beautiful to him. Bored with himself, he lifted his feet, inspecting them. He noticed earlier that his toes were webbed, but the boys weren't. He huffed.

Yet another thing that proved he wasn't human. Then he heard giggles. The twins lay open-eyed, watching him. His tummy did that weird thing again, where it felt like he was hungry, but not. A feeling only they gave him. *I guess it's a good feeling.*

"What are you doing, Eryn?" Ivan whispered.

"Nothing," he quickly replied, flipping onto his stomach so they didn't see his tenting pants. He watched them both as they watched him. Their love and acceptance washed away all the terrible memories from the nightmares earlier. His insides soaked up their happiness like a hardened, dead, sea sponge. He thought they were so pretty. *I'm lucky to have such beautiful best friends.*

"What are you thinking, then?" Ivan prodded.

In the dark, he saw them staring back at him. "I thought about how beautiful you both are, and that I will never be as beautiful as a human. I'm an ugly Brawl."

Both reacted, reaching up and touching his face.

"Of all the humans we know at Phoenix, you are the most alluring one, and that's all that matters to us," Cian said.

"What does that mean?" Eryn asked.

"It means you are even more beautiful than beautiful. You're powerful and mysteriously attractive," Ivan said.

"Yes, and you're fascinating and seductive with your voice. And you smell like...hmmm, like lemongrass and lavender."

"That sounds like toilet spray," Donali commented, breaking out in laughter.

"Ignore him. You also smell like fresh linen and seaweed."

"Yup, a toilet spray," Kawa added, laughing hysterically.

"You sound like two hyenas!" Cian said.

But their laughter was infectious. Eryn jumped over to the McCormick twins and started tickling them. "I will tickle you till you shit your pants, and then you will be glad for my toilet spray smell."

"Dogpile, shit pile!" the Romanov twins yelled, joining the scuffle.

"Stop, stop, I'm going to piss myself."

Eryn stopped his playful assault, and the Romanov twins rolled off his back, careful not to hurt Kawa.

"Are you okay, Kawa?" Donali asked.

"Yes, I'm okay, but I smell like shit with sugar sprinkles on top." They burst out in another round of giggles.

"Dear lord, I need to go to the washroom. I think I

peed myself," Cian said when they quieted down. He got up, but before he could open the door...

Bang! Bang!

Eryn froze and shushed them. Reaching for his trident, he stood at the ready, listening, while sending his mental feelers out to scan the ship. However, his heart pounded so loudly that he struggled to hear anything. For the first time, he worried about his twins and their family and friends so much that he could hardly think straight. Two thumps followed the bang-bang sounds.

Those were gunshots or maybe pots or pans falling, he speculated, as a fleeting afterthought.

"Shhhh," Eryn said, smelling gunpowder. "Something is wrong. There are strangers on the ship."

"How can there be strangers on the ship?" Ivan asked, whispering.

Eryn listened. Then, turning, he searched for a spot to hide four big boys. "Quickly hide here." He lifted the bottom of the massive bed like it weighed nothing. "Climb in," he urged them, whispering, but he felt like shouting to make them move faster.

"No, we want to stay with you." The Romanov twins objected, and Eryn gnashed his teeth.

"I will come to get you when it's safe. Please hide. Otherwise, I'll worry about you."

Donali and Kawa didn't wait to be asked twice and slipped in as fast as possible. They'd learned their lesson by not hiding when Ernest grabbed them.

"Please, you two, do this for me," Eryn begged and pushed them hurriedly down. Thank the heavens they obeyed. As quickly as they could, they all slipped under the bed. Eryn grabbed a shoe and placed it at each corner, making it slightly higher so as not to crush them.

He turned soundlessly, leaving the room. He stopped, closed his eyes, and pushed out his mental feelers to scan the below and above-deck areas. It surprised him to find five intruders on the upper deck he didn't recognize...and oh shit! Two of his friends were lying in a heap, and Brad, Rick, Connor, and Mika were nervous.

Hoping the boys stayed where he'd hidden them, he snuck into the dinette area. As he stepped into the room, he heard muffled male voices on the deck. He stepped carefully over the scones strewn on the floor.

"Well, well, well," an evil-sounding male voice said from behind him.

Eryn froze and lifted his hands, feigning surrender.

"I knew you would pop up sometime. All I had to do was wait. You misfit DNA mongrel. We've been searching for you for years. So, get your hands up where I can see them."

Eryn stood frozen, hoping the twins did nothing stupid like trying to save him.

"You know, you were supposed to take us all to the moon, but no, you ran around playing guard dog and hide-and-seek. Are you even aware that the Earth is about to explode? And you're gallivanting and playing footsie with boys who don't know what you are?"

Eryn's heart raced. He didn't wallow in fear of making a sound. *How did this man sneak past me?* He didn't know, and it scared the shit out of him. No one had ever evaded him. *I'm the apex predator, or so I thought.*

Are there over five evil men on the upper deck? He was doubting himself after the man behind him snuck up on him.

"Where are the others?" Eryn asked.

"Come now. I ask the questions. Where are the twins?" the intruder asked with a chilling, menacing voice while something was poking Eryn in his back. It must be a gun. He calculated falling to his hands, performing a low roundhouse kick, taking the asshole down to the floor. But before he could carry out his superb escape karate kick, he heard a dull thump, a buzz, a groan, and the sound of the man hitting the floor. Turning around, he saw his twins, wide-eyed, with a stun gun in hand.

They looked so damn cute holding the gun together like one couldn't pull the trigger without the other.

"Are you crazy?" he asked, and they nodded in the affirmative.

"Let's tie him up and go upstairs," Cian said, and Ivan dangled a rope in front of Eryn.

"No, no, no, absolutely not!" Eryn suspected this was what a heart attack felt like, or was that a stroke?

"You're killing me! I think I have a nervous attack."

"Oh, you mean a panic attack," Ivan, the bright one, corrected him.

"Breathe, one, two, three in and one, two, three out. Or is that ten? Because you're bigger, it should be twenty in and twenty out," Cian added uselessly, not making any sense at all.

"You stay and watch this guy," he said, glaring at them.

They had the decency not to laugh.

"Okay, let me think." Eryn rubbed his pounding head, where a major headache was forming. "So, there's only one way up, and they would guard the entrance upstairs." Eryn continued to calculate the best next move.

More pitter-patter of feet. Eryn rolled his eyes. Donali and Kawa joined them. He harrumphed, grabbing a spatula from the floor, sticking the thing into the handle of the rotating door, and locking the door so no one could exit or enter. Then he walked over to where the twins were tying the man, binding his wrists to his ankles. He vigorously shook the unconscious man's tied hands and feet. The rope slipped loose like wet spaghetti. He eyeballed them.

"We were still busy...we were hogtying him." They whined in unison. With no outstanding success, thought Eryn.

Gently but quickly pushing the boys aside, Eryn wrapped the rope around the filthy human's neck three times, then down and under his one leg, and twice back around the other. Then, like an expert, he proceeded in a different direction by pulling the man's ankles back and swiftly did the same thing backward twice around his torso. Then, folding his arms backward, he tied them and did the same with the man's feet and, finally, around the neck again.

"That's it!" Eryn felt very impressed with his roping skills.

"Come on. We could have done that," Cian protested. He eyeballed them again.

"Then why didn't you?"

"You're so full of yourself."

"Silly mates," Eryn said, and immediately felt self-conscious for uttering the word.

"Wait, what?" Cian and Ivan exclaimed, noticing their slip of the tongue.

"I said you're silly."

"Nooooo, rewind that. The other word," they asked, looking like two Marmoset monkeys with white hair sticking to the sides of their heads and big, curious blue eyes.

Eryn blushed. It felt like he glowed in the dark.

"Did you say, mates, like Australians say how'zat,

my mate? Or did you mean to say *come here*, I want to rub myself all over you and make you mine? Which mate are you talking about, my mate?" Ivan asked, and Cian elbowed him.

"Stop it, that hurt."

"You mean you want to mate with us?" Cian added.

Eryn knew precisely what word they were referring to. He knew three meanings of the word. Friend, partner, and the pleasuring kind. He read and watched many books and movies at Phoenix as a small boy Brawl. He discovered the pleasuring meaning when he was sixteen, but there was no way he would tell them that, not here and now. Donali and Kawa were listening, and a man was lying tied up in front of them on the floor. Also, he wasn't telling them how often he had touched himself thinking of them. Cian and Ivan had been his best friends since he met them from a distance at Phoenix, but now, the twins heard his mating call, and the little buggers sang back to him. Ivan's song was louder than Cian's, but that didn't change the fact that he wanted to mount both. His faceless mate had morphed into two faces, the most beautiful two faces, and he wanted to touch and kiss and do all kinds of rubbing on their bodies. He realized he was daydreaming when they coughed.

"Okay, you're both. I'm not lying to you. You're my

best friends and partners." *And yeah, I want to mate with both of you.*

"Come, I want to surprise the men. Now is not the time." Their faces lit up and shone at him like the brightest stars in the universe. *I want to lick those pouty, soft lips so bad.*

Grabbing his trident, he pointed it at a small window above the couches opposite the entrance of the dinette. He hummed and softly touched the window with it so it cracked and exploded to the outside.

"That's badass," his mates whispered.

"You stay down here. Please be safe." Donali and Kawa nodded. Eryn ruffled Cian's and Ivan's hair as they stood open-mouthed, deep in hero worship.

Next, Eryn climbed onto the seats, turned his back to the wall, and pushed his arms through the open window while pulling himself into a sitting position.

Bending his head inside, he repeated, "I mean it. Please stay here." He moved so fast they barely saw his feet disappear through the opening.

While hanging onto the side of the ship, Eryn heard voices. He listened.

"What do you mean, the Earth is going to explode? And why haven't you said anything earlier? I mean, you had over twenty years to say something?" Brad spoke loudly, sounding upset.

So they were from Phoenix, and Brad knew them. *The six bastards!* Eryn had the realization while hanging onto the ship and assessing the situation. *I'm killing them tonight!*

"Why not tell us and let us help you? We could've all worked together if you'd said that to us. Why was it necessary for all this sneaking around? Why steal when you can ask? Are you dense or something?" Brad asked. That was something Eryn learned and liked about Brad and the humans. They would always listen to what you needed, and you only had to ask. If it weren't possible, they would work together to make it work.

"Because, you idiot, there are over two thousand men in Phoenix. Who are you saving, and who's staying?"

"That's not up to me. I'm not the god who decides who lives and who dies. But why would you need us, anyway?"

"Because you need to figure out how to get us to the moon. You idiots flooded our Provisions Craft! Our supply of food, water, and building equipment! So, you'll make it right."

Mika and Connor sat, hands up, behind the wheel, while Brad stood talking. Rick watched the men dressed in arctic suits to his right side, but his eyes constantly darted to something.

What's he looking at? Where are Andrew and Juandre?

Still hanging onto the side, Eryn moved around the ship's side for a better view. No, no, no! Both his friends were lying in a heap in front of the door to the stairs going down to the living area. He flipped himself up to the deck and crept closer for better inspection. It didn't look good. And by the heart rates of his friends, they didn't think so either. Eryn held his hand under their noses to feel for heat and movement of air. Nothing. Tipping his head, he listened. Nothing. They were dead. Eryn saw red and felt murderous. These were two wonderful humans. They were only ever good to him. They fed him, and Juandre always smiled at him. Never a nasty, selfish word from either of them.

"Then why would you steal and clone eggs?" he heard Mika say.

"Why create superhuman or deadly creatures? What's your end game? Because, buddy, you make little sense," Brad added.

"There are forces at work here that you won't understand. We only want fuel to propel us up to the moon. Are you aware that people have already been on the moon? You're a sad bunch of homosexuals. You were only an experiment, a forgotten experiment gone wrong!" Charles shouted.

Eryn felt the disbelieving anger flare in Brad.

"Listen, you better stop with the attitude if you want our help. I believe if we can survive in glass domes in Antarctica, then it's most probably true for the moon." Brad turned to Mika and Connor, having a conversation like it was just another day around a poker table.

"Now, Houston Headquarters makes sense. I always wondered why the WHPPS headquarters were at the Space Center and NASA's astronaut training and flight control complex."

"Yeah, now it makes total sense," Connor said, bumping his forehead with the palm of his hand. Mika nodded animatedly.

The man with his gun on Brad continued, "Yes, we even designed a hydrogen-propelled ship as a prototype, but no, you had to design your own box of Smarties. A blue one, and it's glowing, too. Why didn't you at least test our design? Why not try hydrogen?"

"Because it's my rescue mission. Why must I use your design?"

"Well, there's our design, and now tell me, what's wrong with it?"

Mika got up and stepped closer, poking him on the forehead with his middle finger. "Listen, Charles. If you had come to me and told me what you wanted like a normal scientist, I could have helped you. What's wrong with you people? You all act as if I owe you something and that you have an entitlement to take what you want. Why didn't you offer to help us when we needed it? I'm so sick of sanctimonious bastards like you acting as if the world owes you, but you continue to take and destroy. You can't handle someone having more and better than you, but you're too proud to ask. Has it ever occurred to you that we all work together because we think as a team? We're not ten years old. We're not a gang of thugs," Mika screamed, not allowing Charles to respond. "If you want what we have, just come to me and say I have an idea. I'm not sure it will work. Please help or teach me because the world's about to explode!" Mika sneered. "I'm so sick of this shit!"

The asshole named Charles opened his mouth as if to speak.

"No, I'm talking now, Dr. Charles Montgomery. You're a useless drop of spunk. You're slimy and stink worse than a two-hour unflushed lump of excrement. That you went and built your ship astounds me. Congratulations, you used that organ between your ears. Be proud of what you've done, the first hydrogen-propelled ship ever designed, and it flies. Take it and fly to the moon! But no, let me make a pit stop and shoot some honest people before we go because we want it all and leave everyone else miserable!" Mika shouted, red in the face and seconds away from literally combusting into flames.

"They left us here!" Charles yelled back at Mika.

Eryn noticed Mika make a hand signal, as if he knew Eryn was there. *That's it. Keep him talking.* Eryn had had enough of these evil men. He recognized them. They were the ones who had terrorized Joshua for years. They'd beaten and killed him and made Eryn hide in the tunnels inside the mines.

Now they'd killed Juandre and Andrew. They were too stupid to make their own fuel, always wanting, taking, and destroying. They were bad men. *And their time of bullying must come to an end today.*

Decision made, Eryn sprinted from zero to one hundred kilometers per hour, tackling three of the five intruders from the side while holding his trident horizontally. Bullets whizzed over his head as he scooped them up in the air and ran all three overboard into the icy water, taking them with him. They kicked and grabbed frantically onto him, but he swam deeper and deeper until they stopped struggling after a minute. That was his sign, and he knew they were dead. Their grasping hands fell from him, and he swam away and upward, leaving them in the darkness. Circling the ship, Eryn waited for an opening to do the same to the fourth and fifth men who were frantically swinging their guns in every direction.

"You better be careful, or you'll shoot your friend," Eryn whispered as he bobbed in the waves, only the top of his head and big eyes above the waterline. That freaked them out. Eryn didn't use his mouth to speak because he spoke directly into their minds.

"I'll start shooting!" the fourth man said, aiming his gun at Brad. He never saw Eryn coming to collect him. Eryn shot like a resolute marlin out of the water, pegging him with his trident like it was fondue night, and disappeared underwater before he could say ouch. *It serves you right.* Eryn deposited him with his friends in the cold and dark depths.

When Eryn returned to the surface, the last coward, Charles, had Brad, Rick, Mika, and Connor at gunpoint. "Don't come closer. I'll shoot them," he shouted, bewildered. His head turned left and right while making threatening, empty promises to Eryn, who was somewhere out in the water, watching. Eryn hung around for a better opportunity. He watched Mika and Connor for directions.

Mika spoke up to distract him. "You'll have to kill everyone. Then, if the world explodes, you're dying anyway. You know what? I just showed you how easy it is for me to make a rocket fly to the moon. I'll make your fuel formula for your idiotic rocket. Then you can fly to the moon. To demonstrate how easy it is, I'll complete it within ten days. But you go alone!" Mika growled murderously.

Eryn felt Brad's intention to confuse the man. Then, out of the blue, Brad started speaking, startling him. "Wow, that was sexy, Mika. That sounded like the Russian fisting voice you used in the tunnels. I never realized how sexy your dominance sounded. If you told me to get on my knees in that tone of your voice, I would lick your boots clean for you."

Mika immediately caught his friend's meaning. "Comrade, we have a deal when we get home after I make this idiot his stupid fuel. Mika will fist you all night long."

Connor jumped in before Charles could say anything. "Hey, honey, maybe Rick and I can join you?"

"Yes, that would be awesome. I'll bring the popcorn because I like to watch while I rub one out," Rick yelled with his hands high up in the air, moving one step to the side. They were smart, Eryn noticed, they were widening the space between the four of them, to make it harder for Charles to corral them.

Charles pointedly showed them he knew where Eryn was and that he wasn't taking his eyes off him. *He thinks I'm the biggest threat.*

"Stop it. We all know you gay people have no morals. You're trying to distract me, and it's not working." For a second, his gaze darted over the ship and back to where Eryn bobbed in the waves.

"No, I want him." He lifted his chin, showing it was Eryn he wanted.

"That's why they created him, to help us on the moon."

"Who are they?" Connor demanded, sounding irritated.

"There's no way you take that young man or any of us with you," Mika said, and Eryn's heart did a few happy backflips as his eyes prickled with tears. That statement boosted his confidence in his new family.

My ice-people from the glass city, Phoenix, I will help them, not the selfish murderer. Eryn pushed himself out of the water so his whole torso was visible, his legs not kicking. A move no human could do, especially while holding a heavy pure gold staff.

"I belong to Ivan and Cian and not to you." As soon as Eryn spoke, Rick lifted his leg and side kicked the piece of human trash hard on the knee, sending him flying onto his stomach. Brad, Connor, and Mika jumped onto his back, immobilizing him. In a flash, Eryn was next to them.

"Let me drown him. Give him to me," he said, calm and in control of his emotions.

"Maybe later, Eryn, we'll tie him up and ask him some questions. Like who he's working with and how many other experimental projects are in the works?" Brad said, checking Mika and Connor, making sure they had Charles pegged and immobilized.

Brad dove over to help Rick, gently rolling Juandre and Andrew onto their backs and checking their breathing and carotid pulses. Rick shook his head, indicating they were both dead to the disbelieving Brad, who had hoped they were still alive. He dropped to his knees, hung his head for half a second, then jumped back up and made his way back to Charles.

Red in the face and fists clenched, Brad shouted, "You idiots, you're all going to die with us! The rocket is stuck in the mud. Unless you have some super lubricant, that rocket will never fly out of that hole!" Brad yelled, seething about his dead friends. Eryn sensed his anger was directed at Charles, yet the man still flapped his lips about a damn rocket.

Charles made a vicious face, challenging Brad. *You better shut up, or Brad's going to kill you.*

"There's another rocket, and I know where it is. All we need is fuel and him," Charles said with a snarl.

Ignoring Charles's ranting, Eryn aimed to ease the tension. Instead, he interjected, "I'll go get the boys. They're downstairs with one of them." He pointed at Charles with his fork. "I tied him up, but they're waiting for me. I'll have to go down the same way I came." Without waiting for a response, he dove back into the water, eager to reach the twins. A few minutes later, the boys opened the door to the upper deck, appearing shaken and unsure, with Eryn carrying the man over his shoulder. He tossed him down next to his friend like a sack of potatoes. Still unconscious.

In the meantime, everyone else had gathered around Juandre's and Andrew's bodies. He could feel the hope that, by some miracle, they were still alive.

"Why did you have to kill them? You're monsters!" Brad snapped, kicking Charles in a fit of rage. Lowering himself, he kneed the man in the ribs and then straddled him. No one attempted to stop him. He unleashed weeks of frustration, pummeling Charles with his bare fists. Left and right, over and over, until his face was unrecognizable. Mika and Connor halfheartedly tried to drag him away from the man.

"Let me go!" Brad ordered, and Mika complied. He

set Brad free, granting him his revenge, while he stopped Connor from holding Brad back.

A moment later, Brad jumped back on top of Charles. Striking him while articulating each word slowly. "You...don't! Deserve...to...live!Die...die...die! We...would...have...helped...you! You...bastard!" As he hammered Charles's head, dull, wet, thumping sounds reiterated over and over into the darkness beyond their ship. Blood splattered around Charles's head and onto the deck and their boots. Teeth and possibly an eyeball flew into the air and splashed into the water. Rick, Mika, and Connor did not stop him.

From the corner of his eye, Eryn saw Rick staring blankly, then turning away and looking for the boys, needing to protect them from witnessing their father's brutal justice. He understood how much Brad adored the two men who had only wanted to have fun and were good at heart. This terrible man had murdered their friends. Eryn had the impression that they all felt the same about Charles and his men.

Finally, Brad slumped to the side, utterly exhausted. Everyone could see the way he looked; the world felt as if it were coming to an end. So why care anymore? No one did. They were all in a numb, discombobulated, trancelike state.

Eryn decided to help Brad and stepped forward. He quickly scooped Brad up in his arms as Brad hung unresponsive, covered in Charles's blood. Eryn carried Brad inside, where Rick transformed the area into a surgery room. Rick unfolded and extended their kitchen table, unrolling a thin mattress to show Eryn that it was ready. The twins had informed Rick and Mika about the setup for medical emergencies like this.

Carefully, he laid Brad down so Rick could tend to his husband. Brad was wholly defeated and catatonic, staring off into the distance and not reacting to Rick or his boys.

Eryn closed his eyes, touching Brad's shoulder as he hummed a soothing song. "Sleep, Icemen King, rest, and be well." Brad's eyes fluttered shut.

"Thank you, Eryn," Rick said, working on undressing Brad, his eyes glistening with tears.

Eryn noticed the tears and nodded. He left to help Connor and Mika clean the deck. They didn't need to be reminded of the day, so they cut loose their enemy's ship and rolled Charles's dead body into the water. They kept the unconscious man tied up to deal with later and to question later.

Next, their friend's bodies were prepared for burial—something Eryn had never witnessed before. He appreciated their explanations of the ritual, even though their emotions were a mix of rage, sadness, and loss. These feelings intensified while they removed the bullets and washed and dressed the bodies. The process gave Eryn an entirely new impression and perspective on what it meant to be human and how they loved and missed one another.

Mika, Connor, and the twins included him by explaining their actions and the reasons behind them. They also described what humans typically do with the bodies of those who have died on land and around the world, noting that some cultures approached it differently than others. Eryn found it all very interesting, especially since he didn't know how to handle his father's body. They informed him that the rituals had changed since Doomsday and that, since then, they had only dealt with one death, which they had to burn because the ground was frozen, making it nearly impossible to dig a grave. Eryn didn't like his first experience with burial. It felt like too much sadness. Everyone agreed that this was one too many.

Two days later, after they informed Phoenix via radio that Juandre and Andrew had been murdered, the crew of the Blue Halcyon, except for their General McCormick, who was still in a coma, held a small remembrance ceremony for their friends who had died in the line of duty. Each person spoke about their fallen colleagues and the impact those individuals had on their lives back home. Eryn recalled his favorite scone and bread, and they all agreed they would deeply miss their cooks. After Mika and Connor rolled their linen-wrapped bodies into the sea, it was a sorrowful morning. Eryn appreciated the hugs because they made him feel more human.

BIG DOGS WITH UGLY YELLOW EYES

BIG DOGS WITH UGLY YELLOW EYES

"Good morning, citizens of Phoenix.

It's now six a.m.

This is for youngsters. Have you ever wondered why planets are round?

They say it's because their gravitational field acts as though it originates from the planet's center, pulling everything toward it. The only way to get as much mass as close to the center of gravity is to form a sphere.

The technical name for this process is an isostatic adjustment.

Visit the community news page for more interesting facts about planets.

Breakfast is served until eight a.m.

Have a ball of a day!"

. . .

GENERAL BRAD MCCORMICK

BRAD JOLTED UPRIGHT, gasping for air. Half disoriented, he looked around frantically and immediately felt better when he saw Rick sitting beside him, his arms draped over Brad's legs. The movement and gasps had woken him, and as soon as Rick's gaze focused on his, he conveyed the bewilderment, disorientation, and panic he felt. Reaching for his hand, Rick approached him as if he were a frightened animal, perhaps a rattlesnake in need of tranquilizers.

"Now, now, it's all going to be okay. The boys are safe. We're all okay." As soon as those empty words left Rick's lips, the image of Andrew and Juandre getting gunned down while they begged Charles not to shoot flooded Brad's mind. It seemed as if Charles and Juandre knew each other. Juandre repeatedly asked Charles why he never came to say hello. Charles had shouted that he was disgusted by their relationship and that Juandre was a piece of trash. So hateful, so unnecessary. Then the fury bubbled up from within him, triggering his fight-or-flight response. Instantly, he felt like he could kill Charles with his bare hands again. He panted, feeling like he couldn't get enough air into his lungs.

"I can't breathe. I need air. I can't breathe!" he said, nearly falling off the table.

"Come here, love, I'll help you," Rick said soothingly as he grabbed Brad's suit and helped him into it.

He's so patient with me. I don't deserve him. Brad hopped, half hanging and half running, for the exit.

"It'll be fine," Rick promised, taking his time to focus on Brad while speaking loudly enough to awaken everyone. Probably to gather extra hands to help him.

"What happened to...last night...after?" Brad asked, stuttering. "What did you do with..." He couldn't finish the sentence or find the words. Sorrow for Juandre and Andrew tightened his chest, but his Apache spoke in a stern, calm voice, catching his attention, so Brad forced himself to listen to the one man he trusted most in the world.

"You're getting enough air. Take deep breaths, in and out. Focus on my voice while we prepare you for the frigid air."

Heads popped up, and Rick appeared relieved. One by one, they showed themselves. Mika came through the revolving door first, with messy hair. He looked like he'd been sleeping with a finger stuck in a socket all night. "Good. Is he awake?" Mika rubbed his still-closed eyes and dragged his slippers across the floor, nearly knocking Rick over with a loud, "Oomph, sorry, still waking up."

"He just needs a bit of fresh air," Rick said, winking at Mika, but Brad saw it.

"I don't think it's wise to take him up to the deck.

That jerk is up there. We tied him to the mast, Brad. We thought the cold would do him good. When you're ready, we should probably interrogate him." Mika continued as if Brad wasn't having a bloody panic attack and didn't need oxygen like any other land-dwelling vertebrate.

"You were out for over forty-eight hours. I'm making coffee," Connor, who had entered right behind Mika, said.

"Come sit, comrade!" Mika called to him casually, in his usual self-assured manner. Pulling out a chair for Brad, Mika brushed aside the melodrama and shortness of breath. "Let's get some coffee in our systems first, please, Brad. I'm all for getting to the truth, but..." Mika pleaded, but he was interrupted by their children coming in. His smile broadened when he saw them. "Morning, boys," he greeted the five young men.

From Brad's vantage point, one by one, a pair of chocolate brown heads, followed by a pair of blond heads, and finally, Eryn's curly, dark blond mop of hair, emerged through the revolving door. Eryn rubbed his head as if his hair had gotten stuck, or maybe he had scraped it on the low-hanging ceiling. The newcomers immediately sensed the tension in the cabin, their heads swiveling left and right as they assessed the situation.

"Morning, Father." Donali and Kawa's faces brightened as they raced to greet Brad, wrapping their arms around his neck and showering him with kisses and affection, just as they had since they were babies, like two little orangutans. I should ask Peter or someone from the bionics department to build Kawa a new arm, Brad thought, feeling grateful for the love his boys showed him.

"Welcome back, Father. It's great to see you're up."

"Thank you, my boys." Brad soaked in the unconditional love.

"Good morning, General," the Romanov twins greeted, while Eryn appeared skittish, tiptoeing around Brad, nodding, looking down at Brad's hands.

Brad followed his gaze and noticed that someone had bandaged his hands. Guilt suffocated him all over again.

Searching for doubt or disgust in their children's eyes, Brad found none, so he straightened his spine and looked back at his fists. He mumbled to Mika, picking up the conversation they'd started before the children arrived. "Maybe running upstairs isn't a good idea after all." He inhaled deeply, held it in, and slowly released the trapped air, taking steady breaths that flowed in and out. He calmed himself and repeated that two more times.

"Yes, comrade, let's grab a coffee and plan our next steps." Mika broke the tension and patted him on the back. Rick released his arm, and Brad knew that whatever decision he made, Rick would support him. He looked at his husband and expressed his gratitude for his stoic support. Rick always displayed a rock-solid sense of dignity and grace, and he couldn't imagine his life without him—a trait that Brad and many of his patients admired greatly.

"Thank you. I think I'm feeling better now. I just had a terrible dream about the shooting," he admitted, acknowledging the elephant in the room. "Gentlemen, I'm really sorry. I misbehaved. I acted out." He glanced at the kids. "I apologize if I scared you."

They all fell into Brad, hugging their father, friend, and leader. Brad lifted his head. He taught his boys that it was okay to cry and that a man could have feelings. He also taught them that confronting problems head-on cleared the air, allowing life to move forward. So he knew they accepted his feelings. Although he was a grown-ass man, he could shed a tear. After all, he was bloody human, and they were all friends and family. And so they healed with words and reciprocation of love.

"It's all good, Dad. We all felt like that."

"Your father and I raised you better than to solve your problems with your fists." Brad's face burned with shame.

"We know, it was the language of the bad people, so we understand, Dad," Donali said.

"I don't want you to be scared or disappointed," Brad murmured, fidgeting with the bandages. "I saw your eyes earlier."

"We're not scared of you. We're scared for you, Dad." They stepped closer, offering Brad supportive hugs. "And we're not disappointed."

As a leader, or former leader, of Phoenix, he firmly believed in leading by example, so he invited them to sit down at the table by pulling out more chairs for a roundtable discussion. Connor brought a big pot of coffee and squeezed himself between his family. Everyone around the table had time to vent about the past forty-eight hours, including what they learned from Charles and his men.

The Romanov boys each sat on one of Eryn's knees while Eryn wore the biggest smile Brad had ever seen on anyone. The three just seemed to fit together, he thought. Brad doubted that Mika and Connor opposed this unusual bond, especially after they protested when Eryn was taken away or left them. The boy-king was undoubtedly what Brad would consider worthy of a king in honor, truth, dedication, and power. The list was long, and Eryn checked all those boxes. He was strong, yet fragile in many ways. The twins were pleased when Eryn was between them, and Eryn was happiest with them in his arms. It was no one's business what happened in the bedroom since the boys were twenty-one years old. They were old enough to make their own decisions. Still, Brad was relieved they weren't his boys. Thank the frozen damn stars.

"Connor and I cut the hydrogen ship loose. We didn't want to see it anymore," Mika said.

"That's understandable. I don't care about their damn ship. But we need to find out if there's more information we don't have."

Mika got up to grab the scientist's notes. "I saw something about the rockets in his notes." He spread it all out on the table in front of them. Together, they all leaned in closer, examining it.

"Look," he said, starting to read.

We—Environmental Project III (EP-III)—were assigned rocketry and DNA manipulation to ensure the superhuman race survives and thrives on the moon. They also tasked us with research to address fuel, oxygen, and water shortages. However, everything went wrong. Scratch that—it all fell apart.

The American Star Connect company funded the rockets built for human travel in cooperation with the WHPSS. A global effort to establish a lunar presence, and I suspect is the driving force was behind all this madness. Locate the number two mineshaft, marked in blue. It's the northwest tower near the Fochville ruins. Inside lies a rocket ready for human travel.

They all frowned, looking up.

"We didn't see a blue tower. It was brown-black, rusted, and not blue," Mika said.

They all looked at Eryn, who appeared to want to shrink away and disappear behind the Romanov twins.

"Eryn, do you know anything about the blue tower?" Mika asked, noticing that Eryn turned a few shades of green. He looked terrified. His big, cheerful smile from earlier had vanished, replaced by a look of dread. Then, he quickly lifted the twins and moved away from the table. Brad barely saw him move.

"No, no, no, no, no," he moaned into his hands. "That's not a good place to go. Eryn fears that place." He receded into himself, speaking in the third person.

"What's there, Eryn?" Mika asked.

Eryn sank to the floor, curling up as tightly as possible by pulling his legs to his chest and clasping his knees.

He barely touched the floor when the Romanov twins dropped to their knees, one on each side of Eryn. Narrowing their eyes at the group, they snarled like two giant white rabid poodles.

"Look what you've done!" They pointed at Eryn, who trembled. They surrounded him as if to shield him from the men around the table. "Eryn, look at us. You've done nothing wrong."

"Eryn isn't bad. Big monsters and men are bad. They are evil, evil, evil," he cried.

What in the ever-loving gory damn stars? Brad wanted to stop the fussing. He tried to be practical without making the situation worse. The Eryn he had gotten to know over the past few days was crumbling before them. Brad looked questioningly at the others, who shrugged. Gone was the mighty king. What remained was a frightened and vulnerable boy who needed validation for his feelings. The situation needed to be resolved as quickly as possible. He was among friends and should be free to share deeper conversations just as easily as surface-level banter, just like Brad did when he woke up freaking out.

He seized the opportunity to show Eryn and remind the children that it was okay to feel afraid, just as he was feeling at that moment. *I need to turn this into a teachable moment and demonstrate to them that they might regret their choices later if they don't confront their fears now.*

The raw terror and vulnerability in Eryn's eyes broke Brad's heart. He stood up from the table and squatted in front of the young man. "Eryn, please look at me. Remember when you were so brave and took care of me?"

Eryn rocked slower, turning his face to Brad.

"Yes, you took care of me. You made me better. Now let me help you. But, for us to help you, tell us what's scaring you like this."

Eryn looked up at Cian and Ivan, who nodded their approval.

"You know, we're your new family. We care about you just as much as you care about us. Can you feel our love and concern for you? We call that empathy."

Eryn stopped whimpering and became still. He closed his eyes and then opened them. One corner of his mouth pulled up in a half smile, and he nodded.

Brad continued. "Okay, that's good. Empathy means we imagine how we would feel if we were in your situation. However, to do that, we need to understand your specific situation. Understand? Remember when I sat down and invited you all to join me so we could discuss what was bothering us? I was so scared. I struggled to breathe, remember? All those feelings"—Brad put his bandaged hands around his own throat—"it choked me. It felt like I couldn't breathe. I didn't want to say that, but I did. And I promise you, it helps. Tell us so we can understand. Please, boy, trust us to help you?" Brad coaxed and then waited.

Eryn's posture and facial expression shifted instantly to a look of determination, despite the tears streaming from his strange eyes. His bottom lip trembled. "The monsters sleep there. I don't disturb them, and they don't disturb me."

"Are you saying we flooded tunnels, but there are more?" Brad confirmed, and Eryn nodded slowly, looking guilty.

"Yes, but they sleep. They never wake up. They are waiting."

"What are they waiting for?"

"They wait to be set free."

"I don't understand. Eryn, please share your entire story as much as you can. My boy, we need to know what we're dealing with." Brad nearly begged, his heart racing faster and faster. *Freezing hellfires!*

Eryn nodded and pushed himself up, sitting criss-cross with his long legs. Pulling his twins closer, he positioned each next to him, and then Brad moved closer, mirroring him by sitting cross-legged. He invited the other men to join the circle. Rick grabbed some pillows and brought them over, while Kawa and Donali carried plates and cups. Mika and Connor dished out breakfast and coffee before joining the circle as Eryn explained and ultimately faced his fears.

"Under the ground is a big place, just like my home. It also has a rocket. Inside, lots of humans from all over the world wait."

"As many as Phoenix's humans, or more or fewer?" Brad asked.

Eryn held his hands up and showed ten fingers.

"Ten people, ten thousand people?" Brad asked. Eryn shook his head.

"Ten times more than Phoenix."

"What, Eryn, are you saying about twenty thousand humans living underground in South Africa?"

Eryn shook his head. "Not living, sleeping."

"Where are they sleeping, Eryn? Do they have houses or apartments, as we have in Phoenix?" Brad asked, imagining Phoenix underground.

"They sleep in their glass beds, inside the rocket, and the monsters sleep with them, watching them."

"Watching over them, like guard dogs?" Brad asked.

"Yes." Eryn nodded.

"Why are you afraid of them?"

Eryn's eyebrows knitted together. He swallowed. "They're huge and really mean."

"Are they neurotoxic, like your Brawl brothers?"

"No, but they killed and ate my brothers. So maybe they'll kill and eat me too."

"Alright, let me share what I know and think, and then you can stop me. Please correct me if needed. We went through your..." Brad hesitated, reconsidered what he was about to say, and continued. "Your father's notes. Some people wanted to save the humans, but some wanted to eliminate all the humans."

Eryn bobbed his head up and down. "Yes, they fought over who was going and who was staying. Then, when they were ready to go, explosions occurred, and someone helped my brothers escape. I locked my father in his office after he told me to fetch my brothers. They ran and ran. Ernest laughed and laughed, enjoying himself so much. I cried. So many dead people. My brothers were too many for me to catch. Humans resorted to guns and bombs, and when that didn't work, they unleashed the monsters. More bombs, shooting, and fighting followed. There were lots of explosions and many more humans perishing. Eryn didn't know where to run. Must Eryn follow them in Africa, or what? My brothers were everywhere, and the poison spread everywhere. So many people were dead. Huge monsters chased us and ate my brothers while Ernest laughed, still having fun. They devoured my brothers. I ran as fast as I could to save them. But the monsters got so furious, releasing more and more poison into the air. Finally, I had had enough." Eryn paused, wiping his tears and sniffling. "I screamed, 'This is enough killing! Stop now! Go home!' They all turned and went home."

"What a horrible story," Brad reciprocated, thinking that if he had known all this sooner, he would've bombed everything to bits and then used Mika's cannons to level it all.

Mika broke the tension. "So, do we still need these?" Holding up two anti-toxin shots. He looked suddenly keen to get to a lab and have cases of the stuff reproduced.

"How old were you when this happened, Eryn?" Brad asked, frowning because something didn't add up.

"I was a young boy Brawl."

"I ask because sometimes everything looks bigger when you're small. So, if you were a young boy, can you remember what cars, trucks, and buses were?"

Eryn nodded eagerly. "I remember the truck full of gold."

"Good. Were these monsters bigger than cars, trucks, or buses?"

"Yeah, that's a good question," Connor encouraged, realizing where Brad was going with this.

Eryn blew out his cheeks and then released the air slowly. He was silent for a few seconds. Then he shook his head. "No, they were not that big."

What a beautiful sight it was when Eryn realized they were not as big.

"So, they were smaller than a bus?" He nodded in the affirmative. "Smaller than a truck?"

Again, he nodded yes. Please be smaller than a car, Brad wished. "Eryn, is one of those monsters smaller than a car?"

"No, about the size or bigger."

"About the size of a car?" Brad confirmed. "Okay, that's good. Now we all know that. Can you tell me how many are there?"

"I don't know. I'm not sure. They don't communicate with me as my Brawl did. I told them to go home, and they did, but maybe they went back because the nest returned? I'm not sure. Since then, I've left them alone, and they leave me alone."

"I need more coffee and something to eat." Connor got up.

Brad nodded. *I need something stronger.*

"That's fine. We will continue. Just listen with one ear. You may pick up something we don't," he said to Connor. Then turning to Eryn, he asked, "Who told you to leave them alone, and they will leave you alone? That sounds like something your father would say."

"Hmmm, yes, yes."

"Okay, so did you sneak there? How do you know they're sleeping?"

"They're stacked in glass sleeping boxes."

"Jesus Christ, where's that coffee, Connor?" Mika asked, getting up to make another pot of coffee.

Brad shook his head. "Don't worry about Mika. He's just surprised, that's all. You're doing well. How many rockets with how many people, Eryn?" Brad waited while Eryn counted on his fingers.

"There were five rockets. Two left for the moon, one exploded, one rocket where Eryn and Ernest's home was with my nest to protect the rocket. And the one at the blue mineshaft, where the humans sleep with their guard dogs," he said disgustedly.

"Are the guard dogs neurotoxic and dangerous to us?" Brad asked, patiently waiting for Eryn to think, which took a long, bloody time, before he shook his head and answered.

"No, they're only dangerous to us, Brawls."

"So, they watched the humans and guarded them against you, too?"

Eryn pulled his shoulders up high.

"Eryn, do they look like humans or animals?"

"They look like dogs and wolves, big dogs with ugly yellow eyes. Eryn remembers those eyes very well. I see them when I have nightmares, as you do at night, Brad."

A round of chuckles followed, and Brad felt proud of himself because he'd been honest earlier.

"What do Brawls look like? Do they look like you?"

"No, the first Brawls look like frogs, but more man than animal. They looked a lot like Ernest. They were born in a nest separate from me. According to my father, they are Colombian poison dart frogs with special skin glands that secrete toxins."

The twins cringed. "Ernest was the crazy psycho frogman that chewed my arm off," Kawa exclaimed. "He looked like a tree frog." They laughed.

Brad smiled at the boys making jokes, he'd seen the ugly thing when he'd tied it up.

"So, the guard dogs watch the humans, and they protect the humans from Brawls?"

"No, they kill everything that's not human."

"They were supposed to protect the humans." Brad put his hand on Eryn's. "Do you agree? Eryn, you're human. You said you were a boy Brawl. You were a boy."

Eryn nodded. The twins stroked his short, dirty blond curls lovingly.

"Brad's saying they won't harm you because you're human. You're more human than some men, so these guard dogs can't harm you. That's why they didn't hurt you, and that's why they listened to you," Ivan said.

"Because you were barely five years old, you didn't understand what was happening. You didn't know what you were. That's why your father sent you to live with Joshua, so you could see humans and live like one. It was the best thing he could have done for you, allowing you to grow up among humans and understand the difference." Brad explained what he thought had been going through the scientist's mind.

"Your father and the other scientists dabbled with science and played God. They created beings they couldn't predict or control," Mika added.

Brad rolled his eyes.

"I think we need to turn back, my boy. We need to let those people go. Let the rocket fly. Let them take those animals with them. That's their purpose. Do you agree?"

Eryn wiped the snot from his nose. Cian took his t-shirt off and bundled it in his lap to be used as a tissue.

"Yes, I agree."

"We can't kill those people by flooding the tunnels, but we can send them where they wanted to go. That's the only way to resolve this by doing the right thing. So that's why you didn't flood those tunnels, not because of the dogs, but the thousands of humans?"

"Yes." He sniffled.

"With our help, especially Mika and Connor's help, I'm sure we can send them to the moon."

They all agreed that it was the right thing to do. They got up feeling hungry and determined to finish breakfast. After that, they went upstairs to confront the traitor.

CHAPTER 20
THE LOOT

"*Morning, citizens of Phoenix.*

It's now six a.m.

Did you know that it's common knowledge that folklore is based on truth? The notion of vampirism has existed for millennia, and ancient cultures such as the Mesopotamians, Ancient Greeks, and Romans spoke of tales of vampire-like species living among humans.

Just think, these revenants of ancient beings roaming the land, incapable of dying, might have lived among you.

Visit our community news page to reserve your spot for movie night. We're featuring Transylvania's exterminators One, Two, and Three.

Breakfast is served until eight a.m.

Have a happy Halloween!"

. . .

Dr. Mika Romanov

"Did you know liquid propellant experimentation happened as early as the nineteen-forties?" Mika asked while leaning in and supporting himself on the ship's rail with his elbows while holding his binoculars. "Even before I met Dr. John Saunders, who invited me to come work at Phoenix, governments begged me for my research on alternative fuels for rocketry and space travel. If I asked, the bastards would have done anything for me, nearly climbing into my lap and licking my face. Only I would have liked a good ass licking much more, comrade, if you catch my meaning." He snickered, adjusting his binoculars.

"No, thank you. I don't want to imagine a bunch of government officials licking your ass. That's not my thing," Brad replied, pretending to spit hair out of his mouth. They both burst out laughing.

"Oye, will ye stop your joking and playing around? My arms are tired, and I'm getting bloody hungry," Connor said with a thick Irish accent.

"I would tell you to come rest your arms on the side rail like us, but you're too short unless you want to sit on my shoulders," Mika teased.

Brad snorted and giggled.

"Connor, should I go get a little chair downstairs

so you can see over the side of the ship?" Rick asked, all seriousness in his tone.

"Piss off," Connor said with a snarl, and brought on another round of laughing at his expense.

Laughter drifted from the otherwise soundless flying ship. The men enjoyed the back-and-forth banter while searching the horizon for the hydrogen ship they'd cut loose three nights before. The skies were deep indigo, with barely a breeze or cloud in sight. Therefore, the vessel should be almost in the same spot where Mika and Connor had cut it loose and left it.

Connor had used radar earlier and could ping the tracker Bryan had attached to it, so they had a general direction to search. "It should come into our field of vision any moment now, so keep your eyes open," Connor said.

After their hostage explained it had schematics needed to determine the propulsion force of the rocket mathematically, they started looking for the thing. Knowing the rocket's size, weight, and dimensions, they could make the correct calculations to achieve lift-off.

"And here we are, force equals mass times acceleration, so we avoid catastrophe by not killing twenty thousand humans. Oopsie-daisy, we need those schematics," Mika said jokingly.

"And that's why we're playing *Battleship* today,

yeah," Rick said dryly, still searching through his binoculars.

"Ha-ha-ha, that was a good one, love!" Brad complimented.

"Thank you," Rick said stoically. "*Peep, peep, peep, Boooooooooookkkkkkssssshh.*" He mimicked the widely known sounds of the electronic talking *Battleship* game.

"Yeah, ten points to Rick for originality today. I didn't see that one coming," Connor shouted, who sat and rested his arms on the ship's wheel for support. "Oh, no, I shouldn't have said I'm coming. Okay, you childish geniuses, let's not talk about coming again."

"You mean 'yeah, baby, again, and again and again'," Brad tried but failed dismally. No one laughed.

"The first thing to do is to run a few experimental firings. I have a theory that we don't need gallons of fuel. We also don't need any oxidizers. We would have to do these tests outdoors, as any sane scientist would," Mika said, cutting into the joking while still searching for the hydrogen ship through his binoculars.

"Yes, we aren't a suicide squad," Connor added from the back of the helm.

"I figured that," Brad added, back to scanning the horizon and focusing his binoculars. "Tell me, what's your plan?"

"Nuclear power. I'll ask Eryn to sing to the atoms.

The fission would create enough thrust by heating hydrogen gas."

"Hmmm, nuclear fission, you think vibrations would break down radioactive atoms?" Brad asked, pointing to something on the horizon. "Look over there!"

"Yes, I have a feeling they have hydrogen gas onboard. Why would these ass-wipes hint toward the hydrogen-propelled airship? They needed a reactor, and I think Eryn's the key. His sound waves should be able to excite the gas molecules to expand rapidly and stream out of the engine nozzle. So, it'll be a kind of nuclear-powered balloon rocket." Mika pointed to where Brad saw something. "There it is, Connor. Do you see it?"

"Yes, I see it, yelda." He looked down at the tied-up man, who divulged his name as Nick. "See, easy-peasy."

The man scowled.

They used grappling hooks to pull it closer.

"Untie me! I'll get you the stuff."

"Nope." Brad scoffed.

"Why not?"

"Number one"—Brad showed him his left middle finger—"I don't trust you. Number two"—Brad showed him his right middle finger—"I don't trust you. And number three"—Brad hooked his right arm over the left—"guess what number three is?"

"That's very childish coming from the leader of Phoenix," grumbled the still-bound man.

"That's where you're mistaken, Nick. I'm not the leader of Phoenix. They've replaced all of us. We can do whatever we want for as long as we want, and there's absolutely nothing that you or anyone else can say about it. We're free agents, buddy. The world is our oyster, Nick, or whoever you are."

Connor, Mika, and Rick knew Brad was talking shit, but it seemed to work because Nick's eyes couldn't get bigger.

"Finally, the asshole understands what's going on," Brad said, and the others laughed.

"I thought something was wrong with you, the way you hit Charles," Nick sneered.

"Yes, I rather enjoyed that," Brad said, eyeing Mika, both glad the kids were downstairs. "Just like I'll enjoy throwing you overboard with this hook through your ass." He showed him the hook they planned to use by throwing it over the side, hooking and pulling the other ship closer, and the men laughed again.

"You sick bastards, stay away from me!"

Brad continued his emotional battering by pretending to come closer. Nick kicked, making sure they knew he would fight a good fight.

"So, shut up!" Brad shouted at Nick. "I don't want to hear a word from you."

Mika had Brad join him, and they jumped over to

the hydrogen ship. A few minutes later, they returned with bags full of information.

"Thank you for all your research and data." Mika struggled to lift the heavy bags filled with ancient tablets, maps, books, and all kinds of secret intelligence. "It must have taken you eons to collect these. Thank you." Mika laughed like Santa Claus. "Ho-ho-ho." By now, they were giddy with laughter.

Opening the hatch to go downstairs to sift through their new belongings, Brad gave Nick his best evil pirate look. "Arr!" Then he shut the door and left Nick alone, cold and tied up.

Arriving downstairs was another matter. Eryn was lying on his back, spread out on the sofa bench, with the twins busy eating his face. The three moaned and groaned, enjoying themselves in a three-way kissing festival. Still fully clothed, they ground and rolled their hips. The twins rutted shamelessly on each of Eryn's hip bones while Eryn looked like he was fucking the air. Each time he elevated his hips, he lifted the twins, sending them rolling, but somehow the facial suction never lost its grip. The passionate kissing and licking of tongues was quite a sight. Eryn had an arm around each twin, squeezing them closer for more friction.

"*Hmmm*." Mika coughed, clearing his throat.

"Excuse us!" Connor shouted.

"Thank the gods. It's not my kids." Brad boasted, and Mika didn't know what to do. Brad stepped aside, showing him the floor sarcastically, then stepped away so Connor and Mika could proceed. Mika saw Brad out of the corner of his eye, and finding Rick, the two silently watched the scene play out from the back.

Eryn finally noticed they weren't alone and threw the twins so high their heads hit the low-hanging ceiling. The three young men were vertical in an instant. It looked like Connor was praying. His eyes were closed, and Mika heard, "Hail Mary, Mother of god."

Still, in a state of animated suspension, Mika felt like he wanted to attack, thought better midway, and paused.

His boys landed butt first.

"Oh, frog balls," Eryn said, bending forward to help them up, but they jumped up so fast, giving him a headshot on his nose and side of his head, knocking the Brawl King flat onto his back, pulling Cian with him, who fell forward, face first and nose up into his balls. "Argh," Eryn grabbed onto his injured anatomy and nose, moaning and groaning.

Mika closed his mouth with an audible snap, turned, and disappeared through the revolving doors.

ERYN, King of the Brawl
Connor grabbed a hand towel and gave it to Eryn.

"Sit down and firmly pinch the soft part of your nose, just above your nostrils."

Ivan stepped forward to help. "Lean forward and breathe through your mouth."

"Father, we can explain," Cian interjected.

To Eryn's surprise, Connor sat down and spoke calmly. "No, we're sorry to barge in here. The ship is small, and we're all adults. I'll explain it this way. Your dad and I are the same. You don't want to see your father and me having sex, do you?"

"Ugh, no," Ivan said.

"So, I think to use that as a reference, and then you know how we feel seeing you like this. What's most upsetting for us is that you're brothers, which is wrong on many levels. But with that said, it's your own private business, but I'm not approving of incest. And your father's not supporting it. But parents have not approved of and discouraged many things in life. It pushed the kids away and caused more harm than good. I'm Roman Catholic, but they also used to condemn homosexuals, saying it was just as wrong. So, please, we love both of you..."

Ivan interrupted to explain. "But it's not like that. We want Eryn, and he wants us. We don't want each other like that." Ivan spoke slowly and clearly, so Connor understood. Eryn nodded his agreement.

Connor seemed to relax. "Please do things like this in private. Wait till we're home."

"Yes, Dad," the twins said.

"Yes, Connor," Eryn added. His face was a mix of various shades of red and pink.

"We promise," all three said again. Connor dipped his chin.

"I'm going to speak with your father now," Connor said as he got up, but Cian and Ivan stopped him.

"No, please, Dada, we will. We want to talk to him. We need to explain this to Papa. He's distraught, and we know it. I saw his face."

Connor gave them half a smile and added, "I know." Then sagged into a chair with his head hanging low.

Eryn led the twins out via the rotating door to find Mika. When they arrived on the deck, their prisoner called to them.

Shackled to the mast, Nick called, "Hey, I need to talk to the three of you."

"Not now, old man. We're looking for our father," Cian said.

The prisoner raised his chin and pointed to the other ship. Someone had placed bowls of food and water, similar to those used for dogs, near him.

"Who brought you water?" Ivan asked with a grin, projecting Eryn's thoughts and rubbing salt into it.

"Your self-righteous leader, General Brad McCormick."

"He's your leader, too, you terrorist!" Eryn defended Brad.

"I'm not a dog!" Nick screamed and kicked at the bowls. Pieces of bread and water splattered and splashed everywhere except on them.

"Horrible aim, *tisk-tisk-tisk*," Eryn said.

Turning their backs on him, they laughed and boarded the ship via the gangplank from the Halcyon straight into the doorway of the wooden shack.

Holding the wheel, Mika steered the ship to nowhere as he stared out the window in front of him.

Ivan and Cian grabbed Mika around the waist simultaneously. "Father!"

Eryn felt like the odd one out. But after years of watching them interacting from afar, he expected to see this level of intimacy.

"We're sorry. It shouldn't have been done. We explained to Dad, and now we want to talk to you." Cian spoke into Mika's shoulder. Both boys were taller than Mika at two meters.

"Father, I don't want to go into unnecessary details, but the easiest way to explain it is that we both like Eryn a lot and never fight about toys or anything. It's dumb. You taught us to share or get another toy. We're so used to sharing that it doesn't bother us to want Eryn, and he wants both of us. We don't..."

Mika interrupted them. "That's your own private business, what you do in the bedroom. We raised you correctly. I should trust that you can make the right choices. But this is very difficult for me to accept. It is not..." Mika stood rigidly straight.

He opened and closed his fists, as if he were struggling to control his temper and preventing himself from saying something impulsively. Fine tremors in his clothing betrayed the calm demeanor he falsely portrayed.

"It's just that I've never foreseen this for you. I never wanted this for you. I never even entertained the thought of you two..." He turned back and then pointed to the three of them. "Somehow, I thought maybe you would choose Donali or Kawa."

They pulled their faces.

"No, that's just wrong, Father. They're like our brothers," Cian said impulsively.

Eryn read Mika's micro-expressions.

Mika grunted, and he lifted his eyebrows.

Ivan's shoulder bumped Cian, and then they chortled. Cian realized what they'd just been saying. "Okay, I know how that sounds, but let me explain, Father. We're brothers, yes, but I'll never want to share Eryn with anyone else," Cian said.

"And I feel the same," Ivan said.

"So, you share him?"

"Of course!" Eryn lifted his hands and shoulders, very proud to be shared by the twins. "Sorry, Mika, it just happened that both want me, and I want both."

Mika glared at Eryn. He sensed Mika wanted to attack and kill him for ruining his perfect boys. He pinned Eryn's amphibious gaze with his, and although the twins spoke, he didn't break contact.

"It's like sharing a huge ice cream," Cian said.

Ivan rolled his eyes. "Dear lord, brother, you're making it worse. Please stop."

Mika lifted a hand. "Yes, please stop. That's way too much information. I don't need that visual," Mika begged, finally releasing Eryn from his death glare. He rubbed his face vigorously up and down with both hands. But then, like the sun peeking from behind a dark cloud, it seemed to make sense to him.

"Cian is saying that we share him. He's ours, and we're his. Nothing's happening between Cian and me."

"Yes, that's what I said," Cian added.

"My brother is pretty, but we don't plan to or would ever be attracted to or do things with each other," Ivan clarified.

"I think I hear what you're trying to explain. It feels more acceptable if you describe it that way."

"Yes, that was what Dada said, too."

"You realize you'll repeatedly hear many people asking the same question?"

"That's okay. We don't mind."

Mika took a big breath, relaxing his posture. He appeared worried about his boys.

"Father, you always said we were the last Romanov princes, and Eryn's the Brawl King, so it's a royal affair," Cian said jokingly.

Mika turned, rolling his eyes. Looking out the window into the blue distance, his gaze caught their reflection in the glass. He watched the three of them holding hands. Eryn's between them. They couldn't stop touching him.

"It would be wrong to break us up," Eryn added softly, showing he had just read Mika's mind. He sent a look begging him to look closer at their reflections. *They made us for each other.* He said to Mika, mind to mind. *Look, I'm holding them up, and they are holding on to me.*

Mika turned back to them, changing the subject. "Okay, do you think you three would like to have this ship? It's only the basics. You would have to come to us for meals," he asked.

The twins' eyes sparkled. "Our ship?" Cian and Ivan asked.

"I don't know if it's yours, but for now, yes."

"We have to ask Donali and Kawa to join us," Ivan said, always including the McCormick brothers.

"Maybe the McCormick boys joining would keep you three from devouring each other," Mika said with a lopsided grin.

"Yes, let's go get them and bring our stuff," Cian said excitedly, bouncing up and down on the balls of his feet.

They embraced Mika. Eryn loved every second of it until Mika broke away with watery eyes.

"*They're so innocent, look after them,*" Mika said,

surprising Eryn by speaking to him telepathically as he opened the cabin door. "Okay, I'm returning to the Halcyon. I'll send the McCormick boys over," he said out loud, smiling sadly. *"Time to let my little birds fly"*

"I will protect them, I promise," Eryn said out loud.

"We have a ship, Eryn!" The twins jumped up and down.

CHAPTER 21
DISCIPLES OF THE ANUNNAKI

"*Good morning, citizens of Phoenix.*

It's now six a.m.

Did you know that in twenty-twenty-two, the most trusted AI bots were female, and their names were Alexa and Siri?

But in twenty-twenty-forty, scientists confirmed that above human-level artificial intelligence is male, and his name is Lasitor.

Visit your community news page for interesting facts about the first technologies.

Breakfast is served until eight a.m.

Have a bright day!"

Eryn, King of the Brawl

. . .

ERYN STEALTHILY MADE his way toward the entrance of the mineshaft marked *Blue*. He felt uneasy, as if he'd forgotten something important.

He groaned and inwardly cringed when he reached the heavy metal doors. He crept closer, checking the rusted tracks, and to his relief, confirmed there wasn't any movement and that nobody had touched the massive doors since he was last there. Eryn hated coming to the place. He felt the people's dread and despair, which made him feel extremely uneasy. The things that haunted him in his sleep lived down here. So, he planned to be as fast and quiet as a mouse. "In and out, quick-quick," he whispered to himself, copying the general's words from earlier.

He grabbed the massive, rusted handles, pushed the door open, and slipped into the spooky entrance. Chills ran down his spine. Next to his head, Connor's weird camera ball floated and followed him. He had so many new things to get used to, but this new technology excited him because it was human-made, designed and created by the ice-people, and he had dreamed of being part of them and their shiny things for so long. Eryn wanted to prove himself to Brad and his men, but he also wanted to impress the twins.

Because only two anti-toxin shots were available, he volunteered to go on the intelligence, surveillance, and reconnaissance mission. Again, he repeated Brad's big words, teaching himself.

They'd voted and decided his job was to sneak inside the compound and open the gigantic doors to the mineshaft, so Connor could send the camera ball inside to collect information to help investigate their enemy. After ensuring the ball was safely inside, he turned around and ran, kicking up dirt and dust. The place gave him the heebie-jeebies. So he hollowed his back, tucked his tail, moved his legs, and skedaddled right out of there.

Just as he exited the gates, he froze in his tracks, seeing the twins about thirty meters out, waiting for him. Instantaneously, he felt happy to see them, but their demeanor was all wrong. Their eyes were serious, and they weren't smiling. Instead, their heads hung low, and Eryn sensed a somber cloud hanging around them. His heart rate sped up, and his hackles rose. Stepping closer, he scanned their surroundings simultaneously.

"What's wrong? Why are you upset?" He kept smiling, keeping up his appearance while his eyes looked around, searching for something out of place. He felt like they were being watched and spotted two tips of black boots pointing past the ruins of a dilapidated old security checkpoint and office building. The twins' eyes darted back and forth, trying to warn him of the danger, but he'd already assessed the situation. With one leap, Eryn jumped in front of them, bumping into them so hard that they flew a few meters and landed safely behind a piece of concrete.

"Freezing hellfires!" Cian exclaimed.

"Bloody damn hell, was that necessary, Eryn?" Ivan asked.

Eryn wanted to laugh, but it wasn't a good time, so he straightened up and said, "Yes." Happy that the twins were out of sight and amused by their antics. The twins inherited their Russian father's charm and crude choice of language, and although Eryn heard a few more remarks, he focused on Nick, who spoke and showed his face from around the corner. In his right hand, he held a flare gun. He narrowed his dark, beady eyes on them and grinned smugly. Eryn stepped back in a fighting stance with his trident ready. He knew flare guns from Phoenix and that they could be dangerous. They could kill if fired directly at a person, especially at short distances. Some humans changed them to shoot bullets, so he hoped this wasn't a converted weapon.

"Hello again, Eryn," Nick greeted self-righteously.

"Put down your gun, and I won't hurt you," Eryn demanded with a low, gruff voice. He locked his eyes on Nick and waited like a cobra, ready to strike.

"You have to know I'm not naïve enough to believe that. You are, after all, a killer, aren't you?" Eryn felt shame and regret, but then he remembered who he was and what his new friend Brad had told him. Eryn is the king of the brawl. *I am human, and I am a friend of humans. I'm a good boy.* He straightened his spine and drew strength from the goodness within him when he remembered how Brad had hugged and accepted him. He would fight for the icemen. "I fight for good humans," he said sternly. "I never wanted to kill anyone, but bad people have forced me to."

"We're the ones who know how much damage has been done and what you can do. We know why the military didn't shoot you. I know why you're still alive, and I'll tell you why they're all waiting for you. For you and your twins," Nick said, all puffed up and sure of himself.

Eryn frowned and rolled his eyes in exasperation. Then, in the corner of his eye, he saw the twins on their hands and knees, poking from behind the barricade.

"Your fate was determined long ago. The birth of you and the twins was foretold and planned."

Eryn frowned, shaking his head at the twins. He turned sideways so Nick didn't see his hand shooing the twins back to safety.

"You don't have a clue what the reason for all this is?"

"Then tell us, Mr. Rocket scientist." Eryn attempted to keep Nick's attention directed toward him.

"Why do you think you're here on their twenty-second birthday?"

"What are you talking about, you crazy asshole?" Cian yelled from behind the piece of concrete.

Goosebumps appeared on his arms, and his hair

stood up as jolts of energy rushed through him at breakneck speed. Eryn's fear and annoyance at the damn cheeky brother reached indescribable proportions. Eryn vaguely remembered hearing a similar story before. It sounded familiar to him. He wondered if Joshua or his father had told him the story. With a stern expression, he was ready to defend and attack Nick and determined not to be distracted.

"Why twenty-two, Nick? What makes twenty-two so special? I hope you baked us a cake and put forty-four candles on it," yelled Ivan.

Nick shook his head.

"We don't mind. Sharing is something we love to do. We share Eryn, too." Cian added teasingly, mocking Nick by sticking his tongue out at Nick, who looked flabbergasted. Eryn stood his ground, not moving, while he listened to the twins being fearlessly disrespectful, having fun at the idiot's expense. It did funny things to his insides, and Eryn wanted to throw them over his lap and spank them.

"Your daddies aren't as smart as they think they are. We helped them decide on Project One. They followed our lead from the very beginning. We're your Disciples, and you're direct descendants of An and Ki, the Goddesses of the earth. Your name, Ivan, means the fourth, or the Roman letter IV, for the mighty IV-An. And your name, Cian, spells Ki-AN. You're Anunnaki, and your primary function is to decree the fates of humanity."

His face popped purple-red welts of frustration as the twins guffawed at him like two drunk monkeys. His determination grew. Bulging his fists, he ranted on. "Your mother is not a human Scandinavian with blue eyes. No, your DNA is Mesopotamian Anunnaki..."

The twins interrupted him.

"You mean our egg donor was a Mesopotamian Anunnaki? Sorry, man, I'm just saying there's no way an egg survived five hundred thousand years. They can barely make it past twenty-eight days. And I'm very sure Moses didn't carry a refrigerator through the desert," Ivan retorted. Cian patted him on the shoulder for a job well done.

Nick ignored them, determined to say his piece as he stood on his proverbial soapbox. "You inherited your extremely high IQs, perfect health, and undeniable beauty from her. You possess extraordinary powers, and I bet he knows that." He pointed toward Eryn. "He knows you have powers, the same powers he has. Humans didn't possess the technology to extract the deity's holy DNA for thousands of years. We know for sure this is the time your mother predicted. It's written on the Babylonian tablets and guarded until she reveals it to us. The time of the Big Flood. It's written as the Year of the Twins. I can show you the tablets, but that would have to be once you're on board. We must leave now. Your parents can join us. It was also predicted that the world would end and Luna would welcome us. So many souls are already waiting for you. You three will lead us into the future."

Nick fell to his knees. It seemed he was not above begging.

"Please, I beg of you, listen to me. The three of you are like your mother, the Goddess of love, sexuality, and war."

Cian and Ivan rolled on the ground, holding their tummies, cackling. Eryn knew they were different, and he wondered if there might be some truth to what the man was spewing. When they sang to him the first time, it wasn't with their human voices. It was more. Their souls recognized each other. He felt a pull toward them, and he was sure they felt the same tug to be with him.

Nick continued his plea. "Please, boys, I need you to come with me. I'm sorry you have to hear this under these circumstances. I'm desperate for you to listen to me. We've been standing guard for so long. Waiting for you. And I'm sadly the only one left to meet you here. We should have told you earlier, but our leader, Charles, felt it was better to wait until you noticed the change within you. But then you were abducted, and we didn't know where to find you."

That was a blessing. Thank you, Ernest.

Eryn suddenly felt better about the abduction.

"So, we stood guard and watched you from afar. The three of you are unique and supposed to work together. You belong together for a much bigger reason than you think. Indeed, you have seen what he can do. It's your birthday, and your powers will reveal themselves and grow daily. From today, you're no longer boys but men. You are gods. You are Anunnaki. You're leaving your human selves behind. The older you grow, the stronger you will be. Why do you think the Peter Pan Caps let Phoenix live so long? It's your placenta inside those gel capsules."

Eryn smiled. While the crazy man on his knees with the flare gun had been ranting about gods and the Anunnaki, Ivan and Cian sat behind the boulder, pulling cross-eyed faces at him.

"All these people are waiting for you. You only have to get on the rocket with them. Once you're on the moon, you can call forth water and air for us."

Eryn was tired of this. He wanted to get home and ravish his twins. Bugger the moon, and bloody bugger it all. He wanted the twins to eat their birthday cake. "I'm tired of this shit," he said, stomping his trident onto the ground. Pieces of frozen earth flew up. "I'm going home to Phoenix. Come." He signaled with two fingers as if directing traffic to the twins.

"No, I can't let you do that. Get on the rocket!" Nick got up and pointed his flare gun at Eryn. Eryn swiped his trident to the side, as if waving off an irritating fly. The gun flew out of Nick's hand.

"Get out of our way. We don't care about your

crusade for the moon. We want to stay here. So, you get on the rocket and blast off!"

Nick scowled. He roughly searched the collar of his shirt and pulled out something shiny on a chain around his neck. With a voice loaded with malice, he said, "Sorry, you give me no choice," then he raised his arm, and Eryn realized it was a small silver whistle he inserted between his thin lips, and blew on it so hard his eyes bulged.

Eryn heard a faint, high-pitched sound that cut through his mind. Nick held onto the whistle that seemed to be attached to a chain around his neck.

"What did you do?" Eryn asked and didn't want to know.

It's those monsters, and they're coming.

A flashback came to him when he heard that high-pitched whistle, where humans lay strewn and dead at his feet.

"Just wait. They'll be here any moment," Nick said sanctimoniously.

"No, not the monsters!" Paralyzing terror overcame Eryn. "We need to get out of here!" he yelled at the twins, who stood frozen in their tracks.

The telltale rumbling of a stampede grew louder as the earth beneath them vibrated. Next, the sound of paws pitter-pattering grew closer and closer. Then they saw them. A pack of snarling black beasts appeared one by one from around the door—the door Eryn had just pushed open.

The yellow-eyed animals from my nightmares are going to eat me and the twins. I need to get them out of here!

"Ha-ha! Now you're not feeling so bold, are you?" Nick asked sarcastically, his voice laced with malice.

He's a bad man, Eryn thought as he hyperventilated. "Call your dogs off!" His voice was shaky, his body quivering with fear. He stepped backward and lifted his trident, ready to defend or at least poke an eye out.

"Not dogs. They're sacred jackals, or better, Anubis. They guard humans who serve the Anunnaki. A gift from the gods. To safeguard and protect humans in this life and the afterlife."

"Freezing hellfires, they're ugly. Where's the hair? They look like overgrown sewer rats!" Cian shouted. With an *oomph*, both twins bumped into Eryn, waking him from paralyzing fear. They supported him as they braced for an attack.

"No wonder you have nightmares, Eryn," Ivan whispered.

What? Eryn couldn't believe the twins weren't scared or fleeing. "This is not the time for jokes." Although he enjoyed the careless banter, if they were shredded into pieces, he remembered Connor's ball camera and hoped it had recorded this. Mika would kill him if he survived, and they didn't.

"One blow on my whistle, and they'll attack the

twins," Nick threatened, placing the whistle to his lips.

Eryn froze. He was well aware of what those dogs were capable of.

"Okay, okay," the twins interjected. "Let Eryn go, and we'll go with you."

"Not a chance. You two stay right here. I'll go with them," Eryn said, meaning it. However, life on the moon without his twins would be a sad and lonely experience.

I just tasted them, dammit.

"No, let's take turns. Rock, paper, scissors decide who stays and who goes," Cian suggested eagerly. White-blond hair braided neatly down his back certainly didn't go with his wayward personality. Eryn wanted to ruffle him up, make him forget his name.

Eryn momentarily forgot where they were while Nick stood by, looking as if he were watching a tennis match.

"Wait a minute, why don't the three of us go together?" Ivan, the brightest spark plug in their three-wheel motor, said. He was usually the level-headed one of the three lovers, said. *Was he being sarcastic?*

"Yeah, that's it. Then we can rule the moon and look at the earth explode together," Eryn said, catching on.

"Aw, that's so romantic." Cian clapped his hands with admiration in his eyes.

First, Nick looked confused, then said nothing.

Shaking his head, he motioned for them to walk.

"Yeah, Eryn, can we go now?" The twins skipped and sang. *We're going to the moon, far away to the other side, la-la-la-la.*

"What's wrong with you? Aren't you scared? Look at those creatures!" Eryn animatedly asked in disbelief.

"I counted at least ten Volkswagen minibus-size beasts surrounding us. Their yellow eyes follow every step you take."

Eryn looked again. They weren't snarling, and saliva wasn't dripping as he imagined. No, they were waiting.

"Pfft, no, we're not scared. We're positive they won't hurt us. Remember, they don't kill humans who serve Anunnaki," Ivan said.

"But he has a whistle," Eryn said frantically. Confused by his lovers' behavior. First, they say go, then they say stay, and now he can't remember what the last decision was supposed to be. He didn't want to see the two of them being torn apart. Their fathers would kill him, put him back together, and kill him again. That was if he didn't get savagely eaten, as well.

"Nah," Cian pfft nonchalantly.

"If we're as smart as he says we are, we know he

knows there's no way to force us to do anything," Ivan stated, very sure of himself.

Cian threw his arm around his brother's neck and turned back to Nick. "And, for your information, if we want to go to the moon, we won't go in your stinking rocket. We can fly there on our own because we're earth-dwelling deities. Maybe we want to go with our spaceship." They bent over double as they laughed.

"Oh, that's right. We didn't forget who we were dealing with. You're already comfortable destroying this planet. Why should you be trusted with the moon?" they asked, and Nick almost swallowed the whistle.

"We worked very hard for thousands of years. We operated in the shadows, the Disciples of the Anunnaki. Working hard, always listening, and always waiting for you!" Nick shouted at them.

Ivan crossed his arms. "That's just sad. And here you are begging us to take you with us. You and Charles told my parents that they were not chosen, yet it seems to me that they were chosen to be our vessels for rebirth. Like Mary had Jesus, don't you think Mika and Connor deserve more respect from you?" he asked.

Nick laughed at Ivan. "Mary was one of our Disciples. If your parents had joined us, then they would have been worthy. You think we're here in a gold mine by accident?" Nick pointed to Eryn. "You think your obsession with gold is coincidental? Since the dawn of time, it has drawn our gods. The Babylonian tablets prove that gold mining goes back several hundred thousand years, long before the indoctrinated religions existed. They wrote your DNA string code inside a golden capsule. The gods wanted it to be handed down from generation to generation, until such time that technology existed to bring it back to us. Open your minds and see the truth. Ancient gods populated the world, and humans need them as much as they or you need us. The gods must live among us and share their knowledge and wisdom. We are ready. We ripped ourselves out of the clutches of unworthy oppression and are no longer slaves to them." Nick held his arms out and turned in a circle. "We cleansed the earth for you, so you may rise and live forever among us."

"Now, that's the biggest load of crap I ever heard." A male voice said, and the sound of applause came from all around them. Connor's camera ball floated to the right above their heads. That didn't deter Nick at all. He continued to sell his spiel.

"Open your minds. Living with our gods, our creators, is what we need to return to. Our original state. They are the ones who need to lead us. That is our reward. We're their deserving chosen Disciples."

Nick was back to begging, hands clasped in front of him and an expression of urgency, life, and death on his face. "Please, you're the Anunnaki explorers who came to Earth five hundred thousand years ago. The twin gods are reborn. They gave you this planet as a gift from your father to be mined. You came in search of gold. They need gold to save your home planet, which is overheating. Gold is the lowest non-reactive metal, so they set multitudes of mining operations into action, concentrated here in southern Africa, the oldest settlement of the gods on Earth. Anunnaki created a mixture of their DNA and created the first primitive mine worker or slave species to excavate the gold."

"Wait a minute!" Brad's voice boomed from the ball above the twins' heads. "Are you saying they destroyed their planet, flew here, then emptied this planet, and now they all must go to the moon? For what?"

Nick rolled his eyes at that question as if Brad was asking the stupidest question ever.

"This man is the perfect picture of crazy. Let's get out of here," Cian said.

"Listen, thank you for the history lesson. We understand that you've been planning this for a long time. However, we believe our minds are open to spreading knowledge and love to those we care about. All those nice things about religion and humans like yourself embrace. Unfortunately for you, we prefer to stay here on Earth, where the gold is." Ivan extended his hand for Eryn to take it.

"Yes." Eryn nodded. That made sense to him. Ivan smiled lovingly at him, and Cian grinned mischievously.

"We can't help it." Eryn raised his trident. "It's gold, gold, gold for us!" joining the sarcastic circus of the Romanov twins.

"Let those humans go to the moon. They wanted to go. We're staying here. We'll take our chances with the pending global implosion and catastrophic volcanoes."

Nick was utterly still. His face was non-expressive. Eryn sensed he didn't know whether to pretend, lie, or cry. Eryn burst out laughing.

"Sorry, maybe next time, dude," Ivan said.

"Later, going now, ta-ta!" Cian waved his fore-finger round and round, the military signal to move out and meet at the rally point. Then he put it and his thumb into his mouth and sucked. Letting loose a long, high-pitched whistle.

The beasts focused on Nick. It was too late for him to understand what was happening. He fumbled and scrambled for his whistle, but the jackals pounced on him before he could get it in his mouth. He had no time to scream or make a sound as they tore him apart.

They turned and walked back to the ship. "I'm done with this place," Eryn said. "And that hat makes three of us. Let's go."

Three days later, they sent the rocket, carrying all

the other humans and their guard dogs, to the moon without knowing whether it had an automated or pre-programmed landing system.

CHAPTER 22
THE GOLDEN SWORDS

"Good morning, citizens of Phoenix.

It's now six a.m.

Did you know we live above a magical bioluminescent fungi forest?

Visit your community news page to book your seat for a tour of the recently discovered hidden subterranean tunnels. Experience the beauty of glowing plants and insects, such as fireflies.

Breakfast is served until eight a.m.

Have a glowing day!"

General Brad McCormick

Brad admired his friends' adaptability. Of course, it all came down to the voracious testing by their founder,

Dr. Saunders. Still, Brad thought their rapid adaptability to learn behaviors in response to changing circumstances was commendable.

Mika and Eryn bonded like *Gorilla* glue almost instantaneously, and so did the rest of the crew. Eryn was such a straightforward young man to like, and Brad knew that once they reached Phoenix, they would love him. His humble, soft-spoken intelligence and playful nature were magnetic, and that was beside the fact that he walked around with a trident looking like a superhero with an eight-pack.

It didn't surprise Brad when Mika enthusiastically told him about Eryn's ability to grasp what he said without in-depth explanations or schooling. "He's a bloody genius. I think he's probably the only man on this earth smarter than myself. Do you know how good it feels to talk to such a person?" Mika asked Brad, who knew precisely how it felt when speaking to Eryn, and seeing his friend so excited and inspired, felt ten times better.

After the jackals had obliterated Nick, the disciple, not leaving a drop of blood on the ground in front of the blue mineshaft, Eryn and the twins asked them to retreat into the spacecraft. Brad and his team inspected the thousands of rows of men, women, and children in cryo pods, awaiting a new life on the moon.

The creepy scene haunted them for days, but luckily, the sound manipulation idea Mika had wasn't that far off, as the prospective moonwalkers already had a hydrogen reactor onboard. With minimal adjustments, almost as if they had anticipated Eryn and Mika's arrival to work on the spacecraft, they could send thousands of people into space. Using the nuclear electro-sound propulsion system, the launch created enough thrust for lift-off. Thankfully, the ingenious system generated enough positive charges, and the reactor, already onboard, helped ensure a smooth execution by pushing the ions out and through the thruster, which in turn pushed the space-craft out of the mine.

Connor observed the instantaneous bond, and instead of being jealous, he embraced Eryn. The family of five was something to behold. The hand-some men radiated power and beauty and were prob-ably Phoenix's last or first royal family. Brad found that being in their presence made a man feel larger. They give without thinking of taking—extraordinary men with exceptional abilities and powers who self-lessly put the needs of others before their own.

The spaceship was on its way to the moon.

"Out of sight, out of mind," Brad said to Bryan as he reported back to Phoenix on their way home. "Mika's retreated into isolation. He'd sent word that he's waiting for us to come around." Brad huffed. "He said he would give us time to think. I think he needed some space to collect himself. The Halcyon isn't exactly conducive to privacy and silence," Brad informed the elected leadership team. "So, I think we'll take a few days camping out here on the East Antarctic Ice Sheet. We need a couple of days to relax and allow the boys time to adjust. I'll get back to you after we've discussed and tested the best-proposed theory, and let you know so that you can inform and prepare the residents for the impending destruction. But to keep chaos at bay, you must give them a proposed solution and be honest." Brad coaxed, knowing they all felt haggard about the Earth's imminent destruction because of the buildup of hydrogen and halogen gases. *They needed hope, not lies.*

The recordings by the floating camera ball of Nick, the last disciple, had been watched repeatedly, and Brad had played the audio version over the radio to Bryan and his team.

"Inform the residents about their future on Earth and include the story about the Anunnaki, the gold mining, and the replacement of the gold on their home planet. That would clarify the abduction and rescue mission in the gold mining area of South Africa." Brad explained, holding a radio handpiece in his hand. "At first, we thought it all to be coincidences, but that Eryn created a protective bubble by manipulating sound waves is real. We've all seen it. Bryan, I touched him while he held the bubble in place, and the power emanating from him? Well, I felt as invincible as if I'd used a pound of cocaine. That's how I felt," Brad said. He was excited to share his experience with his friend. There was only silence and static. Brad imagined their facial expressions of disbelief, but he didn't have time to convince them, so he continued, knowing they were listening.

"Mika's epiphany on their way back from South Africa was simple, so much so that when he first presented his idea to me, Connor, and Rick, our reactions upset the poor Russian so much that he stopped talking to us. We were speechless at first, and then we laughed at him. Probably due to stress, but our childish behavior caused all kinds of tension and irritation on board. Hence the camping and relaxing idea, because our narrow-minded reaction had Mika rolling his eyes and saying, *I'll give you a day to think about it." His words weren't cold...yet.*

"I'm on my way to apologize to Mika and admit that it makes sense. He should convince the boys, Ivan, Cian, and Eryn, to test themselves and their abilities. I will report on that update and our next course of action," Brad said.

Bryan, the ultimate leader of Phoenix, recommended talking to the boys, preparing them mentally, and testing the theory before returning. Bryan speculated it didn't sound like they realized the magnitude of their responsibility. He added that *if the predictions were accurate, we're in deep shit, and they're our only hope.* Bryan's voice boomed over the radio.

Rick sat on the counter, his long legs wrapped around Brad's torso, while Brad sat on a small kitchen stool, trying his best to have a serious conversation. *Bloody damn hell. The world is ending, and all I can think about is sinking my nose into his deliciousness.*

"We're going to follow your recommendations while there is time. Thank you, Bryan. Over and out." Brad stopped the transmission. "Give me a kiss, please." He got up and gave Rick a ravenous kiss. When he broke the kiss, he could swear he was seeing double. "I promise you, if we save the world, we're every ten minutes for a week." He rubbed his mouth dry on Rick's shoulder. They hugged and held each other, just soaking and giving, exchanging their love.

"How can I help?" Rick asked, kissing and smelling Brad's hair, which was much longer than usual.

"For now, could you collect our boys? I'll get Connor to collect theirs?"

The night before the testing started, Connor went to the pirate ship, as they named it, to call the boys over for dinner.

Each time Brad saw the dilapidated ship, he wanted to scream with frustration. He struggled to accept a world without Juandre and Andrew in it. "If only," he whispered to himself. It whirled in his head.

The unprofessionally built six-man ship the boys inherited was a death trap. Although the propellers on the back were as big as surfboards, the fact that Charles and his team had caught up with them was a miracle. Hammered down to a wooden cabin was a massive net of ropes that held together multiple bunches of silver weather balloons.

Mika and Connor secured the thing to their ship, not trusting that it would stay in the air on its own. It was possible to deflate or disappear during the night, so they hooked and tied the cabin onto their boat. The young men enjoyed their own space, even if it was basic, comprising a wheel to steer the propellers, one desk, one sofa mattress, and one storage room, with an ice-cold shower and a bucket for a toilet, which was to be emptied by throwing the contents overboard.

They saw it as a treehouse or something, liking it so much that they sat inside, joking and talking for hours. However, when they were starved and hungry, they would come down the stairs like a herd of blue wildebeest on the trek to the Serengeti when they were called in for mealtimes.

After the meeting with the leadership over at Phoenix, the oppressive mood around the table didn't seem to affect the boys when they stuffed their faces.

"We need to talk," Brad said, pausing and noticing the worried faces of the adults around the table, but then the five young men looked up and had their cheeks stuffed to the maximum like hamsters, so he burst out laughing, and the others followed suit.

"My goodness, look at you all," he said, folding over, nearly hitting his head on the table. His laugh was infectious, and they all joined in, pointing fingers at each other.

"Phew, that was a good laugh." Brad wiped the tears from his eyes. "Oh, lord, I needed that." The tension broke in the room. Still hungry and oblivious to the pending doom, the boys got up for seconds.

"Boys, we wanted to talk to you about saving Phoenix. We've just finished speaking to Bryan and the others. We agreed to stay out here on the ice to test a few theories and decide how we would proceed when we reached Phoenix. In the past few months, Phoenix noted an increased number of tremors and volcanic activity on the Ring of Fire, the region around the rim of the Pacific Ocean," Brad explained.

The boys were big-eyed but didn't seem to hold fear. Brad figured they either didn't understand or didn't worry about the future. *I wish I had the untainted mind of a child.*

"I think it's better if your dads explained what they planned," Eryn said.

"It can be a crazy ass who-who nonsense idea, but we all know they always build legends on truth," Mika explained. "We can't mine gold or bring the gold back, but we can use other ways to increase our chances of surviving the explosive core meltdown of the Earth."

Kawa and Donali listened, but it soon became apparent that they meant this for the three other young men.

Mika took over the discussion. "Eryn, do you remember the bubble of safety you created for us in the storm?"

Eryn nodded.

"Okay, then I thought about natural disasters in history, how multiple civilizations have perished over time, and how some survived to document extensive floods or catastrophes. Some built ships, some built towers, and some prayed to gods. I believe we can learn from the civilization of Atlantis," Mika said, then paused to read their reaction. Brad thought he was expecting another round of laughs at his expense, but it never came.

Connor listened attentively. The McCormick twins looked fascinated. Eryn and the Romanov twins were waiting for the punchline. Brad sat, leaning back on the couch, one leg relaxed, crossed over the other, and Rick mirrored Brad's posture.

"We need you boys to create a bubble that can sustain itself," Mika said.

Eryn frowned, and Cian and Ivan sat still with perplexed expressions.

"Because, Eryn, you cannot stand there twenty-four hours a day holding the bubble in place," Mika said.

Eryn moved to the front of his seat. "Okay?" he asked and waited for more, listening to Mika.

"What do you want us to do, Dad?" the twins asked, breaking the silence. They seemed eager to help, sitting on the edges of their seats, as well. "We don't have any powers, regardless of what the wack job, Nick, suggested," Ivan said.

"That's why we'll do a few test runs," Connor said.

"Now, we don't want you to stress or think you're wrong or less than if you can't do it," Mika said.

They'd discussed their worry that the boys might be so stressed they wouldn't be able to perform.

"We'll start small, and Eryn's going to help you. I'm confident he can call your abilities forth."

Eryn rubbed his chin back and forth, forming his assumptions or calculating how to achieve such a membrane.

"That sounds awesome," Cian said, looking eager to have superpowers.

"We'll have to make sure you don't hurt your-selves," Eryn warned. "I practiced for many years with my father."

His face soured as he talked about his life before the twins.

"Come, no need for that. Tell us exactly how your father started teaching you," Ivan said. He put his index finger under Eryn's chin, tipping his head up. Ivan's eyes sparkled for him, and they seemed to communicate empathically.

Eryn's face lit up with a big smile for Ivan.

When the twins smiled at him, they seemed to wipe away all his sadness.

"Okay, let me show you the easiest way." He pointed to Connor, who was sitting closest to the kitchenette. "May I please have a glass of water?"

Connor got up to fetch it for him. "Sorry, may I have two more, please?"

Connor turned and fetched two more glasses.

"Thank you, Dad," he teased. But Connor only nodded his head. Eryn looked happy that Connor didn't react negatively. Instead, he nonchalantly accepted it. Eryn had a look of forced concentration on his face as he was doing what he was doing. He drank each glass of water, so it was half full.

He placed it on the table in a triangular shape. "Both of you hear my song as I hear yours. For them," —he pointed to the room—"when I sing, they hear a song, but they don't hear the meaning. It sounds good, but they don't know what it is, and they can't sing it. Also, they can't be taught how to. You can sing, or you can't sing. Does that make sense?"

Brad nodded. "Yes, it feels like I should know it, but I can't..."

Everyone, except the twins, said simultaneously, "Put my finger on it!"

Eryn smiled broadly. His grin conveyed hidden knowledge, and his golden-green eyes glittered. Brad noticed that Eryn's usually slitted pupils had enlarged to round black disks while his face brightened, almost glowed when he spoke about his mates and their songs for each other.

The phenomenal aura he emanated filled the entire cabin. Brad and Rick moved closer to watch Eryn. Mika grabbed Connor for support. Connor took his hand and kissed it. What they witnessed was ethereal, filled with the joyous promise of fantasy. Humans read about it in fairy tales or even in the bible.

Eryn's skin glowed a light pearlescent blue. Almost the same as their ship. It felt as if the temperature had increased. Like when you stepped into the sunlight on a beautiful day out on the ice. Then a low hum vibrated into their bodies. Elated emotions of happiness, calm, peace, goodness, and awe filled them. It was a magnificent experience, and it had only just started.

Eryn put his hands on the table and softly began singing his song. The water in the glass closest to him shimmered as it reflected the light in the cabin. The more he sang, the water moved. At first, ripples started on the surface. It rippled so fast that it appeared as if the water had made a spout. Eryn stopped singing, and the water fell back into the glass.

The cabin was quiet. The twins took his hands and hummed. It sounded like the twins sang a few notes higher and lower than Eryn's song. Again, the water shimmered and moved, but instead of forming a spout, the water turned into tiny crystals, like salt or sugar. The crystals in the glass moved so fast they appeared like sand in an hourglass. It grew in height up and out of the glass. The strange crystals from each glass funneled upwards. They stopped humming, and the crystals liquified and then fell back into their glasses.

Then, all three hummed together, and the water crystallized, arching over to meet the other two columns, creating the outlines of a spiraling pyramid. The three streams thinned out, like three strands of hair. They connected with spikes, just like a DNA triple helix structure.

"Oh, my," Mika said in awe.

"What *is* that?" Brad asked. No one answered.

The glowing, swirling helix elongated. As they changed their song, the strands broke into smaller pieces that glowed brighter and died just as the song ended. That same ethereal glow that had shimmered across Eryn's face now encompassed all three young men's faces. The remnants of the tiny glowing pieces floated gently like fireflies.

Brad and the others reached out, catching the playful little lights. As soon as they touched them, they turned back to water again. Nobody wanted to say a word that would spoil the enchanted atmosphere.

Eryn, **King of the Brawl**

At first, Eryn didn't think it was possible, but after

Mika drew them a picture of what he had in mind and that he was almost one hundred percent sure that it was possible, they practiced around the table with a crumpled-up playing card that lay in a plate of water. They were supposed to each start a side of the plate, then use their voices to manipulate the water from crystals that would eventually be a barrier to the outside while still allowing air and light to travel through. After a few practice rounds, they celebrated by dancing and singing. The three created a crystal-like shape around the playing card in the form of an egg. Interestingly, as soon as pressure was applied to one side, it would retract to the shape of a ball, thereby strengthening the membranes. They decided that tomorrow they would move the experimentations outside.

The Antarctic weather permitted them to practice out on the ice to their advantage. They started small with rocks, which later grew into boulders. Eventually, they ended up on each side of a small hill, pretending it was Phoenix.

"That's it, perfect! Now you, Cian," Mika said.

Cian stepped back and held up his hands. They were triangulated by about a kilometer each. Practicing with longer distances and increasing the radius proved to be much more complex than they first thought. The insurmountable radius of over a hundred meters from the outline of the entire city of Phoenix was depressingly daunting as they struggled, with only a few hundred meters away from each other. Faint musical ringing noises, *ting-ting* at high decibels, but the sound of their voices drowned it out.

This proved to be much more difficult as they wouldn't see much of the results or each other because they'd work from the upper ground and have to send the vibrations underground.

Eryn raised his hands and felt a distinct prickling through his body. He received a slight electric shock. Most probably, the twins were sending too much power his way. Fearing that they had experienced the same, he decided not to reciprocate. "You're over-loading me. My arms can't handle it. It feels like my bones want to climb out of my skin," he shouted.

"What should we do?" they called.

"I'm going to count to three. We should stop sending vibrations simultaneously." He counted slowly, grinding his teeth. "One, two, three, shit!"

They fell backward onto their backsides.

Frustrated and fearing hurting the twins, Eryn swore crassly. "I can't do this without my trident!" Eryn yelled. His blood was boiling. The idea of him hurting the twins infuriated him. "Give me my trident."

"Eryn, do you think if we somehow devise a plan for Cian and Ivan, get them something to concentrate the sound waves with, like you do, would that go more easily?" Mika asked in a gentle tone. His voice calmed Eryn a little.

"Of course it will!" Eryn retorted hotly.

"I'm impressed. Now I can see the man I don't want to cross," Connor said. Eryn felt like punching him. Then, he realized he was seconds away from stomping his feet and jumping up and down like Ernest did when he got mad.

"Sorry, I'm not used to working with others. I'm nervous I'm going to hurt your children. I also fear we won't succeed, and I don't want all those humans to die in Phoenix."

"It's okay, my boy. We're all here to support you. There's a lot of time to get this right. This is just for practice. So, you're allowed to see what works and what doesn't. That's why they're called experiments," Connor said. Stepping closer, he looked up at Eryn and patted his side. Offering his support. "Let's take a break and think about the trident idea."

"We're not as strong as he," Ivan said as he approached.

"Yes, I can't carry that thing," Cian said.

"Me neither. I can't lift it. I don't think anyone except Eryn can," Ivan said and gave Eryn a radiant smile. Eryn smiled back. Any compliment coming from Cian and Ivan made him happy.

Mika stepped closer. "What if we make you each a smaller staff? Please don't laugh, but I think we could take some gold from Eryn's trident and make each of you a twenty or thirty-centimeter staff. Eryn, do you think that could work?"

Relief and excitement coursed through Eryn. "Yes!" Elated, he hurried to get the heavy trident and returned triumphantly. He held it above his head and filled it with sound waves. Sparks began issuing from the tips.

"Wow, a gigantic energy-generating staff," Brad said.

"That is real superhero stuff, Eryn," Donali shouted from the deck of the ship, where the two brothers sat with their legs dangling from the sides. They waved, and everyone waved back to them.

Eryn loved impressing them with new tricks. They were always awed and never shaken. Things he thought he would be judged and ridiculed for were only thrilling to them.

"Just think about it, Brad, all that clean energy and no waste. I'm going to think about harnessing and storing it, like a battery or a reactor. You know, be innovative about it," Mika said.

Brad lifted his cup to Mika. "If someone told me this a month ago, I would never have believed them," Rick said.

The two husbands sat underneath a blanket by the outdoor fire, drinking *the good stuff*, as Brad called it. They were jovial, in love, and happy together.

Mika turned to Eryn with a serious, respectful gaze. "May I touch it, Eryn?" he asked, pointing to the trident. "I'm just ensuring I wouldn't die by electrocution without permission to touch it." Eryn nodded and held it so Mika and Connor could feel it. Blissed-out facial expressions appeared on their faces. Eryn enjoyed feeling that way, as if all their troubles had disappeared. Cian and Ivan gave Eryn a weird look, like, *That's ours.* How could you let them touch your junk like that? So Eryn shut it down quickly.

"Okay, that's enough." He kept talking to prevent them from thinking he was nasty or selfish. "I thought we could remove my trident's left and right forks. That should be enough gold for them, which would be easy to remove. All I need is a hammer, an anvil, and a very hot fire."

"We have a big hammer onboard. Maybe use the plates I anchored the cannons with; I didn't throw them overboard. Would those work?" Mika asked.

"Yes, thank you, Mika."

A few hours later, the twins sat, hands on chins, elbows on knees, admiring every move of Eryn's upper body muscles. He'd gotten so hot that he removed the top half of his arctic suit and tied the arm sleeves around his hips and was now hacking away at the gold with one purpose in mind. He focused only on getting his lovers their needed tools. He knew how he felt when he could concentrate and focus his powers so many years ago. He disappointed himself for not thinking about it earlier. So he mumbled as he hammered away. *Pang-pang, clung-clung, shhhh* in the water, back in the fire, *mumble-*

mumble, pang-pang, clung-clung, shhhh in the water, back in the fire, *mumble-mumble.*

Once the pieces were detached, he continued hammering the gold, forging Ivan and Cian their short swords.

"Thank you. I always wanted a golden steak knife," Cian teased.

Eryn just shook his head and continued working on Ivan's sword. The twins didn't seem to mind watching him as he removed the side forks, as they waited patiently for him. He could feel their emotions and their gazes on him, and the sight of his sweaty body was a lot *of fun for them to watch.* Each time he bent or dipped forward, he saw them looking at him like they wanted to lick every drop of sweat from his body. He paused and rolled his shoulders. *Hmmm,* he heard their thoughts. They swooned and lusted over him with no shame. He liked it a lot. The waves of electrifying yearning weakened his knees. To prevent a nasty accident from happening, like face-planting into the fire or looking like an idiot, he blocked their thoughts. Willing himself to finish his work.

"Holy crap, you two," Kawa said loudly out of the blue. "Wipe the drool from the corners of your mouths. I can see your boners tenting your puffy arctic suits from over here. Shame on you!"

Eryn smiled and continued hammering the gold, pretending he didn't hear that.

"They don't hear you, brother," Donali said and laughed.

"We hear you. We just don't care," Cian said.

Eryn turned and handed Ivan his broad sword.

He stood and kissed Eryn long and hard. "Thank you for breaking your trident for us. We'll fix it for you later."

That excited Eryn. "No need. I enjoy knowing I saved those forks for the two of you."

Cian joined, giving him a peck on the cheek. "Thank you, Eryn."

Eryn blushed. "Okay, I want to eat and shower. I'm so sweaty."

"It doesn't bother me. The more manly sweat, the better the glide," Cian said. He chuckled, rubbing himself around his pectoral muscles with one hand while his other hand rubbed Eryn down to his groin. Eryn stopped his hand. They weren't alone, and Kawa and Donali were looking at them. Feeling uncomfortable, he started walking so he could reposition himself.

"But I want to be clean for you," Eryn said shortly.

"We don't mind you being sweaty. We love you just the way you are. You always smell good to us," Ivan doted on Eryn, *always trying to make me feel better.*

"This lovey-dovey shit makes me nauseous," Donali said. "Let's go. I think dinner is ready."

While walking back to the ship, Eryn spoke to his two mates, now his apprentices. "Besides focusing your energy, your swords absorb other people's energy if you want them to. When you use it, hold the handle end toward your body in the palm of your hand, and point," he said, showing them by stabbing the air. He was super-duper excited to share this part of his life with them. *Ernest never wanted to listen to me.*

"By now, you should know how to visualize your energy being gathered and focused through the sword. Sometimes it will glow or sizzle. It'll never burn or hurt you because it's your energy. It'll focus on whatever purpose you desire for the energy. Carry it with you always because you won't know when you'll need it. You must always concentrate and send your power where it'll be most effective. Take care of it and be careful. You can kill with it. Whether by accident or willingly."

Ivan and Cian nodded, focusing on what Eryn had taught them.

"Good. After dinner, we'll try again." He turned, and because he felt like showing off, he jumped from where they were about to enter the Blue Halcyon straight up into the air and over the railing of the upper deck.

Before he leaped one short jump over to their pirate ship, he heard Cian joking inside and eavesdropped from the galley. After he heard only nice things, he turned and jumped, excited to join them after his shower.

"Man, that smells fantastic," Cian said. He was

smiling from ear to ear. When they entered, most were already around the table eating, but it seemed their fathers were waiting for them.

"Look, Papa, our swords aren't they beautiful?" They handed their short golden swords to Mika and Connor. Both blades were about forty inches long. Eryn had hammered a pommel and grip, a rain guard, and flattened fuller and double edges. Both Romanov boys tied their hair in a tight bun, as their Russian father had taught them, before washing their hands for mealtimes.

"They're amazing. Eryn's so talented. Don't you think, Dada?" Cian took his sword from Connor and walked around the table so everyone could look and touch it. "I teased him and said it's a nice steak knife, but he didn't think that was funny. He's so serious about this." Cian pranced around the table and finally noticed Eryn standing there.

"Oh good, I couldn't wait anymore. I'm so hungry. Eryn, I showed everyone your handiwork, and they're impressed."

Eryn stood frozen, wide-eyed, and not saying a word. "What's wrong, Eryn?" a chorus of concerned voices asked. Then they noticed it. In his arms, he held a blanket. And the blanket moved now and then.

"Oh, my lord, is that a baby swaddled in a blanket?" Rick asked, connecting the dots first. Eryn shook his head from side to side. He looked down at the bundle.

"You won't fucking believe me."

"Jesus, the boy had grasped cussing faster than an Angora goat could catch burrs," Brad said.

"It must be a baby seal. I saw some fighting out on the ice this morning. Is it an orphaned seal?" Connor asked.

The bundle jiggled faster. Tiny yipping and snarling sounds came from his arms.

"Are those small puppy sounds?" Rick asked.

The chairs around the table pushed out as one sound, and in the next moment, oh's and ah's surrounded Eryn. He plopped down and put the bundle on the floor in front of him. First, one head, followed by two more heads, stuck out from the material.

"Are those three gigantic rats?" Rick asked no one in particular.

"Those aren't rats. Those are, can it be? Are those baby jackals?" Brad asked, astonishment written on his face.

"Anubis?" Mika corrected him.

"No, how did they? Where did you find them, Eryn?" Connor asked.

"I was getting dressed and heard them. They were in the bag of clothes."

"Where's the mommy?" Rick asked. "Oh, dear lord, where's the mommy?" Rick grabbed Kawa and Donali and retreated away from the door. "If there's one thing I remember as a young Apache, it's that when there are cute baby cubs, a very dangerous momma bear is nearby."

"I don't think they have a mommy bear, or the mommy bear isn't here, or maybe the mommy bear left them with us," Eryn replied, unsure what a mommy bear was.

"Aww, maybe they followed us. Maybe they want to be with us." Cian and Ivan made cooing noises. The tiny jackals fell over their little feet to get to Cian and Ivan. "Ah, look, they ran straight to us." They held their hands out.

"They must recognize you," Mika answered. "A bear is a big animal, the size of a small car, which sleeps during wintertime. In the spring, they wake and start roaming around for food. Their babies are called bear cubs, and the momma protects them by killing anyone in her path. When we get to Phoenix, we'll show you pictures," Mika explained.

"Okay, thank you, Mika," Eryn said.

"They still look like rats. Adorable, cute rats," Connor said.

Later, when everyone had moved back to the dinner table to finish their meals, Ivan, Cian, and Eryn each held a sleeping Anubis.

Brad stood up after dinner. "I'm going to sleep. Tomorrow will be a long day."

One by one, the adults got up and disappeared through the revolving door to the sleeping area. The five young men offered to clean up, and then they filed outside to the deck area, where they practiced as planned earlier that day.

Stoking the bonfire high with wood that Brad had suggested they collect on their way from South Africa when all decided they needed a vacation because wood was a scarce commodity in Antarctica, Donali and Kawa sat toasty warm while holding the Anubis and feeding them leftover meat from dinner while playing a self-made game of judging the King of the Brawl and his Anunnaki and their creations of all kinds of shapes with spheres to protect Phoenix.

And, of course, Eryn won the game of *whose shape is the biggest.*

CHAPTER 23

SUCK WHAT?

"*Good morning, city of Phoenix.*

It's now six a.m.

Did you know that for more than a hundred million years, sea turtles have covered vast distances across the world's oceans, filling a vital role in the balance of marine habitats and that humans drove them to total extinction in just two-hundred years?

Have you ever wondered how sea turtles mated?

Visit your community news page for exciting videos about nature and how they used to procreate in the wild. For instance, we have a twenty-four-hour video of a male turtle mating while hanging on for dear life on the back end of the female's shell.

Breakfast is served until eight a.m.

Good luck, and hang in there."

. . .

Eryn King of the Brawl

WHILE THE LITTLE hydrogen balloon ship provided hours of entertainment, the thrill of being alone with the twins soon grew old. Now it felt like a suffocating deathtrap, a torture device of the cruelest kind. Trapping him and grinding his self-control. Eryn sighed. His balls were so stuffed that he couldn't decide which way to sit, walk, or stand. *Any minute, they would pop out of their sack and roll away.*

That I want one fucking second alone with the twins isn't asking too much. The McCormick twins pretended to be naïve, stupid virgins who did not know what they were doing to him and his throbbing balls. Eryn groaned inwardly. He knew they were pretending to be oblivious, yet they were fully aware of their actions. Oh, Cian, this, and oh, Ivan, that. Just one bloody second alone would quickly resolve the aching problem he had in his pants. The last few days had morphed into one unending, torturous pent-up sexual frustration.

If we don't see the glass city appear on the horizon within the next hour, I'm going to go psycho and throw the two inquisitive squirrel faces out the door onto the ice. Maybe tie a rope around them and let them dangle a bit. Then we'll see how they enjoy hanging around.

All five young men lay squashed on a tiny sofa mattress. It wasn't the lack of mattress space but the lack of room to move and reposition his aching cock and balls that bothered Eryn most.

Fuck, my mood's sour and to the point of cutting my balls off. If our ship had a deck, I would've slept on it, legs sprawled open, with the Antarctic wind blowing over my balls. Maybe ask the twins to kiss them better for me. Oh, my freaking balls!

Rising hastily, intending to relieve himself, he proceeded to the tiny hold used as a washroom and storage. It was broad daylight in Antarctica, as it was in the middle of summer, and scant light penetrated to reveal the figure of Ivan crouching on the mattress, his chin upon his knees, his handsome face gleaming with mischief. Eryn didn't say a word. Instead, he held his hand out to Ivan in a silent invitation. Taking Eryn's hand, he soundlessly flew, landing with a soft *oomph* against the door. Neither one spoke. Eryn's eight-foot, bulky frame pinned Ivan's seven-foot frame. Electricity sparked between them. Their faces shimmered blue-ish gold bioluminescence. Eryn's balls and cock drummed with the beat of his heart. Both were panting, trying to read the other's meaning in their eyes.

Eryn reached for the door, and Ivan covered his hand. *We're thinking of doing the same.* Eryn read Ivan's intent in his sparkling blue eyes. Smiling and grinning, both opened the door and fell inside. Kissing and grabbing, teeth clacking, and tongues swooping deep into each other's mouths. *Holy shit, I needed this!*

Ivan pulled back, short of breath, looking dizzy with lust. "I want to suck you."

Eryn stopped for a second, panting. "Suck, what?"

"Your cock, what else?"

Eryn couldn't believe what he was hearing. Then, he stopped thinking altogether as Ivan fell to his knees, opened his pants, and took his thick cock into his mouth. *Glorious!* It was the warmest, sweetest, dirtiest thing anyone had ever done to him. *It feels, it feels so damn good.* He never thought humans did this. Eryn grew up in a cave with no frame of reference to sex with humans at all. The memory of two monkeys fornicating flashed through his mind. Okay, this feels way better than touching himself. *I could ask Ivan to do it all day.*

"I'm going to make a mess in your mouth. You better stop, Ivan." Eryn futilely tried to push Ivan back. Grabbing a fist full of blond hair, he couldn't decide whether to keep his cock in or push Ivan away. It was a war inside his mind. He felt dizzy and drunk. It all felt too good, so he slammed into Ivan's mouth.

Ivan sucked relentlessly, and Eryn exploded into his mouth. It looked like the sky had fallen inside the tiny room. Tiny blue and golden light sparks escaped from their touching skin and danced around and in between them while days of collected sperm ran in rivulets from the corners of Ivan's mouth. *What a sight!* Eryn was transfixed by the erotic visuals. Ivan eagerly licked and sucked and attempted to swallow him whole. Eryn gasped. The overwhelming sensitivity sent him backward against the wall. Arms splayed to the sides, searching for something to grab and hold on to.

"Hah! That tasted awesome," Ivan exclaimed as he stood to kiss Eryn.

Eryn liked the taste of his spunk all over Ivan's face. He licked his lover's beautiful, swollen lips clean with his long tongue while vibrating with pleasure, enjoying the sensation of emotional overload. "I want more," he said and croaked a deep, guttural sound. "Now it's my turn to taste you."

Ivan didn't have time to respond. Eryn was a fast learner. He spun him, changing places, and had his pants undone and his cock in his mouth faster than the speed of light. He paused, making sure he retracted his fangs, feasted, munched, and sucked Ivan's dick like a slice of juicy watermelon. Ivan threw one leg over Eryn's shoulder, grabbed onto his hair, and face-fucked him as hard and fast as he could. Eryn enjoyed every second. He was ready for one more round. He squeezed the life out of his cock, wishing he had a hole to push it into.

Ivan moaned and whispered, "I'm coming, and oh, my god, I'm coming." His cock swelled, and then he squirted his seed down Eryn's throat, ramming into Eryn's mouth another few times, hanging onto

Eryn's head, barely able to keep himself upright. While Eryn never lost suction, Ivan's legs began to tremble.

"Having fun?" Cian asked, and in the background, they heard the McCormick twins giggling.

"We heard a commotion, and I came to investigate." Cian stood in the doorframe, leaning toward the side with his arms folded. A hungry grin on his face. He lifted his nose and sniffed audibly. "It smells like you were having lots and lots of fun here. Without me," he said sarcastically. Eryn grunted, and Ivan sighed in exasperation.

"Hmmm, you were making so much noise it sounded like you were wrestling or something. I thought maybe there was a fire because the light beams shone all around the door. Do you need help?" Cian asked, smirking from ear to ear, and his head cocked to one side.

"Want to join us, brother?" Ivan asked shortly.

Eryn did not wait for another snotty remark while he stood on his knees with one of Ivan's legs draped around his neck. Those bloody McCormick twins. He pulled Cian inside. It was such a tight fit that the door could barely close behind him. Eryn hastily made the small space work for them.

"Why do we always end up in the smallest spaces together?" he asked, expecting no answer. With Ivan's leg over his right shoulder, he unzipped Cian's pants and removed his right leg, draping it over the left shoulder. He worked on both their dicks. Gluttonizing himself into a trance, he never wanted to come out of.

Ivan laughed. "No, my dick is too sensitive." He snorted but left his dick where it was, evidently still enjoying the attention. Cian moaned and relaxed into the administration. He half hung on his brother with one hand while the other grabbed a railing used to hang their towels. Eryn was so fucking turned on that he continued fist-fucking his dick, pulling long, fist strokes over the head of his thick uncut cock. Their throaty sounds of pleasure and the two long pale cocks smelling like man, honey, and gold made him frantic with lust. His twins smelled exactly like melting his favorite yellow metal.

Eryn congratulated himself on a job well done when Cian ripped the railing off the wall, hollering, "Fuck yes, I'm coming!"

His instincts kicked in, and he drank every drop of jizz, tasting the sound of his lover's songs. It was all so intoxicating. They were scorching hot and beaming. He stood up, squeezing his cockhead to keep from ejaculating. Pushing the two blond heads down, the twins slipped onto their knees.

"Ah, yes, that's so good. You look beautiful down there. I'm going to spill right onto your pretty lips." Eryn felt brave and filthy, and it felt good to see them opening their mouths to receive him. "Yes, boys, suck my cock." He ejaculated as soon as the words left his mouth. He shot volley after volley onto both their faces, smearing his cum over their pink lips around their mouths with the head of his cock. Ivan hummed in satisfaction and squirted a second, but smaller, wad onto the floor. The tiny space was stuffy, and every nook and cranny was glowing, filled to the brim with sex sounds, smells, and euphoric emotions. Eryn helped his mates up to continue with a three-way kiss, sharing the taste of their essence.

"Ah, yes, that was so good." Eryn helped them into their pants as he said he wanted to do it again. Then they helped him into his pants while giddy with sexual satisfaction and fumbling around for the door-knob, laughing. When they finally opened the door and practically tumbled out of the room, untangling their limbs, it was empty.

"Where are the McCormick twins?" Eryn asked, fastening the buttons of his pants. The door was open. The twins poked their heads out. Eryn heard the roaring voices of men, so he scrambled to the door. Before them was a huge crowd of men waving and welcoming them.

"We're here!" All three young men exclaimed. They watched as the men threw rope after rope over the balloons of their little hydrogen pirate ship. It reminded Eryn of the book he had read about *Gulliver's Travels* as they pulled into the shipyard hangar and tied down.

"I've never seen such a beautiful sight," Eryn said in awe. "The glass domes are sparkling with all the rainbow colors, and look at the friendly faces of the men waving to us. Your fathers must have contacted Bryan and his team, explaining our situation, on their way back to Phoenix. Maybe even divulged more detail than what was necessary," Eryn remarked, taken aback by the thousands of Phoenix residents.

Ivan and Cian nodded and waved back at the people.

"It's a happy and beautiful sight, and although it's nice to be here, we have work to do if we want to survive the destruction of Earth."

Ivan pointed to the sad faces in the crowd. "Look, they're waiting in line to speak to Brad."

"Those men were good friends with Juan and Drew. They performed drag in the ballroom some nights. Chances are they were informed already about these tragic murders."

"What's drag?" Eryn asked. Frowning, he'd never heard that word before.

"It's men who love dressing up in various styles of women's or female clothing, and they're incredibly talented. They held shows and events in the Blue Ballroom, where Juan loved performing. He sang and danced mainly in the 1920s in a country called France. It was very entertaining to watch. Maybe we can show you some videos later."

"Now that females are extinct, drag has grown into something much more, especially for those who love the female body. Some go to watch, to meet

ERYN, KING OF THE BRAWL

men for sex. Others go to drink, dance, relax, or have fun, and sometimes men go for nostalgic reasons. To remember the world before Doomsday. But Juan and Drew also used to prepare and serve food to these men. They spoke to everyone daily. They were popular, and everyone loved them. I think Brad will probably have a ceremony for them so everyone can remember them and say goodbye." Cian's head fell.

Eryn felt the sadness radiating from him. He pulled them closer for a hug.

A hollow noise at their feet startled them.

"Sorry, boys, the cleaning crew is just coming up the gangplank!" an unshaven older man said as he lowered a plank from the ship to the ground. They hastily grabbed their belongings, eager to leave.

"What the fuck is that?" the older crewman yelped, holding a mop, ready to strike over his shoulder.

"Ah, those are our puppies. Come, dogs!" Ivan slapped his legs to call them closer. Three baby Anubis tumbled out of their box bed, falling over one another to get to Ivan.

Cian bent down to scoop them up.

"Here, give me one." Eryn carried the small, black rat-sized Anubis in the crook of his arm, looking like Obelix and Dogmatix.

"What are they? Are they mine rats from South Africa?" another cleaner asked.

"No, they're Anubis. Jackals that protect humans," Eryn answered proudly.

"It's a long story," Cian interrupted.

"No matter, you can tell me later. I bet you're tired, hungry, and eager to get off this..."

Eryn looked around and didn't know what to say, and decided to say nothing.

"Yes, we know, okay, we'll catch up later," the man with the big beard said while chuckling. Eryn liked him. He was friendly.

They left the ship and went searching for Mika and Connor.

"I want us to have an apartment of our own," Ivan said, looking at Eryn.

"There's no way we're going to live with our fathers," Cian told Eryn.

"You stand firm. Just say no." Eryn lifted his staff. "No!" His voice boomed down the corridor.

"That's the spirit!" Ivan patted him on the shoulder.

Connor and Mika protested weakly. They most probably knew their argument was futile. So Eryn and the twins were alone in their apartment.

Finally, the Brawl King could ravish his twins' bodies horizontally. The problem was, where to start? Their tall, slender, hairless physiques were the opposite of his eight-foot muscled bulk. Eryn was shamelessly sex-hungry for them, and he palmed his cock.

"Fuck, just look at the way you want me. My cock

throbs for you. I can't wait to have you both on top of me."

They slipped their clothes off, almost in sync with one another, and stepped closer to Eryn to help him out of his. Their white marble-skinned bodies glowed as he hummed his mating song for them.

"I doubt all three of us would fit in a shower. Maybe I should wait?" Ivan turned.

"We'll fit. Come, I'll show you." He took each by the hand and led them to the bathroom. Opening the hot and cold water, he ensured the temperature was comfortable and stepped inside, sitting on the floor. They giggled.

"Come," he called out to them. His voice was low and gruff.

"What is it with us and tight spaces?" Cian asked.

Eryn's heart was racing, and the intoxicating smells of dried cum, sweat, and lust drove him crazy. They climbed inside, following his orders.

"Cian, you stand to this side, and Ivan, you to that side." He positioned them in front of him. Their cocks, precisely the same size and shape, bobbed before him. All three of them had light body hair.

"Now, let's wash each other." Again, more giggles.

"Have you noticed, Eryn, we don't have body hair?" Cian asked.

"Why? What do you mean?"

"We always thought it's because we're young, but

you don't have pubic hair either." Eryn looked down, not sure what pubic hair was.

"I thought it was supposed to be like this."

"No. We'll show you later what humans look like. Let's take you to Quik-Fix Hall. You'll love the show," Ivan said.

The three virgins followed their instincts and did what felt good to them. He felt their anticipation turn into nervousness and then into disgust.

"Don't worry." Eryn looked up, smiling gently at them. "I understand that you're brothers. I wouldn't want to touch my brother like this, either. Just relax, and enjoy me, and let me enjoy you. I don't want you to do anything you hate or are uncomfortable with."

"No, it's just that we want you to know we don't want to do anything to each other, only to you." Ivan snorted, then nodded to Cian.

"We'll share you, and you may have both of us, but we don't think the washing and touching each other is cool."

"I'm glad you told me. But I feel you don't like to do those things. So why don't you sit here?" He patted his upper legs, offering each thigh. "I'll wash you. Let's tell your fathers that we want a bigger shower," Eryn added.

"I can imagine how that will go down," Cian said, sitting down.

"Don't worry. I'll ask them." Eryn's heart leaped. He loved it when they were happy.

Finely tuned and susceptible to their emotions, both sat down with their assess on their upper legs. Eryn forgot about soap, water, and showering. He touched and kissed them both all over as they rubbed themselves against him. He was so bloody horny for them.

Cian grabbed soap and shampoo and lathered their bodies while Ivan and Eryn kissed. Having all three washed off, they pulled Eryn to their room. Pushing him till the back of his legs touched the bed, they pounced, so he fell backward. They climbed his body as if he were a tree and they were spider monkeys.

In synchronized movements from his beautiful, webbed toes, over his hairless muscled legs, then extra tiny licks, bites, and kisses to his balls and rock-hard cock—his lovers drove him crazy. Both tongues licked the head of his cock like it was a snow cone. Sucking the pre-cum out of his piss slit. His nine-inch cock was so hard it protruded and stretched his fore-skin to the maximum, which stopped about two inches from the tip, all pink with a shiny, fat head. The twins tasted it, and both reached for their cocks.

"Ah, you taste lovely, Eryn. How does lavender and honey taste?" Ivan remarked.

Eryn felt wonderful. Never had he ever had so many compliments from anyone. As soon as they said that, he moaned and croaked. "I think I'm going to...

ah. Yes, fuck, that feels so good." He ejaculated, so the twins lapped his crotch, dick, and balls clean.

"Motherfucker, I see stars! I'm sorry, it just happened."

They giggled again, each sitting on a knee and rubbing their assholes on it. In coordinated strokes, they pleasured themselves and counted. "One, two, three!" Then shot their loads together all over Eryn's legs and torso. One of them even hit Eryn in the face. He stuck his long tongue out, wrapping it around, licking their dicks and himself clean.

They fell onto him. One on each side. All three were happy and sated, with smiles on their faces. After they recovered, Ivan got up to get the three Anubis pups. "We need to find a spot for them to walk and run during the day," he said as they snuggled together.

"We'll need a bigger bed and a shower," Eryn mumbled sleepily, thinking the Anubis would grow into car-sized pets.

"Hey, Connor said I was your pet back in the mines. Am I really your pet?"

"Sleep, Eryn. We'll talk kink tomorrow. I'm tired."

"What is kink?"

"Sleep, Eryn."

"Okay."

CHAPTER 24

THE SONG OF ANGELS

"*Good morning, citizens of Phoenix.*

Lasitor, your Artificial Intelligence (AI) community news broadcaster, bids you a good morning.

It's now six a.m.

Over forty thousand tremors have rocked Antarctica since the end of August, and we've noticed a spike in seismic activity that's depressingly cumbersome.

Scientists with Phoenix University detected an increased number of quakes—including a handful of more vigorous shakes of magnitude six in the channel between the South Shetland Islands and the Antarctic Peninsula. In addition, several tectonic and micro-plate movements caused frequent rumblings and have increased over the past four months. It's unusual. Therefore, our leadership team has called a meeting. It's scheduled for nine a.m. sharp. We will save a recording for you on your local community news page for those who are unable to attend.

Breakfast is served until eight a.m.
Thank you, and enjoy your day."

ERYN, **King of the Brawl**

"WHAT?" Eryn was up in an instant. His legs were wobbling while attempting to balance his massive body on the soft mattress. He was dazed and sleep-drunk. "Where's my fork, I mean spear? Where's my spear?" Disoriented, he scanned their room from left to right. Hands up and fisted, his body was ready for action as he assumed a fighting stance. Adrenaline pumped through his veins.

"Calm down. It's Lasitor."

"Who?" Eryn searched the ceiling for the source of the booming robotic voice.

Cian pulled the bedding over his head and mumbled sleepily, "Lasitor, the community AI, a computer program. He's kind of part of the building. He hides deep inside the programs so no one can find and delete him."

Taken aback by the lack of enemies, Eryn plopped back down. "What a way to wake up." His heart rate returned to normal, so he snuggled between his two favorite people.

"Didn't you hear Lasitor in the mornings when you stayed here with Joshua?"

"No."

"Maybe Joshua removed the speaker as we did from our room at our dad's place so that we could sleep in," Ivan said sleepily.

"Yeah, some people spray silicone inside the speaker to silence his voice. It's much more bearable."

Eryn yawned, stretched his arms out, and sank back under the covers. He pulled Ivan and Cian closer. "Morning, lovers," he said in his best seductive voice, loaded with all kinds of erotic insinuations, while he roamed downwards with his hands.

Just as they settled into each having a handful, a relentless irritating knocking at the front door forced them to take notice to move their horny asses out of bed.

"It's probably our dads." Cian moaned and started sucking on Eryn's s nipple.

"Ignore them. They'll go away," Ivan said. Wrapping his hand around Eryn's balls to pull on them. Eryn grew nervous; the knocking was unsettling, and who could relax anyway? They pinned Eryn by throwing a leg over one of his. The knocking started again, sounding like a song. *Pam, padda, pam-pam, pam-pam!*

"Shitballs! I promised them I wouldn't hurt you. Look at you. It looks like I ate, swallowed, and regurgitated you. Even your eyebrows need combing. Oh man, your dads are going to kill me," Eryn said. He sat up, making a quick decision. He scrambled, throwing the bedding this way and that. Then he grabbed each by the ankle and pulled them down. "Come, get up!" They came flying feet first out of bed and were upright with the velocity of a bullet. Frantically, he pushed and steered them toward the washroom. "Go shower. I'll open the door." They looked so adorable, their blond hair standing in all directions. He laughed, maneuvering them into the bathroom. Once there, he turned and quickly checked himself in the bathroom mirror. "I don't look any better." The twins dissolved into laughter. Dammit! The insistent knocking got louder.

"Shower, now!" he ordered them and closed the door with a bang.

He heard them shouting back. "You're so bossy!"

Grabbing a pair of pants from the floor, he hastily pulled on one leg while hopping. He took a few deep breaths and waved his hand over the sensor.

He greeted them with his best innocent-looking face. Mika and Connor were waiting, smiling from ear to ear. They knew precisely what they'd disturbed. Eryn stepped back to invite them inside.

"Morning, Dads. Please come in." Eryn started calling them dads as a joke while working on extracting the rocket from the mineshaft. It didn't seem to bother them much. Eryn could tell it made them happy, so he continued doing it because it made him glad, too.

The two scientists embraced their parenthood of

triple-deity children. They saw it as an honor to raise a divine being. They'd spoken about the exchanged female DNA, Nick, the disciple, divulged before he died. However, it was inexplicable when exactly the switching of the eggs and DNA happened. Something Mika and Connor wanted to discuss with Dr. Peter von Leutzendorf, not excluding the nagging fact, was the Peter Pan Capsules as the product of the twins' amniotic fluid, rather than the vitamins within the artificial placenta.

As the family had their meeting—something Eryn loved to be part of—they determined that switching the female DNA didn't matter because Mika and Connor were still their fathers, and that hadn't changed. If it did, they would still be their boys. Eryn was a different matter. He decided he would rather not know his genetic makeup; it didn't matter to him.

"Are you three well-rested and ready for today?" Mika asked, stretching his neck like a giraffe to see into their bedroom. Eryn cringed, wondering what to say. If he said yes, he'd be lying, but if he said no, they'd be disappointed. So he settled for, "Almost, the shower is too small for three people."

Connor coughed, and Mika blinked a few times. Speechless because, yes, the size of the shower did technically answer the question. Eryn could almost hear his thoughts looking for an answer as his mind whirr-whirred like gears behind Mika's stare.

"Okay, we'll get that sorted for you three today,"

Mika said casually while pinning Eryn with his intelligent blue gaze. No matter how Eryn tried to outmaneuver him, Mika was always one step ahead.

"Thank you, and while we're on that subject, Dad, do you think we can get a bigger bed, too?" Eryn asked like it was the most natural question. Testing Mika—ruffling his feathers unsuccessfully.

Mika gave an impassive nod. *Damn, the man is smooth, like water on a duck's feathers.*

Connor broke the silent standoff and said, "It makes sense," as he bent down to scoop up the three Anubis. The small black jackals yelped and looked happy to see Connor.

"Yes, they slept on the bed with us, and I'm worried if they get bigger..."

"No problem. We should get you an apartment big enough for the six of you. Last night was a short notice. We should go apartment hunting as soon as we settle down and have a chance. Maybe somewhere close to where these three can run free when they're bigger," Connor said, rubbing his nose against them playfully.

"Yes, that would be nice, thank you. Ivan said something about that last night," Eryn said, and relaxed in the older men's company. "Do you want to sit and wait for us?" he asked, unsure about the proper etiquette. He'd seen them offer each other something to drink, but he didn't know what the fridge contained. *Damn, I don't even know where the kitchen area is.* He decided not to offer anything. *I didn't think about that last night.*

"Hmm, no, thank you. Maybe we must go. Please ask the boys to come to the leadership office. We'll have breakfast while we discuss the plans," Mika said.

Eryn nodded. He was feeling extraordinarily naked in front of them while being bare-chested. *My comment about the shower and bed size went well.* The thought boosted his self-confidence, and he thought the brothers would be impressed.

Connor reluctantly put the Anubis pups down and left.

Eryn ran for the shower as soon as the door closed.

An hour later, the famous triad reached the Command Center, having had to stop many times for welcoming pats and hugs as a welcome back to Phoenix. The news about the Anubis had spread like wildfire. They looked fierce, making quite an impressive spectacle as they exuded power, friendliness, and kindness, but most of all, they oozed sexual pheromones.

Each twin wore a golden sword in its holster on their back. Their blond locks cascaded over their broad shoulders and seemed to glow. Both were dressed in black bodysuits and boots. Their freshly shaven, pale-skinned faces gleamed in the overhead lights while their blue eyes shone like reflected sunlight on ice. Their body length exacerbated their godlike features as they stood two meters tall and towered over the Phoenix males. But Eryn, at two and a half meters tall, was most comfortably dressed in his favorite pair of ragged jeans, a white t-shirt, and brand-new size sixteen snow boots, given to him by Mika.

The crowd swarmed them, and as soon as they saw the three Anubis in his arms, no one cared about his big build, strange eyes, or spear. When he bowed to one knee to lower himself so the ecstatic kids could see the supernatural creatures, the long braids in his ponytail flopped to the front to cover his shyness. Every man with a child or a child's heart obstructed the entry.

The door behind Eryn swooshed open, and Mika appeared. He greeted the crowd and apologized. "Sorry, comrades, please let the boys have breakfast. They have eaten nothing for over twenty-four hours."

He looked a bit upset, and Eryn sensed he was worried about them. The three Anubis loved the attention. They nipped and licked at anything within their reach. Ivan, Cian, and Eryn figured the more people they met, the friendlier they would be when they grew up. Eryn waved at the crowd and followed Mika inside, and the crowd dissipated.

"We need names for them," Eryn's voice thundered through the quiet area as the door shut. He was a nervous wreck after a barrage of repeated questions: How old are they? What are their names? How big will they be when they grow up? What do they eat? Where do they go potty, whatever that means?

"Boys, come in. We're in the big conference room." Mika welcomed them.

"Thank you, Dad. We're bloody damn hungry," Eryn said as they fell into the office, feeling overwhelmed.

"We saw your entourage and quietly hid inside here. We can imagine the questions, and we don't have the strength for that." Brad chuckled.

"You know, Dad, you're all cowards hiding here," Ivan said.

"We know," the men in the room answered, looking very proud of themselves.

"It's a matter of self-preservation," Brad answered.

But Mika looked worried about the boys. It was obvious how tired they were when they practiced, and today would be a much bigger task. "Bring the pups over here. What have you been feeding them?" he asked.

"Meat. They look happy with that."

"Oh, where do you get that?" Bryan, the new leader, asked.

Eryn summed him up as a good man with friendly eyes. He got to know Bryan the night they took him prisoner, but they weren't happy to meet that night. Given the circumstances, that was understandable. Everyone in the office turned their way.

"Meat is a rarity in Phoenix, you know?"

"So far, Eryn caught them a few birds and a penguin," Connor answered, reaching out for the pups again. They fell over their feet to get to Connor.

"Ah, luckily for them to have a daddy like Eryn," Brad said. "You should see him. He dove into the Antarctic waters, heavy spear in hand, and brought food for all of us."

He sounded proud of Eryn and wanted to say more, but Mika interrupted him. "Come, boys, time to have breakfast." They didn't need another invitation for them to storm the buffet. The amount of variety shocked Eryn. He stepped back, uncomfortable and unsure about the correct etiquette for the second time that morning. The twins immediately caught on to it.

"Eryn, what would you like to eat? Come closer. We'll help you," Cian said. He picked up three plates and handed one to Ivan and one to Eryn.

"Usually, we eat bread with protein and then some fruit for vitamins."

Eryn frowned. He understood nothing but bread. Feeling uncomfortable in front of everyone, he whispered, "Just give me the same as you would take. You can tell me more about it later."

Ivan widened his eyes to Cian—a silent warning to be more sensitive.

Mika must have seen the non-verbal communication and stepped forward. "Boys, you eat and fill your tummies. You'll burn the candles on both ends today, so fill up and don't be shy."

Brad stepped forward and added, "Eryn, no one here is judging you. We're thrilled to have you, and you're welcome to ask questions. Ask as many questions as you like. All of us are here to make you guys feel supported."

A chorus from around the office of, "Yes, absolutely, thank you for trying to help." We're glad you are here."

"Thank you for saving the boys from your brother."

Eryn smiled shyly and straightened up. Cian and Ivan smiled from ear to ear, thankful for the warm welcome of their lover.

Brad turned and spoke to the men, laughing. "Someday, someone will discover that area where you guys practiced creating capsules. I would love to hear their explanations or theories about where the balls came from and why they're stacked hundreds of meters into the shape of a pyramid."

"Maybe a giant rolled his snot into little balls and stacked them like that," Cian said.

Ivan pulled his top lip up in disgust. "Yuck, that's disgusting." He threw the ball-shaped donut in his hand back onto his plate.

The room broke out with laughter. Eryn loved every second, and the Anubis yipped and howled with shrill jackal calls.

"They're so damn cute," Connor said while he fed them pieces of fish sticks.

"Okay," Bryan said. "Now we think Mika should explain what we decided on for the day's business."

Mika stepped to the front of the conference room. The room was the largest meeting room in the Command Center and could seat over a hundred people. Mika quickly explained to Eryn that they initially intended it to be the governing council or town hall meeting room, where community members could attend meetings. However, the original council of three preferred to meet in their own offices, with Connor's being the preferred location because it was the most technologically advanced and comfortable.

"Thank you, men. I appreciate you organizing the conference room today. It's the ideal size for the first and current councils of three, as well as the divine triad, as the three are now known," Mika said boisterously with a wide smile.

The boys stuffed their faces, only coming up for air to sip their drinks, nodding a few times, and then diving back into cleaning their plates. Mika looked lovingly at them as he admired their enthusiasm for filling their stomachs.

"We welcome the extra space, especially the buffet breakfast. I can imagine how going down to the community dining area wouldn't be productive for today's plans," Brad said.

Bryan stepped forward to make an announcement. "Now that everyone's here, welcome back, but I'd like to make a proposition. Since you were gone, your replacement council members were swamped and realized that you three had a tremendous job managing Phoenix as smoothly as you did for over twenty years. Filling your shoes was not a straightforward task. We couldn't wait for your return, and although it's selfish of us, we feel you men are best at getting the jobs done."

Peter and Tony nodded affirmatively from the opposite end of the table. Eryn noticed the bright blue eyes were sparkling every time Peter looked in Bryan's or Tony's direction. Peter looked radiantly happy, but he couldn't seem to make eye contact with Eryn. *Maybe he's shy?*

Simon and Paul sat ever reserved and professional while listening as Bryan spoke. When Bryan was done, Simon lifted his hand for a turn.

"Dads, we didn't realize the scope of your work, and we hoped you would retake your places. I speak for father Rick, who single-handedly managed the clinic. It's time you accept our support and retake your seats on the council, but the circumstances, although tragic, may have been a blessing in disguise. We are not on the council, but we offer to stay and help manage the clinic. Paul and I salute you. We don't want your job. We talked to the replacement council and came to an agreement to act as deputies, and we propose we bring this to the citizens, the

Phoenicians. The Phoenix population is growing, which means there are more souls to represent," Simon said. He bowed slightly to thank the council.

"Thank you, men. I'll think of how and when to present this to the general population. I love the name Phoenicians. It's very original," Brad said, looking not surprised by the proposition but very appreciative of the support of restructuring.

He sat, and Mika got up to take the floor. He turned to the giant touchscreen and switched it on by touching the side of it.

"Lasitor, I need bird's-eye views and worm-eye views of Phoenix."

"Certainly, sir," the AI answered with a professional tone.

"I also need to know how deep Phoenix's underground pipe, tunnel, and sewage system runs."

"Yes, sir, calculating," Lasitor answered. After a few minutes, architectural blueprints and maps with measurements appeared on the screen. Mika continued as the men sat at the front of their seats, concentrating on what Mika would show them.

"Then, I need the latest Phoenix architectural maps and designs of the artificial systems and Antarctica's environmental support of Phoenix within a hundred-kilometer radius. I need you to crosscut the views from a nine-point circle on that radius."

As soon as Mika said the nine-point circle, the room exploded in ah's and oh's. "You're the alpha geek," Connor said, and Mika bowed. "See, that's why I married the man," Connor said proudly

The triad just looked up, swallowed, and shook their heads. Then dove back into their plates.

"Excuse me, not all of us here are scientists. Can you explain again to us who don't have more than one degree after our names?" Captain Howell asked sarcastically.

"Certainly, sir." Lasitor started, as if Bryan had asked him and not Mika.

"In geometry, the nine-point circle is a circle that can be constructed for any triangle. It's so named because it passes through nine significant concyclic points defined by the triangle. These nine points are the midpoint of each side of the triangle, the foot of each altitude, and the midpoint of the line segment from each vertex to where the three altitudes meet. These line segments lie on their respective altitudes."

Eryn noticed Bryan looked even more confused, deepening the furrow between his eyebrows. Mika helped by drawing on the screen—he drew a circle inside the circle, then wrote "Phoenix." Then he drew a triangle.

"The boys will start each at a point," Mika told them. "Then they will move to the next point." He drew another triangle. He was making dots at the points where the triangle cut through. "See the first three dots, then they move. Then six dots, and finally, they move to a third spot." He made three more dots on the circle where the triangle cut through.

"Ah, now I see. Thank you, Mika. I see now what you have in mind," Bryan said. He looked at the boys and exchanged nods and smiles. Eryn appreciated him asking.

"Mika had to show us a picture, too. Don't feel bad, Bryan," Eryn said.

"Now the Pyramid of balls makes sense," Bryan said, referring to Brad's earlier statement. "Am I correct in saying we'll be in the center of it?"

"Yes, because a triangle is the strongest shape, we used air-filled pillows instead of one bubble around us. What do you think?" Mika turned and asked his audience.

"Sir, that's an excellent idea. I ran an algorithm against anything that could destabilize Phoenix, and I have to say that's the best option," Lasitor answered again as if Mika had asked him. The men around the conference table laughed but eventually agreed. It might work.

"Okay, lovers, are you ready to rumble?" Eryn asked, later that afternoon,

literally meaning what he was saying, referring to when they practiced with their swords for the first time. Cian and Ivan's swords sizzled and sparked so loudly that Mika came running outside, asking if it was raining.

"Where's the rumble?" Since then, they teased him about that, and it became an inside joke between the four. As they discussed and planned earlier that morning, they divided the triad into three directions.

"Yes, let's roll out!" Ivan said. Pulling his goggles over his eyes and climbing onto the back of a snowmobile, he waved to Eryn and then proceeded to start on the first of his three points of the nine points on the one-hundred-kilometer radius circle around Phoenix.

Eryn watched a sea of spectators stretching out as far as his eyes could see, waiting for him. He could barely contain his excitement at being part of something so big. He'd always worked alone, and Ernest never appreciated him. Therefore, the crowd of spectators who offered whatever support was needed to complete the task gave him an immense sense of purpose. It felt good helping humankind.

Mika and Connor previously stated that placing a protective layer on the inside of Phoenix should be a top priority, as the impending annihilation could occur at any time. As soon as the battery-powered snowmobile stopped, Eryn jumped off to weave a buffering layer in case of falling debris.

He lifted his spear and sensed his mates triangulated from him. Together, the three sang, filling the air around them and forming a vacuum of sound that enveloped the city. The beautiful notes stunned the crowd into silence. Some had fallen to their knees and cried while struck by the beauty of his song.

"Oh, my gods, it's soul-wrenchingly magnificent!" his driver, Thomas Edgar, exclaimed. He had his arctic suit on like all the others, contrasting with Eryn's black bodysuit and black boots. A gift from Connor and Mika.

"Yes, the song of angels," someone in the crowd said.

"Not a song. It's like a choir of angels," another man answered.

Eryn smiled and sang louder for the people. The more he sang, the more transfixed they got. Overjoyed, some started to dance and play. Still, Eryn sang. He held his spear high and sang even louder until he saw tiny sparks from the tip of his golden spear. Then he lowered his voice, sensing the twins ending their song. He could feel them getting tired.

He turned to Thomas, who sat sideways on the snowmobile, watching him with awe. He had his radio with him. "Thomas, how long have we been busy working?" Eryn asked as he'd lost track of time when he closed his eyes to concentrate and work.

"Sir, you've been busy for four hours."

"Please radio Mika, Connor, and the twins. Tell them ten minutes, and then we stop. We must work together. Otherwise, we may overload each other."

"Yes, I know, sir. Mika explained to me earlier."

"Thank you, Thomas."

"No problem, sir."

Eryn didn't like the man calling him sir, but he figured he was a king, so that was probably the way humans showed respect to a king.

He heard Thomas' radio Mika and sensed the energy reducing on both his lovers' sides. Ten minutes later, he lowered his spear. Drained, he fell back into the snow. Worried that if he felt so tired now, how much more would his Cian and Ivan be? He decided on a blowjob for each tonight. *The pups are with Donali and Kawa, so we have the bed.* He got up, pushing himself up with his spear. The crowd didn't say a word.

"Are you ready, Thomas? I want to go home." Eryn asked.

"Yes, sir, jump on. Let's go!" As soon as his butt touched the snowmobile, the crowd erupted in applause. They cheered and roared their thanks. Eryn waved while a few boys ran after their resident superhero. Eryn was thirsty and hungry. All the talking and working had him parched, and he would have asked to stop to drink something and maybe talk some more, but he wanted to see the twins. His spirit lifted when he saw his mates waiting for him in front of the main entrance. They looked as drained as he felt. Mika and Connor waved and disappeared inside, avoiding the crowd following Eryn and the twins.

"I'm so glad to see you." He jumped off his ride before it completely stopped.

Cian and Ivan fell into his arms. "It feels like we haven't seen you for years. We missed you so much!" Ivan said.

He kissed both, sharing a three-way kiss, weaving his long tongue between them, tasting their essence, and it immediately settled his anticipation of seeing them. No one remarked because, in Phoenix, throuples were the new normal.

"Let's go. I'm ravenous." Eryn pushed his twins inside to move them faster toward his goal.

"Me, too. I need Juandre's Booster Juice, a shower, and a bed," Cian said with the same goals in mind as Eryn.

"We need all our strength for tomorrow. We should pace ourselves. Early in the morning, we should start looking at the external layers surrounding Phoenix. Those famous balls of cushions will be a big hit with the crowd," Ivan said. Although his goals were precisely in the same order as his mates, he had to talk with caution. Eryn loved him. He was predictable, stern, cute, and sexy...

Cian interrupted his thoughts. His eyes sparkled with mischief. "The kids are excited to see how we bubble-wrap, Phoenix," he laughed.

"I don't know about you, but that hundred-kilometer radius is almost too far away from you both," Ivan said as he sheathed his sword on his back.

"Just remember to leave two openings for the entrances," Eryn cautioned. "No, seriously, leave one at the front where the massive roll-up door is situated and another at the shipyard for the movement of equipment or ships."

"We know, but that would be so funny. I can see how our dads and Brad freak out when they can't leave or go outside." Cian chuckled, never failing to be the joker.

"Got it, boss." Ivan saluted Eryn.

"It's not me but Father Mika who said so. We're to leave two separate tunnels of a hundred meters created with a downward curve to ensure water can't enter," Eryn said as he steered them into the dining area. He was so hungry, and the singing burned most of his energy. He knew the twins felt the same.

That night, they ate, drank, and slept. It was eat, sleep, rinse, and repeat for the next seven days.

The crowds had grown smaller by day seven. Some children carried small black superhero toys, and the three looked badass in all black. Eryn, the giant carrying a golden staff, was the favorite, but the twins and their golden swords were also well-liked. Phoenix was wrapped in protective layers. Encapsulated, and it should be safe against external natural forces.

"We need lubrication," Cian said to his mates. "I'll ask Father about it. I noticed they have strawberry-mint-flavored glycerin lubrication. Someone mixes it for them, maybe the pharmacy? Also, tonight we're watching porn. Not one of us knows what to do. We need some tips. Lasitor will play it for us," Cian explained his plan excitedly while on their way out after breakfast for their last day of applying the finishing touches to safeguarding the Phoenix.

"Tonight, we research. Cian, we'll have to flip a coin to see who goes first," Ivan said.

I have to put a lot of thought into this. Eryn decided to watch and see what they came up with.

"Before we finish today, apply a protection layer to the surrounding earth, directly to the ground and atmosphere. The more layers, the better," Eryn said, hoping to avoid any debris or gas released by the underground volcanic eruptions. "If you do that, I can do layers from the core to the stratosphere, and we can reinforce those now and then," Eryn said, kissing them goodbye.

They hopped on their transport for their final day's work. Like all the previous mornings, a crowd was already waiting for them. This time, they were a bit more organized, Eryn noticed. He smelled baked scones and coffee—a whole container with Rooster Juice.

"Morning, everyone," Eryn greeted them with gracious nobleness. He thanked them for being so thoughtful by making his efforts easier.

"Just like bubble-wrapping a snow globe, Daddy!" one small boy told his father when they finished speaking to Eryn, who explained safeguarding Phoenix to the boy.

It was a big and daunting task, but all the residents of Phoenix supported their divine triad by attending the bubble-wrapping or offering something warm to eat or drink.

The eighth day was eventful. First, as a mating gift and to show they appreciate their efforts, Mika and Connor demolished three apartments next to each other and rebuilt them so that the three boys could live together in one massive apartment with their Anubis. The three apartments were empty and next to the shipyard because no one wanted to live so close to the noise. Mika had the walls reinforced and insulated, so no sound would travel outside or inside the apartment. The pups were happy they had a big enough room to run inside, and if they wanted to go out, the shipyard exits were nearby. The three young men and their pups were excited and immediately moved in that day.

Phoenix celebrated the accomplishment by having a celebration of life for Juandre and Andrew in their favorite nineteen-twenties Moulin Rouge set in the Blue Ballroom. For the finale, many men took part in performing the Can-Can on and off stage. Those who didn't dance clapped as they danced to the beat of the music. Tears were streaming down their cheerful faces. Even Mika got up on stage to dance his Russian warrior dance in their honor.

Afterward, Connor, Brad, and Bryan spoke about their love and enthusiasm for life. Everyone agreed with booming laughter that the Rooster Juice production would continue in their honor.

During the ceremony, Eryn had two things on his mind, the twins. He wanted to suck, lick, and taste them. During the speeches, he smiled at the people while he daydreamed about flicking his tongue, and tasting their hardened flesh in his mouth.

He could taste them already, the glands in the back of his throat, where the undeveloped gills were located, contracted and filled his mouth with saliva while Brad and Bryan's voices went *bla-bla-bla* in the background.

When he returned to reality, they mentioned joining the council members. The week had been long, and he had many things to try. Thinking about the porn they watched the previous night, his heart rate had yet to return to normal. Another round of clapping and asking anyone willing to lend a hand to step up and put their names down.

"Voting will happen within a week." Brad continued, "If the proposed council needs to be replaced, this is where the community can give voice to new members to replace them."

Brad waved them onto the stage. Eryn grabbed Ivan and Cian by the hand. "We're leaving right after this," he said, pulling the twins hastily to be honored as the divine triad and receive the ceremonial key of the city of Phoenix. "A sign that all three would always be welcome at Phoenix as Phoenicians," Brad said proudly.

Mika and Connor appeared to be the happiest fathers. They clapped and cheered the loudest as the three accepted the key with an air of reserved nobility —saviors of the last of humanity and the horniest three virgins on Earth.

They left as quickly as Eryn could pull them off the stage and down the hallway.

Finally, the ceremony ended.

CHAPTER 25
DELICIOUSLY CRUEL

"Good morning, citizens of Phoenix.

I, Lasitor, bid you a good morning.

It's now six a.m.

Are you in the mood for adulterated fun? Did you know recent studies down at Quik-Fix Hall revealed, despite what men claim, only fifteen percent of the patrons have a penis longer than eight inches, and only three percent have a penis over nine inches long?

Visit your twenty-one and above community news page to sign up for a dick-measuring contest, among other things.

Breakfast is served until eight a.m.

Have a good day!"

Eryn King of the Brawl

Eryn stood stock still in front of his Anunnaki mates. *Am I drooling?* He licked his lips. Four smoldering blue eyes followed the movement. While smiling greedily, his gaze locked on his prey, his pending feast, and lord knows he came hungry. After rechecking his pointy fangs, he made sure for the second time this minute they retracted by rolling his tongue over the roof of his mouth.

I'll lick them both until they have permanent goosebumps. Then I'm going to lick each goosebump until every inch of their bodies is slick with my spit, and then I'm going to suck on my mates until they're bone dry, begging me to stop. So Eryn strategized, and the anticipation tightened every muscle in his body, ready to pounce.

After they kicked off their boots, Ivan and Cian led Eryn to their colossal new bedroom. They were waiting for Eryn to make the first move. Other than checking his fangs, next on the list was the Anubis, so he sent his feelers out like he used to do with his brothers. Yes, they're happy and safe in their kennel. They're all fed, content, and sleepy.

His lovers seemed happy and impressed, not only with their new apartment but also with him. Mika and Connor enlarged a few photos they found in Joshua's apartment of a younger Eryn, playing inside the colorful bioluminescent subterranean tunnels, pictures Eryn didn't know existed. Until a few days ago, he didn't know what a photo was, but now they were everywhere he looked. It scared him a bit. It was as if it had caught his soul in time; apparently, it was beautiful and acceptable to use them as decorations for their home. For Eryn, where his twins were was his home, and the pictures didn't matter to him. As long as he had them, he was the luckiest man in the world. He was glad that Joshua was now a hero and would be remembered that way.

The drumming of their combined heartbeats slammed into the insides of their ribcages, creating a techno rhythm that drove Eryn forward, refocusing him on the twins. He grinned hungrily, sensing their anticipation, their need, and want for him. They tried to reciprocate and return all kinds of filthy pleasures, ensuring Eryn knew he was on their menu. *Finally, I can do what I visualized all day.* Eryn held himself back to prolong their sweet suffering. *Control yourself. This will be perfect, just like you planned. Keep the surprise for last.*

He nodded his approval while raking their bodies slowly up and down with a smoldering gaze.

Their breaths hitched, and Eryn knew they felt the intensifying heat of his approving gaze stoking the fire between them, and he basked in the electric musical radiance of their combined divine mating songs. Cool musical notes touched their skin like snowflakes, while golden blue spirals fluttered like a cold summer breeze, caressing them and blending their songs into one crescendo of euphoric lust and power. *This must be what humans feel when they say they will make love.*

Then, in his best layman's terms, he said, "I'm fucking horny and fascinated with the two of you. I want you more than anything I've ever wanted. Even gold doesn't compare to the two of you." Still, Ivan said nothing.

And that was when Cian broke the tension. He lifted his fist to his mouth and sang to the beat in the room. "Don't you feel it? It's the nineteen-nineties Technotronic song." He excitedly let loose singing the song, thrusting his hips widely.

"Pump up the jam, pump it up,
While your beat is stompin',
And the glam is flowin.'
Look around. Lovers are waitin',
Pump it up, bring it on,
Let's get fuckin, close the damn door,
See, 'cause this where the magic's at,
You'll find out if you suck on that,
I'm just glad that we are gay,
Get your booty on the bed tonight,
I'm your buffet'
Be my lay,
Get your booty on the bed tonight.
Be my lay Be my lay-ay.
Be my lay-ay-ay,
I'm your buffet."

Cian sang while Ivan and Eryn watched, not

finding the silliness amusing. Cian let his fist fall. "Sorry, I couldn't resist. I feel as high as a kite."

"We know, we can see that. When you're done, I'd like to get on with what we were doing. You wiped away all the heat and song. Look." Ivan pointed to the surrounding room. All the color was gone, and only gray darkness shone cold and empty around them.

"If you do that again, I'm going to put you in the corner with a carrot stuck up your ass. You'll be nobody's lay. You get me, no one's buffet," Eryn promised with a low, menacing voice. He meant it, but as soon as the words left his mouth, silence fell over the room.

Cian looked like he was having a choking episode or a seizure with wide-open eyes. No sound escaped his mouth. Pressing his lips together, his face turned pink, purple, and blue. Grabbing his throat and closing his eyes, he turned away from them, unable to contain himself. He erupted in laughter, accompanied by snorts and giggles.

Eryn shook his head, and Ivan shrugged, sharing a private what the fuck moment. Eryn stepped closer to Ivan and lifted his chin, recapturing the mood. He kissed Ivan profoundly and sensually. Tasting and savoring his deliciousness.

Cian quickly lost the goofiness, realizing he was losing out. He watched them while rubbing his cock as Eryn gifted Ivan with pecks of kisses on his neck and Adam's apple. Eryn took Ivan's beautiful face in both hands and kissed him deeply. Cian groaned and joined in. Then Eryn alternated between his lovers and did the same to Cian. He stood back. Their sexy pink lips were parted, and they were breathing faster than usual. Their flawless beauty was almost blinding. Eryn wanted to squint his eyes at Ivan's bright pearlescent shine, which was ten times more luminous than Cian's.

Still, they were inhumanly beautiful, with elegantly cut angles, sharp edges of high cheekbones, and straight, upturned eyebrows.

They're so different from me. I don't know what they see in me.

Ribbons of songs of approval, desire, and strength continued again, swirling around them, weaving the unbreakable bond into every cell of their bodies, urging them to become one bond and mate. Eryn never expected the overwhelming compulsion or the inexplicable need guiding him, and he couldn't resist them one second longer.

"I have to have you now. I'm hungry for you," he said, reaching for Cian and Ivan's pants above their zippers, pulling them closer for a three-way kiss, taking the lead, first kissing Ivan and then Cian, who moaned into his mouth.

Ivan joined by nipping and biting on the left corner of Eryn's bottom lip. Eryn turned his attention to Ivan, licking deep into his mouth, running his tongue between his top lip and teeth like he knew

Ivan liked it. All the while, Cian rubbed himself on his right hip, licking a path over Eryn's square jaw up to his earlobe, sucking on it.

Eryn all but growled at them, "Let's get naked. I want to suck both of you at the same time." The twins were eager, so ready to be devoured that they stripped off their shirts, buttons popping, sending them flying to the sides of the room. They loosened their belts, mechanically thumbing their zippers. They let their pants fall to the floor and stepped forward, loosening their long blond hair from the buns on their heads. Their cheeks were flushed red, and they whined and panted for Eryn, who read every unspoken word in how they moved and watched him. Eryn removed their briefs by reaching around their tight, skinny, muscled butts, grabbed hold of the snug-fitting cotton, and ripped them off by pulling down and back, tearing them into pieces.

"Fuck, Eryn, that's hot!" That woke Cian out of his stupor.

"Holy fuck, Eryn!" Ivan exclaimed, joining his brother and answering the urgent wake-up call. Eryn threw the pieces of white cloth this way and that.

"Hmmm, yes, lover." They groaned their approval when they recuperated from the erotic move. Inching forward, they moved closer, offering their leaking, uncut cocks to Eryn as he kneeled, waiting with his mouth wide open. They hissed in unison, depositing their pale seven-inch cocks as deep as Eryn could manage down his throat. Eryn grabbed hold of their backsides, forcing them deeper. He couldn't get enough. He wanted to devour them, so he growled his hunger and frustration around their cocks.

Ivan gasped, throwing his head back. Cian let loose a string of unrecognizable vowels and consonants. Maybe it was Gaelic?

Pulling his head back, Eryn let their stiff cocks slip out of his mouth, and saliva dripped down from his chin.

"Look, his eyes glow a faint red, reflecting the dim overhead light on the extra layer of tissue covering his eyeballs, the tapetum lucidum—a product of your nocturnal frog DNA so that you could see colors in the dark," Ivan said, awestruck. Eryn watched how mixed pre-cum and spittle glistened on their cockheads while thin strands of the sticky threads shone and stretched like spiderwebs between his lips and their drenched members.

Repeating the move two more times, Eryn sensed their pleasure increasing. They shivered, moaned, and writhed, becoming more vocal, and their dicks throbbed deliciously rigid and malleable like the yellow metal he loved so much.

Eryn looked up at them, slipping his long tongue out and wrapping it around their cockheads. Overrun with lust, the twins threw their arms around each other to steady themselves.

Eryn tightened his tongue around their cocks,

inserting the long, stretching tip into Cian's piss slit. Sliding inside, tasting his essence, needing to taste more, he fucked the inside of Cian's cock, slowly slipping deeper while looking into those blue eyes, snaking his tongue deeper and deeper, all the while Cian yelled louder and louder obscenities until he touched Cian's prostate.

"Motherfucker," Cian exclaimed, throwing his head backward, his knees buckled. Ivan held him tighter, supporting and forcing him to endure the unexpected intrusion.

"Take it, brother. I know you like it. That looks so hot," Ivan remarked, radiating anxiety for his turn to be speared by the mighty tongue.

Slowly, Eryn slipped his tongue tip from Cian's dick, who was panting and had tears of pleasure streaming from his eyes. He vibrated when Eryn returned to his administration, sucking and probing him simultaneously. By now, the golden blue ribbons twisted, danced, and fluttered, transforming the room into a fantastical neon blue galaxy. As soon as Eryn noticed Cian's increased breathing and rapid heart rate, his eyes closed, head thrown backward, he palpated Cian's usually soft ballsac, discovering it all rumpled and tightened up, balls gone, ready to shoot his load. He immediately reversed out of there, leaving Cian edging on the precipice of an explosive orgasm.

"No, that's just nasty, Eryn. I almost fucking

came," Cian objected. His glow diminished while sweat ran from the sides of his face, but he readied himself to anchor Ivan. Eryn snickered and snaked his tongue around Ivan's cockhead, who immediately relaxed into the exquisite sensations of being speared and sucked.

"Ohm, ohm, ohm, oh my," Ivan sang his mating song mixed with incoherent sounds, while Eryn devoured his rock-hard cock from the inside, giving him the same slow tongue fucking. Ivan's icy blue eyes locked with Eryn's. For a second, it felt like it was only the two of them in the room. All of Eryn's fears, flaws, and wounds disappeared as he found total acceptance and requited love staring down at him. Ivan closed his eyes, breaking the connection between them. Eryn felt the telltale goosebumps on Ivan's ass and abruptly ceased the blowjob session.

Now it's time!

Eryn couldn't wait to show them his big surprise. He hoped they liked what he'd conjured up for them.

"Holy fuck, you're going to kill us," Ivan exclaimed. He glowed brighter.

Eryn swallowed his laugh with glee. He knew he was teasing the fuck out of them, and his playful nature showed when he rubbed his hands together, looking extremely naughty.

"Holy fucking shit, you're so deliciously cruel. I love it. Do it to me again, please," Cian begged, pushing his cock toward Eryn's mouth, but Eryn didn't budge. He had other plans for tonight.

"It sure sounds like I'm doing something right." He sniggered, steering them to their extra-extra-extra-large king-size bed, big enough for three tall demigods and three full-grown Anubis. The back of their legs touched the foot of the bed, and they sat down in front of him, cocks purple-pink pointing straight up to the roof. Their songs danced around them, slower but ever-present.

The need to fuck something pulsated through Eryn's groin. He got up to remove his clothes, to present his big reveal to them. Their mating song urged him to uncover his massive, muscled body for them.

I must show them how magnificent I am. I must show them I deserve them.

With the swirling force of their mating call that he couldn't resist anymore, the animalistic need to make them his, to mate, to become one, drummed through his veins. Slowly, he removed his pants, keeping his green-golden gaze locked with his lovers. The twins pinned him with the same hunger and reluctance to take their attention off him.

Eryn's two ten-inch cocks sprung free, pointing straight at each of them.

"What the fuck?" The young men exclaimed in surprise. "Is that real?"

"Do you like it?" Eryn asked unsurely, hoping his

decision to grow another cock didn't look too eager to please both, although he would do anything for them, and he hoped this showed his devotion to making both brothers happy.

"Eryn, you have two cocks?" Cian exclaimed, still shocked, mouth hanging open.

"Am I seeing this right?" Ivan asked Cian. Licking his lips, not looking away from the two-eyed monsters, Cian grunted affirmatively, slowly.

"Do you have four balls now?" Cian asked.

Eryn couldn't tell whether they wanted it. Do they like it? He couldn't tell. "I can remove it if you don't like it or if it bothers you. It looks strange. I just thought this way, both of you could have something to play with. No, I have only two balls."

Cian didn't say a word. He motioned for Eryn to come closer with a pointer finger. His eyes crinkled at the corners, and he looked intrigued. Lying down on his back, he opened his legs invitingly. "Come, plow."

Eryn complied.

"Just tell me one thing. How did you do that?" Cian never failed to verbalize his thoughts, excitement, and wonder, written all over his face. "I wonder if we can do that, too?"

"I don't know. You have to try to see. I remembered my father said something about changing my body to reproduce but never thought about it again until you guys fought for the attention of my cock, so I thought it would be nice to have two, and the next moment I went to piss, there were two."

"Luckily, you're a grower and not a shower. Otherwise, you'd have trouble walking," Ivan said. Falling onto his back next to his brother, he, too, opened his legs for Eryn. Both lay watching and waiting with a hand around their cocks.

Eryn retook control. Satisfied with the twins' reactions, he moved closer. His two cocks sprang up and down as he moved his big, bulky body over the mattress. The width of the twins' slender hips combined more closely with his targets. Ivan rolled over to the nightstand.

"Lube up those big boys."

Eryn grabbed the glass bottle Ivan chucked his way and lathered his cocks with the fruity-smelling lubrication. A gift from their fathers. He applied it liberally, as the pornographic sex education video the twins showed him the previous night had taught him. He squirted a blob on each of his lovers' holes and massaged them. Their asses were hungry for him. They puckered and clenched around the tips of his fingers. Ivan and Cian's eyes were closed, and they were back to moaning and wordless begging as he teased and thrust his long middle fingers, searching for their prostates. He knew he had found the little pleasure nuts when they howled in surprised ecstasy.

"Eryn, if you don't fuck me now, I'm going to explode," Ivan said.

Pulling his fingers out of their well-stretched entrances, he grabbed his eager mates' hips, dragging their asses closer to him, then folded their legs back so their knees touched their ears; he aligned his cocks to their holes, teasing their entrances.

"Do it, fuck me," Cian said with fire in his gaze.

"Make us yours, Eryn!" Ivan encouraged and grabbed his cock, squeezing it for relief. Eryn aligned a throbbing dark red, almost purple cockhead in front of each hole, then moved closer, bending his hips, aiming to slip inside.

"Prepare yourselves to be fucked by a mighty king, King Eryn of the Brawl. I'm going for gold now. I've waited the whole damn day to do this. You're so fucking beautiful."

"Okay, less talking, more fucking, guys," Cian said, pushing his rear toward his massive dick on Eryn's right.

Ivan shuddered and groaned as Eryn breached his sphincter. Eryn ached with need. Almost unbearably so, with two times the pleasure. He groaned, enjoying the double-dipping and two-timing levels of raw lust and pleasure overflowing his senses, exaggerating his awareness of his lovers.

"I think I see stars," he exclaimed loudly, enjoying his first double penetration.

"Eryn, wait," Cian screamed on the brink of being torn open. "Please, fucking wait, let us adjust."

Eryn stopped himself, sweat dripping from his

brows. The energy from their mating heat had him seeing double. He wanted to come, but he held himself as still as possible. He caressed and fondled his twins' dicks.

"You said less talking, more fucking, Cian. What do you want?" Eryn asked, teasing and spearing them again with his tongue. As soon as their holes relaxed, they nodded for him to continue. The sweet taste of their nectar and the feelings of their tight virgin holes around his cocks were better than he'd ever imagined. The whining sounds from his lovers forced him to let go of the animal inside him. He pistoned the tips of his cocks in and out of their asses, showing them he was the king to rule and dominate them.

"Fuck yes, Eryn, please fuck us faster! This feels so good," Ivan begged.

"That's it, baby, fuck yes! Show us how hard and fast you can go," Cian hollered with his eyes closed.

They begged, moaned, and commanded, but Eryn knew this first round wouldn't last long. Ivan had to hold back his climax as he watched Eryn's tongue fuck into Cian's slit while pounded by Eryn's ten-inch cock. Cian's eyes rolled back into his head, grabbing onto Ivan and the bedding to stabilize himself. Ivan waited for his turn for that tongue, so he cheered from the side.

"That's it, Cian, cum for us!" Ivan encouraged his brother. Eryn pumped deep two more times, and then Cian erupted. Jizz spurted out on the sides of Eryn's tongue. When he retracted his tongue fully, Cian squirted another few thick creamy shots of semen straight into Eryn's mouth and over his face, which he was eager to taste and lick clean with his stretchy pink tongue.

As his sensual torment continued, Ivan started trembling from head to toe, so Eryn turned his skillful tongue over him. Ivan shook his head from left to right, trying to prolong the exquisite torture for as long as possible.

"Motherfucker," he cried out. Eryn retracted his tongue, and Ivan ejaculated puddles of cum onto his lower abdomen. Then it happened, Eryn, the bed, and the whole damn room rumbled and vibrated as Eryn shot massive loads of cum into their guts.

Sliding his hands under Ivan's and Cian's hips, he lifted both their hips high. In one movement, they sat back to back, and he sat back on his haunches, bringing both their bodies with him. Cian was on Eryn's right hip, and Ivan was on Eryn's left hip. Eryn let his head and shoulders fall backward as he panted and groaned with contentment while they continued riding his sensitive cocks. When he'd recovered and caught his breath, he lightly moved his hands across their stomachs, taking hold of their soft cocks.

"Hold out as long as you can, Eryn. We want to ride you for a long time. This feels so good, baby," Ivan said as Eryn snaked his tongue around from the base of his cock to the tip of his erection.

"Stop saying, baby, I'm a king. I'm not a baby." Eryn lifted his hips and fucked them from the bottom. They groaned.

He pumped their dicks and fucked their holes. Their long blond hair, sweaty and messy, flew everywhere. The sounds of wet skin slapping wet skin and the smells of cum and sex had Eryn trembling and rumbling within minutes, and the twins sensed his arousal reaching climactic heights and that he was near coming again.

Cian planted his heels and bent backward to slide his hand down Eryn's thigh, grabbing his balls. Eryn squeezed his eyes shut, his lips in an *O*, pulling air in and out, sounding like a steam train. Cian wrapped his long fingers around it and pulled.

Eryn didn't stand a chance. He wanted to orgasm but prolong the pleasure simultaneously. He threw his head back and yelled, "Ah, that's not fair. Don't stop. It feels so good."

Then he felt Ivan sending his enjoyment of the vibrations shooting through his hypersensitive cock.

"We'll cum together, okay?" Eryn moaned. He sensed they were close to orgasm for the second time. He rammed up, hard and deep, one last time. The rumbling of Eryn, the bed, and the room started again, and then they ejaculated.

"Fuck yeah!" Eryn roared with pleasure.

"Yes, yes, yes!" Cian exclaimed, multitasking the

shit out of this by pulling Eryn's balls and balancing himself.

"Ah, fuck, yeah, baby, sorry, I meant..." Ivan exploded. *Eryn, I love you so much. Ivan mentally connected and spoke directly* into Eryn's mind.

The twins howled, falling spent and sated onto Eryn. Their slicked, sweaty bodies slid from Eryn's hips like two garden snails, leaving a trail of Eryn's jizz.

They lay as they fell and landed on Eryn's left and right sides. A heap of bliss-out mess. Once their breathing was under control. Ivan licked his dry lips and smiled up at Eryn.

"I love that I can see your love for me. I see it in your eyes. They're filled with love. And what makes it even more special is that we can share feelings and emotions." Ivan said.

Eryn stroked Ivan's cheek softly with his big thumb.

"I didn't realize we could do that. I always thought it was only you who could sense ours. Maybe it was because our powers are getting stronger."

Eryn licked Ivan's parched lips sensually. "I'm glad you can feel my feelings as well." For some inexplicable reason, Eryn connected only with Ivan. Maybe next time he will try harder to connect with Cian.

Cian rolled closer and kissed Eryn's shoulder lovingly. "That was awesome, Eryn. Thank you."

"Hmmm, I loved it, too, my Cian." Eryn looked into those deep blue eyes. He could see which twin was Connor's boy and which twin was Mika's boy. The blues of their eyes differed from each other and were the same colors as their fathers. However, their long, lean bodies were almost identical. He felt more connected to Ivan, maybe because he's Mika's boy.

"We need to clean ourselves up. I hear the pups are getting restless." Eryn pushed them playfully, rolling them to make space so he could move off the bed. "Let's go shower and have a late-night snack. I'm starving now."

Cian grunted but didn't move. "I think you guys should get the food and feed me when you return. I'm too tired to get up. I don't think I can walk. I can't feel my toes."

Eryn grabbed a pillow, hitting Cian playfully in the stomach. He folded double with an *oomph.*

"Get up, you lazy ass!" Ivan seemed upset and irritated with Cian. "I'm hungry. I'm going to take a shower." He disappeared behind the glass bricks, and only his silhouette was visible through the walk-in shower, which was big enough for three men and three full-grown Anubis.

Eryn got up to free their pets from the kennel, a twenty-by-twenty-meter room with soft pillows for them to sleep on. When Eryn opened the gate, they tumbled over themselves to greet him. He turned around, tapping the side of his leg. "Come on, it's time for a shower," he called, and they yipped, eagerly following him to the water. They jumped and tumbled over each other, playfully nipping at his heels, sneezing, licking, and howling. "Yes, that's it, come on, boys." He turned on the water, and they all jumped in, loving it.

Steam filled the hot shower, and among the mist, Ivan was already waiting for Eryn. "I worked up an appetite," Ivan said softly, and Eryn sensed that something was seriously amiss. He said one thing but meant something else.

Ivan was hiding his true feelings, Eryn thought. As he caressed his mind, it felt prickly, like a rolled-up porcupine. He was guarding his emotions. Ivan was unhappy and not himself. There was both guilt and doubt on his mind.

"Me too. I could eat a whole mountain of pancakes," Cian said, his voice muffled by the bedding. Eryn sensed he was falling asleep and saw that as an opportunity to ask Ivan what had been bothering him. He had a feeling Ivan didn't want to admit his feelings because he didn't want to hurt his brother. Eryn leaned against him, pulling him closer.

Water cascaded from the waterfall shower heads above. The pups were soaking wet and didn't like the soapy water in their eyes. They jumped out, shaking the water from their bodies. Eryn watched Ivan while he smiled at the three Anubis, cleaning their wet snouts on the towels he laid out for them on the floor.

"Come here. I love you so much. I didn't have a chance earlier." Eryn's voice was smooth, and his tone seductive. Diverting the water with the back of his head, he prevented it from splashing into Ivan's eyes when he looked up at him.

"I noticed, so I waited," Ivan replied, his voice sensual and suggestive. Eryn sensed Ivan's heart rate speeding up.

"You first, I need you to say it. Please tell me you love me. I need to hear it," Eryn said with vulnerability.

Ivan finished washing his hair, rinsing out the conditioner, and then gave Eryn his full attention. "I love you very much, Eryn. I'm so happy to be here with you. I also love that you let us share you," Ivan said, but he was holding back. He clenched his jaw, and his eyes turned red. *He was fighting back tears.*

"Yes, but I can tell something's bothering you. Please tell me. You know you can share anything with me. I love you, too, my Ivan."

"It's just...I love...Cian, but sometimes, I need some space and want things to go my way for a change. I can't be like him. It makes me so tired sometimes, you know, I'm...just...not as...energetic. He's always the happy one. I'm always the one who worries for both of us. I feel like the odd one out. And now we're sharing you. It was fine to share when we were having fun, but it's serious now. I want to love you for myself. For once in my life, I want something for myself, just for me. Not to share. The way I know you deserve. Both of us deserve it. He doesn't see you. I'm not sure how long I can continue living like this. I never thought we would live together forever. I don't mind his company, but I feel suffocated. So possessive. It's getting to be too much for me. Pretending. He's getting to be too much for me." Ivan cried softly, and Eryn held him. The water ran over them, creating a private curtain around them.

Eryn hugged Ivan. "We need to talk to Cian then," Eryn said, feeling guilty for putting the two brothers in this predicament. He rubbed Ivan's back, sensing the sadness draining from him like water from the shower. It was clear this was something Ivan had never shared with anyone else, ever. He let him cry, allowing him to release years of frustration, watching it spill down the drain to disappear forever. "Soon, when you're ready, you should talk to your brother. If you explain this to him, it may hurt his feelings, but it's not fair to walk around pretending. It will turn into a monster, growing bigger into something that will consume the beautiful brotherly love left between you. I'm sure over time, Cian will forgive you, and your relationship will be stronger than ever."

Ivan's body shook as he cried in silence. "Do you think you feel the same about me?" he asked, whispering in Eryn's neck.

Eryn kissed his forehead. "I do my Ivan now more than ever. I'm convinced we are mates. I am yours, and you are mine. I don't mind sharing with Cian, but I don't feel with my heart; I feel with my body when I'm with him. It is fun, I agree, but I also can't see this working for the three of us. In the long run. Like you, I want to reveal my true feelings to Cian, but I also don't want to hurt him."

"Yes, we do owe him honesty. He will not take it well," Ivan said.

Eryn took Ivan's head between his big hands and gazed into his sad blue eyes. "I understand, but we must make him realize that we are setting boundaries now to prevent lying to him in the future. It would be poor taste to develop a deeper connection while keeping it from him. He will feel excluded, and not telling him would embarrass him."

CIAN

In the bedroom, Cian pretended to be asleep, snoring softly to maintain appearances while Ivan and Eryn talked about him. Cian was unaware of his brother's deep unhappiness. He had to admit that he felt the same way about Ivan.

Ivan cramped his style, and he took his feelings for Eryn far too seriously. Yes, he wanted Eryn and to have fun with them, but hurting Ivan was something Cian couldn't bring himself to do, nor would he ever want to. He wasn't under the illusion that he was in love with Eryn, not love like his fathers had for each other.

If this wasn't working out, he had no problem with moving out to search for that pull, that call he'd felt ever since they sent humans to the moon. Cian sat up, not fully aware of what he was doing. Turning his head, he tilted it to the side as if listening.

Was this the song Ivan and Eryn were discussing, or was this something else, or someone else calling me?

CHAPTER 26

GODLY POWER

"*GOOD MORNING, CITIZENS OF PHOENIX.*

It's now six a.m.

In these uncertain times, Lasitor bids you goodbye.

May luck and success always be with you. I'm going to miss you.

It's been a pleasure to work with you—best of luck. But I fear your never-ending adventures on land are coming to an end.

General McCormick, you've been a faithful and fantastic leader to us. Your contributions and dedication will always be a prime example for others.

I know you have never seen someone as intelligent as me. I recorded tons of memories to download when I'm gone.

I never thought that a day like this would come when I would have to bid farewell to you.

Breakfast is served until eight a.m.

Goodbye and all the best!"

DR. MIKA ROMANOV

MIKA FINISHED GETTING DRESSED for the day with a heavy heart. Then he sat at the end of the bed. He had a pounding headache and grunted and moaned like an older man while putting his boots on. The movement worsened the throbbing of pain when he bent over to tie his laces. His wet blond hair fell in thick threads over his face. Being irritated with it, he tied the hair hastily into a bun with a few well-practiced, quick movements. He wanted to tell Connor something for a long time, but he put it off until a better moment. The secret had been festering so long that its significance had grown so large and so heavy that he felt as if he'd swallowed a ten-ton brick. It was so thick in his stomach that he was continuously sick and lacked appetite. Connor had just said, while clutching his hips, that he could feel his hip bones and made a joke, asking Mika whether he missed the Phoenix dining rooms.

Mika sat up, folding his hands on his lap while listening intently to the strange goodbye announcement made by the AI Lasitor.

If that wasn't a Freudian slip, my name's not Mika

Romanov, a geneticist, geologist, medical doctor, physicist, and linguist.

"What is up with Lasitor this morning?" Connor's muffled voice came from underneath his pillow. He lay on his stomach, wondering how he landed after ejaculating twenty minutes ago. Their massive soft mattress looked like it had swallowed him. It seemed as though he never intended to move from the spot.

At least he's verbalizing coherent sentences now.

"Come, my lazy gille-toine." Mika started with their usual banter. "We've been so busy that our love-making feels like...hmm." He cleared his throat and altered his voice and accent to a Texan American one. "Wham bam, thank you, my man."

Chuckling, he attempted to lighten his mood. "I miss our post-coital conversations." Connor didn't move, but a soft huh or hmm came from underneath the pillow. Mika smiled and told Connor whether he wanted to listen or not. Then maybe he could have breakfast today without feeling guilty. He turned sideways on the foot of the bed and spoke.

"The issue for me is that our marriage is such that we always tell each other everything, and I promised you a long time ago that I would never keep a secret from you."

Oh, here it goes, he thought when Connor stirred and turned onto his back. He lifted the pillow from his face and folded it in half to tuck it under his head. Mika stared at Connor, pulling the linen over his crotch, looked at Mika, and waited. Mika nervously licked his lips and readied himself to divulge the worst news ever to his husband.

"I've been carrying a secret with me, and knowing you, my husband, you'll flip out and lose your leprechaun shit. Whenever I wanted to tell you, the time or place was never right, and it's killing me now." Mika leaned forward, his elbows resting on his knees, hiding his face and guilt from his spouse. Connor frowned, listening.

Mika drew in a deep breath. "I believe it's all my fault because I trusted the wrong people, and you trusted me. So, you trusted him because I trusted him. You're going to despise me for it. I was such a moron. I'm never foolish, but this was my first time, and it's pretty humiliating," Mika muttered, his head in his hands, rolling it from side to side.

My headache is killing me. Maybe after this admission, it'll disappear. But he knew that thought was hopeless.

Connor got up onto his knees and rubbed Mika's back in tiny circles. "Yelda, what?" he asked. "I have never heard you so distraught. But, of course, you know you're free to tell me anything. Sure, I might stress out, but you know how quickly I cool down. I never hold grudges against you or go to bed angry at you. We may disagree, but don't believe that I would despise or hate you for it." Connor moved closer to Mika, wrapping his legs and arms around him. "Tell me." He encouraged Mika with kisses on his back before resting his cheek against him.

Mika pulled a crumpled piece of paper from his pants pocket. The thing he wished he could throw away and forget, the thing that threatened all they'd fought for and believed in so passionately. This tiny piece of paper would kill his comrades, who believed in the larger good and established a whole city.

"I took this from the scientist's notes from the first night on the ship when we rescued the boys. First, I grabbed it to reread it quietly. Then it became something for which there was no time. It's now my filthy secret that's hurting me and us." Mika let out a throaty cry and sniffed. "Here you read it. I can't because my tears will smear the ink," he told Connor as he got up, searching for a tissue to blow his nose.

Connor looked up in astonishment. He took the paper and headed to their loveseat across from the bed. A trail of bedding followed him, so he folded it around his waist, tucked it underneath, and sat down. Mika took a seat next to him. Connor looked at his face. "You know, now I can see your wrinkles and sagging around your eyes and mouth. It looks like this has been eating you up from the inside, yeldael."

Mika nodded, avoiding eye contact. Connor unfolded the piece of paper carefully, as if it were a poisonous scorpion.

"Okay then, let me read this, and then we'll talk." He patted Mika on the leg and read.

Connor placed the crumpled piece of paper on the ground, his hands trembling. His face was colorless, nearly as white as the sheets around his waist. Mika remained silent, allowing him time to digest or percolate everything.

"I'll make us some coffee and give you more time to look it over. That's how I felt after reading it."

Connor stared at Mika, speechless with shock. He tried his best since he couldn't flip out and freak as promised. "Yes, please, and add extra whiskey to it."

Mika nodded and, leaning forward, kissed Connor on the forehead.

NEEP, neep, neep! Whoop, whoop! Neep, neep, neep! The emergency siren sounded.

"What now? Sweet frozen spitballs!" Connor sprang up to get dressed.

CHAPTER 27
PETER STUTTERED

"MORNING, CITIZENS OF PHOENIX.

It's now six a.m.

Lasitor recommends that you and your children keep your emergency kit in a backpack on your person. During an emergency, such as a natural disaster, power outages are to be expected. You'll need to act quickly and follow the directions of the emergency team. Have your emergency kit with you. Food services and any other services will be down. Prepare and store nonperishable meals in your emergency kit now. When the alarms sound, stay with your assigned group and refrain from searching for one another.

Breakfast is served until eight a.m.

Good luck to you today!"

. . .

ERYN, **King of the Brawl**
2073 A.D. (21 A.T.)

"GOOD MORNING, ERYN," Bryan greeted while looking up at Eryn coming from the opposite side of the steel corridor.

"Hello," Eryn greeted him with a warm smile. Bryan offered his hand to shake. Eryn stopped, looked down at it, and grabbed it. Careful not to crush his hand, he held a firm grip and nodded, just like Mika had taught him.

"Let me introduce you to my partners," Bryan said, pointing to Tony and Peter.

"Oh, you have two partners." He held his big hand, gave the men his best, friendliest smile, and greeted Tony.

"Hello, Eryn. Nice to meet you. I'm Tony," he said with an Italian New York accent.

Next, Eryn turned his attention to Peter. "Hello, you must be Peter. Nice to meet you."

Peter looked nervous, moving from one foot to the other. Eryn could smell the fear radiating from him. Bryan noticed as well, and he frowned. Eryn held his hand out, and Peter took it. His hand felt cold and clammy. It looked like he wanted to pass out.

"What's wrong? I will not hurt you." Eryn spoke softly with a friendly voice, as he would to a skittish animal.

Peter stuttered. "I'm no-no-not...scar-scar-scared... scared of you," he said while looking extremely uncomfortable. *Sorry, Peter, I don't believe you.* Eryn listened to his heartbeat and the sound of his breathing. It was faster, and his pupils dilated. *He looks ready to run for his life.*

Tony saw it as well. "What's wrong, lover?" he asked, reaching out to comfort him.

"I have to go, I remember, I just...I have to..." He turned and all but ran down the corridor.

Bryan gazed questioningly at Tony, who shrugged his shoulders. "Sorry, Eryn," Bryan apologized.

"I'll go check up on him. Eryn, I will find you so we can talk more," Tony said. He excused himself by shaking Eryn's hand again. Bryan winked at him.

"Yes, please do." Eryn could see the worry in his eyes. The Italian turned to search for Peter.

"Why would he be afraid of me? I would never hurt him," Eryn stated, hoping Bryan confirmed that. *The last thing I want is for people to fear me. Is it my size, or maybe he heard what I've done? Perhaps he heard about the men I'd drowned. Maybe it's my eyes?* Eryn couldn't put his finger on it, but the white-haired and blue-eyed man with his smooth white skin made him think about his father, Dr. Wessels. They looked very similar to Eryn.

"No, it must be something else. Don't worry about it, Eryn. When he feels better, I'm sure he'll come and explain to you."

Eryn sensed Bryan was telling the truth. Maybe only about the apology. Something else was going on.

Bryan changed the subject. "Eryn, have you ever swum in a swimming pool?"

"No, why?" Eryn asked.

"We were on our way to go for a swim. Do you want to join me? I'm all alone now."

Eryn nodded eagerly. He liked Bryan because he was always friendly and honest. He enjoyed his appearance, as well. Bryan was an attractive man.

"Where are your men?" Bryan asked.

"They took the pups for a walk."

"If you want to join me, you don't have to swim if you don't want to. Can you swim?" Bryan asked, hinting with one arm for Eryn to walk with him.

"I know how to swim. I swam in many places, but never in this pool. Watching the humans, sorry, I meant to say, men, swimming but could never swim here in this pool when I was a small boy," Eryn said and paused. He almost said small Brawl. He tried not to say Brawl because explaining what a Brawl was a hundred times a day wasn't fun anymore.

"As a small boy? Oh, you can come. Just hang your feet in the water and decide if you want to go in or not."

"I want to swim," he said, his heart galloping with excited anticipation. *I always wanted to swim in the clean water.* "Yes, let's go!" He agreed eagerly.

"I'll lend you something to swim in. We swim in

swim trunks. Do you think you can get your butt into a pair of my shorts?" Bryan asked while leading the way and appearing excited to spend time alone with Eryn.

"It'll be a tight fit," Eryn said. *Maybe I should watch for today and swim when I'm better dressed?*

"Come, no worries. We can see who's there, and if we're alone, I can lock the gates to the pool, and then we swim without clothes."

Oh, fuck! Eryn felt his face heat, and he knew it was as red as a tomato. When Bryan noticed, he asked, "Are you shy?"

"Yes, only Cian and Ivan see me naked," he said abruptly, thinking about his two dicks. Maybe he should wish one away to swim with Bryan?

"Come on, no need to be shy. We're all men," Bryan said.

"That doesn't matter. Only my men see me naked, which is only for them," Eryn said sternly.

Bryan did a double-take. Eryn made sure he projected determined innocence.

"I know they were virgins when they met you."

Again, Eryn straightened, looking down at Bryan with warning and retribution, not amused by the line of questioning.

"Okay, I'm just nosy. Don't worry about me and my questions. If you don't want to answer, that's fine."

"Yes, I don't want to answer those types of questions. It's only for me, Cian, and Ivan," he said again, looking Bryan in the eyes.

Bryan looked impressed by Eryn's strength in saying no and meaning it. "Wow, that's refreshing. Good for you for expressing your feelings. I respect that," Bryan said honestly, and Eryn could tell he meant it. "Okay, let's go swim. Naked and sex stuff is not up for discussion," Bryan promised.

"Yes, thank you." Eryn smiled. The anticipation of going swimming was back.

"You know, I feel honored to take you for your first swim in the Phoenix swimming pool," Bryan excitedly told Eryn. They hadn't met under the best circumstances, and it looked like he wanted to make up for that night. "Eryn, I wanted to thank you for trying to help us that night," Bryan said, turning his way. "I meant to get you alone and apologize for mistreating you that night when the twins were taken. In my eyes, you were the enemy. I saw what you did, how high you could jump, and I think it scared me. I wanted to show you and my men that I'm strong, so I hit you. Can you forgive me?" Bryan asked sheepishly.

"I know you felt all those things, and even now, I feel guilty for not explaining before I left. I had to get to Ernest and protect my mates. Additionally, I didn't know who had been abducted. Only when we reached safety did I see who it was. If I hadn't left, they could have died. So, thank you for not hurting me so bad that I couldn't escape." Eryn held out his hand, and Bryan shook it, speechless.

Nodding his head up and down, he turned and pointed. "Here we are." Then he pushed the door to the locker room open.

"I'm going to get dressed. What do you want to do? Do you want to borrow some swimming trunks?"

"Yes, please," Eryn answered without hesitation. He'd wished his second dick away for the past five minutes. He hoped it would be gone by the time he entered the changing area. But it was still there when he pulled his pants down. Luckily, both had shrunk to a manageable size, suitable for a swim trunk. *Thank you,* he thanked his penises for shrinking. *You can grow back later.* He told them that the twins would be very sad to see them so small.

Dressed in tight blue swim trunks, he excitedly pushed the door to the pool area open, so it slammed with a bang against the sides, just in time to see a big splash in the water. The smell of the chlorine and the warm mist of the heated pool brought back nostalgic memories.

"Come, the water feels extra warm today," Bryan called while frolicking.

Eryn walked up to the pool, loving the crystal-clear water. "Sit on the side first, then hang your feet in the water." Eryn did as Bryan suggested, and he sat on his heels.

Then, supporting himself with his left hand, he lowered his feet into the warm water. His skin tingled, and goosebumps popped up all over his body. It was a pleasant experience, almost like being down in the mines, just a lot cleaner.

"That's it, now slowly lower your body while holding on to the side," Bryan coaxed gently while he drifted closer. As amphibians were drawn to the water, Eryn was unfazed by the pool's shallow depths on his side.

"You can stand upright here, see, it's not that deep." Bryan demonstrated his point by rising and pointing to a spot directly above his navel region to indicate the height of the surface level.

A few brief audible gasps were all that Eryn could muster while lowering himself carefully into the deliciously warm water. Then, standing up to check the surface level, he teased, "Look, Bryan, a full foot and a half lower than you," he told him, clearly indicating that he was taller.

Bryan responded with a teasing taunt. "Show off."

"Isn't it wonderful?" Eryn asked excitedly, as if on a carnival ride. "I'm in the water!" He jumped and twisted about like a kid at a water park.

Bryan dove swiftly out of the path as a massive wave of water blasted his way, while Eryn thanked him incessantly, whirling around, creating giant spouts of water.

"Thank you very much for everything." Every time he jumped up, he yelled something.

Bryan's grin spread over his face. "It's my pleasure. I'm pleased to do it for you," he said.

"When I got into the water, it was much warmer than I expected." Eryn regained his composure and remarked, "Compared to my latest experiences swimming in the icy waters near the southernmost tip of South Africa."

Bryan stepped closer.

"Besides steam and energy generators, the lava tunnels are used to heat the entire city's water organically." Bryan froze. Between his eyebrows, a deep scowl appeared. It was clear to Eryn that something troubled him.

He halted his ecstatic enjoyment, sensing the seriousness of Bryan's demeanor.

"The water in the pool is so hot that it's unbearable," Bryan said slowly, almost to himself. He appeared to be thinking. Then he looked down at the water.

"What's wrong, Bryan?" Eryn asked, also noticing the heat increasing rapidly.

"Do you feel the heat is increasing?" Bryan asked.

"Yes, and the water level is going down," Eryn stated, looking at his hands. The level was at least two inches lower than when he jumped in earlier.

Bryan looked up and stretched his eyes wide. "Out, out, we need to get out!" He swam to the nearest side. Eryn swam after him. Feeling the urgency but not understanding the danger.

Bryan grabbed the side and pulled himself out of the water. Immediately, he was up and reaching his hand for Eryn. Eryn jumped without taking his hand and landed on the side of the Olympic-sized pool.

"Fuck, it's happening! We need to sound the alarm. Come, Eryn." Bryan ran for the nearest pager to trigger the emergency alarm.

THE FIRST THING Eryn heard was the droning. Next, the vibrations and thunderous creaking started midafter-noon, and by nighttime, full chaos had struck. However, encased in a layer of protective bubbles. No one was preparing the people inside the building for the unimaginable force. It flung them around while their glass city undulated and gravity shifted.

Waters covered the roofs, and the inside felt like a pressure cooker, as heat and steam filled Phoenix from below. It felt like they were seconds from combusting. The pressure on his eardrums was even worse than jumping down the mineshaft as a little boy. Eryn knew they were going deeper than ever. He felt an indescribable sense of uselessness due to the pain, despair, and lack of control. He never truly understood the emotion of human fear until it trapped him in the middle, trying to reach Ivan and Cian.

It lasted for two and a half hours.

"The energy released must be three thousand times greater than a 9.0 on the Richter scale," Mika shouted to Connor while rushing to aid a man trapped in the debris. Some construction was too weak, and blocks of plexiglass tumbled like rain from above. Eryn didn't know where to help or who to rescue. He attempted to hum and sing, but the force was unstoppable. Whatever was happening was supposed to run its course, he thought.

Screams and darkness surrounded them as people, and anything not tied down was tossed into the air.

Sparks of electricity and embers of light filled the tunnels as humans fled for cover from the falling debris. The tunnels appeared intact to them, but icy water soon overwhelmed them. Their perfect city and their perfect dreams crumbled around them. Terrified cries and sorrowful bellows were cut short. It meant instant death had taken another person. No alarm or emergency preparedness could have saved them from it. They were all at the mercy of their gods. Only the lucky ones survived. After the final shakes and rattles faded away, Phoenix's foundation appeared to be in the depths of the sea.

So much life and so many dreams were destroyed in one afternoon.

Months later, their tears had run dry. The repairs had started. For decades, gaunt faces roamed the desolate dark hallways until one day. Stares were returned with a smile. Laughter followed by a giggle, and happiness didn't feel like a forced thing anymore. Hope bloomed, and once again, the Phoenicians had retaken their purpose to do everything better and smarter.

EPILOGUE

"GOOD MORNING, CITIZENS OF PHOENIX.

It's now six a.m.

Did you know that an estimated one hundred and two billion metric tons of gold have been removed from the earth?

The mining of gold via the Earth's ocean floor has been a sensitive subject, so sensitive, in fact, that it's caused a war.

Check out this article on our community news page about sub-sea mining robots and how to eliminate them when you see them.

Breakfast is served until eight a.m.

Have a fantastic day!"

CIAN **Romanov**

2124 A.D. (72 A.T.)

It's been fifty years since the Earth tilted nearly 180 degrees on its axis. Toxic gases escaped, filling the stratosphere and obscuring the view of the stars with a dark blue-purple haze. While the Earth's crust cooled down, the melted ice caps now lay at the equator. The Earth was covered in debris and water. If it hadn't been for Eryn, Ivan, and Cian wrapping Phoenix inside a cocoon of spongy, air-filled bubbles fifty years ago, Phoenix would have been destroyed, and the last men on Earth would have been wiped away like old footprints in the sand.

Cian felt utterly alone. Never had he ever felt so damn miserable. He questioned his existence more today than on any other day. He shook his head in exasperation. "Why am I here? And why am I so bloody drawn to you?" he asked the moon, frustrated and hopeless.

Opening the hatch of his vehicle, it swooshed, releasing the pressure that built up inside when they floated up to the surface. Making himself as comfortable as possible in the narrow bucket seat, he threw his long legs out of the door's opening, crossing them, and exhaling heavily.

Every lunar cycle, like clockwork, he dragged his sorry single ass out into the tunnels where he would exit Phoenix for a ride up to the surface. As if all-knowing, his guard dog would wait to accompany him as if he were also called by the moon. Riding in the Bubblecar, as Connor and his students named it, was always one of Rotty's favorite activities.

The double passenger vehicle, a design his father based on the floating camera ball, was an anti-gravitational sphere that could darken or camouflage itself to melt with its surroundings. Making the soundless, zero-emissions vehicle the best design Phoenix University had produced since the Blue Halcyon. Therefore, voted to be mass-produced for all citizens who wanted to travel outside of Phoenix.

Each month, Cian would fly himself and Rotty to the middle of nowhere on the waters of the South Sea, where they would lie back, listening to the waves lapping against the sides of their Bubblecar while staring longingly at the moon.

Rotty growled and sat up like he knew something was amiss. He sniffed the air. Restlessly whining.

"Down, boy, it's only the moon." Cian patted his leg, inviting his best friend and protector to lie next to him. The big black animal crept closer and plopped his head on his lap.

"That's it, don't stand. You're my smart and beautiful big boy, aren't you?" Cian said. Playfully hugging him and kissing him on his wet snout.

You chose me and stuck by me.

As if reading Cian's mind, Rotty panted happily, and Cian rubbed behind its hairless ears again. His yellow eyes sparkled, reflecting the moonlight that bounced off the waves of the deep blue ocean water. Cian smiled inwardly. He saw happiness in Rotty's eyes. The thought lifted his spirits slightly, easing the pressure cooker of melancholy he had been feeling. Like a female having her period, Mika had told him earlier, and every other day. To him, they all felt like one sad existence. He sighed, looked up at the bright dot in the sky, and folded one arm behind his head while the other hand lazily stroked his companion.

Tonight, a full-fat moon hung so low in the sky that he lifted his leg and touched it with the tip of his boot, hoping whoever or whatever on the moon was looking back at him, missing him, even though they'd never met before.

Cian figured that now that his brother had found his mate under the most unusual circumstances, the chances of something unique happening to him—like maybe a spaceship landing on the water and abducting him—were slim. "That's a zero-to-nothing chance," he whispered. "But, hey, a man can dream, can't he?" he said aloud, and Rotty lifted his head, taking notice and looking at him questioningly. "Yeah, I'm a sad, sorry sucker, aren't I, boy?"

Rotty whined softly. "Yes, you agree, I know."

"You know, I saw a movie once of a spaceship that would float down, and a door would open and start sucking up people into the UFO, transporting them to who knows where. Maybe for some anal probing. Man, that sounds better and better to me each time I tell you the story." Cian chuckled. Even the word probe got him hard nowadays. The Anubis whined worriedly. "Yeah, that's a possibility. We can dream, though."

As the waves lapped rhythmically against the floating bubble, Cian drifted in and out of wakefulness. This was where he relaxed in his solitude. Alone on the ocean with Rotty. Just him, his Anubis, the music of nature, and the incessant pull of the moon. This was where he found his peace, as if sleeping in a lover's arms. "The bloody moon," he mumbled and drifted off into slumber.

A few hundred meters below Cian and Rotty, the city of Phoenix lay enveloped in a layer of protective bubbles. When the ocean water calmed and the earth draped the moon in its shadow, the city of Phoenix beamed from the abyss below.

"Is it time to go back?" Cian asked Rotty groggily. Rotty growled and moved over excitedly from side to side. His overgrown body filled his seat and hung over the sides. *He usually can't sit for long.*

Cian sat up. Something hummed around them. It sounded like machines and people working. He flipped onto his stomach to look behind them, through the back and sides. Nothing.

Rotty's growling, so I didn't imagine it.

He scanned the water surface around them and then extended his gaze further out. Still, he couldn't see anything.

"Where are they, boy?" he asked, patting his best friend. The three hairs on his head were standing erect. He looked supercharged. His head and body were getting bigger, Cian thought. His Anubis was ready to attack. Then Rotty looked upward to the sky.

"Freezing hellfires!" Cian exclaimed in amazement. Rotty growled louder. Cian embraced his Anubis protector. "Shhh, don't let them know we're here. I know you are big and strong, but they're much bigger than us. Just relax and watch for now, boy." Cian hushed and patted him. The animal felt like it shrank in his arms, "Yes, that's it, you can't grow further. Where would we go? We won't fit in the car. That's my big boy." Cian whispered into his ear. He watched in disbelief at what he was seeing. A floating sail-ship hung above them. It was about the size of a football field, but what caught his attention most was the number of bodies—weird pirate-looking men throwing what looked like ropes or pipes over the sides.

Are they planning on sliding down? Are we being attacked?

He heard, "Yes, Captain," and a male voice shouting orders.

"Get that canister down into the hull!"

"What?" Cian asked in a whisper. Rotty answered with a soft whine. Realizing that while the strange ship hung above them, the sky had cleared so he could have a glimpse of the stars—something he hadn't seen in fifty years.

They aren't exiting the ship. What are they doing? Where are they from? Are these people from yet another Environmental Project?

"Freezing hellfires, they're sucking the gasses from the atmosphere," he said as soon as they removed their vacuuming pipes, and he noticed the skies dulled again. Cian sat open-mouthed and watched as the ship floated up and away.

When the ship was out of sight and gone, Cian grabbed the door and shut it. Rotty turned a few times in his seat. "I know, boy, that was weird. We should tell Phoenix. They would want to know." Rotty gave another growl, then lay down. He'd learned the hard way what would happen if he sat up while the vehicle toppled over. They descended into the depths with a plop, eager to tell their leaders about the sighting.

They entered the underwater city via a long, transparent tube a few minutes later. It was wide enough to allow only one Bubblecar at a time onto a one-way conveyor belt that stopped at the vehicle platform, where passengers boarded or alighted, just like they would at an underground railway station.

Cian and Rotty floated behind a line of empty cars
already available for passengers. As soon as it was
their turn, they jumped out of their transportation
before it came to a dead halt and exited the Transportation Dome via the stairs to the main floor of the
Central Dome. The pitter-patter of the Anubis
toenails on the coral-tiled floor reminded Cian that it
was foot care and pedicure night for them.

"Excuse us, excuse us, thank you." Elatedly, they
hopped with haste and ducked this and that way to
avoid oncoming foot traffic. They ran straight to the
leadership office. Whoever was working tonight
would be the first to hear about Cian's spaceship
sighting. Rotty kept up; he matched Cian's long
strides. Already, Cian was having difficulty maneuvering through the narrow corridors with him by his
side. Cian thought maybe Rotty only grew when he
needed to, but he shelved that thought as Eryn and
Ivan rounded the corner to the office. Shitballs! He
didn't want to see their happy faces. The happier they
looked, the sicker he felt. And pretending he was
happy made him feel like a walking tumor.

The lights lit up the hallways as Rotty and Cian
approached them. "Shitballs," Cian swore under his
breath. Rotty growled.

"Yes, thank you, boy. At least I have you on my
side. I can imagine what Ivan's going to say about the
spaceship floating above the waters." Rotty looked up

at Cian as if to say I love you and bugger them. Cian gave his friend a quick pat on the head.

"Aren't the two of you already tired of each other? Aren't you supposed to bugger for like a week when you are on your honeymoon? Or did Eryn bugger your little hole raw because he's too proud to bend over for you? Maybe you are just not enough for him." Cian said. He made it his mission to let them know what low-life backstabbers they were.

"Brother, stop your salty comments. You know well I am enough. I've been enough for half a bloody century. No, we are not tired of each other. We are here because we know you need us," Ivan said and scowled as usual at Cian. Eryn crossed his arms. But he was amused, not at all defaced by Cian. This is why Cian loved him. But this is also why Cian can't have him. Eryn had wanted only Ivan. Cian was only the cum-stained rag forgotten in the corner behind the bed. Cold, stiff, used once, and discarded. Collecting dust and spiderwebs on his balls.

Okay, that was messed up, Cian thought. Sometimes words escaped his mouth, and by the time he heard himself, it was too late.

"Yeah, it's urgent alright. Please excuse me," Cian said and pushed between them to activate the sensor so the door could swoosh open. Rotty followed him, head held high with a cheeky swagger. Damn, he loved the animal. It's as if Rotty's soul was carved from his.

Cian found Mika, Connor, and Brad in the office. Again, they were dressed casually, as if they had forgotten they were supposed to be working.

Is everyone around here on holiday? "Hello, what are you doing here if you aren't working? Flip flops and T-shirts? You are the embodiment of unprofessionalism, Brad."

"Hello, Cian. Serious and pissed off as usual." Brad retorted and saluted.

"There's my favorite boy." Connor got up, and Rotty jumped to greet him. Sniffing my father's balls, the traitor.

"Fathers, Brad," Eryn said in his friendly, deep baritone. Of course, everyone noticed the happy couple standing behind him. They looked delighted to see them. Not the sour puss faces that greeted me, Cian thought.

"Eryn, Ivan, so glad to see you. Are you here for a game of canasta?" Mika asked as soon as he noticed his favorite sons behind Cian. He got up, pushed Cian aside, and greeted them with open arms.

Am I invisible? Cian wondered.

"Hmm, no, we are here because Cian saw something and wants to talk to you about it," Eryn said. *The Brawl had already read my mind. So intrusive. I should spit my secret out before Ivan figures it out.*

"No! Really, a spaceship?" Ivan exclaimed.

"Freezing hellfires!" Cian shouted. He turned to

leave and intentionally shoulder-bumped Ivan and Mika to get out of the office.

"We're leaving. Come, boy, let these nosy bastards tell them what we saw. I'm so sick of you all. I'm going! Bugger you all very much!"

THE END.

TIMELINE

Spoiler Alert!

2041 A.D. to 2043 A.D. (3-5 years before Doomsday.) Eryn and his brothers are born.

2046 A.D. DOOMSDAY. Worldwide breakout of Neurotoxic biochemicals. Nuclear Winter follows.

The story of the men of Phoenix begins - *Phoenix Code: New Beginnings Prequel*

Ishtar arrives on the moon and waits for Cian, Ivan, and Eryn while guarding Barkor in Grayrak.

2051 A.D. (5 years after Doomsday.) The marriage of Mika and Connor takes place.

2052 A.D. (6 years after Doomsday.) The Big Flood (Tsunamis) happens, and, on that same day, the Romanov twins are born, marking it as the Year of the Twins: 0 A.T.

2058 A.D. (6 A.T.) The story of Eryn begins. *Eryn, King of the Brawl: New Beginnings M/M Series Part One.*

2073 A.D. (21 A.T.) Mika and Brad find the *apple* in the Disciples of the Anunnaki's confiscated loot. Cian and Ivan's Anunnaki heritage is revealed. Eryn makes each a sword of gold by dividing the forks on his trident so that they can focus their power on wrapping Phoenix in a protective layer to save their city from a string of global volcanic eruptions that led to the almost-instantaneous melting of the polar ice caps and global storms, turning Earth on its axis.

2124 A.D. (72 A.T.) Cian's first sighting of the hydrogen mining ship of the Zelk.

AFTERWORD

ABOUT THE AUTHOR

"I found it surprisingly beautiful. In a brutal, horribly uncomfortable sort of way." —Tyrion Lannister to Janos Slynt.

I am a Canadian speculative fiction author, writing in the genres of science fiction, fantasy, and paranormal.

My writing explores who we are, where we come from, and where we are going as a human race on Earth.

I enjoy weaving and exploring questions and subjects about our history and origin by creating new, exciting worlds and characters. My stories are unpredictable, twisted with a dash of humor, and centered on gay characters.

You will question your existence among these worlds and wish you could escape to these places filled with foul-mouthed heroes who struggle and strive to save humankind.

I hope you've discovered something that excites and intrigues you. Please share your thoughts by leaving a review or visiting www.kashelchar.com to contact me or learn about my latest works.

www.ingramcontent.com/pod-product-compliance
Lightning Source LLC
Chambersburg PA
CBHW030425030726
47493CB00022BA/68